Demi stalked to the desk and sat, crossing her long legs, well aware of the effect that usually produced....

She reminded him of one of his sister's cats. The creature was usually graceful as a ballerina, but once in a while she'd take a leap at the kitchen counter and miss—scrabbling ignominiously down the woodwork to land in a heap on the tiles. The cat would stalk off in high dudgeon, tail on high, quivering with suppressed fury, every line of her body declaring, "Who me? I had *no* intention whatsoever of making that leap. And if anyone suggests that I *had*..."

Demi widened her dark slanted eyes, then narrowed them like a cat. Clearly she was used to men stumbling over themselves to please her. How could she not be, looking like that? Leaning closer, she rested one graceful hand on his good knee.

"I need help right now—need it *desperately!* And you won't be a help, you'd be an added burden."

No way! he thought. *I'll get this job and walk again if I have to walk on my hands!*

Dear Reader,

Did I ever wander into a fascinating and glamorous world this time! I've always loved perfume, but never known a thing about it. Where it comes from, who makes it or how? To answer those questions, this shy but inquiring author had to go down to New York City—brave the subways, talk to strangers. (Generally, I'd rather talk to a familiar dentist with drill in hand than interview a stranger!) But each and every one turned out to be marvelous—passionate about fragrances, wonderfully exotic (French accents, Russian accents), and delighted to share their world with an interested novice.

If, after reading this book, you'd like to learn more about perfumes or becoming a nose (a creator of fine fragrances), you should contact the Fragrance Foundation in New York City at (212) 725-2755. That's the official public relations clearinghouse for the industry and it's very helpful.

Finally, if you'd just like to dabble in some wonderful scents, the following are considered the classic perfumes of this century: L'Heure Bleu and Shalimar by Guerlain, No.5 by Chanel, Arpège by Lanvin, Patou's Joy, Femme by Rochas, Christian Dior's Miss Dior, L'Air du Temps by Nina Ricci, Opium by Yves Saint Laurent and Trésor by Lancôme.

Meantime, thanks as always for reading my tale!

Peggy Nicholson

THE SCENT OF A WOMAN
Peggy Nicholson

Harlequin Books

TORONTO • NEW YORK • LONDON
AMSTERDAM • PARIS • SYDNEY • HAMBURG
STOCKHOLM • ATHENS • TOKYO • MILAN
MADRID • WARSAW • BUDAPEST • AUCKLAND

ISBN 0-373-70770-3

THE SCENT OF A WOMAN

To Jane Robson, good friend, *great* editor. Love and bon voyage, P.

And with heartfelt thanks to the following:

The wonderful people at Quest International Fragrances.
Herb Kelhoffer, your patience and enthusiasm overwhelmed this
shy author. Thanks for all the time you took answering my
questions and for those marvelous books. Your favorite scent,
chocovan, inspired Demi's love of chocolate. Thanks to Claude Dir,
Quest's senior perfumer, for some terrific background info. And to
Francis Kurkdjian, for creating a *muguet* fragrance just for me.

Bob Elias of Elias Fragrances, who allowed me to pick his brain and
prowl his factory on the last frantic working day before Christmas.
Tatyana Petrakov, head perfumer at Elias, whose passion for scents
and exuberant creativity became the paradigm for Demi's drive to
make magic in a bottle. To all the Elias lab techs and chemists who
let me watch them work.

Patrick Firmenich of Firmenich Inc., bemused but gallantly helpful in
spite of a nasty sore throat. Robin Mower, for all the New York color.

To Ron, for sitting up late into the night with me, drawing floor plans
of motoryachts and brainstorming ways to disable them.

And to Land Grant, Renee Auriema and Damian. I shall never hear
the "Hallelujah Chorus" again without groaning. Thanks for your
hospitality, one last apology for my burglar alarm disaster, and a big
hug for old-time's sake.

And to the two amiably tipsy Brooklyn cops in the Santa Claus hats,
for not arresting me as a burglar and for not taking a hammer to the
burglar alarm.

And I can't forget the junior con man or self-styled taxi supervisor.
With your flair for spinning tales, you really ought to stop rooking
tourists and take up writing, guy. You're a natural! And to the
Jamaican cabbie who rescued me.

A belated Merry Christmas to you all, and bless you each and
every one!

CHAPTER ONE

THE VIDEO STARTED without credits or soundtrack. This was no Hollywood production. Opening shot—the camera in tight focus on two taut, darkly shining curves.

Jon Sutton's pulse skipped a beat, then settled to a brisker rhythm, as his recognition reached conscious level. A nicely rounded derriere! Clad in something black and silky, moving away from the camera with a lazy-but-irresistible "Follow me, boys!" bump and sway.

One question was answered, anyway. The FBI agent pointing that hidden videocam was male.

He tore his eyes from the view to glance at his brother.

Slouched low in his seat, Special Agent Trace Sutton kept his gaze fixed on Jon's TV screen. But the corner of his mouth visible from his sibling's vantage point kicked upward in a familiar *gotcha!* curl.

Jon turned back to the show. "You've switched to interstate porn rings?" But no, this was a class act. The camera angle had widened. He could see the whole woman now, following a maître d' through a crowded restaurant—five-star, judging from its tablecloths, the candles and flowers, the dress of its clientele. Heads turned in her wake, women's as well as men's, though the women's eyes narrowed where the men's went wide.

"Nyet."

Jon translated this particular denial to mean that Trace was still investigating the Russian Mafia and its burgeoning links to the U.S., his field of interest for the past two years.

"She's Russian?" The camera hadn't caught her face yet, but from the back, he'd have guessed Eurasian. Despite the curves she was wonderfully slender, with straight black hair cut in a gleaming bell shape to swing just above wide shoulders.

"Egyptian, French, and pure Brooklyn Heights," Trace corrected.

"American as hot dogs and apple pie," Jon murmured. The Suttons were mutts, too, from fiercely proud West Virginia hillbilly stock with a dash of Cherokee on their mother's side, and methodical German farmers and polished English gentry on their father's.

Turning her head to follow the maître d's swing to the left, she gave her audience an elegant sweep of jaw, a small ear with a pearl catching the light of a chandelier, just the tip of her nose jutting past a high cheekbone. If she turned out to be merely cute, he'd be mightily disappointed. *Watch it, pal,* he reminded himself. This babe was the bait in whatever game Trace was inviting him to play. And he was in no mood for games. Hadn't been for months—the whole past ugly year.

"Look beyond her," Trace commanded.

Seated alone at a table, a broad-shouldered man in a dark suit faced the camera lens.

"The maître d' blocked his view of her till this frame," Trace noted. "Now he spots her. What's he feeling?"

"A snake in his trousers. Ask me a hard one, Watson."

"So we know he's heterosexual and older than eight. What else?"

Jon obediently turned back to the screen. "Surprise. It's just dawning that this package is for him. And it's not what he expected."

"Anything else?" Trace hit the Pause button, and the man froze halfway to his feet.

"Aside from good manners and a great tan?" Jon eased

his wheelchair a foot toward the screen, then back again. "He's feeling...regret?" Or maybe Jon was simply projecting. Gorgeous women took *him* that way nowadays.

"Stubbed his toe as he stood," Trace countered, not buying it. He continued the action, and the man straightened to his full height. Big, fit and graceful. Suave—he took her extended hand, but instead of shaking it, turned and dropped a kiss on it. The woman's head tilted.

"Conclusions?" Trace prodded.

Beyond the fact that he loathed the lucky stiff? "First meeting," Jon summarized. "But it can't be a date. This woman never answered a personal ad in her life." Not with that "See me and weep" walk, as if she knew her own worth to the penny. Angelina had carried herself that way.

Still does, he reminded himself grimly. If he cared to look. Every day at four o'clock, Channel 10. He forced his mind savagely back to the problem at hand. "Sophisticated. Shows in the haircut and the way she took that kiss." That wasn't the first time a man had kissed her fingers, and it sure wouldn't be the last. "This is business," he decided. "That little black suit says she's serious. And...she's very good at whatever she does."

"How d'you figure that?"

"She's dressed for work, but she's confident enough to play it her way." The suit was silk, and it was tailored to subtly celebrate every curve. The skirt was cut short enough to show that her thighs would match the rest of her. "She's way past pretending she's one of the boys with boxy tailoring and sensible shoes." This one was feminine to her toenails, and those would be polished—to match her silk undies from Paris.

"Anything more?"

"He's not your standard frat boy, either. More than a passing resemblance to Omar Sharif." *Blast him.* "And he knows it, witness the mustache. Spanish? Or maybe Arabic?"

"American." Trace grinned at his brother's grunt of disgust, then relented. "But his father was Syrian."

"Ah...and he has money, of course." Like Angelina, this one would expect money as her due. "This restaurant will cost him—she's not the type to split the tab. And look at his signet ring. And that suit, hardly off-the-rack." He glanced at his brother. "I could go on, but you know this already."

Trace nodded. "But anytime you want a job in analysis, bro, I'll put in the word for you."

"I *am* in analysis." Archeological chemistry was all analysis, not that he'd seen the inside of a lab in months.

"Really? I thought you were into brooding these days."

"Back off," Jon said as lightly as he could manage, stretching his fingers wide in a feigned stretch. He turned blindly back to the screen.

Any other man he'd have shown the door for that crack. Only his brother could push him to his limit and beyond. They'd saved each other's asses time and time again, but after their latest transaction he was the debtor.

Because it was Trace he'd called after his accident, and it had taken only a shakily casual "Guess where I am?" to send his brother flying halfway round the world, to collect Jon from a tiny clinic in southern Chile, then oversee his medevac back to the States.

He'd ditched a long-anticipated vacation to do that—a ski trip to British Columbia—and with it a budding relationship, Jon surmised. Trace dodged all his questions on the whereabouts of Hilda whenever he tried to ask. Still, Jon counted her as part of his bill, and no small part. Trace didn't pair up easily.

"So...what's her link to your interests?" he asked, relieved to find his voice sounding normal again.

"Probably nothing." Trace sounded as elaborately un-
concerned. "She's more of a sideline we uncovered in our
travels, just somebody we're wondering about. Likely no
more than a scenic detour."

But you want to be sure, Jon added silently. Was that
where Trace saw him coming into this? *Then think again,
friend.* If Trace imagined pretty women were any sort of
inducement... *Burn me twice? Not in this lifetime, thank
you.* Still, though she wasn't for him, he was scorched, not
dead, and therefore remained curious.

"Where'd you run across her?"

"It's a long story. And a dry one." Trace stopped the
film again.

Jon tipped his head toward the kitchen. "Bring me another one, too. And watch the bar," he added automatically
as Trace reached the doorway.

"Considering it's eye level..." Trace ducked his head
and passed under the chin-up bar. "You can reach it
from...?" His voice trailed off and a light gleamed around
the corner as he opened the refrigerator.

"Yeah." Foster, one of his ex-students now teaching
over in Botany, had lowered it to its present position for
Jon. He was up to eighty chin-ups a day, and those were
harder than the normal sort, his legs unable to straighten
and weighted down by casts.

"So tell," he demanded when Jon had handed him a
green bottle, and lifted his own in wry salute. "What's her
story?"

"It starts with a motor yacht belonging to an American
heiress that cruised through the Black Sea two months
ago...."

The Russian connection at last. "And?"

BY THE TIME HIS BROTHER had finished, the couple in the
restaurant was dallying over their after-dinner coffee. Not

once had she turned Jon's way. Trace hit the Pause button and ambled off to the bathroom. Jon shifted irritably in his chair—no position was comfortable after three months— and looked from her smooth dark head to the Fast-Forward button on the remote. Or was that what Trace wanted him to do? So he'd wait.

Meanwhile there was the puzzle. A package passed in the dead of night to the yacht *Aphrodite*. At least, the CIA's informant *thought* it had passed. Its carriers had rowed off into the darkness with the box aboard, then rowed back later without it.

"They could also have chucked it into the water. Or passed it to any of the fishing boats at anchor," Jon had pointed out.

But all other vessels in the harbor that night had been local boats—hence the snitch's conclusion that the package, an unusual event, went to the unusual boat, the one capable of smuggling it abroad.

And maybe it did. *Or maybe not.* To wrap a riddle round the puzzle, nobody knew what was in the box. *This is what my tax dollars go for?* To buy information like this? Heck, he would speculate for free for them if it would help with the national debt. *Anybody consider that it might have been somebody's clean laundry they were delivering?* But, no. Trace said the deliverymen were the baddies, foot soldiers for one of the Moscow Mafia syndicates he'd been following. Ugly customers.

Challenged to guess what they might be smuggling aboard a yacht, he'd had suggestions, some of them down-right chilling.

The simplest being that the package contained gold or other currency, the ill-gotten gains of some ex-Communist politico, or the worse-gotten loot of one of the Moscow gangs. Considering the shakiness of the country, anyone

who had the means to move their hoard to an offshore bank
might well do so.

By the same token, the box could have contained stolen
artwork. Rumor had it that many a masterpiece that vanished in World War II had ended up in Russia. Tight as
the times were over there, now might be the time to sell
that Degas or van Gogh sketch on the international black
market, and again, bank the proceeds offshore.

Or use them in a modern-day version of the triangle
trade. "Money, artwork or stolen arms from Russia buys
opium in Burma or cocaine in Colombia," Trace elaborated. "Pays for the ships to smuggle it to the U.S. and the
bribes to slide it across our border. Profits are astronomical.
Some of the money is banked offshore—a comfy retirement
nest egg. The rest buys legitimate technology and goods to
be shipped to Russia to earn more money, then round
again."

"And who says they don't understand capitalism?" Jon
rubbed three days' worth of bristles, then grimaced—if he'd
known Trace meant to drop in on him, he would have
shaved. "What else might it be?"

The box had been just large enough to contain a human
being, curled up. Willingly? Somebody emigrating the hard
way? Or unwillingly? Because VIP kidnapping was another
racket the gangs were exploring.

"But to an American yacht?" Jon had protested, realizing as he said it how naive that sounded.

"The *Aphrodite*'s half as long as a football field, with a
crew of four plus owner and guests. It's likely our heiress
never sets foot in her engine room or the crew's quarters.
She could know all—or be entirely in the dark."

As were they. And the dark bred bogeymen. Black imag-
inings. Trace's final surmise was the worst of all. Pluto-
nium, ripped off from a Russian missile works? Bound for

one of the renegade nations that yearned to join the atomic club or for terrorist bomb-makers here in the U.S.A.

"You really know how to cheer a guy up!" Jon glanced bitterly at his TV set. From a beautiful woman to world-wide death and destruction in one short hour. Two thumbs down on *this* show. "But what's her connection to this?"

"Him—'Omar,' whose actual name is Richard Sarraj." Her dinner companion had first appeared when the *Aphrodite* returned to the Med and stopped off in Lebanon. By then, the CIA had traded info with the FBI—nothing ever came for free, apparently—and Trace's cohorts were watching, too. Sarraj had come aboard for a week while the yacht was in port.

After that he'd traveled throughout the region for another month. "Syria, Arabia, Kuwait, Egypt, Algeria. Skipped Israel, which might tell us something. Our background on him—deep as we've dug—says he's an ex-stockbroker, reputable Manhattan firm. Now self-employed as a consultant—for which read 'fixer.' Helps rich Saudis spend all that oil money. They prefer to invest in stable countries like the U.S., and they need to diversify. Find other sources of income before the oil runs out. Half Syrian, Sarraj can walk both sides of the line. Brother Arab offering trust-worthy advice, or insider American who knows his way around the wilds of Wall Street. There're plenty of others playing that game, plenty of them honestly. Or—he could have found himself the perfect cover."

"For?"

"For international terrorism. Either as a player or as their loyal errand boy. He can carry messages across borders, meet people in power with the perfect excuse, move huge sums of money around the world and justify every penny."

"But you've got precisely zip on him, except he came aboard the *Aphrodite*. Could have been social. Or maybe he was drumming up business?" He didn't even like the guy; why was he defending him? "How many people have come and gone since you started watching?"

"Roughly fifty," Trace had admitted.

Which means you're busier than the long-tailed cat in a room full of rockers if you're trying to watch all of them, dig into their affiliations, their backgrounds. Even the FBI had limits on the resources it could bring to bear. Which was where he came into this? Amateur hour? Trace had used him for a brief consulting job once before, strictly behind-the-scenes analysis on a chemical bombing.

This time I'm not in the mood. I just want to hear the end of the story, then it's good night, Irene. "Can we get to the babe?"

"Sure." Trace's grin was instantly banished. "When Sarraj headed home at last, he stopped off in the Cayman Islands. Opened a bank account for a blind syndicate, naming himself as the managing partner. No other names specified, simply code numbers for the other members. Since the bank never knew in the first place, we can't find out who's backing him. But twenty million dollars was wired to that account from a bank in Malta a week ago today."

Jon whistled. "Payoff for whatever was in that package?"

"Could be. Also could be entirely unrelated—legitimate investors pooling money for him to use on their behalf. Whichever, the next day he went out and bought controlling interest in a small company in Brooklyn."

"Hers?"

"Nope, but you're getting warm. It's a firm that specializes in putting perfume into those sample strips in magazines. They've patented a new process that supposedly makes the strips airtight."

Jon nodded. "People with chemical allergies have been complaining. If they've solved the scent leakage problem, and the process is protectable, they should be golden. Maybe we should ask Sarraj for a hot tip?''

Ignoring that gibe, Trace aimed the remote at the screen. ''Here's what he did next.'' The subject broke his frozen pose with a broad smile at his companion and a few brief words.

Her head tipped to one side, a black bell tolling. Then slowly she shook it. *Bong!* A deep brazen note, Jon felt its reverberations in his stomach, not his ears.

Her hands rose into view again—she talked with her hands, he'd noticed. Long slender fingers, graceful gestures, dark-polished nails. ''Whatever he's proposing, she's not buying.'' *Tell him no, babe.* If he interested Trace and his pals that much, she ought to steer clear.

''Give it a minute.''

Whatever her disclaimer, Sarraj was the one who wasn't buying. He smiled again, a dismissive, ''There, there, little girl, leave the worries to me'' kind of smile, and reached into his suit jacket. Withdrew a checkbook. Jon made a noise deep in his throat. *Don't!*

She sat very still while he filled in the check. As he ripped it off the book, she shrugged, reminding Jon that she was part French. She reached to take it, glanced down—and went very still.

''How much?'' Jon asked grimly.

''Half a mil.''

Jon let his breath out in a low whistle. ''What's he buying?''

''That's what we want you to find out.''

Jon ignored that for the minute. Refusals would come later, but now... ''But supposing he is what he claims to be and the deal's legit?''

''Then he just bought her nose.''

CHAPTER TWO

DEMI COUSTEAU HAD ALWAYS imagined that should an angel come to your aid, he'd come smelling of stale garlic and cheap wine, disguised as a shabby beggar. Or perhaps as a cripple.

His rags and misfortune were a test: *Are you compassionate, oh, Demi? And thus deserving of a heavenly helping hand? Or will you pass this beggar by and never see the wings beneath his cloak?*

Well, so much for expectations! The angel seated across the table smelled of Givenchy's Xeryus, with its soul notes of musk and leather, and he'd traded his rags for the sublime attentions of a London tailor. Far from haggard, he was as darkly sleek as a movie star, hardly starving after the sherried lobster he'd just consumed, and he'd had a manicure more recently than she had.

And he was offering money from the outset, not begging for it. Under cover of her lashes, Demi counted the figures on his check again. Six. The wine had not addled her wits.

She held in her hands the answer to all her prayers— well, all but one. And the man himself might be the answer to— She swerved away from that thought. *Keep your mind on the money, my girl!* The last time she'd mixed romance with business, her heart and her pride had taken an unaccustomed drubbing. She wouldn't make that mistake again.

But perhaps it would be a mistake to accept this miracle at face value. Perhaps this was precisely the heavenly test she'd been set—would she take advantage of a newcomer to her world? Not a good way to start their association, and besides, he'd learn soon enough. She set the check on the table between them. "This isn't the usual way it's done, Mr. Sarraj, creating a new perfume."

"So?" He didn't retrieve his offering. "As I said, I'm a novice in the field of fine fragrances. Please instruct me."

"The process starts when a fashion designer, or a cosmetics firm, or a celebrity with her own perfume line—an Elizabeth Taylor or a Paloma Picasso—decides that a new scent is needed. Perhaps a fragrance to match the changing trends in fashion—sporty or fresh or romantic.

"Or perhaps the instigators hope to capture a new slice of the market—say, they want a perfume for women from twenty-five to forty, professional women who need to project an image of success and competence at the office. Girlish honeysuckle wouldn't suit a corporate lawyer, you see. So, first of all, the client issues a brief."

"Yes, I know about briefs." Without turning his head, Richard Sarraj snapped his fingers at a passing waiter, then pointed at their half-empty coffee cups. "The man for whom I speak knows the type of perfume he wants, how much he is willing to spend, what slice of the market he means to capture. We'll go into those details at a later date."

"Very good." Demi smiled at the waiter who filled her cup. He gulped as their eyes met, then disappeared from her circle of vision, like a man toppling backward on his heels. "But once the specs of the brief have been determined..." Here came the hard part, her test. "Then the brief is usually thrown open to several of the perfume manufacturers. Major players like International Fragrance and Flavorings, Quest, Firmenich, Elias. Their Noses will compete to create a fragrance that best fulfills your brief."

She drew a breath and refused to look down at the check. "And up to the point that someone wins that brief, whether it takes a year, two years, or even five, everyone works for free. We all seek your business, you see."

But unlike the big boys, she couldn't afford to go on for another year or two eating her costs and overhead, gambling that at the end her fragrance would win the day. She hadn't enough cash on hand to keep her lab running another two months, much less two years. Why, her lab tech's salary alone...

"Yes, we know that, too. But..." Richard Sarraj lifted his cup and drank, holding her gaze over its rim. With those dark, liquid eyes he looked extraordinarily like Omar Sharif—and he had an actor's knack for delivering a line. "But my prince wants *you*."

An angel sent by a *prince* was offering to save her? Demi cast aside all doubts and surrendered to the miracle. It would be churlish, after all, to turn down manna from heaven. Still, she lifted one eyebrow—a gesture she'd spent months perfecting in the mirror after seeing her first Garbo movie at age thirteen.

"A Saudi prince," Sarraj answered the silent inquiry. "Not in direct line to the throne, of course, so he wishes to make his mark in business. And like all Saudis, he's a romantic. Longing for the glory days, spice caravans across the desert. Arabs were the earliest perfumers, you know."

"'Fill the tent with a variety of perfumes,'" Demi quoted softly. "'Ambergris, musk and all sorts of scents, rose, orange flowers, jonquils, jasmine....'" The recipe for a seduction from *The Perfumed Garden*, a fifteenth-century book of erotica—a successful seduction.

Her reference sparked no answering glint in Sarraj's eye.

He must not know it. "Exactly so. Even Shakespeare wrote of 'all the perfumes of Arabia.' My prince would rather spend his money in an effort to restore his people's lost art than invest in plumbing supplies or ulcer medicine."

"Of course." Anyone with soul was captured by perfume, its heady sensuality, its ancient glamour. "But why did he choose me?"

Sarraj showed his excellent teeth. "Modesty is a great virtue in woman! But we have followed your career. That pheromonic cologne you created for Pherotics last year— Irresistible? It was very well named."

"Thank you." But she hadn't proved irresistible to her client, Reese Durand, owner of Pherotics. He'd chosen Nicola—Nic—instead, and Demi was still hurt and bewildered by his choice. To her mind, she and Reese had seemed made for each other. And worse yet, she'd met no one in the year since who could knock Reese out of her heart. Having once seen Paris, how could you settle for Poughkeepsie?

"Besides your obvious talent, there's another reason," Sarraj continued. "The prince must deal with the Western world, that is the reality of the marketplace. But when possible, he is most comfortable doing business with his own people." He inclined his dark head in a courtly half bow. "Such as you, Ms. Cousteau."

She hid her urge to laugh aloud behind a wide, brilliant smile. "The prince is most kind." If a trifle misguided! The last time *she'd* seen a camel was in the Bronx Zoo. Just because her grandmother was Egyptian, or—

Oh, please! Surely they couldn't know about Ali? Her first true crush—not counting her mother's doorman—Ali had been a gorgeous twenty-four to her smitten fifteen. She'd had two delirious months showing him the city. She'd even attended mosque to prove her devotion. Then he'd learned her true age and dumped her overnight. A diplomat's aide couldn't break the laws of the country in which he was stationed, he'd explained, wiping her tears for her. *"But when you grow up, Dark Eyes—"*

For which she'd slapped him silly and stormed off. How

dared he suggest she was not a grown woman? That their affair could be anything less than true love everlasting?

He'd been right, of course—her heartbreak hadn't lasted four months. But even so, he'd been a gentleman to his gallant chauvinist toes, not a kiss-and-teller. *So figure that one out later.* "I see." She flicked the check with a tapered nail. "And so this is for?" It was best to be clear.

"The first installment toward your fee." Sarraj's knowing smile assured her—he understood the final bill would be much, much higher.

"Should I decide to accept your brief," Demi reminded him, eyes wide and guileless. It was never wise to surrender yourself easily or cheaply, even when you were hell-bent on surrendering. She'd learned that rule by age eighteen. *Always hold something back. Let them come to you.* The last time she'd forgotten that, with Reese—

"Quite. And should you do so, there are certain terms we must insist upon." A suave crack of the whip, reminding her who was the boss here.

The golden rule—he with the gold, rules. If Sarraj was an angel, he was a tough one, more of the avenging sort than the heavenly-choir type, she suspected. "Yes?" She allowed her eyes to slide to his wrist, with its massive gold Rolex. Let him think she wasn't worried—was in fact bored, perhaps preparing to leave him, not hanging anxiously on his every word. *What terms?* She'd known this was too good to be true!

"First..." He steepled his stubby fingers. "First, money is no object. You must use only the finest of ingredients in creating this perfume. The prince wants the very best."

"I...believe I can live with that," she said gravely, laughter fizzing like champagne within. She'd worried for a minute? This was a twenty-four-karat-gold miracle drawn by a team of matched Rolls-Royces! It was always the cost-cutting that limited a perfumer's creativity. With a client who didn't fret about the bottom line, she'd create a miracle to match Sarraj's own. *Magic in a bottle!*

"And second," Sarraj continued sternly, "you must allow us to use your name in any publicity we choose to generate. The prince has no wish to pretend that he created this fragrance, only to reap its rewards."

Were they mind readers, to answer her every wish? This was the main reason she'd left her secure and well-paid position as senior perfumer with one of New York's finest fragrance houses, to start her own company. The traditional insistence on the Nose's anonymity...that obsequious collusion in the fiction that the designer or the celebrity had created *her* work of art... Her realization that no one outside the discreet walls of the industry would ever know her name.

But no first-rate composer or painter would have denied his soul's children for money. Why should she?

So Sarraj's prince offered her this? The right to sign her masterpiece? The right to stand proudly before the world and say, *This is mine? I made it, a fragrance that gives millions a glimpse of heaven? A classic perfume women will be wearing a hundred years from now?*

Demi Cousteau reached for the check. "Mr. Sarraj? I believe we can do business...."

RAIN, THE OILY STREETS of Manhattan slick and gleaming with it... Traffic like a stampede of wet sow-bugs jammed carapace to carapace in the depths of a dark canyon... Horns echoing off stone... Air thick with diesel fumes. Sodden people scurrying through puddles, their faces harried or desperate or glum. God, he hated the city—any city! Why had he ever let Trace talk him into this farce?

Jon Sutton looked from the unmoving traffic beyond the windshield wipers to his watch. He was twenty minutes late for his appointment with Demi Cousteau already. A swell way to start a job interview.

The driver of the disabled car service had caught that movement in his mirror. "Wha'd I tell you? There's a grid-lock alert on."

"So next time I'll take the subway." *Right. In a wheel-chair.* He should be home in Princeton, holed up in his apartment, not dealing with traffic jams, crowds and a downpour when he couldn't even walk. They weren't three blocks from his destination and, at this rate, it would be noon tomorrow before they arrived. "Okay, what's my bill? I'm out of here."

"Hey, just be patient, buddy. I'll getcha there."

Doctors, lawyers, friends and colleagues had been advising him for months to be patient. Patience had gotten him precisely nowhere. "Out," Jon repeated in a voice that worked equally well with Princeton freshmen and Third World bureaucrats. It wasn't the volume, it was the tone....

"Okay, okay, that'll be twelve." The cabbie closed his door with a slam and stomped around to slide open Jon's, then activate the hydraulic platform that lowered him to the street.

"Give me a receipt for fifteen." Jon handed him two bills and waited, rain drizzling down his collar, dribbling through his ludicrous new haircut. Maybe it was the hair, not the weather or the city, that had wrecked his mood. That and the extra-thick glasses made with nonprescription lenses he was supposed to wear.

"The little things count when you're working under-cover," Trace had said to justify his transformation after the woman he'd brought in to cut Jon's hair had gone away again, giggling. "We want you to fade into the woodwork. Can't have Cousteau and her pals taking you seriously," he'd added straightfaced—then passed him a mirror.

No danger there! Not that he'd ever been much to brag

on, but now? He looked like a sheepdog who'd gone thirteen rounds with a weed whacker. He looked like— Jon drew a steadying breath. *Like precisely what I've agreed to be for the next few weeks. A nerdish loser looking for a job he's barely qualified to fill. Mr. Milquetoast with his marvelous chemistry set.*

"Here." The cabbie handed over a receipt, then stepped behind him. "Let's get you up on the curb. I could lose my license, letting you out here."

"I'll be fine."

"The hell you will. Next ramp's at the corner."

Teeth clenched, Jon allowed himself to be tipped skyward, raindrops smacking him full face, then heaved up onto the sidewalk. "Thanks." Grimly he set off down the block. *Big Wheels on parade.* He could have been home, warm and dry, watching cooking shows on the tube with a beer in his hand.

Feeling sorry for yourself! an inner voice jeered.

Sorry—and dry. It was all Demi Cousteau's lab technician's fault. Beautiful women could take care of themselves. Beauty was an impenetrable defense—none should know better than he—but her lab tech… "You did what?" he'd demanded, not believing his ears.

Trace and his Fibbie friends had had the guy, a Filipino working in the States, hauled into Immigration the day after that video of Cousteau had been filmed. A question of some unspecified irregularity in his papers, they'd told the man.

On the archeological digs every summer in Pakistan and Turkey, Jon had seen for himself what it was like in the poorest countries. A man crawled up from such poverty only with the greatest determination and sacrifice. "Haven't you people ever heard the words 'There but for the grace of God go I'?"

Sure they had, but words like "national security" chimed louder in FBI ears. Hector Domingo had been whisked from the country before he could catch his breath. And the lab tech had been warned that if he wanted to return to the States once his mysterious irregularities had been cleared up, then, in the meantime, he'd best keep his mouth tightly zipped indeed. In particular, he was not to contact his ex-boss, who had unspecified difficulties of her own with Immigration.

Jon had been told too late to save the lab tech. But at least he could cut a deal on his behalf. Trace wanted him to apply for the man's job? All right, he'd do it. He wasn't doing anybody much good, he had to admit, sulking around his apartment. Might as well go skulk for God and country. It probably beat nature shows, watching hyenas munch Bambi.

But in return—on the *very* long shot that Cousteau hired him—his salary must be passed on to its rightful recipient. Let Trace and his buddies sweat, cooking up some plausible excuse for paying the guy.

And once this investigation was completed—always assuming Demi Cousteau wasn't residing behind bars in some federal prison—the man must be restored to his job. "Take it or leave it," he'd said bluntly, hoping Trace would leave it.

Instead, Trace had accepted his terms. Three days later, here he was, his wheels splashing through puddles in midtown Manhattan, on his way to apply for a job he didn't want in a city he hated. All the lab tech's fault, blast him.

He found the address he'd been given with no trouble—a midsize, midblock building of dingy stone in the West Side middle Fifties. Negotiating the lobby's heavy glass door would have been trouble, but, as Jon maneuvered his chair to one side, someone opened the door from within. "Thanks." He looked up into a man's dark and cheerful face, somebody in maintenance, judging from his well-washed gray uniform.

"Anytime." The custodian returned to his push broom.

Jon wheeled over to stare up at a glassed-in directory hung between the elevators. Cousteau had given the name of her company as Alluroma, International when he'd responded to her help-wanted ad. At least he suspected that had been Cousteau. The soft voice on the phone had held the faintest suggestion of an exotic accent and a cool authority.

"Help you find somebody?" the maintenance man asked just as Jon's eyes lit on her company's name and its floor. *Twenty-three.* "No, thanks. I'm set." Jon jabbed the Call button. Why did people leap to the conclusion that a man's mind wasn't functioning just because it rode in a body that didn't perform according to the norm? Had he himself been this insensitive? If so, never again.

The elevator doors slid open and he rolled inside, then closed his eyes in frustration. It would be a bitch to reach over his left shoulder and hit the control panel. *Should have backed in, dammit.*

The closing doors rebounded as the janitor grabbed an edge and leaned into the car. "Hey, mister?"

Jon contained a snarl, refusing to look behind him. "I'll manage, thanks." Accepting help often came harder to him than muddling through difficulties in his own way, at his own speed.

Mr. Helpful didn't retreat. "You wouldn't have a brother whose first name begins with *T,* would you?"

Jon turned his head sharply but still couldn't see him. "I...might."

"What's the rest of it?" The speaker's voice had changed subtly, sharpened, its consonants no longer slurred.

"Trace—Allan Tracey." *And if you're not one of his friends, then I'm an idiot.* Had he just fallen for—

"Thought so," came the crisp response. "In that case, don't look for Alluroma on twenty-three. Go to twenty-nine.'' He released the door, leaving Jon to press his own buttons.

He elbowed fourteen, giving himself a moment to consider as the car rose. Cousteau's floor number in the directory had read twenty-three, no mistake about that. But a directory number was easy to change if you could open the case that enclosed it. *Shouldn't be much of a feat for a G-man.*

So every other applicant for this job had gone to the wrong floor? He'd been wondering why Trace was so sure he could have the position for the asking. And Cousteau would be unlikely to check the number herself any more than he verified his own address every time he returned home.

But when the job seekers didn't find her office on twenty-three, wouldn't they ask somebody? The doors rolled open at the fourteenth floor. Jon back-jabbed the button for twenty-three. *Let's go see.* Like most scientists, he suffered from a double helping of curiosity. And now that he was forty-five minutes late for his interview... *Might as well be hanged for a sheep as a lamb.*

Minutes later, he stopped his chair outside a door on the twenty-third floor. Alluroma, International. The neat black letters on its glass panel were as fresh as if they'd been painted yesterday, which they probably had.

And if he opened that door, ventured within to apply for a job? Would he meet a woman claiming to be Demi Cousteau, possibly even resembling the real one? Not that they'd find a face to equal the one he'd seen on Trace's video, not if they searched for a year.

But was there some woman within who'd accept his résumé, then inform him sweetly that she was *terribly* sorry, but she'd hired another applicant not an hour before?

Jon was tempted to put his theory to the test. But there was no sense in confusing your own allies, and besides, he was now fifty minutes late. He was going to have a tough enough time placating the real Demi Cousteau, up on twenty-nine.

CHAPTER THREE

WHEN HAD PEOPLE GROWN so undependable? Too angry to sit, Demi Cousteau prowled her office. Jon Sutter was nearly an hour late, which meant he'd be a no-show like the others. "Six in two days!" What had happened to common courtesy? Not one of them had bothered to call and cancel his appointment! "People like this I didn't need to hire anyway!"

But she needed someone, and she needed him yesterday. She stalked back to her desk to stare down at her computer screen, which displayed the formula she was developing. She could have mixed it herself, but with time being of the essence... And it was, it was, it was. Sarraj had forgotten to mention one very "minor" matter at their dinner meeting Monday night. He'd told her two days later when they met again to discuss the terms of his brief. And now it was Friday.

Sarraj's princely client demanded the finest, most luxurious, most heavenly scent ever created for a woman...and he wanted it in two...short...*months.*

"Two months!" she'd cried aloud. "Guerlain's Chant d'Arômes took seven *years* to develop!" Who did the prince think she was—a composer of dime-store colognes or room deodorizers? *Pah!* She couldn't make a perfume to please a cat in sixty days!

"That is his absolute, irrevocable time limit," Sarraj had stated austerely. "Carved in stone. So if you cannot do it, then—"

Then she could return his check and lose Alluroma—and go crawling back to whichever fragrance and flavoring firm would have her. Then maybe she *would* be working on room fresheners a month from now.

And, oh, but wouldn't they laugh? She'd been warned that it took deep pockets to survive the cutthroat competition of the perfume world. That sheer talent wasn't nearly enough. That no one made it alone nowadays. That pride goeth before the fall. She could just hear them all saying, "Poor Demi, we told you so!"

So she'd swallowed the heart in her throat and told Sarraj, "Of course I can do it." And she would, if she gave up sleeping for the interim. But first she needed a lab tech, and she needed him now. "*Damn* you, Jon Sutter, and the horse you rode in on!"

A low chime sounded like a mocking retort—Demi jumped guiltily. That was the doorbell she'd installed to warn her of callers, since she could afford no receptionist. Instead she maintained the fiction that she had one who'd just stepped out. She glanced at the clock on her wall. If this was Sutter, he was an hour late. This one she would not hire. An undependable perfumer's assistant was much worse than no assistant at all. She stalked to her office door and threw it wide.

Her eyes haughtily swept the air of the opposite doorway at the expected level—and then dropped. A wheelchair was jammed in the entrance, its occupant pink-faced with his efforts to free the contraption. His glasses had slipped to the end of his nose. A rather square jaw was clamped tight with exasperation.

"Oh, *here!* Let me—" Hurrying to the rescue, she caught the uprights beneath his armrests. The doorjamb prevented him from extending his elbows past the wheels to get a decent push, that was the problem.

"I can manage, thank you." A muscle fluttered below

his cheekbone. He smelled of wet wool, rye toast and Old Spice.

"No, I insist." Leaning forward to get a better grip, she insisted, and he popped out of the logjam—his metal footrest ramming her ankles. *"Ouch!"* Bent nearly double, she bunny-hopped backward—then tipped forward over her toes, her hands sliding down the metal uprights as her weight shifted. Her fists landed on his thighs, or something extremely hard where his thighs should have been. There she balanced, nose to nose with the man. *"Oh!"*

Looking up into her reddening face, he laughed aloud. "Quite!" Not three inches separated their lips. His eyes were pale blue above his slipped spectacles. One lock of her hair brushed his cheek.

Hands clamped on her forearms—big hands—and for a horrid instant Demi realized that, should he choose, he could keep her in this humiliating pose indefinitely. Unless she was prepared to plant one knee between his own for leverage, then wriggle, she remained entirely at his mercy.

The wicked smile on a rather nicely shaped mouth suggested their minds moved as one. Then his fingers tightened and he lifted her gently and very efficiently toward the vertical.

She tottered backward on her high heels, then stood. "Well..." She whirled, retreated a step, then spun back again. It was *his* fault. If he'd arrived on time or in a narrower wheelchair— And his amusement wasn't helping at all. Who was he to laugh at her, looking like that? "Whoever gave you that haircut, I trust you shot him?"

The insult bounced right off. "That's why I was late. I had to run him down, then back up over him a couple of times to make sure." He swiped a hand through the light brown disaster, then down again. It looked no better. "That bad, huh?" He shoved his glasses up a straight nose.

"Worse." No way would she consider hiring a man who

looked like a tornado-struck haystack and smelled like a damp sheep. Reese Durand wouldn't have been caught dead wearing pink socks with a brown suit—or pink socks with anything.

She stalked to the reception desk and sat on one corner, crossing her long legs, well aware of the effect that usually produced. But she needed a little leverage here. For a man who couldn't even walk, come asking for a job, he was terribly self-possessed. "I suppose you're Jon Sutter?"

She reminded him of one of his sister Emily's cats. The creature was usually as graceful as a ballerina, but once in a while she'd take a leap at the kitchen counter and miss—go scrabbling ignominiously down the woodwork to land in a heap on the tiles. At such times, you'd better keep your laughter to yourself. The cat would stalk off in high dudgeon, tail on high, quivering with suppressed fury, every line of her body declaring, *Who, me? I had no intention whatsoever of making that leap. And if anyone suggests that I had...* Usually an intense grooming session would follow, the cat acknowledging no witnesses until her ruffled fur and her pride were back in order.

Cousteau straightened the cuffs of her jacket, smoothed a hand down her skirt and lifted one elegant eyebrow. "Well?"

It was hard not to burst out laughing, but laughing at her would be the nail in his coffin. "I am. And I'm sorry I'm late."

"I find tardiness *very* unprofessional."

He'd always thought promptness a highly overrated virtue. But this wasn't the moment to say so. All the same, if she was waiting for him to make an excuse, she'd be sitting there waving those wonderlegs for quite a while. He didn't believe in excuses. Jon smiled gently instead.

His nonresponse made her widen those dark slanted eyes, then narrow them like a cat. Clearly she was used to men stumbling over themselves to please her. How could she not be, looking like that? "And you might have told me...saved us both the inconvenience."

He felt his amusement fade. "Told you what?"

"That you—" She uncrossed her legs with a sizzle of nylon, irritated that he'd force her to say it. "That you don't—won't—fit, Mr. Sutter. Not the position as advertised, and certainly not my door."

"Oh? I seem to be on the inside." He rolled his chair forward a foot to demonstrate.

"If you think I'm going through *that* every day—!" A tinge of rose darkened her high, honeyed cheekbones. Like the cat, she'd sooner pretend it never happened.

"No, I suppose not." He wheeled the chair around to study the doorjamb. Good, it was wood, not metal.

"I'm really sorry, Mr. Sutter," she said behind him. "And I do thank you for coming. I know it must have been a nuisance on a day like—" She stopped as he reversed and trundled over to the inner doorway.

Wood, as well. He swiveled to face her. "Give me a saw, some sandpaper and ten minutes, and I *will* fit."

She let out her breath in a hiss. "I don't particularly care to have my woodwork hacked up. And that's the least of the problem—"

You, babe, never met a problem in your life, I bet, beyond deciding which shade of nail polish to apply. Was this how people would be seeing him the rest of his life if he never walked again? As an incompetent? Somebody who wouldn't fit the plan, whatever the plan might be? "I don't know the precise disability laws, Ms. Cousteau, but I imagine you're breaking them. Shall we ask the state labor board?" He felt his temper rise at the thought of doing so. This wasn't his way, to seek shelter behind the skirts of the law's petty bureaucrats. Was this what the future held for him? *No way! I'll walk again if I have to walk on my hands.*

"Look..." Demi Cousteau slid down off her perch. She caught the wheeled chair placed behind the desk, swung it close to him, then sat so they were on a level. "I'm sorry. Truly I am." Leaning closer, she rested one graceful hand on his good knee. "But I need help right now—need it *desperately!*" She widened those extraordinary eyes in mute appeal.

Jon sucked in a breath, her touch arrowing up his thigh. At least she didn't find his present status repulsive if she'd touch him. Or was this simply honey to make the medicine go down?

"I need help," Cousteau repeated. "And you won't be a help, you'd be an added burden. *Believe* me, if there were any way—"

"I want an interview." And he wanted her hand off him this second, before he embarrassed himself. Barring family and nurses, no woman had touched him in months, and none like this.

Cousteau wasn't used to having her pleas ignored, not by men. "Fine!" She shot to her feet. She was tall for a woman. Standing, he'd have topped her by no more than five inches, but he would settle for that and gladly. "Come into my office." She opened the inner door with an ironic flourish.

Rule one for any man with an older brother: Never turn down a dare. Jon rammed his chair into the gap, lifting his fingers at the last possible moment. It stuck halfway through and he swore.

"Oh, *please...*" She caught the chair handles from behind and shoved, while he forced the wheels. Metal scraped across wood—he popped into her inner sanctum.

She let him go instantly, and Jon wheeled on alone to her desk. *It's you,* he wanted to say, looking around the room. Colorful, dramatic, faintly exotic. The walls were painted something between straw and buttercup—reminded him of a tent he'd lived in one summer, the desert sun glowing through its canvas. He'd bought a woolen rug to lay over the sand, though nothing so sumptuous as the ruby-toned Khorassan presently spread under his wheels. And he'd fantasized piles of silk pillows strewn around, a dark, velvet-soft woman to lie with him on those pillows.... That would have been the summer before he married Angelina. *Lesson being that fantasies beat reality every time.*

He looked back to find Demi Cousteau glowering at her scratched doorway. "I'll fix it." She wasn't just being a bitch. There wasn't one object or color out of place in this room, not a note of discord. A perfectionist, at least in the visual realm.

"You will—if I hire you." She snatched a form off her desk. "Fill out this application. And you brought your résumé?"

She prowled over to the corner where a north window met an east to read it, stood silhouetted against the light and the saber blades of a potted palm. *A nose like Nefertiti's,* he'd thought the other night when she'd risen from the table and turned at last toward the hidden camera. "You've held only the one job since college?"

"That's right." He remembered to print Sutter, not Sutton, in the name blank, then penned in the false social-security number Trace had given him. *Not exactly a swashbuckling career, is it?* Caspar Milquetoast, small-town pharmacist, content to count pills and dispense bottles, imagining no higher calling. He bet she dated CEO's of major companies. And maybe airline pilots. *Would you be any more impressed if I told you I'm a full professor at Princeton?* Probably not. Probably she considered teachers dull.

"Why did you leave that position?"

Because I'm only happy working outside. The lab work, the teaching, that's just the price I pay to get back to the

desert, the mountains, a sky blazing with stars at night.
Another thing about him that Angelina had never understood. This one wouldn't, either, another city girl.

"Umm?" He glanced up from his task as she stirred
impatiently. "I didn't—not willingly. My pharmacy was
bought out by a national chain. They had their own personnel to plug into the spot." *Jon Sutter's a loser, just a
useful pair of hands. Let me fade into your woodwork, be
the humble fly on your wall.*

Instead, he'd started by scarring her woodwork. *Nice going, Jon!* He wasn't subtle enough to be a spy. And lying
left a bad taste in his mouth, even when it was for national
security.

"Do you know *anything* about perfume chemistry, Mr.
Sutter?"

"No." *But your last assistant, Hector Domingo, was
also a pharmacist back in the Philippines, before you took
him on.* "But I'm a quick learner." He was, that. "And I
can measure and mix with precision." He'd been cramming
perfume texts for three days now. Had learned enough to
know that that was the essence of what she'd need from
him. He finished the application and rolled over to present
it.

Her eyes flew down the page. If what he'd garnered
about world-class perfumers was true, then facts on paper
wouldn't sway her decision. Noses were artists, their works
composed not with pigments or notes of music, but with
chords of fragrance. Passionate, creative, often imperious,
they were the divas of the fragrance world.

No matter how smart she was, Cousteau would lead with
her emotions and instinct, not cold logic. Were her instincts
now warning her against him? *Something about me doesn't
ring true? I smell fishy?* He met her gaze with a hopeful,
puppy-dog smile. Somewhere along the way he'd decided

he did want this job. Opposition always brought out his contrary streak.

"I..." She let his form drop to her side. "I couldn't help noticing..." Again that faint, sexy bloom across her cheekbones. "That you seem to be wearing casts, Mr. Sutter. Does that mean that..."

"That this isn't my normal state of affairs? That's right. I had an...accident." Or rather, ran to meet one.

The river welled up from where it lived in his memory—and his nightmares. The silken rush of the water beneath the skin of his kayak lifting him, cradling him, sweeping him onward... His early pride and exultance fading mile by spray-drenched mile... The mocking voice of the cascades. *You wanted risk? Came to* me *for forgetfulness?* His rising terror as he realized that, quick learner or no, this time he'd overreached himself as chute followed chute, down, down, faster and faster...toward the roar of falling water...the rocks... The devastating, *astounding* pain...

"Car wreck!" he muttered, fighting upward toward the air, toward his script. Trace had suggested a car wreck. It was a much more likely form of misfortune for Mr. Milquetoast.

"I see." She frowned, picking her way delicately. "It's not...permanent?"

"Not the casts." Which were due to come off in three weeks. But beyond that? If his right knee didn't work, and the doctors held out little hope... That one at the clinic in Chile had wanted to amputate.... *The hell, you say!* But if it wouldn't bend, then would come the fallback position—more surgery, an artificial knee. Then more months trapped in this chair. *No, it won't come to that. I won't allow it to come to that.*

But after the river, Jon had the full measure of human

will—and its limitations. Sometimes you were a leaf on the dreadful current.

"I see," she murmured, though her tone said otherwise. But at least she stopped probing. "Come see the rest of my setup."

She shoved him through another doorway—he winced at the sound of splintering wood—to show him a warren of small rooms branching off an inner corridor. Bathroom to the left, storerooms and a small, well-equipped kitchenette with a table to the right, everything neat as a pin.

"There's just you and the receptionist?" he asked, remembering the jacket draped across the back of the secretary's chair in the waiting room, the vase of flowers, the phone and the pens set out on the desk.

"Err...that's correct." He glanced back at her sharply. She gave him a breezy smile. "You have just one more door to brutalize, Mr. Sutter. Let's not stop here."

He gritted his teeth as she rammed him into the laboratory—not a large one, but cheerfully businesslike—and he understood her resistance at last. His chin didn't come up to the black Formica countertops. And as for the shelves and shelves of bottles rising to the ceiling on three sides of the room—the essential oils and absolutes that made up the perfumer's palette... He turned to find her waiting, one eyebrow raised. "I can't say it'll be easy," he acknowledged, and rolled closer to the shelves filled with their green, blue and brown glass bottles. Every scent that man had found useful or pleasing over the last three thousand-plus years. *Beethoven had eighty-eight keys to work with, she has thousands!* There were seventeen distinct scents for roses alone, he'd learned.

"But..." He reached for the reshaped coat hanger that he kept in a sling hung from his backrest for just such contingencies. Raising the wire to the top shelf, he hooked a bottle—and yanked.

Barring her screech of mortal anguish, it would have been an easy catch. Instead the siren blast at his ear made him jump and he nearly muffed it. His fingers frantically juggled the prize—then clamped round it at last, and he caught his breath. Swung to offer up the bottle with a modest smile. "But you see it's doable."

"*You...!*" She snatched it from his fingers and cradled it to her breast. "Absolute of *tuberose!* D'you know what this *costs*, you—you barbarian?"

Slowly Jon shook his head. But if she chose to murder him here and now, he might go willingly. With her cool sophistication in tatters, she was a blazing goddess. *Slay me with one bolt, Dark Eyes!*

"More than five hundred dollars—per *ounce!*" Demi Cousteau set the four-ounce bottle on the counter beside her.

Ulp. Smart move, hotshot! "Umm, maybe you could hand me the bottles I'll need, in that case?"

"*Pah!* As if I have nothing better to do? I'm supposed to be the perfumer's assistant's assistant? If you knew how little *time* I have—" She spun on her heels to glare around the room. "And even if I had time, how do you propose to reach the—" She stopped herself and smacked a gray metal instrument topped with a glass tube. "What is this?"

"Gas chromatograph."

"And this?"

"Flashpoint machine."

"And this?"

"A heater-stirrer." Cramming had been a good idea.

"So, at least you know what they are. That's better than the only other—" She paused.

The only other candidate you've seen? Because if Trace was really clever, he wouldn't just keep applicants away from her. He'd send in a few ringers, as well. People clearly not qualified to fill the job. "I know what they are and I can use them," he agreed. "And as for how I'd reach them…"

This would hurt, but he could think of no other way to prove his point. Rolling his chair to where a center island jutted within four feet of a side counter, Jon spread one hand on each surface. They were higher than he liked and the gap wider, but— Pressing down, he groaned with the effort.

Cousteau yelped a protest and lunged to stop him, but he was rising already. The first twelve inches were the bad ones, then he got his elbows locked and the rest was easy. They faced each other, Jon looking down at her finally instead of up, his thighs held parallel to the floor, Demi with her beautiful mouth dropped into a delectable "Oh!"

"Move my chair and bring me that stool," he panted.

"But—"

"*Do* it!" Did she think he could hang around all day?

Making a low sound much like Emily's cat when you stepped on its tail, she kicked his chair out from under him, then snatched up one of the stools shoved under a far counter and scurried back to position it beneath him. *"Here!"*

"Ooof." He settled onto it gratefully. "That…would be roughly the procedure," he added mildly while she glared daggers but didn't find her voice. "Except I'd get a stool with wheels so I could move easily around the room. And I can come up with a simpler way to chin up to the stool. One that won't require your help."

"You…really want this job, don't you?" Her voice vibrated with some deep emotion.

Fury? In part, anyway. Still, she was impressed. Jon nodded, well satisfied. Sometimes showmanship made your best point. He'd learned that years ago as a teacher.

A chime sounded in the distance, startling them both.

When she turned back from the sound, her smile was too

sweet. "Well, I'll give you my full consideration. But right now...I have another applicant to interview."

So close—another minute and he'd have had her! And whoever this interloper was, he'd already proved himself clever enough to bypass the trap on twenty-three.

"Wait here a moment, please, then I'll help you back to your chair."

Jon sat, swearing under his breath. When had he decided he wanted this job?

A minute later she floated back into the lab on those wonderful gams. "Can you do it again?" When he nodded, she rounded the island, caught his chair, wheeled it behind him. Jon raised himself high enough to let her whisk the stool out from under him, then he lowered himself.

They scraped woodwork all the way back to the reception room without speaking. No further questions; clearly she was already focused on her next candidate. He'd lost the moment and the momentum.

Wheeled into the reception room, Jon met the eyes of her next applicant—and blinked.

Clad in a dove-gray business suit, silk burgundy kerchief peeking elegantly from a breast pocket, this morning's custodian met Jon's gaze with a bland, butter-wouldn't-melt stare.

Not bothering with introductions, Demi Cousteau propelled Jon into the corridor, then held out her hand. "I'll be calling you with my decision some time this weekend, Mr. Sutter."

"I look forward to hearing from you." He kept it solemn, fearing a smile would widen to a grin. But that was one nice thing about playing on the fed team. They always had depth in the backfield.

CHAPTER FOUR

BY THE TIME JON MADE it home, his spirits had taken a swan dive. After calling for the disabled van with the portable phone that Trace had given him, he'd gone outside to wait on the corner, and it had turned into a long, wet wait indeed. But he'd been too stubborn to retreat inside, and now he was chilled to the bone. *Springtime in the city.* Acknowledging an outgoing tenant's help with the doors with a noncommittal grunt, he rolled into the lobby of his Upper West Side co-op. A sublet Trace had found for him, its three-month lease should give him plenty of time to do this job.

But she won't give me the job. By the end of their interview, Demi Cousteau had been only too delighted to show him the door. Didn't matter that the guy coming after him was an FBI ringer who'd probably claim he'd flunked high-school chemistry. *I came on too strong, showing off like that? Or maybe not strong enough?* Whatever, something about him had rubbed her wrong.

The elevator door opened to reveal two laughing young women. Their startled eyes dipped to his face, then shot away. They edged past his chair with smiles aimed above and beyond him, then hurried off to the exit. You'd think it was catching, the way people pulled their skirts aside.

And this was why Cousteau hadn't wanted him, he told himself as he entered the car. She'd want her men whole, big and capable, like Sarraj. Why should a beautiful woman settle for less, even in her flunkies? She was a perfectionist. Maybe it pained her to look at him?

And deeper than that—bone deep—her rejection would be instinctive. And justifiable, as all instincts were in the brutal end. Whether they were choosing mechanics or husbands, women chose men who could protect them, protect their babies.

Shuddup! You don't think about— He reached back over his shoulder to punch the button—hit the wrong one and jammed a knuckle, then shook his fingers out all the way up to six. *Snap out of it, Jon. Look at the worst case. She doesn't hire you, and you get to go back home.*

But thinking of his apartment in Princeton didn't cheer him. He'd moved there after his divorce, only a month before his ill-fated jaunt to Chile. It wasn't home, just a hole he'd crawled into while he sorted himself out, a place to stow the boxes and books he'd carted away from the wreckage of his marriage. But after his accident he hadn't had the energy to find better, cheerier digs—a house of his own, since he never willingly shared quarters with strangers.

Speaking of which... Jon winced as he passed a door on the way to his own at the back. The baseline of a disco beat buffeted his eardrums, then gradually diminished as he rolled on. Funny how birdsong, the sound of waves or wind in the trees meshed with your mind, soothed it, while manmade sounds battered and distracted.

I don't belong here. What am I doing here? He'd call Trace and tell him to forget it. That he'd failed. Mr. Milquetoast with his not-so-impressive chemistry set had riled the lady rather than wowed her. *Find somebody studlier to ring her chimes.* Maybe she *would* hire that ringer if he knew the first thing about chemistry.

He maneuvered through the door to his apartment, then paused, staring bleakly down its darkened hallway. *Honey, I'm home!*

He grimaced and switched on the lights. Funny to think that Angelina might be only a mile or two away from here. Not that it was ever the mileage that had done them in. *Ain't the miles, hon, it's the values.* They were worlds apart when it came to what they thought mattered in life.

Shuddup. Stop whining. Transferring himself by chin-up bar to the wheeled stool he used in the galley kitchen, Jon rolled to the sink, filled the kettle, set it on the stove. Swiveled to contemplate the refrigerator—frozen pizza for supper, or chicken pot pie?—then blinked as he saw the note on the counter.

"Trace?" he yelled. His brother had warned him that he wouldn't visit on the off chance that Jon might be watched at some point in this game. But apparently he'd made an exception. He had a key to the place, just in case. "Trace?"

Too much to hope for. He unfolded the note and read.

Won't be seeing you for a few weeks—gone hunting. But a message to that number I gave you will reach me anytime, anywhere. Meantime, good luck with Gorgeous, but don't get too lucky....

"Yeah, yeah, yeah," Jon muttered. They'd discussed this already, consorting with the enemy—or, at least, a subject under surveillance. Unwise. Bound to skew the judgment. *But don't worry, friend. Even if she'd have me, I'm immune. You don't go looking to catch smallpox a second time if you survive the first.*

TAKE ONE GIANT LEAP forward, then stumble two steps back. Demi Cousteau rubbed her aching temples and stared blankly at her computer screen, which displayed the eighteenth variation of the first formula she was exploring for Sarraj. She shouldn't take this any further tonight. Tired as she was, everything smelled like yesterday's oatmeal.

She shouldn't fiddle with this formula at all till she'd actually smelled it. For which she'd need someone to mix it. *One minute I win the brief to die for, the kind of commission perfumers spend their whole lives dreaming about. Then the next thing I know, Hector disappears like a rabbit stuffed down a magician's hat! What is this—some kind of cosmic joke?*

And to replace him I have my choice of a maniac on wheels or a murderer? Not that Greenley, the applicant after Sutter, had admitted to murder. He'd claimed he'd been imprisoned for embezzling a very modest sum from a former employer. Prison was where he'd earned his B.S. in chemistry by correspondence course.

But if he thought embezzlement was an acceptable crime to admit to, then what did he really do? She hadn't bothered calling his reference—the prison warden—to ask. Because embezzler or ax murderer, Greenley wouldn't do.

Which left her with Sutter—undoubtedly intelligent. Also late, rumpled and possibly a lunatic, considering that stunt he'd pulled with her tuberose absolute. And there was something else about the man, something she couldn't put her finger on that disturbed her all the same. "Eight million people in New York and these are my choices?" Maybe a few more would trickle in come Monday, but could she wait?

She could not. *So, ax murderer or haystack man?* Demi glanced over her shoulder at the dark doorway leading to the lab. With whom would she rather work late, night after night, with nobody else in the building? She sighed and reached for her phone.

But when it rang at his end a dozen times without a pickup, she frowned. He didn't even own an answering machine? That wasn't a good—

"Hello!" He sounded breathless and more than a little annoyed.

She had a sudden picture of him bumbling frantically across a room on wheels. This would never do; he hadn't the mobility for the job. But to hang up on him now... "Mr. Sutter? Demi Cousteau..."

"Oh..." A note of surprise. "Yes, I...wasn't expecting a call this late. Can you hang on a minute?"

The phone thumped in her ear as he set it down, and she glanced at her watch. Ten. Time always flowed when she was composing. Still, that wasn't late for the city on a Friday night. She often set out on dates at this hour. But then Sutter came from the country. His pharmacy had been located in a small town in western Connecticut.

That's another thing. Why, if he's such a stick-in-the-mud, worked in one town all his life, did he suddenly uproot himself, move to the city to look for a job? Not that there was any place else in the world to live and work, as far as she was concerned.

"Popcorn," he stated, coming back on the line. He had a nice voice, midweight, neither tenor nor bass. "Had to turn it off."

Nobody else there to turn it off for him? She hadn't even thought to ask this afternoon if he was married. *With that haircut, how could he be?* No wife would let him out of the house looking like that.

"You're calling me to tell me thanks but I won't do," he said into her silence. "That's very kind of—"

"I was calling to say that you might do, actually." She hurried to add, "I haven't checked your reference yet. But assuming that's satisfactory, I was wondering if you'd consider working on probation for a week?" That would give her time to interview more applicants. And meantime maybe she'd find that he *could* fill Hector's shoes. Stranger things had happened. "To see if we suit each other..." she continued when he didn't respond.

"You want me to temp," he said evenly.

Was he insulted? "To temp *temporarily*—and at full pay. It's not a matter of money, it's..." And it wasn't his immobility, as much as that worried her. It was something else. She hadn't gotten a handle on him yet, when usually she could sum up men at a glance. As she pictured him now at the other end of the line, he almost seemed to...*waver,* like a mirage. "It's that I'm looking for a long-term relationship. You'd be my right hand. If we aren't in tune..."

She couldn't have tension in her lab. To do her best work she needed to reach a plane of vibrant peace where she could focus all her senses and energy inward. Hector had freed her of all the petty office drudgeries to work like that, and he'd had olfactory talent, as well. She'd found she could bounce ideas off him. His opinions had really meant something.

"And I forgot to ask you today, are you willing to work late when we're on a deadline, as we are right now? I'll give you comp time later on, but when I need you... For instance, I'm still at the office."

"But it's after ten. Is there anybody else in the building in case—" He cut that thought short. "And how do you mean to get home at this hour? Nobody will be out on the streets when you—"

She laughed softly. What was he proposing, to come rolling to her rescue? If a mugger accosted them, she'd end up protecting *him!* Still, he was sweet to worry, whatever else he was. "When I work this late, I call a car service. I'm careful, believe me."

"I damn sure hope so."

His disapproving growl made her smile and suddenly decide. *He just might do.* She'd never minded gallantry in her men.

"All right," he said, suddenly decisive, too. "I'll work

a week for you as a temp if that's what you want. When d'you need me—tomorrow?''

"You'd come in weekends?" Then he definitely wasn't married and— She reached out to touch her computer screen. If she could smell this tomorrow, start building on that... "That would be wonderful!"

APPARENTLY, PROMPTNESS was a trait Demi Cousteau required of employees, not the boss. Portable phone at his ear, Jon glared overhead at her building's northeast windows. *Where are you, dammit?* The lobby doors were locked for the weekend; she'd said to phone her when he arrived at noon. He'd been calling off and on for some twenty minutes, and though it was sunny today, it was cold. He should have guessed that, like Angelina, she'd assume the world set its clocks by her schedule, whether she was running early or late.

The roar of an engine ending in a screech of tires made him snap his head around. The yellow cab's driver sprang out his door and hurried to open his passenger's, a courtesy Jon had never seen before in the city.

Long shapely legs pivoted to the pavement. Demi Cousteau gave her hand to the cabbie, rose gracefully to her high heels—and smiled. The man stood transfixed—as if she held *him* up—then he roused himself with a start and bustled off to open his trunk.

"Jon, I'm so sorry I'm late!" She joined him on the sidewalk, flushed and breathless as if she'd run a mile to meet him. Her hair wasn't bell smooth this morning, but curling and tousled. He imagined her rising from her bed to give it a sleepy shake. "I didn't think it would take so long to—" She shrugged blithely and turned as the cabbie arrived with the long box he'd pulled from the trunk.

"Where would you like it, my lady?" The man's accent

was something Middle Eastern. The glance he shot Jon was pure Othello.

"Give it to Jon, here," Demi commanded, unlocking the lobby doors. "And thank you *so* much, Jafar."

Jafar clutched the four-foot package tighter to his chest. "Lady, I will carry it."

And welcome to it, buddy. Two years of playing step and fetch it had been enough for Jon. Besides, saddled with that package, he wouldn't be able to turn his wheels.

"*Nonsense.* You have people to meet, fares to collect...." She tapped the wheelchair's armrest invitingly. "Jon can handle it."

And so now what did he do, claim he couldn't? Grimly he accepted the burden—earning himself a drop-dead scowl from Jafar—and balanced one end between his knees. With her conquest almost bowing them through the door, Demi pushed his chair into the lobby while she called cheery farewells over her shoulder and assurances that, yes indeed, if she ever needed a cab again, she would call no one but Jafar.

"Whew!" She laughed as she rolled him toward the elevator. "I'm sorry I left you out in the cold. This took longer to find than I expected."

He didn't take the bait and ask her what she'd bought as the elevator carried them upward, though he should have. Jon Sutton would have.

He'd started out this morning reminding himself of the part he was supposed to be playing—eager-to-please, harmless geek and nerd, not to be taken seriously. He had a feeling he'd dropped the ball once or twice during their first interview. So today he would stick to his script.

But he hadn't counted on her using him as a shopping cart, dammit. And there was nothing he hated more than to be pushed. He spun his own wheels. Chose his own path at his own speed.

She must have caught something of his mood, because she stopped talking abruptly. He could feel her eyes on the back of his neck. "What time did you get home last night?" he asked to break the charged silence.

"About midnight. I went out for a bite after I talked to you."

Alone or on a date? he found himself wondering. Though even if she'd started out alone, the men of Manhattan would have seen she didn't end that way.

Unlocking the door to Alluroma, she declared, "First of all, I'll give you a rundown on the project we're working on."

"Nope. First comes access." Jon set her box to the side of the door and reached for the satchel he'd jammed into the seat beside him. He pulled out a small backsaw and a chisel.

"But—" Her brows drew together as she swung to face him.

"I've brought some primer." He made a cut mark on the doorstop and stuck his pencil behind his ear. She'd want it done right, he knew her that well already. "But if you have any more of this trim color stashed away, you might want to find it. A bit of paint and no one will ever notice this." He heard her hiss something wordless, then her heels rapped out a retreating rhythm of irritation. He smiled to himself and finished the cut.

By the time he'd chiseled out a neat gap at hub height in the first two doorjambs, then sanded and primed the raw wood, he was feeling better. Demi Cousteau prowled wordlessly from the computer on her desk to the lab and back again, casting him dark-eyed, speaking looks each time she passed, but he simply ignored her. *Good for her character.*

Remembering her package, he wheeled out to get it. "This is for me?" he asked, noting the description printed on one side when he propped it against her desk. She'd purchased a stool, assembly required, wheels included.

"It is." She met his eyes, held his gaze with cool reserve.

"Thanks." *And truce?* He ventured a smile, and after a long moment she returned it, then swung away to study her computer screen.

Truce. He was a surly bum nowadays, hardly her fault. He started on the door leading from her office to the back rooms. "So tell me about this project," he murmured, his eyes on his saw blade. This would be Sarraj's venture, he assumed, the reason Trace had dragged him into this—her check for half a million.

There'll be some perfectly innocent reason. Demi Cousteau was no more a conspirator than Emily's cat, he was willing to bet, and for much the same reason. Because if you lived your life by the feline credo All That I See Is Mine, then why conspire? Why not simply stand midfloor and meow till your minions stumbled over themselves to bring you your current desire?

She floated across the room to prop herself against the wall beside him, arms casually crossed. "I've won a brief—a commission—to create the most *wonderful* perfume in the whole world!"

She's been dying to tell somebody this, he realized, glancing up at her. Her face glowed—or was that just the dress she wore, the color of French marigolds, reflecting off her flawless skin? "You can do that?"

One brow rose in haughty surprise. "But of course. I'm one of the five best Noses in the world!"

Jon smiled in spite of himself and reached for his chisel. "So how does a Best Nose set about making the most wonderful perfume?"

"Well, aside from genius and inspiration, it takes world-class ingredients. No penny-pinching to make the product more profitable. And in this case they've given me a mandate to use the best of the best. Money is *no* object.''

Except that money was always an object—*the* object—in business. She might be in this game for love, but the businessmen who hired her? Jon knocked out a section of wood and reached for his sandpaper. "How can they do that? Don't they want to make a profit?''

"How they can do it is that they have oodles of money. My client has bottomless pockets.''

Greeks bearing gifts, darlin'. Don't you know there's always a catch? Of course, the catch might be something as simple as Sarraj overpaying her in hopes of buying the rest of the damsel, along with her world-class nose. Hardly a reason to call in the FBI.

"As to the why,'' she said, sounding a little nettled that he hadn't oohed and aahed yet, "it's a marketing ploy, and a brilliant one, I think. Every perfume needs an angle—a hook to make people try it in the first place. After they sniff it, they're mine, of course....''

"Of course.'' Could she really be that good?

"But to make them pick up the tester that first time, the launch campaign will tout the fact that my perfume is the most expensive perfume in the entire world—twice as costly as Joy. Everyone who's given a chance to smell it will want to, just to see if it really could be worth all that money.''

"That is clever,'' he agreed, and marked the other doorstop. "The equivalent to offering a man a chance to test-drive a Maserati. All his life he's been wondering, is it really *that* much better than his old clunker? No guy would pass that up, even if he couldn't afford to buy one.''

"Precisely!'' She splayed her long, slender fingers and touched fingertips, played them against each other in a little drumbeat of glee and excitement. *Now you're getting it!* her tone said.

Getting it? He was ahead of her, seeing pitfalls wherever she turned. The saw's tiny teeth bit into the jamb. "But what happens if, after people sample it, they aren't impressed?" Using the best of the best ingredients, she had no excuse for failure.

"Pah! That won't be a problem."

If you say so. "But what if your clients have priced it too high? Priced themselves right out of the market?" If no one could afford to buy her perfume, what did it matter how fabulous the fragrance might be? And still she'd be associated with a failure—the most expensive flop in the world? *That'll do her rep a lot of good!*

"I'm sure they've done their market research," she said coolly. *Not my department, price-setting,* her tone said, and of course it wasn't. No more than Pavarotti was expected to make sure the caterer brought enough sandwiches for the chorus at the dress rehearsal. *She* put the "wonderful" in the bottle, somebody else stuck on the price tag.

His second cut completed, he reached for his chisel. "Who, by the way, is 'they'?" If Trace had gone hunting, this was what he sought. *Who are your deep-pocket pals?* Inquiring federal minds would like to know.

"A consortium of investors headed by a Saudi Arabian...*prince.*"

That impresses you, does it, Dark Eyes? Like Angelina, she thought money made the man? And as for *titles*... He knocked the scrap of wood out with one vicious blow of the chisel. "Does the...prince have a name?"

But she must have caught the mocking edge to his voice, because she answered with one of her own. "I'm sure he does."

But if you know, you aren't telling me? Jon risked a glance up and over his shoulder, and found her standing with her arms tightly crossed—which did wonders for her breasts, though that clearly wasn't the intention of her body language. She was shutting him out. Head tipped to one side, her sooty eyes narrowed, she regarded him with wary interest. As if a garter snake had just grown a rattle on its tail.

Uh-oh, Caspar Milquetoast wouldn't be giving her the third degree, would he? And princes *would* impress him. Jon gave her an ingenuous smile and swiped a hand through his hair.

After trying that a few times in the mirror, he'd learned it only made matters worse. *Stork* terror was the general effect. He'd never known he had cowlicks before Trace's friend with her magic scissors laid blade to him. "Well, gee," he said mildly, "this is really exciting, isn't it, a prince and all?"

Taking off his glasses, he pulled out his shirttail to polish them, then left it hanging out. He set the specs back on the tip of his nose, where they made him look earnestly bookish.

She'd relaxed again. Her lovely mouth was pursed beguilingly in her effort not to laugh at him. "Yes, it is," she said gravely.

"The most important guy we ever had come into our drugstore was the U.S. secretary of agriculture. He was touring our part of the state last summer, and he got heartburn. I mixed him the special antacid I use myself. Fixed him up in minutes."

"Really?" She opened her big eyes and contrived to look impressed.

To keep her looking at him like that, Jon was tempted to fabricate further. He could tell her about the secretary's bodyguard, who was a martyr to bunions. Or the pack of condoms the secretary stole on his way out of the drug store.... But he got a grip. He'd just be trying to impress her, like any other fool who hoped to hold her attention by babbling. "What am I supposed to call you?" he blurted out instead, then cursed himself. Caspar would have waited to be told.

"When clients visit us, Ms. Cousteau, of course. But when we're alone, Demi will do." She gave it the French pronunciation, the "d" bedroom-soft, her lips shaping a perfect kiss as she exhaled on the "Duh," then widening to a smile as she accented the *"ME."*

"*Deh*-me," he repeated, saying it wrong on purpose, just for the pleasure of watching her repeat that kissable "Duh."

"No!" She laughed and shook her head. "Listen, it's Duh…*me*. Demi."

If he'd been standing, he'd have dipped his head at that first sexy syllable to cover her mouth with his own. Wouldn't have been able to stop himself. If he'd been standing…

Realization was a bucket of ice water dumped over his head. He looked down, ran one hand down his thigh— hardness, instead of warm flesh. He couldn't have reached her mouth if it meant his salvation. "Demi," he said blankly and quite correctly. *And to kiss you would be crazy, anyway. For any number of reasons.*

"Very good," she said above him, then, "You know, Jon, it's almost two and I'm *starving*."

"Want me to run— To go out and grab us something?" He was the perfumer's gofer, after all. And suddenly Jon needed to get away from her. To look up at the sky and breathe deep. "I noticed there's a deli across the street."

"There is, but I'll go. You stay here and finish that last doorway, then we can get to *work*."

Fair enough. He sawed out the lab door in record time, then checked his watch. He'd ordered a hot Reuben to delay her, and throwing that into the equation, she should need at least twenty-five minutes to make her round trip.

Which left him now with seventeen sleazy minutes for

spying. *National security, pal, remember?* After this, his debt to Trace would be more than cleared. Gritting his teeth, Jon wheeled into her office.

CHAPTER FIVE

JON STOPPED HIS CHAIR by her desk. So many places to search, so little time. Absently he drew a new notepad from his shirt pocket—he'd bought it specially for his first day on the job—then found his pen. The $500,000 question could be broken into two parts, he supposed.

"One," he noted on the first page, "who's her sheikh sugar daddy? Is he really an Arab prince? A prince with millions?"

Which brought up issue two. He inscribed the numeral, then, "And what is the prince's half million really buying?" Jon's eyes roved the room, vivid as its absent owner. Was the prince's cool half million financing the world's most wonderful, most expensive perfume? Or something nastier? Say, a terrorist attack like the World Trade Towers bombing?

Trace had several alternative theories as to where and how Demi might fit into such a conspiracy, but— Jon glanced at his watch. *Get moving!* He'd start with phone messages. If she was part of a terrorist plot—ridiculous notion—then the plotters had to communicate with her. He wheeled to the counter that edged one wall, where her answering machine sat with its red light blinking.

Her first message started with a time mark announcement. "Time, 11:00 a.m., Friday." Yesterday's news. Either she hadn't collected her messages or she didn't erase once she had. He flipped his pad to the next page, inscribed, "Her Friday Callers."

"Demi-doll!" A man's voice spoke abruptly in a too-brash, too-cheery baritone. "I've been trying to reach you all week! Call me? 679-8020."

Jon copied the number down. This one could be exactly what he sounded like—Mr. Too-Hearty, No-Class Swinger hoping for a last-minute date. Or he could be a mad bomber, disguising himself as the former.

"Time, 12:10 p.m., Friday."

"Uhh...Demi? Maybe you won't remember me, but I'm the guy who sent a drink to your table last Tuesday? At the Monkey Bar? You said I could call you sometime?" Embarrassed laughter. "So, well, I'm—here I am. I—uh, guess I'll try again. Later. *Oh,* this is How—" *Beep.*

Howard? Jon wrote the name on his pad.

"Time, 1:20 p.m., Friday."

"Demi, this is Kyle," sang a woman's voice, "and that hunk you sent me, Richard Sarraj, just walked out my door! *Sooo* my question is, was that really business—or entirely business? I mean, even if he is just a potential account, I owe you *big* time, kid. We'll definitely make a proposal. But is there any chance that you're matchmak—" *Beep.*

Sarraj! And where had Demi sent him? Not that this Kyle sounded like any kind of menace to national security, herself. "Account," she'd said. Banking account? Ad-agency account?

"Time, 1:22 p.m., Friday."

"You couldn't—in my dreams!—be matchmaking, could you, Demi?" Kyle's exuberant contralto continued. "Because if you are, well, I never minded castoffs, not from you. What a *stud*—I've had a thing for Omar Sharif ever since I saw *Doctor Zhivago.* So would you *please* call—" *Beep.*

So that was how women saw Sarraj. All it took was muscles and a mustache and dark, soulful looks? *You, too,*

Demi? Or was she harder to impress? Jon hoped she had enough taste to dump Sarraj on—

"Time, 3:43 p.m., Friday."

Someone called to say that he couldn't get orange flower oil, would sweet orange neroli do instead? Could be a real ingredient supplier or that question could be code— This was impossible.

"Time, 11:45 a.m., Saturday."

"Ms. Cousteau, this is Pete Ruggles in Connecticut, returning your call of nine o'clock this morning," said a rasping, elderly voice. "Concerning my former employee, Jon Sutter?"

Jon sat bolt upright, then slowly he grinned. *So*—she'd called that phone number Trace had given him for a reference!

"I can't tell you what a nice young fella Jon is. He's hardworking, clever, honest to a fault. All the customers loved him. Beats me why, when our drugstore was bought out, they didn't keep him on. Me, I retired, but Jon—" *Beep.*

Thank you, Federal Bureau of Investigation. I'll ask you guys for a recommendation anyday. So…had Demi heard this yet, and would it be enough to boost him from probationary status to permanent?

"Time, 1:15 p.m., Saturday." They'd been here in the office when this one came in, yet he hadn't heard the phone ring. She must have the entire system set on Mute.

"Demi, it's Jake. I've been trying to say this all week. You wouldn't let me say it the other night—not that I'm complaining about how you stopped me…" Husky, uncertain laugh. "But still, I've got a question to ask you—a big one. The biggest. I guess you know what I mean. So would you call me, darling? I left a message Thursday, by the way, but maybe your answering machine is full, or maybe it's brok—" *Beep.*

The question, was that what he meant? A marriage pro-posal? *Don't do it, sucker! If she isn't even returning your calls, then she doesn't give a damn. Probably gets three proposals a week—five if you count bus and cab drivers. Listen to one who—*

The chime sounded for the corridor door, and Jon's head jerked around. Holy crap, she must have flown! He bent over her machine, desperately scanning the buttons.

"Time, 2:02 p.m., Saturday."

Stop, where's the damn Stop butt—

"Richard Sarraj here, Demi. I—"

There! Jon jabbed the Stop button, hit the Rewind, then spun his wheels backward—and the back of his chair slammed her desk. *Damn!* He swiveled, sprinted off toward the lab, then braked as a man paused in the doorway to the reception room. Richard Sarraj stared at him blankly.

You! Jon found that he'd been holding his breath, and now it rushed out in a *whoosh!* Up to this second, Sarraj had been fiction—a voice recorded on a machine, a figure trapped on videotape. Omar Sharif playing the part of the suave Muslim terrorist.

Now here stood the reality, larger than life, giving Jon the cold-fish eye. He remembered this same gut-punched reaction the first time he saw a moose outside of a picture book, strolling across his parents' front lawn.

Between strange men caught in awkward encounters, at-tack was the best response. "Can I help you?" Jon put a bite to the question, then abruptly recalled his place. If any-one was an actor here, it was him, and his role was the wimp. "Umm, what can I do for you, sir?" He smiled sheepishly and tweaked his damnable glasses.

Sarraj let the question hang as his eyes traveled coolly and quite deliberately over Jon's head, then around the of-fice. In spite of his resolve, Jon felt his temper rise and his smile harden. *Only lackeys need answer questions*—was that the guy's tack?

And what had he heard from the outer room? That last aborted message had been Sarraj's own. Had he recognized himself speaking? *Okay, okay, so James Bond I'm not.* "May I—"

"Where is Ms. Cousteau?" Sarraj cut in.

Definitely don't like him, Jon decided. The hall door opened, then closed, and Sarraj spun with an athlete's easy grace. *Fast.* Jon filed that fact away.

"Richard!" Demi's cry of surprise and delight carried easily from the reception room. "What are *you* doing here?"

"WHO'S HE?" JON ASKED in an undertone, minutes later in the kitchenette, nodding back toward her office.

Demi poured out a glass of the Pinot Grigio she kept on hand for best customers and a glass of seltzer for herself. "That's Richard Sarraj, the point man on this brief I was telling you about." She placed the two Waterford crystal goblets on an antique silver tray. "Eat your Reuben before it gets cold. I'll be back soon." And meantime, she hoped her stomach kept its complaints to itself. Sarraj wasn't the type to be amused by human frailties.

As she closed her office door and brought the tray to her desk, Richard Sarraj turned from the window. "Who is he?"

She'd been dreading this question. Demi smiled and handed him his drink. "Jon's a new lab tech I'm training."

Sarraj's heavy brows drew together over his hawk nose. "You mentioned a Hector when we first talked. The assistant you said was so talented. So then this one is...?"

The last thing she needed at the outset of a major project with a new client was to seem unstable or disorganized. "A new man who's willing to work weekends." Let him think that Jon was additional staff, not that she'd lost her right-hand man just when she needed him most.

Sarraj took a sip of his Pinot Grigio, made an appreciative face, then persisted levelly, "And where is your other assistant?"

Blast, he had good instincts for a dodge! "Hector was called home unexpectedly, to the Philippines. He'll be back soon." At least that was what his friend had said when he'd called Wednesday night to explain Hector's vanishing act—that Hector would return as soon as he'd straightened out this confusion with his work permits.

But who was this friend? No one Hector had ever mentioned to her before. Demi switched her attention back to Sarraj and smiled brilliantly. "Meantime, we're making *excellent* progress. I should have the first samples for you by early next week." Surely he didn't think she'd have them already? "But was there something I could help you with today?"

If he recognized the change of topic for what it was, he let it go. "I called earlier, but I suppose you're not monitoring your phone calls?" He turned to give her machine a long look, then turned back. "But as I was in the neighborhood, I thought I'd drop by. To tell you about my progress this week, interviewing ad agencies...."

News that could have waited till their scheduled appointment. Still, Demi settled back to listen. Maybe he truly wanted her advice, which was well and good. The marketing of a new perfume was almost—almost—as important as the fragrance itself. If she could help him choose the best agency to handle his account, she'd be delighted to do so.

Or maybe this was just an excuse. *If he's come to ask me out?* She studied him over the rim of her glass. He really was an attractive man.

Not quite as sharp as Reese Durand, she thought, who'd

always reminded her of a commando knife her French grandfather owned, and no doubt had used—elegant, functional, exquisitely balanced. Reese had been the perfect mixture of street smarts and savoir faire. Like her grandfather, a slum boy who'd climbed all the way to the top.

This man was as polished, if not so finely honed. Still, there was that hint of danger and competence about him that always called to her. If he'd come to ask her out, she would go, even though her usual policy was to refuse last-minute dates.

And her resolution to never again mix business with pleasure? Demi smiled ruefully to herself. *I'll worry about that...tomorrow.*

When Sarraj departed with the promise to collect her at her apartment at nine that evening, she stood thinking. He'd couched their date tonight in business terms, a need to discuss possible names for his perfume. *So who's kidding whom, here?* She shrugged and turned toward the kitchenette and her overdue lunch, then remembered his remark that he'd called earlier. She hadn't taken her messages lately. She left the machine muted to avoid intrusions on her concentration when she was composing, and sometimes she forgot to switch back.

She stood listening by the counter, her stomach grumbling. Eric Somebody-or-other, who was a lout, had called. One happy-hour drink with him had been unhappy enough, thank you. Howard—she'd forgotten that one. Then Kyle Andrews, creative director at Madison, Hastings and Gurney, the ad agency she hoped Sarraj would choose in the end—a young, lean, cutting-edge firm.

Demi picked up the phone, punched numbers decisively and reached Kyle's voice mailbox. "Since when d'you need *my* help, Kyle? As for Zhivago, far as I know, he's up for grabs. May the best woman win." She smiled as she hung up. Maybe later she'd care if Kyle captured his heart, but right now? She was just going through the motions. He looked perfect on paper—handsome, monied, capable—but as for ringing her chimes? Not yet. *Damn you, Reese Durand, you're a spoiler.*

She started the machine again and snorted. The *nerve* of the man! Who did he take her for? Substitute sweet orange neroli for orange-flower oil? "In your greedy dreams!" She made a note to call another supply house come Monday. Then Pete Ruggles with high praise for Jon Sutter.

Good... Demi stopped the machine for a moment, considering. Call Ruggles back for more? No, really, what he'd said was enough. Sutter was smart, apparently he was honest, now it only remained to see if they were simpatico. Because something still niggled at her. He *seemed* nice enough, but she couldn't quite find her balance with the man. As unsophisticated as Jon patently was, he should have been eating out of her palm by now. And yet...

But he wanted to kiss me when I was pronouncing my name. She was familiar enough with the signs, that blank-eyed, sledgehammered look men got at the exact moment a jolt of testosterone zapped their brain cells.

Not that she minded Jon's feeling that way as long as he understood it would never go further. She definitely did draw the line at mixing pleasure and business in her lab. It was one thing to flirt with a man with the certainty that you could end the relationship the instant you chose, but quite another to know that you'd have to endure the languishing sighs—or pouts—on a daily basis from an employee you depended upon. That you hoped to keep for years.

She pushed a button again and winced. "Jake, what do I do with you?" On their first date, he'd laid out his ground rules with fierce precision. Newly divorced, he was out for fun, not a meaningful relationship. She could take it or leave it—and if her clock was ticking, well, she'd better

run for her life! She'd laughed and taken it; she was much
of the same mind.

But now, not a month later? Damn, why did he *think*
she'd ducked his heart-to-heart the other night, but to save
his pride? "This is rebound, you idiot! You don't propose
on the rebound! Someone will take you up on it if you're
not careful."

Not my fault if the man's an idiot. A sweet idiot. She
stalked gloomily to the window to stare out toward the
sliver of early green that was her view of Central Park,
beyond the skyscrapers to the north. This past year, she'd
been cutting a wide swath through the men. Trying to forget
Reese? Trying to prove to herself that even if *he* didn't
want her, she hadn't lost her power or her touch? She
wasn't quite sure. It was no more than she'd done before
she met him.

But now something had changed. It wasn't as much...
fun...anymore.

Maybe because she'd never taken men's feelings seriously before? She liked so many men—old ones, young
ones, brash ones, shy ones—she'd always assumed they felt
the same. Why settle for one any more than you'd settle
for one pair of shoes? You needed one pair for the opera,
another for scuffing around the house, a third for walking
thirty blocks downtown to prowl the antique marts. So
when a man she didn't want fell for her, she brushed him
off kindly, with thanks for the compliment, but without
much concern, assuming he'd find someone else as easily
as she changed from heels to sneakers.

But now that she'd finally felt the pain of wanting someone she could never have? Someone who made other men
look like broken-down penny loafers? It wasn't much fun
realizing she might be inflicting that same pain on somebody else.

But what now, if playing the field had lost its charm? *Where do I go from here?* And with whom?

Her last message was Richard Sarraj, wondering if she was free tonight. *Free tonight—and for the rest of my life?*

Her stomach growled dolefully. Why worry about the rest of your life when a crab-salad sandwich on rye was only two minutes in the offing?

There was truth in that! With a rueful smile she headed for the kitchen, then the glories of her lab beyond. If this was all she ever had, it was enough.

WANTING COMPANY WHILE she ate, she carried her lunch into the lab. Jon leaned down from his chair, tightening a screw on the nearly assembled stool. His hopelessly ragged hair hung on end, obscuring his face. As she brought another stool over to the counter beside him, he straightened, pushed up his glasses, and his blue eyes fixed on her sandwich. "No. Not in my lab."

Whose lab? "I beg your pardon?"

He didn't back down, simply glared at her like a wind-blown stork defending its nest. "That's a very bad habit. There are toxic materials all around us. You don't want to risk picking up something on your sandwich or your fingers, and I don't want you possibly contaminating any of the formulas I'll be mixing. Scoot."

This was what confused her—he was an eager-to-please, mild-mannered nerd one moment, and the next? Demi opened her mouth to blast him, then shut it again. He'd stopped working on his stool, and something in the way he sat there, his screwdriver calmly clasped in both hands, assured her that he didn't mean to start again till he'd won. And here it was half past three and they'd yet to mix *one* trial!

The phone rang in her office. "Excuse me." She snatched up her sandwich and retreated, dignity barely intact, and saved her snarl for the telemarketer who'd chosen this unfortunate moment to call. Hip propped against the side of her desk, she ate her sandwich in several savage bites, barely registering that it was rock crab instead of snow crab, as billed, and glared back over her shoulder toward the lab. Come Monday, there had better be more responses to her help-wanted ad. This one just wouldn't do.

When she ventured again into his—her—*the* lab, he'd completed the wheeled stool and somehow gotten himself atop it. Imagining what a fall to hard linoleum might do to him, she hated to even think how he'd managed that. Or how she'd have picked up the pieces if he'd failed. He was thin but not small—easily would have stood six feet, she estimated, if he could have. "I *wish* you wouldn't do that."

His hair was even wilder now, and he looked up from cleaning his glasses on his shirttail to give her a bashful grin. "Almost done," he assured her, ignoring her plea. He'd somehow pulled himself around the perimeter of the room to the doorway of a large supply closet on the end wall. He lifted a cordless drill from his lap and attacked its jamb.

Demi closed her eyes, took a deep breath, smelling sawdust—red oak—then opened them when the racket stopped. "*What* are you doing?" Hacking and sawing and drilling her poor lab, like some modern-day beaver run amok? Her first instincts had been right. He was mad.

"Installing a chin-up bar. Which reminds me, I left it hanging from the back of my chair. Mind bringing it over here?"

Only for a week, she reminded herself grimly, finding the steel bar hanging from a sling on the back of his wheelchair. Meantime, she looked helplessly at the essential oils and aromatic crystals she'd set out on the counter near his scale. Might as well start mixing the first trial herself.

She found the ten-gram bottles, pipettes and a pencil in

the drawers beneath the counter. Brought her printout of formula variations over by the digital scale, then reached for the first ingredient. Lifting the stopper from the bottle, she closed her eyes and inhaled.

Fields of lavender baking beneath the noonday sun of Provence. She was five, riding her grandfather's shoulders, savoring the scent of his pipe tobacco, his good, clean, masculine smell of sweat and garlic and lemon soap—the fragrance of happiness and safety and love without end or condition. Smiling with the memory, she opened her eyes—turned to find Jon watching her, his drill poised in midair.

"That was a good one," he observed quietly.

Did he understand? That odor was memory—experience caught in a bottle? On impulse she brought the container to him, her hand covering its label. "What is this?" If he had a nose, she could forgive a lot.

"I can't—" He caught her wrist to bring the essence closer.

"No." She resisted, halting its progress six inches from his nose. His hand was very warm. And large—his fingers encircled her bones with inches to spare. "Rule one in *my* lab, Jon. You don't stick your nose into an unknown substance. Some of the ingredients here are incredibly concentrated. They could damage your nasal membranes or your lungs. And some of the ingredients are poisonous in quantity, as you said yourself. So you sniff first at a distance till you know what you're sampling."

"All right." His thumb moved against her pulse point. "Thank you." He dipped his shaggy head and sniffed. "I don't—" His smile was regretful, a child peering through locked gates.

"What d'you see in your mind?" she prompted. "The very first thing?"

He laughed and shook his head. "My mother's bureau?

An old bird's-eye maple thing... Its top two drawers are
open.''

She tipped her head, considering, half her awareness
trapped by his fingers' warmth on her skin, a lazy, tingling
sensation creeping toward her elbow. He had a grip that
surprised her. She could picture him lifting her up a wall
or a cliff, not finicking with pills and bottle caps. "She
kept her lingerie in the top drawers?''

He nodded, still not releasing her. His left eye had a tiny
splash of gold in its iris. Kite in the blue.

"Did she use sachet or potpourri?'' Demi started to
smile.

"I think she—lavender?'' He laughed aloud. "She did,
I'd forgotten that! Little packets done up in lace and cal-
ico.''

"*Very* good.'' She pulled away and he let her go. Turning the bottle, she showed him its label. And he was as
pleased as she was. Somehow the pleasure rebounded between them, a bright Ping-Pong ball bouncing back and
forth. "That's just how you do it, too—identifying an odor.
Don't expect a billboard to pop up in your brain with the
word 'lavender' printed on it. Look for an image or an
emotion that springs to mind, then figure out what scent
you've associated with it. For instance, every time I blow
my nose with a certain brand of tissue, I think of ham-
sters.''

He had a nice laugh, easy and open and warm. "Okay,
I give. Why?''

"Paper is made from wood, you know, and apparently
this company makes its tissue from cedar scraps. And when
I was a child, I had a pet hamster for a few weeks. Ferdi-
nand. The bedding in Ferdie's cage was cedar chips.'' She
smiled mistily at the years-distant pet, not at him, and
swayed back to the counter.

He could picture her not yet grown into her enormous

eyes or her beguiling grace, cupping a beloved hamster. "What happened to Ferdie?"

She looked up from the scale and her face darkened. "Oh…Mother made me give him away. She said our apartment smelled of animals."

He nodded curtly and turned to stab the point of his drill bit into its mark, let it rip. Damn the woman. No child of his would ever lose— He found he'd sunk the bit almost to the chuck and pulled it out again. Blast, now the screw wouldn't bite. "Demi, bring me a pencil, would you?"

She angled her head and narrowed her eyes at him, thinking what, he couldn't guess. He finished the other two holes for the end piece and then she was beside him, holding his request plus another bottle. "Thanks." He jammed the pencil into the too-deep hole, broke it off. Redrilled to the proper depth. "What d'you have there?"

"This one isn't a single essential oil, it's a perfume. Mine."

A world of pride in that single word. He hoped he liked it. As she offered the bottle, this time he controlled his impulse to touch her. Too damn long since he'd touched a woman. *But not this one.* Next time, if there ever was a next time, he'd choose a reasonably pretty woman, not a heartbreaker. Only a fool cried for the moon. Dutifully, he closed his eyes and sniffed her creation.

Firelight dancing across bare skin…. Leaves blazing red and gold on the trees, raked up in drifts and burning…. The ruddy gold of sunlight probing your closed eyelids at the beach, the heat´ of the sand cradling your body…. Pumpkins with cinnamon, baking…. The smell of a woman's shoulder after you'd made hot, sticky love on the hottest day of summer.

He laughed shakily and opened his eyes. "It smells… hot…golden…sexy."

"You do have a nose!" She looked like a cat given mice

and cream. "My name for this one was Firefly. It's an amber-floral fragrance. And that's one of the things I'm known for in the trade. Cleavage." She laughed as his eyes automatically dropped, and shook her head. "In the *juice*, Jon. To say a perfume has cleavage means it smells sexy." She danced away to put the bottle back on a shelf, then returned to her measuring.

So she *was* good—very good. Not conceited, but justifiably proud of her talent. Even with the bottle withdrawn, naked images twined across the back of his mind. He shook his head abruptly. "I've never heard of Firefly. But then I don't know much about perfumes." Angelina had wanted only Chanel No. 5 and Joy. If it cost top dollar, that was enough for her.

"It was only launched a month before Christmas, but it's selling gangbusters." She named a designer that even fashion-oblivious Jon knew well. Angelina had modeled his line in her peak years, and partied with him still, or so she claimed. "He bought it—and renamed it, of course." She sniffed and went back to her work.

"You get royalties, I hope?" With a winner like this one...

She shook her head. "That one I created on spec, between briefs. I sold it for a flat fee, I'm afraid, and he got it dirt cheap. Six months ago I needed the money and he knew it."

Jon made a note to punch the weaselly tightwad, if he ever encountered him, on her behalf. He dropped his chin-up bar into its end slots, then frowned. If Demi had been hard up for money a few months back, was she hard up still? Had she been sweating it till Sarraj came along waving his check?

He found it hard to imagine her helping terrorists, but people did all kinds of things for money, some of them incredibly vicious. *Who are you really, Demi Cousteau?*

Would you hurt people for money? To save your business? Alluroma was her baby, he could see that already. And women would kill to save their babies—at least some women would.

He found it hard to believe—well nigh impossible—but then, what did he know? Like Angelina, she was so lovely you couldn't see her clearly; at least men would not. She walked in beauty like a spangled veil. No man could look beyond it to her heart. All he could ever hope to do would be to judge her by her actions. And for those he must watch and wait.

"Jon, if you're *quite* finished mooning there, would you come mix this?"

"Yeah, boss." Those big eyes across the room were flashing danger signals. It was high time he produced. "Coming." He caught the nearest shelf and dragged himself along the wall, working his way toward her.

"In this *life*time, I meant! We only have two months to make a miracle." Half laughing, half exasperated, she swept across the lab to meet him and caught his hand. "Come *on!*"

Hauling him along behind her, she reminded him of Emily, the baby of his family, who'd towed him wherever she willed when she had something urgent to show him.

He had a sudden overwhelming urge to spin the woman back like a top to face him, and tell her to cut it out! He was nobody's pull toy. He clenched his teeth, instead.

She let him go as they reached her mixing station. "Now, as you can see, I'm mixing two trials at once." She nodded at the two tiny vials positioned on the pan of the scale. "That's because variations one and two are identical down to…here." One burgundy nail tapped the last three ingredients in the two formulas, which were laid out like very long cooking recipes. "It's faster to measure one ingredient, zero out the scale, then measure the same amount again for the second vial. Also saves you a pipette, since you must—on pain of death, Jon, are you listening?—you *must* throw away the pipette after it has touched an essential oil. To dip it into any other bottle would be to contaminate the second essence.''

"I hear you," he agreed, remembering her five-hundred-dollar-an-ounce tuberose oil. One mistake like that and she'd tow him straight to the elevator shaft, then shove, no need to wait for a car. He reached for his notepad. Jon Sutter would be taking careful notes when she lectured, even if Jon Sutton wouldn't.

His fingers patted an empty pocket and he blinked—then remembered, his heart free-falling as if he *had* stepped into an empty elevator shaft.

He hadn't used his pad for a couple of hours—not since he'd taken note of the messages on Demi's answering machine.

CHAPTER SIX

JON PICTURED HIMSELF jabbing buttons as Sarraj approached. *I set it aside to do that!* He must have left the pad behind—twelve kinds of blithering idiot!—when he sprinted away from the counter.

So where was it now? Still lying there, open to the incriminating page? This was the end, and it wouldn't be a pretty one, not with Demi's flair for the dramatic.

Demi lifted one eyebrow. "You understand, Jon?"

She wouldn't look that way, friendly but puzzled, if she'd found he was spying on her. "Uh—yes," he agreed—to whatever she was asking.

"Good. So finish mixing these two trials, being *sure* to check off each ingredient as you measure it, then call me."

His eyes followed her elegant, sexy sway as she left the lab. Going back to her office? One glance toward the machine and she'd surely— He let his breath out as he heard the bathroom door open and close. So... *Think fast, Sutton.* There was no time to switch back to his chair, then beat her to the office. *Cool, gotta be cool.* And lucky. If the phone didn't ring in the next few minutes, then maybe...

When the lav door opened, Demi's heels ticked away down the corridor. Blast! Jon measured, zeroed the scale, measured again, flung the pipette in the trash and grabbed the next bottle. Four more ingredients to go—or wait... Did he dare?

Ten minutes later he'd still heard no shrieks of outrage from the far room. Back at the chin-up bar, he transferred

himself to his wheelchair, then raced to the counter to collect her first two trials.

At the door to her office, he stopped, looking in. Ab-
sorbed in a massive, technical-looking text, Demi sat at her
desk, absently massaging her temples, her computer glowing in the dusk. Artist hard at work. Jon rapped on the door
frame, then entered as she jumped and turned.

"Jon, I told you to call me!"

"Who's the gofer?" He set the two vials on her desk.

"You don't bring me the bottles, silly, we need *mouillettes.*" She rummaged through a drawer and brought out
several spears of white cardboard. "Smelling strips," she
explained, handing him one. "Cut from blotting paper. You
label them to match your vials...." She printed a neat name
on two strips. Sheik 1, Sheik 2. "Then you dip just the tip
of it into your formula. And *that's* what you sample." She
dipped the first *mouillette*, set the vial aside, brought the
strip to her nose. Her feathery lashes drifted shut, her
breasts rose as she inhaled....

Tearing his eyes away, Jon glanced at the counter. His
notepad was nowhere in sight, but from this angle—

"Hmm." Demi shrugged and opened her eyes. She set
the strip aside.

"Well?" he demanded as she dipped the Sheik 2 *mouillette* into its corresponding vial.

She smiled without looking up. "You think it's that easy,
that we'd find it in one? We may do this a thousand, two
thousand times before we get it right. I was ten months
making Firefly, and that was very fast."

He held his breath as she brought the second sample to
her nose. *How good are you, babe?*

Demi sniffed blindly again, then...the shadow of a frown
crossed her face. Her nostrils flared, her eyes snapped wide.

"Something's missing."

"Can't be," he lied. "I was very careful."

"Not careful enough!" She brought the strip to her nose again—then threw it over her shoulder. "It's the ylang-ylang. You left it out!"

You beautiful bloodhound, you! Had he included it, that ingredient would have been less than a hundredth of the whole. Nevertheless, Jon shook his head. "I'm sure I—"

She shot to her feet. "You doubt *me,* one of the five best— Pah!" Her hands flew wide, tossing him and all incompetents to the wind. "I should have hired the ax murderer!"

"Huh?" But she'd already swept up the vial and stormed off toward the lab, growls of wrath trailing behind her like the mutterings of a thunderhead drifting off over the horizon.

Hoo boy! Jon supposed he could take his notepad with him when she fired him. Still, now that he'd gone to all the effort… He rolled over to the counter—and found that it wasn't there.

Can't be! He lifted the answering machine to check behind it. *Where is it?* He searched the floor, leaned down to peer under her desk. No notepad anywhere—*crap!* But if she'd found it, this current tantrum would have looked like a firecracker set against Mount Saint Helens.

So…what? *If Demi doesn't have it, then where the hell—* It hit him just as she swept back into the room, brandishing her printout.

"You *see?*" She thrust it under his nose. "You didn't check the ylang-ylang off on number two—you skipped it! Are you always this absentminded? This—this—?"

"No…" He stared blankly down at her formula. Sarraj had it! But why hadn't he shown the pad to—

"Jon, are you *listening?*" Demi tucked the back of her hand under his chin to nudge his face up. "Hello?"

He caught her wrist and pulled it aside. *And did anyone ever spank you when it would have done some good?* His fingers tightened at the subliminal flash of a hot, plush curve beneath his palm. "I'm listening," he said evenly, "and I'm sorry. I don't usually make mistakes like that." *But if you think you can handle me like a child or a puppy, you, babe, are making a bigger mistake.*

"Jon..." She dropped gracefully to her heels before him, bringing their faces near level, her hand still trapped in his.

"I cannot have this. You could wreck everything! If I hadn't caught that— Don't you see? I might reject a trial I would have accepted if you'd mixed it correctly. Or worse, accept a trial we could never replicate."

"I see." He let her go. Maybe he was doing her an injustice, too, not taking her work seriously.

"Do you? A mistake like that could cost us *weeks,* and we don't have a minute to waste! I have to have perfect accuracy. *Can you give me that?*"

He drew a deep breath and met her eyes squarely. "Yes."

No excuses, no sniveling self-justification. Demi searched his face. It was a good face, wide across the cheekbones, square of jaw; his blue eyes were deep-set but very direct. Small, deep lines bracketed his lips, as if recently his mouth had schooled itself against pain.

Is he in pain now? she wondered, staring at him. He'd been very active today, stooping and bending and using his ridiculous chin-up bar. And pain or no, the work must have tired him. Perhaps that explained his mistake? She swept her hair back with one hand, smiled at him—all the apology she owed or would give—then stood.

"You know, I'm rather tired," she lied, knowing instinctively that if she asked him how he felt, he'd swear he was fine. "It's almost six and I have a date tonight. Maybe we should wrap this up?" It would be at least an hour before she calmed down enough to be able to compose, and that would be too much, asking him to stay that late.

"All right. I'll shut the lab down." He tucked her formulas to one side and rolled toward her door, then stopped and looked back. "Will you want me tomorrow?"

"If you can spare the time, yes, please." Had he no life of his own to lead, no one to meet on a Sunday in spring? "That would be very helpful," she added gently. And perhaps it helped him, too, having someplace to go where he was needed? He was a newcomer to the city, she reminded herself. If he was lonely, that could account for it.

She moved to close Poucher's guide to fragrance materials, then paused, rereading an entry. Myrrh. She'd never played with it before, but the Wise Men had brought it as a gift to Bethlehem. The ancient Greeks said that a perfume fixed with myrrh would last ten years. She marked the page. *Tomorrow.*

Jon knocked and entered on his way toward the reception room. He must have swiped a hand through his hair again; it stood up in comical spikes. "Guess I'll go now. Would ten in the morning work for you?"

Demi was careful not to smile. If she was crazy enough to keep him past Friday, she'd have to do something about that hair. "That would be wonderful. Good night, Jon." She looked down, then up again as he cleared his throat.

"I...suppose your date is with that guy who stopped by? Sarraj?"

She supposed it was none of his business! She and Hector had traded gossip about each other's dates, but Jon was not her friend, not yet. On the other hand, if he harbored any wistful little notions about her, now was her chance to tactfully quash them. She gave him a radiant smile. "Yes, it is. And *you* have a good night, too." Implying that hers, with Richard Sarraj, would be quite satisfactory, thank you.

Odd that she felt no stir of anticipation, thinking of what tonight might bring. Just a vague sense of...loss as Jon rolled out her door.

Jon DIDN'T REALIZE HE HAD company until he was tucked
up safely inside the special van. As the driver walked
around the front of the vehicle, a voice drawled from behind, "How goes it?" The man moved up to a seat beside
him. "Call me Greenley, by the way. How's it going?"
The FBI agent had traded his job applicant's suit for jog-
ging shorts and waffle treads tonight, as if the taxi had
snatched him off some suburban track.

Jon shrugged to cover his shock and pitched his voice
as low. "It goes." He'd already reported last night, by
phone to some neutral-voiced, noncommittal woman, that
Demi had hired him for the week.

That arrangement would probably end tomorrow—if she
didn't call him from a restaurant somewhere this evening
to tell him he was fired. All it would take was Sarraj's
passing his notepad across the table and he was toast in
Demi's book. History. *My six-hour career as perfumer's
assistant to the world's most passionate, most beautiful
Nose.* Someday it would make an amusing story to tell over
drinks around a fire, out on some dig. Someday…

But now? If Trace had come to meet him, he'd have
confessed. But looking like a fool in front of Greenley,
whom he didn't know? *Left my spy notes out in full view
of the enemy….* He'd wait till she'd fired him, then he'd
tell Trace.

Still, he did have news to report, he realized belatedly.
While the driver cruised uptown, his head bobbing in time
to the reggae beat on the radio, Jon described Sarraj's visit
and Demi's date tonight. And all he'd learned about her
unnamed Saudi prince—precisely one fact more than
zip—that he existed.

Greenley took no notes. "That's all?" he asked when
Jon stopped.

All he'd admit tonight. "Yup."

"Okay, keep in touch." Greenley leaned forward to tap

the driver. "Next corner. Pull over." As the van slowed,
the agent sidled around Jon's chair. "Oh, and Trace said
to tell you... Gorgeous attends mosque—least she did in
her teen years." He slid the door open, jumped out and
slammed it behind him. Headed crosstown toward the park
in a ground-eating lope.

So what? Jon wanted to yell after him. *That's supposed
to convict her?* Some of the most honorable men he knew
faced Mecca five times a day. *What am I doing, working
for a pack of federal paranoiacs?*

Not, he reminded himself grimly, that he'd be working
for them much longer. Once Sarraj had whipped out his
notepad... *Maybe I'd better pray to Allah myself.* You
would almost think that he wanted this job.

"IF YOU'D EXCUSE ME a moment?"

"Of course." Watching Richard Sarraj walk away toward the back of the restaurant, Demi drew a breath in
relief. For some reason the conversation was not flowing
tonight, but proceeding by fits and starts. It almost felt as
if they were at cross-purposes here—her trying to learn
more about her date, him sticking determinedly to business
topics. *So maybe I was a fathead, thinking this was more
than business?*

Yet two or three times this evening she'd glanced up
from her plate to find him staring greedily, almost incredu-
lously, at her. When she caught him out that way the conversation would stumble, then lurch off again in another
dead-end direction. Richard seemed almost irritated at some
of her questions, but how else was she to get him talking
if he wouldn't volunteer?

She'd tried the trusty feminine ploy of going first, offering bits of her past in exchange for his. Her tales of a
childhood split between the south of France and Manhattan
had wrung a few corresponding facts from him. He'd

grown up mostly on a ranch in Idaho, reared by a foster father, playing with a foster brother, after his mother had died in some unspecified way—a way that had tightened Richard's lips and sent the conversation lunging off in search of a safer topic.

Such as names for the perfume? Richard declared that his prince favored Seventh Veil.

Sexy enough, Demi had to admit. Nice flavor of the Near East, Salome's dance. Should appeal to the bad girl in most women. And she liked the image of veils dropping one by one, unfolding in the same way a perfume unfolded on a woman's skin over time—from top note to heart note, till at last its soul note lay revealed, but...wasn't the image of seven veils a little...hard-edged? Salome was a Bad Girl with a capital *B*.

So Demi had countered with Sheik. Simple, sexy as Errol Flynn, with aural associations to chic. Easy visuals around which to design an ad campaign. She didn't say so, but give Richard a burnoose and he'd do for a model. But Richard had shrugged her suggestion aside—almost contemptuously, she'd felt, which hadn't sat well with her—and said that, in the end, his prince would choose.

For better or worse! She bit her tongue not to say it. But now that Richard had broached that topic, and since he'd previously mentioned that the prince liked to deal with his own people, *well*, then... How did Richard himself fit into that picture? The name Sarraj was...?

For one awkward moment she'd thought he'd simply clamp his jaw against her prying and refuse to explain. Then he'd relented, but minimally, as if she'd extracted his words syllable by grudging syllable. His father had been a pilot, a captain in the Syrian air force. Come to the States to train on American military jets, since the U.S. had sold a shipment of the planes to his country. Met Richard's mother, an art student studying pottery, in San Diego...

Gave her a baby, then went back home again, Demi surmised, filling in the gaps. Cross-cultural marriages were tough to pull off in the long run, though her grandparents' was the exception that proved the rule. She'd started to say as much—and Richard had promptly excused himself.

Drumming her nails, she looked up with a start when he returned.

"How, by the way, did you come to hire—what did you say his name was?"

Yet another twist in the conversation, back to business *again*—and she hadn't said. "Jon Sutter." Demi turned her wineglass on the tablecloth. "I hired him because he was the best applicant." Out of a ridiculous three, but no need to say so.

What followed seemed closer to inquisition than conversation, with Richard asking her Jon's background, his qualifications, how he'd come to apply. Had she carefully checked his references? And why would she even consider hiring a man whose disabilities must surely disqualify him?

Sarraj had bought her skills and her undivided attention for two months, not her company or the right to preempt her business decisions. Demi's smile hardened ever so slightly and her answers grew vaguer. Jon had worked last at a pharmacy, but she'd forgotten its name, or its town. Was that important? She widened her eyes at him guilelessly, daring him to say it was. Because if he did, then *she'd* ask why?

They stared at each other, two fencers with épées at the cross, just the faintest quiver of steel connecting them—then the answer sprang to mind. This wasn't business at all, was it? Richard was jealous of Jon!

She almost laughed aloud with the absurdity of it—*Jon*, with his hair on end, his weak eyes and his gentle bookishness? Her Big Bird on wheels? A man patently without ambition or daring—measured against her grandfather, who'd fought in the Foreign Legion? Or Reese Durand, who'd taken Wimbledon at twenty-one and his first million at twenty-five? True, she liked Jon very much—maybe very much indeed—but in that way? *If that's what this is all about, you have nothing to fear,* she almost assured him. Instead she merely smiled. "And now, if you'll excuse *me?*"

She allowed herself a laugh in the mirror while she re-colored her lips and pinned a few wisps of her smooth French twist back in place. If Richard Sarraj was silly enough to see Jon as a rival—well, then, why not let him? A little competition could do wonders for a budding romance. *But Jon?* Pity there was no one to whom she could tell the joke.

"SO YOU'LL STICK AROUND for fifteen, twenty minutes?" Jon reconfirmed as he added an outrageous tip for just that favor.

"I'll circle if I can't stand," the chauffeur of the special van agreed before hustling back to his driver's seat.

Jon had waited up till midnight for her call, telling himself that after she fired him, he could sleep late on the Sunday. But his phone never rang. *She'd rather scalp me in person?* Why should that surprise him? Jon stopped before the locked doors to her building, drew out his phone and sighed. *Here goes nothing.* He'd once ridden out a hurricane on a barrier island just to see what such a storm was like. He supposed this could be no worse than that.

The phone rang twice—a slender, golden-skinned hand descended over his shoulder to whisk it out of his grasp.

"Allur-oma," Demi purred into its mouthpiece, her head cocked and her eyes dancing. She handed it back to him. "*And,* for being on time..." She presented him with a white paper bag. The odors of cinnamon, fresh bread and coffee rose between them.

The condemned's last meal? he wondered, sniffing hungrily as she held the lobby door. He hadn't had much of an appetite for breakfast. "I usually am," he defended himself belatedly.

"Oh? Not *my* first impression," she teased, and danced on ahead of him to summon the elevator. Dressed in a snappy little red suit with a cropped jacket, she lit up this gray April morning like a Chinese dragon. But why wasn't she breathing fire?

Sarraj hadn't told her, was all he could think while they shared coffee and pastries at her desk. Either that or she was one hell of an actress?

"Palmiers..." Demi closed her eyes and took a delicate bite of the flaky pastry. "There was a tiny bakery in Grasse where my grandmother took me when I was little. I'd always have a *palmier* and *café au lait.* The baker was an old, old man who was in love with my *grand-mère,* I think, the way he fussed over her. But then, everybody was. Is..."

If she's anything like you, then I know why. A golden crumb clung to her full bottom lip. Jon hung on to his own mug with both hands to keep from reaching. "I thought you grew up here in the city?"

"I did, mostly." She took another luxurious nibble. "But my father was French—well, half French. My mother would send me summers to stay with his parents when she traveled. Grasse is the heart of the perfume world—has been since the sixteenth century."

"The Cousteaus are perfumers?" The talent ran in some families for seven generations or more, he understood from his cramming. There were perfume houses in France older than the Napoleonic Wars.

"No." She flicked the crumb out of temptation's way with the tip of her tongue. "My grandfather is a broker of raw materials for the trade. He founded his own business after the war, in the fifties. He speaks many languages—

Arabic, Hindi, Swahili—and he loved to travel, so..." She took a sip of coffee and licked her lips again. "Attar of roses from Bulgaria, sandalwood from India, myrrh from Somalia... My grandfather finds the best sources at the best prices and brings it back to the makers. But he has a very fine nose. And he trained mine from the cradle."

And he spoke Arabic. Jon knew what Trace might make of that. "And your grandmother, whom the baker loved? Is she a Nose?"

"No—she's an Egyptian." Demi smiled at her own joke, then the smile grew pensive. "Grew up in the gutter, I think, though they've never told me. Just what I've guessed from the bits and pieces a child overhears. He found her in Cairo in '42, while he was on leave from fighting. I have always thought, from things they've said—and not said— the way she looks at him, that maybe he saved her...from something." Her eyes darkened, their pupils pools of expanding ebony.

"Something?" he prodded gently.

"Something...awful." She shrugged, suddenly very French, and then smiled. "But in the fifty years since, I think she saved him, too, from himself. Without her he would have been a hard, hard man."

And with her, a lucky one, Jon imagined. Some men got lucky. But which grandparent did Demi take after? he mused as he went on to the lab and set to work. The lovable waif saved from the gutter? Or the hard man—the fighting man who'd founded a company? *And how is Grandpa at poker?* Or his granddaughter? *If Sarraj did show her my notebook last night, could she hide it?* Would she?

Didn't seem possible. She was a quick-fuse lady, not a smolderer.

But then the alternative was equally disturbing. If Sarraj had *not* shown her...then why not? What was he waiting for?

CHAPTER SEVEN

"No," SAID DEMI a half hour later, stopping short in the lab doorway. "*Absolutely* not. Not in my lab."

Jon stretched his last piece of shock cord around the hook he'd screwed into the far wall, then turned it back on itself and tied a series of half hitches. "Got to if I'm going to move around here with any speed." He demonstrated by pulling himself hand over hand along the line, rolling on his wheeled stool. "See?"

"This is a lab, not a spider web! The first time I hit one of these…"

"You won't. I'm hanging red flags everywhere to remind you."

She ducked under a cord and stalked to his mixing station. "Did you happen to recall, while you were remodeling, that you're on probation here?"

"But if I'm to give my best while you're deciding, I have to be able to move around." *No more pull-toy, babe. I pull myself.* "You said we had no time to waste."

"We haven't, not a minute. Have you formulated *anything* yet today?"

"Was just about to start." Jon pulled himself lengthwise till he came to a cross guy, then he swiveled the seat of his stool and changed direction, ending up at the counter beside her.

She sniffed, not impressed. "Add the ylang-ylang you left out to Sheik 2, then do the rest of the versions on that printout." She smacked another set of papers on the counter. "Then here are your next half-dozen."

She'd composed these already this morning? He was careful not to groan aloud as he set the Sheik 2 vial on the scale. Demi leaned back beside him, elbows propped on the counter. "If I'm still on probation," he murmured as he sucked up ylang-ylang in a pipette, then measured it drop by drop into the vial, "then are you interviewing more candidates?" When she hadn't fired him this morning, he'd started feeling as if their arrangement might have some legs to it, after all.

He discarded the pipette, then glanced at her sharply. On second thought, what if Sarraj *had* shown her his notepad last night? But instead of sacking him for spying, she'd decided to oust him this way? Simply claim his performance wasn't satisfactory, then replace him with whoever came along?

"Of course I'm still interviewing," she said coolly. "And if I find someone who isn't having a bad-hair year, then—"

Then it's the old heave-ho, huh? "What's wrong with my hair?" He brushed a hand up through it.

"Tell me what isn't?" She flicked a cowlick. "Pah! For every one you smooth down, another pops up! This looks like revenge, not a haircut! You'd almost think someone did it on purpose."

Now *that* was too close for comfort. "So I'll cut it if you hire me."

"You will. The first designer who walks in our door and sees *you*—phtt—he's gone. He'll take his brief elsewhere. How can we claim to be artists, creators of beauty, with you sitting there looking like a—a half-blown-away dandelion?"

Ouch! And he'd wondered if she could be vicious? Jon capped Sheik 2, shook it, then offered it to her in wounded silence. She rummaged through one of the under-counter drawers, then brought out a handful of smelling strips. He started on her third formula, but when Demi closed her eyes to sample Sheik 2, he allowed himself the luxury of stopping and staring.

His eyes couldn't get enough of her. If this was all there was to spying—staring at Demi Cousteau—he'd sign up forever. He turned back to his scale hastily as she breathed out and came back to earth. "Well?"

"Mmm…nice top notes. I'll play with that, but the rest…" She pulled a pencil from behind her ear, changed amounts of two ingredients on the printout. "Mix it again for me, like this, and call it Sheik 2A."

So this was why it could take years to create a new perfume. "Sure. What's a top note?" He knew, but he liked the sound of her voice.

"A perfume is structured to unfold over time. First you smell the top notes, the lightest, most volatile fragrances of the juice. They fly out of the bottle at you, or up off your skin. And like most first impressions, they'd better be good ones. Why else would a woman stick around for more?" She aimed a mischievous glance at his hair.

Why indeed? He grimaced and reached for his next ingredient.

"If she does wait around another fifteen or twenty minutes," Demi continued, "then sniffs again, the heart note—the middle note—will start to step forth. This is the heart of the fragrance, your essential sense of its character. Oh, it's rosy, but with a spicy note beneath. Or woody, with a hint of citrus. You should smell the heart notes for, oh, four hours or so.

"And then, like the last petal of a flower unfolding, the soul note unfolds—the heaviest, most persistent scents that give the perfume its depth and longevity. In a really fine fragrance, the soul notes should linger on into the next day.

That's why I'll smell these *mouillettes* again and again. I'll learn new things about them over time."

"You keep saying we have no time to waste." He un-stoppered another bottle and reached for a fresh pipette. "What exactly is your deadline?"

"Two months." Her voice was too light, too casual.

He nearly dropped the bottle. "Two months! Is that even possible?"

She sighed. "If Sarraj wanted just a pleasant perfume, then there would be no problem at all giving it to him..."

"But a really fine perfume, a classic, like L'Heure Bleu or Joy?"

"If it can be done, I'm the one who can do it." She turned to the shelves, began collecting the essential oils and absolutes and aromatic crystals he'd need for her next trials.

"But why the rush?" Jon wondered aloud as he worked. If a perfumer required a year or three to develop a really fine fragrance, then it would be foolish to rush her. *Assuming that a fine fragrance was really your goal.*

Demi smacked down two bottles beside him. "Because the prince wants it yesterday, okay? He didn't tell me why and I didn't ask. I imagine waiting isn't something royals do if they can help it—and they can."

If they didn't want Demi to make them a fine fragrance, what did they want her for? That was the FBI question in a nutshell.

But the question that interested Jon more and more was: Was Demi in on their scheme, whatever it might be, or was she simply the innocent tool they were using? And for what?

THE REST OF THAT SUNDAY, then Monday and Tuesday passed in amicable hard work. Jon was hitting his stride—he could mix her formulas almost as quickly as Demi could compose them. It became a contest, who would take the lead. Jon would draw close to completing his list in the hours while Demi sat staring into space or with eyes closed and chin lifted as she sniffed an imaginary fragrance that wafted through her mind. Then just as he was mixing the last trial on the last page of her printout, she'd snap out of her trance and launch into ferocious activity, composing ten or twenty variations on her latest theme, and again he would fall behind.

As fascinating as her world was, he could almost lose sight of his real purpose in being here. And even when he remembered, she didn't leave him much time for spying. He snatched a half hour both days when she went out to fetch their lunches. Finding her business accounts, he'd crunched the numbers till he concluded much what he'd expected. Alluroma had been tottering on the razor edge of bankruptcy for the past six months. Which meant Demi might have been vulnerable to any proposal to bail her out, legal or otherwise.

But what? he wondered, closing her ledger and putting it back in its drawer. He jumped guiltily as the phone rang—then started for it. One of his duties was to answer the phone in Demi's absence if he was near enough to catch it. He'd finally realized there was no receptionist at Alluroma, though every morning Demi slung a new jacket on the imaginary one's chair in the front room. His boss was a perfectionist even in her petty deceptions.

"Alluroma, International," he said, picking up. If this was an applicant for the lab-tech position, then he or she was out of luck.

"Yes. Give me Demi, please." The woman's voice was low, beautiful and imperious, with a decided undertone of *Hop to it, buster!*

A fashion designer, he bet. "Ms. Cousteau is not available at the moment. May I take a message?"

"If Demi is there in the office, then call her. Now, please. I'm in the midst of rehearsals and—"

"One moment, ma'am, I believe— Yes, here she is." Jon put one hand over the mouthpiece.

Demi floated into the room, cheeks rosy from hurrying, one brow lifting as she spotted him. "Who?" she mouthed silently.

"Queen Elizabeth?" he whispered back.

As he wheeled toward the kitchen he heard Demi cry, "Mother?" on a note of glad surprise. "Where are you? But I thought— When did you—" She subsided into silence while Jon brewed a cup of tea for her and coffee for himself, interjecting an occasional "But—" or "Yes, all right" into the conversation. Jon smiled to himself. Interesting to hear Demi getting the worst of an encounter.

"Yes, of course, I'll be there," she snapped finally.

"But you might have— No! No, *please,* don't do that! I can find my own— *Mooother...* All right. I'll meet you after, then. Yes, I love you, too." She hung up the phone with more force than the act required, then stalked into the kitchen.

"Moms, huh?" he observed sympathetically to draw her out. The evil one who gave away her hamster, he remembered.

"Mothers," she agreed in a throaty growl that sounded just like the woman on the phone. "Mine's singing at the Met tonight, replacing the second soprano, who's ill, and she forgot to tell me. She just assumed I'd know. I suppose she thinks all New York City's talking about it. *Phtt!*" She smacked the bag of sandwiches down on the table. "As if I don't have worries enough of my—" She threw up her hands, then sat, glaring into the middle distance.

"Your mother sings opera?" he guessed as he unwrapped his sandwich.

"Mother is Liza Hansen," Demi said flatly, as if that explained it all.

"She's a diva?"

"You could call her that. *She* would call herself…" Demi moodily picked an onion slice out of her sandwich and flung it into the trash.

And she'd come to town to sing without telling her daughter. Blithely assuming she'd know. And that she'd drop everything to attend?

"Sooo…" Demi glanced at her watch. "I'll have to quit by five to make the performance. Meantime, we have Richard Sarraj coming at three."

Great, Sarraj. Jon found he'd squeezed a gob of egg salad out of his sandwich. Maybe today he'd show Demi Jon's notepad? *What the hell is he waiting for? He likes playing cat and mouse as long as I'm Mickey?*

AT 2:45 P.M., DEMI prowled into the lab. "You haven't finished Sheik 32 yet?" She gave a tiny *tsk* of irritation and turned to the lineup of labeled vials arranged at the back of the counter, choosing several. "Finish it if you can. I have hopes for that one." She opened a vial, Sheik 7, sniffed, nodded to herself, then held the vial to her left wrist.

"You're going to show that one to Sarraj?" And show him not on a scent strip, Jon realized as she nodded. She would offer Sarraj her wrist.

The image was as joltingly vivid as it was unwelcome— *Sarraj's nose lingering against her skin, the man breathing in her scent.* Jon didn't need to feel this way—had sworn off women who could make him feel this way. He swiveled his stool—and his hand brushed the vial on the scale. "*Crap!*" The half-finished formula spattered across the counter, a hundred dollars or more of ingredients in a worthless puddle.

"Sorry." He set the vial upright, then sat very still.

What was it to him if Sarraj smelled Demi's wrist—or her navel? He'd already told himself she wasn't for him. *Dog in the manger, is that what I am? Clumsy damn dog.*

"So you should be," Demi said coolly, handing him a roll of paper towels.

"You can dock my pay." *And let me go at the end of the week?*

"Pah!" She selected another vial, Sheik 14B, and applied it to her other wrist.

A tiny muscle danced in his cheek. Sarraj would have a pleasant afternoon indeed. It was a wonder he wasn't coming round twice a day for show-and-smell! "How many are you going to let him sample?" he protested in spite of himself as she applied Sheik 22D to her left inner elbow, where the skin would be petal soft.

"Four, if you'd be *so* kind as to finish that one?" Demi glanced up as the entry chime sounded. "Bring me 32, as soon as you finish it."

He finished the formula in record time. Transferring himself to his wheelchair, he rolled silently down the corridor and stopped in the kitchen.

"...be delighted to escort you." Sarraj's voice carried easily. "I take it the occasion is black-tie? Excellent. When shall I pick you up?"

"Seven would do nicely. And Mother's inviting us out after her—" Demi looked up as Jon appeared in the doorway. "After the performance," she finished, rising to meet him. "Richard, I don't believe you've actually met my assistant, Jon Sutter?"

SO THEY'D NEVER BE BEST friends, Demi told herself ruefully an hour later, after she'd seen Sarraj to the door. The encounter had been awkward from start to finish, Jon becoming totally tongue-tied, all blinky and smiley—she hadn't realized how shy and socially inept he could be.

And Richard had been stiff as a board—probably embarrassed, recalling the way he'd challenged Jon's qualifications the other night?

Or absurd as that seemed, he was still jealous. If so, give him a point for possessiveness. She liked that—so far and no further—in her men.

And deduct a point from Jon for his lack of social finesse. With a minimal outfit like Alluroma, she needed a lab tech who could wear more than one hat. Hector had been delighted to entertain clients if they strolled in when she was out. He'd handled himself well at launch parties, too, dancing attendance on the women with which the perfume industry was filled while Demi charmed the men, then flirting with suave discretion with the younger male designers, who were his real interest. She and Hector had made a good team.

But she and Jon? Yes, she enjoyed his company when they were alone together, but if he couldn't handle their clients... *If only I had a few more applicants to choose from!* No one had called today, or yesterday, to apply for the position. Which was strange when she thought of it. Entry-level jobs were scarce and usually much sought-after in this industry. Her eyes fell on the *New York Times,* which she'd purchased at lunchtime. Maybe IFF or one of the other biggies was hiring this week, luring away all her candidates? Idly, she flipped through the paper till she reached the classifieds.

Half an hour later, Demi walked into the lab, her heels clacking ominously. She had to duck twice under Jon's lengths of shock cord and, with each dip, her temper climbed a notch. Jon pushed his oversize glasses up his nose and blinked warily through them, owl under glass.

"*Who* canceled my want ad?" She halted beside him.

"What?"

"You heard me! I've been on the phone for the last half hour, going round and round with some idiot in the *Times* classified section. She claims I canceled my ad Friday afternoon!"

"You didn't?"

"I did not. But do *you* have any idea how that might have happened?" He was turning pink under her narrow-eyed scrutiny.

"No."

Then why did he look as guilty as a husband caught with strange lipstick on his ear? "You didn't cancel my ad?" It didn't seem like a trick he'd pull, but that blush...

"No, I didn't."

His words held the ring of truth...his cheek muscle fluttered. Was he just one of those hapless types you could make blush simply by saying "You're blushing"? Or was he mincing words with her? He'd have needed a woman to cancel her ad.

If you didn't do it yourself, do you know who did cancel it? Suddenly Demi didn't dare ask the question. Because if she found out that he had, then he'd have to go. And she didn't want him gone....

A little late to be realizing that! She swung abruptly away, toe tapping as she thought. She'd been stupid to leap into this confrontation before thinking it through. Stupid to accuse with no proof and no way of proving. She glanced back at Jon over her shoulder. His cheek muscle fluttered again, and she had a sudden impulse to whirl and press her palm to it. *You do know something!* She let out a long, slow breath. "D'you want this job that much, Jon?"

"I did *not* make that call, Demi," he insisted behind her.

He had a good voice, strong and sure of itself, moving pleasantly along her nerve endings. It didn't go with the goofy hair or the sometimes-silly grin. Close your eyes and you'd say it came from another man entirely. *Who are you, Jon, and why don't your pieces fit?* Maybe that was why she couldn't see letting him go, angry as she was. He was a puzzle to be solved. She shrugged. "If you say so."

Without looking back, she stalked from the room. And maybe she *was* being unfair. Maybe he was entirely innocent. The phone rang and her steps quickened. Maybe that was the *Times* Classified, calling to say it had all been a mistake, a computer glitch?

No such luck. After she'd hung up, Demi leaned back in her chair to stare up at the ceiling. Wonderful! Obviously this was not her day, and it had hours yet to run. She swung her head at the sound of a throat clearing.

Jon sat in the doorway. "Look, if it bothers you this much, then maybe I'd just better resign."

No. For no reason she could fathom, she wanted him here. "It's not that. My date just finked out on me. Richard found out he has to fly out to L.A. to meet with one of his most important clients." And she'd *so* been looking forward to seeing him in a tuxedo—and watching her mother try to find a flaw in this one. Even she would have had to admit that Richard was near perfect.

"Sorry." Rolling over to her desk, Jon set four *mouillettes* upon it, his latest formulations. "That must be... disappointing."

So was his reaction, or lack thereof. Hector would have crooned his outraged sympathy, then fixed them both a good cup of hot tea while he assured her that all men were undependable rats, not to be lived with—or lived without. Well, she might as well get used to the fact that Jon was not Hector, or anything like... "Not so much disappointing as disastrous. Mother will insist on fixing me up with one of her admirers. The last time I let her do that, she gave me a fifty-something thigh pincher. I had to spike him under the table in self-defense, then Mother wanted *me* to apologize.''

She glanced at her watch. Maybe she could still rake up somebody? Not Jake. She'd made it plain to him last night that she would not marry him, or even date him again till he came to his senses. Now if Hector had been here... She blinked. Well, why not? "Jon...how d'you feel about opera?''

''Double-wide blondes in chain mail and cow horns? Yodeling?''

There was no sneaking up on him, he was there already—*and* remembering that only ten minutes ago he'd been falsely accused. ''If it were Wagner, I wouldn't even ask,'' she said coaxingly. ''But if you've never tried it, Jon, it's really rather nice, and our tickets are free.'' Her mother would be appalled, but so what? Served her right for not giving her time to find a real date.

''That's not a problem.'' He sounded even stuffier.

''Then what is?'' Was he going to make her crawl? Send him a written apology? ''If it's your clothes...'' She paused. He probably didn't own a tux, and couldn't have climbed into it if he did. She'd noticed that he always wore trousers that were acres too large, slipped over his casts, then belted to stay in place. ''I'm sure they won't...''

''Hold me to the usual standards? That's nice of them.''

He was normally so uncomplaining, she forgot how he must mind. But there was nothing she could do about that. ''Please, *please,* Jon? Save me from the thigh pinchers?'' And it would do him good, too, she assured herself, a night on the town. Better than sitting at home, lonely, in front of the tube.

He shrugged and ran a hand through his hair—and she tried not to wince. What her mother would think of his hair...

''If you put it like that...'' He sighed, then gave a grim nod. ''When shall I pick you up?''

CHAPTER EIGHT

SAVE HER FROM THE THIGH pinchers, Jon thought savagely as his van neared Lincoln Center that evening. Did she even have a clue that he was male? *Oh, lady, if you think your thighs are safe with me...* For a split second he could see himself drawing his tongue from the back of her knee to the shivering softness at the inner top of her thigh—then delivering one well-deserved nip to the tendon, right where the nerves ran shallow, just to show her who was boss. Of course, since in his fantasy she still wore her spike heels, this maneuver was not without danger—but definitely worth the risk. *Yeah, and very easy to do from a wheelchair!*

"Duct tape holding up?" his driver inquired.

"Fine so far." This was the same driver who'd picked him up from Alluroma a few hours ago. A nice guy, he'd been happy to double-park and run into the tux-rental shop they'd passed on their way to Jon's co-op, and then into a hardware store. Broke the usual monotony, he'd assured Jon.

"That's the place, over there." Demi had insisted he meet her at one of the outdoor cafés across from the center. Jon hadn't liked it. He'd been raised to collect his dates properly and see them home safely, but pressed for time as he'd been, he'd reluctantly agreed.

And there she was, sitting at a curbside table with *two* men, one of them flirting nonstop while the other one alternately glared at his rival and fixed a fatuous, hopeful smirk on Demi.

The van stopped almost under her nose. Jon started to protest, but the driver had slid out his door already.

She'd never seen the whole production before. He couldn't help glancing her way for a painful instant. She'd spotted him all right, was watching his slow descent with a troubled look, staring right past the guy who was trying desperately to hold her attention. Jon looked away, praying she'd have the sense not to try to help him—and wonder of wonders, she didn't.

When he wheeled over to her table she gave him a radiant smile, then her hand. "Jon!"

For just a moment it was a real date. Her fingers were fine boned and small in his, and he could almost have sworn they returned his reflexive squeeze. As their eyes held and the moment stretched, her beautiful lips parted in surprise. Then his focus widened to include her gaping admirers. *Yeah, pals, she's been waiting for me.*

But before he could make that crystal clear, Demi routed them herself with charming thanks for entertaining her while she waited. *It's my legs that are broken, not my tongue, my brains—or my...* he felt like telling her, then bit his tongue. He'd set out to convince her not to take him seriously—and he'd succeeded, so he had no one to blame but himself. *Get a grip, guy. Impressing her is not what you're here for.*

"You look—" Demi inspected him from head to toe "—*wonderful,* except for..." She reached to brush a lock of hair behind his ear. "But how did you get into..." Her eyes moved over his trousers.

"Scissors and duct tape. Just don't make me laugh too hard." Tomorrow he'd have to explain to the rental agency that he'd bought their tux. But tonight it was worth every penny. She hadn't dressed down in expectations of match-

ing him, as he'd feared she would. She wore a simple strap-
less job in red velvet, with a black velvet jacket slung over
it, her hair shining and loose, diamond studs sparkling in
her ears. There must be half a hundred men at the surround-
ing tables who wouldn't give him a Heimlich should he
suddenly need one.

"That's a promise! And meantime, I think we have time
for a drink." Before he could get it for her, Demi raised a
slender arm and a waiter came running.

Seventeen days, Jon reminded himself grimly while they
waited for their wine. Seventeen days till the casts came
off. *Meanwhile, count your blessings.* Here he sat with a
beautiful, brainy woman on the warmest night yet of this
year.... City lights washed out the stars, but still, he was
surrounded by happy people, waiting to hear wonderful
music. He did like opera in spite of his pretense at ignorance. His father had been a music teacher before he became principal of the high school in the small Vermont
town where he'd raised his family. All his children had
been well-grounded.

"So..." Demi lifted her arm and rotated it gracefully
beneath his nose. "Sheik 14B after five hours. What d'you
think?"

I think I'm in trouble. He caught her wrist and held it
pressed to his nose for a moment, his eyes drifting shut as
he savored her scent. His heart gave one gigantic pulse,
sending blood shooting down to his toes and all points in
between, then surging back home again, a comet slinging
round the sun. "I..." *This is the soul note?* He'd given up
on that kind of music. "We're not talking business tonight?"

"Why not?" She slipped out of his grasp and reached
for her drink.

Why not indeed? That was their entire relationship, as
far as she knew. She had no way of knowing he was stalk-

ing her, judging her... Wanting her? *I'm just the harmless geek in the wheelchair*. Jon's eyes lit on the dog.

"So what *do* you think of it?"

"I..." He scowled suddenly as a man kicked at the dog's shoulder, driving him away from his table. The dog took it without complaint and shuffled humbly on to the next prospect. Stood there, gazing up with dark, soulful eyes.

The people at that table ignored him. "It's...very nice." Jon scrounged in the side pocket of his chair, then pulled out the package of cheese crackers he'd bought days ago and never finished. "Here, boy!" He waggled a cracker and, three tables away, the dog picked up on a friendly voice. "Come on. Come over here."

He came worriedly, hesitantly, then in an incredulous rush as he caught the scent. He picked the first cracker delicately from Jon's fingers—someone had taught him manners—then inhaled it and looked for more.

"Jon!" Demi laughed.

"Been a while, huh?" Jon observed as the dog gulped down the second cracker. Under the dirt you could count his every rib. After the third cracker his tail remembered its function, and he whacked Demi across her shins. "Sorry!" Jon lured him to one side. He was a god-awful mix of Airedale, retriever and basset hound from the look of him, conceivably with a touch of alligator, low-slung as he was—goofy and starving and very lost in the big city.

"He smells like a *dog!*" Demi wrinkled her nose and moved her legs hastily aside as he danced his clumsy gratitude.

"And so he should." Jon was out of crackers. He rubbed the dog's head in apology and the mutt leaned against him, groaning and moaning. A sympathetic ear at last. "Poor ol' boy. Lost your way, huh?"

"I'm so sorry!" The waiter swooped down on them to

catch the dog by the scruff of his neck. "He's been mooching around all night. Come here, you!"

"No problem." Jon detached the man's hand. "He's with me now." He hadn't had a dog in years—didn't want or need one now. But this one needed him.

"But we— Oh, *ugh!*" Demi exclaimed as the dog reared up to rest his paws on one wheel of the chair and Jon leaned over to touch noses—the only way to properly cement a canine relationship—and received a slurpy, full-face kiss.

Angelina had never liked animals, either, he remembered, sitting upright and wiping his face. "I'm sorry." Sorry that she felt that way.

"Anyway, he's too young to appreciate opera," Demi pointed out, "and it's time."

It was. Couples were rising all around them and strolling across the square. "True." Jon laid a bill on the table. "I don't suppose your mother would let us stash him—"

"In her dressing room? You haven't met my mother!"

"All right, let me think." As they left the café, the dog kept pace with his chair, anxiously glancing up at him every step or two. A smart one, though he'd have been wiser not to walk between them. He bumped against Demi—who shied away and brushed at her dress.

"Watch it, boy—here." Jon snapped his fingers, and the dog hurried to heel on his far side. "You know, he's *really* smart."

"So he's Einstein. Can't you just give him a fiver toward his college fund and wish him well?"

"He's hungry, Demi. Haven't you ever been hungry?"

"Three times a day for thirty-one years." She blew her breath out in a disgusted *whoosh*, consulted her evening watch, then, swinging to face him, she crossed her arms. "We have precisely ten minutes to find our seats, of which there are two. *So*...it's me or Rover, Jon. Which will it be?"

Even though the evening was based on false terms, he'd wanted to spend it with her. And setting his own disappointment aside, he *had* agreed to escort her and he tried not to break promises. But beauty could take care of itself, Jon had long since learned. An empty seat at her side would be filled in minutes. Demi didn't need him. No one had needed him in years, he realized, looking from dark, exasperated eyes to dark, hopeful ones at knee height. "Him, then," he said, "if I have to choose."

"Fine." She wheeled and walked off, head held high.

He stared hungrily after her—she swayed more when she was angry—then glanced down as the dog nudged his knee. "Yeah, thanks a lot, pal. You could have timed this better."

Or maybe he was doing Jon a favor, barging in. Yes, he wanted her, but he damn sure didn't need a woman who recognized only her own needs, her own desires. *Been there, done that, and once was enough.* He groped in the side pocket for his phone, then flipped it open. With any luck he'd get another driver, another van. He was in no mood to explain his date swap.

But as he punched out the numbers, elegant black heels stepped into his circle of vision. He took his time following them up Demi's showgirl legs, past the clinging shimmer of crimson velvet, to her rueful scowl.

"I'm being a selfish brat, aren't I?"

Just so long as you know it! He gave her the warmest smile he ever had yet—then grabbed the dog's scruff as he tried to greet her. "Well, it's not every night your mom sings at the Met. Look, I had an idea." He glanced around, then lifted an arm toward the line of cabs that were letting out a string of latecomers to the performance.

MINUTES LATER THEY watched a cab drive away. At the first light, its driver leaned over to roll down his right-hand window. A long canine nose popped into view, pointed back in their direction. Demi laughed and shook her head. "Fifty dollars to drive a mutt around Manhattan all night! What makes you think he won't simply pocket that fifty, then drive him straight to the East River and drop him in?"

"The other fifty I'll give him when he brings Rover back here at midnight."

"You are *insane*, Jon Sutter! Utterly, certifiably, indubitably—"

"Don't you think we'd better hustle?"

"I do, which means you, sir, will to have to put up with *this!*" Stepping behind him, Demi caught the chair's handgrips, then aimed him at a near run up the ramp.

HE'S WITH ME NOW. Such simple words, but they rang in Demi's head louder than the golden voices that soared and swooped on the stage below. *He's with me,* and therefore a muddy, misbegotten mutt had nothing more to fear, the lucky dog. He fell under a man's protection now, a man who spoke with such quiet assurance that it was almost invisible.

She was still half wondering if she'd imagined it. But, no, when she'd tried to bend him to her will, make him choose between them, the steel had shown again.

Stubborn, that's all he is, she told herself. *Just an obstinate, sentimental dog lover. What's the big deal?*

He's with me, and so was sheltered henceforth from a world that frightened even her when she found the courage to look at it straight on. A world where a woman might walk forever alone, unsheltered by love, with no one to take all the love she had to offer. *I'm sitting here, jealous of a dog?*

Of a dog who'd been promised protection by a man who clearly couldn't even take care of himself? A man trapped in a broken body and a hopeless haircut, dependent on *her* undependable whims for his livelihood? A man content to be employed, not employer? If anything, Jon was the one in need of protection. Pity the hound wasn't something serious, like a Rottweiler or a Doberman. How typical of him to take on a sad, four-footed clown instead. What a pair they'd make!

He's with me now. The words rang in her head with serene, simple authority. *Shut up!* She stole a glance at her companion, who sat beside her in the aisle.

With his eyes fixed on the singer, Jon's face was rapt and very still. He might not know opera from a polka, but the emotion in the music had touched him all the same. The soprano's aria trembled, spiraled to its heartrending conclusion, grief rendered into silvery sound, and his head jerked up as the audience exploded into applause. He glared at one of the chandeliers overhead, his sandy lashes batting desperately, the strong column of his throat convulsing as he swallowed.

Why, you big softie! She had a sudden, ridiculous urge to catch his hand and lift it to her lips. If he'd been a real date, she would have, because he really was sweet. Her own eyes teared up as she watched him fight his emotion, and she turned hastily to the stage—in time to catch her mother's grand entrance. "That's her!" she hissed, digging him in the ribs. After that, she kept her mind fixed firmly on the music. Because afterward, there was always a quiz.

"*THAT'S* HIM?" HER MOTHER demanded, peeking out through the gap in the curtains. "In the wheelchair?"

"That's why I didn't bring him backstage." Demi glanced at her watch. He was supposed to collect his mutt in twenty minutes. It had taken her longer to drag her mother away from her admirers than she'd predicted.

"Surely you could have done better than that?" her mother burst out. "If you'd left it to me..."

"He's just a *friend*, Mother—and a very nice man. Come meet him, and please be nice."

Watching the two size each other up as she completed her introductions, Demi felt her tension slowly ease. Jon wasn't as overwhelmed as she would have expected after his awkwardness with Sarraj. When her mother offered her hand knuckles-up, he'd kissed it gravely and with no hesitation at all. Only Demi had noticed—or had she imagined?—that glint of wicked amusement in his blue eyes. And when her mother demanded Jon's opinion of the Met's "little entertainment," he'd interpreted that modest question correctly, responding with the apparently sincere opinion that Liza Hansen made a magnificent Leona. Her duet with the tenor in the second act...so *bel canto*...so...

Demi cocked her head and narrowed her eyes at him. He'd surprised her once again. And really, he had a wonderful mouth when you noticed it, though his hair or his glasses usually trapped your attention. It was strong and solemn, but with a smile lurking always at its mobile corners. She started as her mother hooked a possessive arm around her waist.

"So you really won't mind if I snatch my girl away tonight?" Phrased as a question, it was clearly a command. "I haven't had a chance to chat with her in months—I'm fresh off the plane from my South American tour. And we'd love to have you along, but there's a question of access, I'm afraid. If I'd known, I'd have made reservations elsewhere, but..." She shrugged, a wide, graceful gesture, big enough to be seen from the boxes.

"Not a problem," Jon said agreeably. "I've gotta see a man about a dog, anyway." His eyes met Demi's and shot away before she burst out laughing.

"Oh... *Oh,* well, in that case we won't keep you. The rest of my party is waiting backstage, so..." Her mother's hand urged her toward the steps to the stage.

"You'll have someone to see you safely home?" Jon asked quietly.

"Of course she will," her mother cut in as Demi opened her mouth. "Or else she'll stay at my co-op, in her old bedroom."

Jon nodded, apparently satisfied, and Demi felt an odd rush of warmth. He took his duties as her escort so seriously, even if he couldn't have been much protection should the need arise.

"See you tomorrow then?" he was saying. "And thanks to both of you for a wonderful evening."

She opened her mouth to tell him to wait, but he turned his chair and headed purposefully up the aisle. *He cares more for that darn dog than he does for me!* Not that she had any right to complain. He knew he was just a stand-in, not her first choice, either. Jon was probably grateful to her mother for freeing him of the burden.

"Well, *that* worked out nicely," her mother said with satisfaction. "I have the most delightful man I want you to meet—a major donor here at the center, though he's English, not American."

This was the world she'd been raised to enjoy, the people with whom she'd mingled since she was a child. Here she was Liza Hansen's charming, obedient daughter, though Liza insisted that most people took them for sisters.... She patted her mother's hand. "Thanks, Mother, but I can't, not tonight. Shall I call you tomorrow?"

"*Nonsense,* there's no reason you can't—"

"There is." Though just what her reason was, Demi could not have explained. Just a feeling. But as Jon disappeared through the doors to the lobby, she felt a sharp pang of anxiety. *Wait for me!* She kissed her mother on both cheeks— "You truly were magnificent. Now don't stay out all night—" then hurried up the aisle.

No need to run, she reminded herself, but she had the

sudden, wild impatience of a child set loose on the last day of school—running free toward the summer, shedding textbooks and hair clips and shoes as she ran. *Hey, wait for me!*

CHAPTER NINE

"SO INSTEAD OF bouillabaisse at one of Mother's chichi little bistros," Demi related to Kyle via her office phone the next morning, "I end up chowing down on chili dogs in Times Square, along with Jon, his dreadful mutt—who ate four—and the driver of his van. How's *that* for a first date?"

Kyle giggled. "Not quite what you imagined with Richard Sarraj, I take it? Still, it sounds charming—you and the three chili-dog brothers!"

Demi snorted. "When they dropped me off I tried to kiss Jon good-night—just a peck on the cheek since he'd been such a dear, standing in for Richard. But when I leaned down? His brute nailed me *square* on the mouth—a chili-and-raw-onion kiss from a dog! I marched straight upstairs and stood in the shower till the hot water ran out."

She glanced at the clock on her wall. Speaking of Jon, he was late.

"SARRAJ'S OUT WEST," Jon reported to Greenley as the van sat in a traffic jam some six blocks north of Demi's office. "Short notice, apparently. About three yesterday he accepted a date with Cousteau. Then he called back to cancel, told her he had to fly out to L.A. to meet with a client."

"She told you California, huh?" Greenley reached down to scratch the dog lying between them. "That's interesting. 'Cause Sarraj flew east, to the Canary Islands."

Jon's stomach gave a nasty lurch, or maybe it was simply

the van, lunging into a gap in the next lane. "You're sure of that?" And had Demi known? Or was she in the dark, too?

"Well, it's your brother who says so. He's been tracking the *Aphrodite* by satellite since she left the Med. He was there waiting when she pulled into port last night. Then Sarraj flew in this morning, went aboard."

Jon nodded blankly. A little of the sparkle that had remained from last night winked and died out. *Demi, did you lie to me?*

"Anything else?"

He'd already reported on her precarious financial state earlier this year. "She has an unusually tight deadline. She's contracted to deliver the juice in two months. Ten months would be about the tightest gap you'd expect. Two years wouldn't be abnormal at all for a top-drawer perfume."

Greenley pursed his lips. "She give any reason for the hurry?"

"I don't think she knows." Whatever was going on here—if it was anything underhanded—Demi didn't know, he felt that in his bones. Yes, she was demanding, perfectionistic, imperious—after last night he could see where it came from—and a bit of a brat, even, though she had the honesty to admit it, then back down. But a hurtful liar?

"Have you gotten a chance to go over her inventory?"

"Not yet. For a fake lab tech, I keep pretty busy." Her inventory was a major point of interest in this investigation.

Seemingly innocent chemicals of the right type and the right quantity could make a fearsomely powerful bomb. Or provide the components for a gas attack like the one in the Tokyo subways. "Hey, by the way, that cute trick you guys pulled, canceling her want ad, nearly got me fired. Don't do anything like that again without telling me."

Greenley shrugged. "You've a better chance of looking innocent if you are, Sutton. Basic rule of the trade."

He wasn't grateful for his education. "Next time, I want to *know*. And if she places that ad again, leave it in. I'll take my chances." The happiest ending for him might be if she let him go at the end of this week. If he was wrong and she was in on this, he didn't want to know, much less catch her.

"YOU'RE FORTY MINUTES late!" Demi called when the hall door opened. Surely he wasn't going to presume on her goodwill after last night? If so, she was here to disabuse him of that notion. Within the walls of Alluroma she was still the boss—and Jon was still on probation.

"I know." Jon appeared in the doorway. "I've been sitting in traffic for the past hour. Finally got out and rolled around Sixtieth or we'd be sitting there yet."

"We?" He wheeled into her office, and behind him, tail waving shyly, plodded— "Oh, *please!* In your dreams, Jon Sutter! You march that—that spotted crocodile right out of here this minute!"

"Demi, a dog needs to be walked at least three times a day. This way he gets it going and—"

"And a perfumer—this perfumer—needs a fresh, clean environment with minimal disgusting intrusions of the nasal variety."

"I'll wash him tonight, I promise. We overslept this morning."

"You'll brush his teeth three times a day? He had tuna for breakfast and, trust me, he forgot to use mouthwash." The hound was sniffing some invisible trail across her carpet. He reached her desk and looked up at her doubtfully.

"I'll buy him dry food at lunchtime. That'll fix that."

"He's not *fixable*, Jon, short of drowning. The answer's no!"

"Love me, love my dog?" he tried, edging toward the lab.

What was this, blackmail? "I don't mean to love either of you, just work you to death. He'll be a distraction."

"Burton? He plans to snore in a corner all day. You'll never notice him."

"You are utterly *besotted* if you think he looks anything like Richard Burt—*erk!*" Demi jumped as a cold, damp nose touched her hand. *"Pah!"* She yanked a drawer out, seeking alcohol and cotton to clean her fingertips.

"Not the actor. The Burton who searched for the head-waters of the Nile. My hero when I was a kid. He had a talent for getting lost, too."

"Maybe a crocodile Burton *met* on the Nile..." Long, spotted nose lifting as he caught the scents from the kitchenette, the mutt trundled off down the corridor. "Jon, this is a class establishment. Possibly an Afghan or an Irish wolfhound—but that?"

"Okay, okay." He ran a hand through his hair, further reducing their class quotient by three defiant cowlicks, then consulted his watch. "I'll take him home. Should be back about noon, traffic willing."

She'd made a breakthrough this morning, pivoting on one chord of Sheik 32 and heading off in a new direction entirely. She wanted to smell it now—yesterday—not sometime this afternoon.

And there were shadows under Jon's eyes, she noticed as his glasses slipped down his nose. He hadn't gotten his eight hours last night, as she should know. Everything she took for granted, from dressing to catching a cab, must be a drain on his vitality. It was a wonder he was as cheerful and patient as he was. "No," she said as he snapped his fingers for the dog. "You're here, so stay here. I can stand it for one day.

"But *keep* him out of my office!" she added fiercely as

he gave her a wide, happy grin. For just a moment, cowlicks and all, she could picture him at twelve. The image
stayed with her as he gave her a thumbs-up, then wheeled
off down the corridor.

Jon at twelve, and his hero had been an explorer of deepest, darkest Africa? How did a boy like that grow up to
work in a pharmacy? *What happened to your dreams, Jon?*

Dreams were what made the man, in Demi's view. She'd
never yet fallen for a man who didn't dream, and why
should she? She dreamed big; shouldn't her lover dream
even bigger? It was that ambition, that restless yearning
toward the far horizon that seemed to her the heart note of
masculinity. That most enticed her. Reese Durand had had
it. Her grandfather had it. She suspected Richard Sarraj had
it, though so far he'd kept his dreams held tight to his vest.

But Jon? *What happened to you, Jon, satisfied with such
an unchallenging, go-nowhere job? Such a loser mutt?* She
sighed, pinched the end of her nose—and winced at the
smell of her fingers. Reached for the alcohol again. And
why was she even thinking of Jon in terms of her men? He
was an employee, not a romantic prospect.

WHILE DEMI COLLECTED the top-shelf bottles he'd need for
formulations that day, and Burton sprawled in a corner—
raiding garbage cans in his dreams, from the way he licked
his chops—Jon tracked down the rest of the essential oils,
A through Z, around the lab. "You never told me what
Sarraj thought of your trials? Did he like any of them?"

Demi's shoulders did their Gallic dance. "Oh, he liked
them all."

What man wouldn't, sampled off Demi Cousteau? "He
didn't prefer one in particular?"

"Thirty-two, I suppose. At least, that's my choice." She
brought a box of bottles to his counter, then offered her
wrist. "What do you think? Can you still smell it?"

He'd be happy to try for a day or three! Holding her, he sniffed, her pulse thumping past his fingers with discouraging regularity. She didn't see him as a man at all, to offer herself so easily. Didn't she realize that he only had to tighten his grip and he had her, to have and to hold as long as it pleased him?

Or maybe she went him one better. She'd sensed he was a civilized man, no threat to her whatsoever. Unable to feel pleasure unless he also gave it. *And she goes elsewhere for hers.* He let her go abruptly. "It smells...nice." If heaven smelled nice. "But maybe that's just you?"

"No." She brought her wrist to her nose. "It still lingers—just. And I can do even better with the fixatives once I've settled on my top and heart notes. I want it to meld with the odor of the skin, not ride on top of it. A fragrance should seem the scent of a woman herself, not something she applies."

"Hmm." He worked for a while in silence, Demi fidgeting at his side. Sarraj... "So he had no preference?" For half a million, you'd think he'd have an opinion.

Demi shrugged. "Sometimes a client wants to direct the process every step of the way, if he's knowledgeable and knows what he wants. Or if he has too big an ego to realize he knows nothing, that his advice will hurt more than it helps. Others—the ones I prefer—stand back and let the perfumer guide the process."

Or if the client simply didn't care? If creating a wonderful perfume wasn't the point of the game? *But if not that, then what?* Jon finished the first of the day's trials, then reached for a *mouillette* and a pen. "This is Sheik 32B or 33?"

"Call it Veil 1. We've zigzagged to a new concept I'm working out. We're dropping most of the amber notes, going more floriental."

Now that felt like progress. "Veil?"

"Richard says the prince might call my juice Seventh Veil. I may as well get used to it."

"Salome..." he mused, dipping the *mouillette*, then offering it to her. "Not bad." Biblical seductress, hypnotizing King Herod with her dance, veil by dropping veil, until he gave her— The hairs bristled at the nape of his neck, his fingertips tingled—he glanced at her sharply.

Scent strip held to her nose, lashes brushing her cheeks, Demi breathed deep, her head falling slowly back like a woman looking inward, searching for the first ripples of her own ecstasy. He could imagine her kneeling above him like that. Her lips parted in a sigh....

Response was inevitable. He stirred and hardened—and spun his stool before she could see. *Get a life, Sutton!* He shoved across from the counter to the nearest shelf to stare blankly at the bottles before him. Herod. He'd never felt one shred of sympathy for the guy before, but now he could almost—almost—see it. *You want what, honey? John the Baptist's head on a platter? Drop that last veil and we have a deal....*

Nasty, but what would *he* give for the right to unbutton that silk blouse she wore today, button by fumbled button, till her last, soft mystery lay revealed?

Everything? Which turned out to be far, far too much the last time he offered it. Because beautiful women didn't give back. Didn't need to. He worshiped at their shrine no more.

Liar, liar, pants on—

"Now *that* has possibilities," Demi murmured behind him on a note of buttery satisfaction. He heard paper rustle, then her pencil busily scratching.

Translation: three dozen more variations for me to mix. Jon pulled at his baggy pants and decided he was decent.

"What are you looking for over there?"

Peace and sanity? "Umm..." His eyes lit on a bottle set

alongside the bottle of Firefly, the perfume she'd sold to the tightwad designer. "What's this—Irresistible?"

"Oh, *that*..." She sounded embarrassed. "That's a men's cologne I created for Pherotics, up in Boston. A pheromonic fragrance. It contains hormones to attract women to men."

"I heard about this!" All his male students had been wearing it last fall in their perpetual hope of getting laid. And Angelina had come back from some cast party, he recalled with a sharp stab of distaste, claiming she'd met some heavenly man who wore a pheromonic cologne. She'd always enjoyed making him jealous. Why she hadn't realized that if you stretched a man on that rack long enough, he went numb... He hadn't bothered to ask if the stuff worked. "Does it work?" His hand hovered over the bottle.

"The man I composed it for says so. But if it does, it's subtle. It might give a guy a slight edge, but it's no guarantee. So demand's growing, but growing slower than we'd hoped, which is too bad for me. I get a ten-percent royalty on it for five years, and it's been out almost two. It may make Reese's fortune in the long run, but it won't make mine."

Reese. Demi stood very still for a moment, waiting for the old pain, the old humiliation to jab her in the same sorely accustomed spot.

It didn't. She cocked her head, scarcely daring to breathe. It was gone, just like that? No pain left, just its fading memory? Now when had that happened? *Blame it on Richard Sarraj, I suppose!* She swiped her hair back behind her ear, turned to beam at Jon. *I'm free!*

"That's too bad," he was saying, lifting the bottle to his nose. He sniffed cautiously. "*Nice*... I remember driving in a jeep, up in the mountains of..." He stoppered the bottle abruptly. "Someplace. It's nice and outdoorsy, but I don't feel any different."

"You wouldn't, silly. It's supposed to affect women, make them notice the man who wears it. To you it's just another fragrance. Now, would you get *over* here? I've changed the second variation, see? A little more iris, two milliliters less of the synthetic civet..."

THEY WORKED HARD ALL afternoon, barring a short break when Jon walked the dog and fetched their sandwiches. Burton ate two ham with Swiss—he was well on his way to becoming insufferably spoiled. Jon reported that the temp had climbed to the low sixties. Spring, her favorite season, was happening out there beyond their windows...the smell of sun-warmed earth and swaying jonquils, the wind backing from north to south to blow off the ocean, hints of dried kelp and ozone sailing through the town... Now, if you could capture *that* in a bottle...

At three Demi couldn't stand it anymore. If she declared victory, then they could retreat with dignity. "Now this..." She waved a *mouillette* under Jon's nose, Veil 16. "This is another turning point, I think. No more gardenia—too heavy, no matter how I lift it with the aldehydes. We're going with jonquils, and speaking of which, let's go smell some."

"Huh?" He looked at her as if she'd gone mad.

I'm that much of a slave driver? "We're done for the day, Jon. I have to smell springtime. Want to walk home with me?"

"Uh...*yes!* I mean, sure, why not?"

While he closed up the lab, Demi went back to her office to change to walking shoes. A thought hit her as she tied her laces, and she turned to the phone. Minutes later they were sauntering uptown, three abreast, no doubt one of the odder trios in a city that had seen it all—fashion-plate woman, at least down to her high-top sneakers, haystack on wheels, furry crocodile, and all of them grinning like teenage truants.

"Walk through the park?" Jon suggested when they reached Columbus Circle.

"Definitely!" They turned that way; the wind eddied around a building and she sniffed suspiciously. "Did you—" She bent to put her nose to his cheek and sniffed. "It *is* you!"

Startled, Jon jumped and swung toward her—their cheeks brushed. Clean-shaven though he'd started the day, his bristles scratched. The sensation starred out across her face, a tiny, electric shock.

His pupils widened, his eyes seeming to darken from sky blue to cobalt, with that single speck of gold in the left one—kite against storm clouds. She straightened abruptly. "You're wearing Irresistible, you sneak!"

He turned the color of the pink hyacinths in the window boxes of the café they were passing. "Yeah. Thought I'd field-test it."

"On whom?" A sudden, fierce emotion swirled through her, like the wind shifting to the warmer south. He was *her*—Demi blinked—lab tech. *He's just my lab tech.* Gee, maybe the stuff did work? Reese and Nicola had always sworn that it did. "On *whom* are you going to test it, pray?" Not that it was any of her business, but—

"Not that it's any of your biz, boss, but there's this cute woman at the store where I shop."

She sniffed. Not good enough for him, something told her. Men were such romantic fools when it came to choosing, and Jon in particular seemed an innocent. *I should check her out for him.* "Where do you shop?"

"Why?"

Aha! He is serious! she thought, catching the defensive note. She would definitely have to see this woman. "I thought it might be the same place I shop. Maybe we'll bump into each other sometime.''

"Oh... Uh, the Korean's, on Broadway near Eightieth.''

They'd pass it later on—she'd see to that. But first Demi glanced at her watch and picked up their pace. His appointment was for four-fifteen.

Still they had time to watch Burton romp across the park with a miniature poodle—Burton gallantly galumphing, his lop ears lifted as comically high as he could hold them and his tail swinging in stiff, placating arcs, the beribboned poodle running rings around him and yapping shrill contempt till her scandalized owner called her away. There was time to laugh at the pigeons, bowing and strutting and cooing their springtime courtships along the walks.

Demi crushed grass and smelled it, then held it under Jon's nose. Picked violets, whose scent enchanted, then vanished in a heartbeat, and dandelion leaves, so deliciously green and bitter that her mouth watered.

Jon challenged her to sniff his closed fists, then professed himself astonished when she could identify not only pine needles but privet. *And also your skin,* she thought, but didn't tell him so. His knuckles smelled of the essential oils he'd been handling, the lab soap he'd used at the end of the day, Burton, whom he thumped in the ribs every time he galloped back to Jon's chair. And an odor that was simply Jon, a hint of musk, a trace of leather, a color in the mind that reminded her of sun on warm limestone—rocks she'd stretched out on above a running stream somewhere in her childhood on some wonderful day. An odor henceforth labeled Jon in her encyclopedic mental catalog.

They exited the park at Sixty-sixth and she led them crosstown to Columbus Avenue, then north to her haircutter's. "Precisely on time.''

Jon peered through the plate glass at the chairs with their

towel-draped occupants, the hairdressers hovering behind them. "You're getting your hair cut? I like it how it is."

"No, silly, you are. You have an appointment with my favorite cutter."

He shook his head decisively. "I have my own barber."

"Who moonlights as a hedge trimmer? You go back to him and you're fired, Jon Sutter!"

He pushed his glasses up his nose. "Can't be. You haven't hired me yet."

Demi saw the trap she'd walked into too late. She lifted her brows haughtily, but he wouldn't be cowed. He simply waited, laughter dancing in his eyes.

She drew a deep breath. Well, really, what *was* she stalling for? She hadn't a single other prospect, and wouldn't have, since she hadn't replaced her ad. And Jon was amusing to have underfoot. She could talk to him, a real bonus when he was the only one she saw at work for days on end. And except for his one mistake, she couldn't fault him in the lab. *So...?*

There was just that niggling, unnamed doubt that all was not quite as it should be...as it seemed....

Though he seemed humble and ever-eager to please, he wasn't quite as under her thumb as she would have expected by now. As would be wise to have him. Because the lines of command had to be crystal clear. *It's my company and I'm the boss.* "I said I'd tell you on Friday."

"So I'll get a haircut Saturday—or not."

But she wanted to see him *now*. She'd been looking forward to this transformation, planning and gloating for the past hour. And given his taste in barbers, she definitely meant to supervise the event. Alluroma had an image to uphold, after all. She blew out her breath. "Okay."

"I'm hired?"

Oh, don't! some deep-down instinct cried. He was trouble. Somehow, some way, goofy grin and all, Jon Sutter was trouble. Change. Chaos.

Of course, trouble had always attracted her, though not during business hours. And what alternative had she—an ax murderer? "On the condition that you give me carte blanche on this haircut—you're hired."

His grin sprang from hiding. Really he had a wonderful, wicked smile. A pity he used it so rarely. Then Demi took its meaning—she'd missed a trick. She should have added a condition about the dog, if you could call Burton that. *I'll take you—but not him!*

"Deal!" Jon said as she opened her mouth to amend it. Then let her hold the door for him as he wheeled inside.

CHAPTER TEN

"THE SAME LENGTH ALL over," Demi specified while Gretta prowled around Jon's chair, surveying him from all angles with fascinated outrage.

"A crew cut?" Gretta whisked off his glasses and set them aside.

"Longer if you can salvage another half inch or so."

"Help, Burton, they've got me!" Jon called plaintively, and Demi turned to see his mutt reared up with his nose to the plate glass. He barked, cutters and clients burst out laughing and Gretta picked up her scissors.

Demi crossed to the chairs along the opposite wall and pretended to read a magazine. But she kept sneaking peeks as a new man emerged, swath by falling swath. And she couldn't help noticing how—how inappropriate Gretta's hand looked, resting familiarly on his shoulder, or how broad those shoulders looked in contrast to her hand. Really, did she have to touch him so much? This was a hair-styling, not a massage!

"There," Gretta said with satisfaction at last. She brushed an imaginary wisp off his shoulder. "You know who he looks like?"

What he looked like was embarrassed and exasperated, plainly resenting their discussion of him in the third person. And he also looked slightly...apprehensive...when their eyes met in the glass. Or could Jon even see her at that distance without his glasses? He looked so new and different that for a moment Demi felt an odd pang of loss. No more Big Bird. Would he still make her smile? Yet he looked...competent. Nerd no longer. And good. He looked *surprisingly* good. She hadn't realized...

"Like Kevin Costner in *The Bodyguard*," Gretta crowed. "I knew he had the bones to carry it off!"

"Gimme a break!" Jon snatched his glasses off the counter and jammed them on the end of his nose. "But thanks all the same, Gretta." He retreated with all haste to the door while Demi paid. This was a business expense, she'd assured him earlier, window dressing as much as the palm trees in her office were.

But as she made out her check, Gretta whispered, "Hey, is he taken?"

Demi pursed her lips and concentrated on finding her balance. Not as far as she knew, Jon wasn't. But Gretta wasn't right for him, any more than the woman at his grocery store would be. Gretta was an airhead. And callous with her men, judging from the tales she told Demi while she cut her hair. Jon needed someone.... *Someone else.* Someone kinder. He'd be a lamb to Gretta's body-snatching wolf. "I'm afraid he is." She ripped off the check. *By me.* She needed his full attention for the next seven weeks, till they'd fulfilled their contract.

SHE KEPT GIVING HIM odd little looks as they wandered on through the West Side. Jon had never been much of a judge of his own appearance when he looked in the mirror—about average, he'd have said. So now he had no idea if Demi had improved him or only changed him. You had to discount Gretta's crack about Kevin Costner—she'd been waiting for her tip. And he'd never understood what women saw in Costner anyway.

At least she'd returned him to the range of normal, which was a relief, but then why was Demi staring? Not that she was the only one out looking on this fine spring day. He aimed a "Keep-off!" scowl at yet another approaching ogler—they were averaging four per block—who ate up Demi with his eyes as he neared. The guy grinned unabashedly—*You'd do the same, pal!*—and swaggered on his way.

Maybe he could train Burton to attack on command?

Attack food vendors' carts and toddlers with ice-cream cones, maybe. "Burton!" he yelled as the dog stopped before just such a hapless mark and raised his nose toward the dripping prize. "Get over here, chowhound!"

And now he'd lost Demi, he realized, looking behind him just in time to see her waving to him from the doorway of a shop, then slipping inside. A vintage clothing store, he noted, wheeling back to it.

She floated out in ten minutes or so with a bag tucked under one elbow, a look of guilty bliss, and a brown fedora tipped over her elegant nose. "You like it?" She pirouetted for his approval.

He could imagine her wearing it beside him in Paris on their way out to a dig in the Mideast. He'd do the museums, she could hit the perfume houses and the boutiques, they'd meet for wine and cassoulet in a little bistro he knew in Montmartre. Afterward they'd walk back arm in arm through the long purple twilight to their hotel. Make love by candlelight.

"You don't!" She pouted and walked on ahead.

"No, I do!" He could see her wearing it to bed, perhaps with a pair of black hose and garters. *Did* she wear proper stockings? Or those horrible panty-hose things? No way to ask her. "It's nice. *Très chic.* Racy?" he called after her. And apparently that was the right word, because she turned back with a dazzling smile and let him carry her package for her, tucked into the side of his chair. A nuisance, but for Demi...

"Why are we stopping here?" They'd reached the Ko-

rean's, a grocery store he favored because of its wide aisles
and easy access.

"Don't you need anything for supper tonight?"

"Not a thing." He hated shopping even with two working legs.

"Bet you need a paper," she insisted. "Have you
checked the lost-and-founds for Burton yet? Somebody
might be missing him terribly."

Don't you wish! But it hadn't occurred to him, and happiness faltered as he considered it. Burton didn't deserve
an owner who'd taken no better care of him than to let him
stray. Still. "I s'pose I should...."

Once inside, Demi didn't settle for a paper, which could
be had by the door. She insisted on cruising all four aisles,
picking up cans and packages then putting them down
again, glancing around impatiently. They rounded an aisle
and met the proprietor.

"Mr. Chicken Pot Pie!" The owner grinned at Jon,
bobbed his head at Demi while giving her a lightning once-
over, then bustled away.

"Mr. Chicken Pot Pie?"

Jon shrugged. "Guess that *is* the main thing I buy here."

"That's disgusting. Don't you cook?"

"Well, I don't eat 'em raw."

"Ha—let's get out of here." She chivied him to the exit,
then appropriated his paper when they hit the street. Scanning the classifieds as she strolled beside him, she murmured, "I didn't see your girlfriend."

He started guiltily—he'd already forgotten the woman
he'd invented. "Uh, I guess she only works nights?"

"Student?" Demi asked with elaborate disinterest.

"Dunno." *What do you care, Ms. Nosy? Can we drop
it?*

Demi sniffed and turned a page. "D'you think he's a
Lab-shepherd cross?"

"If I'm half Eskimo."

"Angora tomcat?"

"Closer, but there's something about his ears.... Face it, nobody wants him."

"Well, I don't want him at Alluroma." She folded the section, then thrust it at him. "Don't you *dare* bring him in tomorrow. I mean it, Jon."

"You're just scared of the competition. He can smell rings around you, you know."

"Oh, *please!* I'm one of the five best—"

"Noses in the world. Yes, I know. That means you have maybe one-third the olfactory ability of a brain-dead Chihuahua, to say nothing of Burton. Just look at this apparatus!" Burton shuffled back to see what they were on about, and Jon tapped him on the snout, then dodged his tongue. "How could you match that? You're jealous."

"Of that? I can identify a thousand or more scents. All *he* knows is pastrami, tuna and roadkill."

"I could stump you in five."

"In your dreams!"

"Care to put it to a test?" Beyond the next cross street he spotted Zabar's, the deli that was Mecca to every foodie in Manhattan. "You miss one in five and Burton's welcome in the lab."

Demi glanced from the store to Jon, then down to the dog—who promptly sat and leaned against her shins, gazing up at her adoringly. She retreated one fastidious step and he collapsed. "You'll leave him home when I win?"

"If."

"When. You've got yourself a bet, mister!"

They left the dog out front in the charge of a street musician who tootled Jewish klezmer music on an alto sax to the passersby. With Burton sitting mournfully by his open instrument case, nosing each coin as it bounced onto the blue velvet, Jon figured his tips would double.

Meanwhile, rules of the game were simple. Demi was honor-bound to keep her eyes closed, and he made her tilt the fedora over her nose to remind her. With her holding on to the wheelchair's handgrips, apparently pushing, Jon was the actual navigator. He led Demi to the end of the short block, reversed direction to pass Zabar's again, then turned once more. There were two entrances to the deli, and it was best she not know which one they entered. "We're turning left now."

The inside of the store looked like the sack of Rome—frantic shoppers bumping and elbowing each other while they juggled briefcases or wailing babies with their over-loaded baskets, snarling and snatching goodies from under each other's fingers. *Big mistake,* he thought, staring at the riot. Rush hour at Zabar's.

Still, he wouldn't find a more exotic collection of scents outside the Bronx Zoo. Edging into the fray, they rolled into an almost-visible wall of aroma—cinnamon, baking bread, fresh-ground coffee. Could Demi smell the garlands of dried peppers and garlic hanging overhead?

"Cheeses to the left," she noted smugly at his ear.

"Smoked cheddar, pecorino Romano, Gruyère..." They circled counterclockwise around that island, Jon surveying his choices while trying not to run up the heels of the shoppers ahead.

Stilton? No, even he might get that one. Argentinian fontina? Something more exotic. He grabbed a yellow, plastic-wrapped chunk, stopped the chair and held it up to her nose. "Number one, hotshot."

She sniffed, frowned, sniffed again. "*Mmm...* Austrian Tilsit."

"You're peeking!"

"Poor sport. That's one." Taking it from him, she dropped the cheese into his lap. "I am utterly *starving!*"

So was he, but not for food. He turned again toward the

back of the store. Something harder for his beautiful blood-hound... The cases to their right held refrigerated pasta. He snagged a package. "And this?"

"Pasta." Her nose grazed his hand, and he curbed the impulse to brush her cheek with a fingertip. "It's made with pumpkin. And they used nutmeg and cardamom to spice it."

"Pumpkin tortellini," he agreed. *Burton, old boy, I'm doing my best.*

"Get it," Demi commanded, "and if you see any Alfredo sauce..."

"Here's some. We should have taken a basket." But there was no turning back now with a dozen shoppers hard on their heels.

Back of the aisle were candies and other dried sweets in bins. Jon scooped up a bagful, took out a piece and nudged her mouth with it. "Now this is *not* one of your five." Maybe the taste would confuse her, he told himself. But it was for his own sake, not Burton's, that he offered his fingertips to the warm dampness of Demi's delectable lips.

"Yum...too easy. Chocolate espresso beans. Buy me some?"

They turned along the back of the store, passing dried sausages on their left. He grabbed one called Love and Garlic and held it to her nose.

"*Gack!* Salami, take it away, you sadist! And that's three. I hope Burton likes soap operas."

"You haven't won yet." *Okay, get serious, Sutton.* They rounded the end of an aisle and headed toward the front of the store.

"Fish on our right," Demi sang out. "Sardines... smoked salmon...smoked brook trout, fresh perch."

"Braggart. You know that 'cause you shop here."

"Avocados on our left," she noted as they turned cross-store, "none of them ripe. And the pineapples are too ripe." They turned again. "Breads to our left. Buy us one, will you, Jon?"

Us? It was a magical, wistful word, but she didn't mean it that way. "How about this?" He held a loaf of whole-wheat sourdough to her nose.

"It's stale."

A worker stacking a pyramid of loaves looked up indignantly. "It just came in today!"

"Came in stale," Demi said with the blithe tactlessness of the native New Yorker. She reached blindly to pat a pile. "Let's get one of these with the rosemary."

Jon added a crusty Italian *ciabatta* to the mounting heap in his lap, then guided her back around an aisle to a case of prepared foods. *Could* she be peeking? He might have a terminal case of the hots for the woman, but that didn't mean Demi played fair. Hell, his brother thought she might be a terrorist—and he worried she might *peek?*

Even if she wasn't cheating, maybe she was cuing herself geographically? Careful not to slow or stop, he snatched up a pint of dip.

Ahead were barrels and barrels of coffee beans. Demi patted his shoulder. "Get some Blue Mountain Kona, half pound, fine drip grind?"

While a clerk ground their beans, they retraced their route against the surly traffic to fruits and vegetables. Demi chose salad greens—mixed organic—and balsamic vinaigrette *maison*. Jon waved a basket of fresh lingonberries under her nose—and she shot him down. "That's four!"

They went back for their coffee, then the last aisle funneled them to the checkout counters with their long, fuming lines. "And your last effort?" Demi said with kindly condescension. "I'd like to open my eyes."

Grimly Jon opened his half-pint container of dip and held it up to her face. "Number five."

The faintest shadow moved over it. She sniffed, bit her lip. "It contains garlic...olive oil...parsley."

"With a head cold I could tell you that! What's the main ingredient?"

She scowled, then jumped as a woman nudged her with a basket from behind, calling, "Hey, would ya move up there, please?"

They moved and he offered the container again. "Well, champ?"

"Can I taste it?"

Cheating! he started to say, but even for Burton he couldn't resist. "Sure." He dipped a forefinger into the stuff and held it to her lips.

For just a second she hesitated, her eyelashes fluttering, then clamping down again to fan against her cheeks. A tiny, private smile flicked across her mouth. Then she opened to him, sucked it thoughtfully from his finger.

Heaven would feel precisely like this, except in heaven she would never stop. He couldn't catch his breath. She took her time, using her tongue, savoring the dip—savoring him, it almost seemed.

"If you two lovebirds would *move*, then the rest of us could—"

"*Eggplant!*" Demi cried, opening her eyes. "*Baba gannoujh!*"

"*What* did you call me?" the woman behind them demanded.

"You peeked!"

"Did *not*, you sore loser!" Demi squeezed past his chair and looked back, laughing. "And for that, you get to pay!" She tipped her hat to him and the grump behind. "I'll go tell Burton the bad news." She danced on out to the sidewalk, leaving him with a bill for thirty-three dollars and seventeen cents. And a forefinger that he would have had gilded as a memento if it weren't still attached to his hand.

MAYBE IT WAS GUILT that made her offer to cook supper. Demi's glee at winning had faded while she watched Burton and Jon's reunion outside the store. Jon might have been gone for a year, the way the brute capered and whined, then reared up against his wheel to lick his face. Jon's pleasure had been less demonstrative, but just as obvious. Demi felt like the Wicked Witch of the West for plotting to part them.

Or maybe it was just that the day had been one of those rare, magical ones where happiness rode like an angel on your shoulder. Call it spring fever, call it Jon's good company, whatever, she didn't want it to end yet.

Or maybe it was just that she was starving and Jon had paid for the food. So it was only fair she cook it. Still, for a moment as they neared his co-op, she hesitated. What if he took her offer wrong? These past few days she could hardly help noticing how he watched her when he thought she wasn't looking. Or back there in the deli, the excuses he'd found to touch her.

Not that she'd minded. She was finding him attractive, too, now that she could see past his hair. Surprisingly so. Blame it on springtime, blame it on her Irresistible cologne or blame it on the delightful day they'd shared together, she felt...drawn to him this evening. Surprisingly drawn.

Still, attracted or not, she had no designs on his bod or his heart, none whatsoever. *Not my own lab tech.* A silly fling like that had a guaranteed messy ending. And some instinct warned her that, no matter how he joked, Jon was vulnerable. She liked him much too much to toy with his feelings.

So this is supper—and nothing but! she told him silently, since there was no way to say so aloud without hurting his pride. "So what d'you think?" she said casually. "Shall I come up and put this feast together?"

She'd expected instant, eager agreement. Instead he went blank.

"Nothing fancy," she elaborated when he continued rolling alongside her in silence. "Just a simple salad and the pasta." Heavens, it almost sounded as if she were the one needing company rather than granting him the favor of hers! *Come on, Jon. What's the matter?*

"Umm," he hedged at last with no hint of enthusiasm.

"Or has your apartment been declared a bachelor's disaster zone?" That would explain this hesitance.

"Not at all." He sounded offended. "I'm very neat—well, neat."

"Then you *are* mad at me for winning. And here I've been thinking you're such a good sport!" They stopped as they reached his co-op.

"No, I'm not. But Burton may never forgive you." He shrugged. "You know, I guess I am sort of tired tonight. Maybe some other time?"

But don't hold your breath! she thought, recognizing his tone. She'd used it herself so many times, on men she had no intention of dating. "Oh." No one—well, no man before or since Reese Durand, had ever refused her company. She blinked, as startled as if he'd bopped her on the nose.

He held out the bag of food. "You should take this. You picked it out."

For us to eat together, she realized with a sharp pang of loss. She'd really been looking forward to seeing his place—seeing what it revealed about Jon. Had looked forward to simply sitting across from him at a table and talking lazily, maybe sipping a glass of wine and letting him make her laugh as the twilight closed round. "*No,* thank you. You paid for it."

Her disappointment was showing. She managed a dazzling smile. "So you eat it. And don't you *dare* settle for a pot pie tonight!"

"All right," he said soberly.

A nasty, green-eyed thought leaped out of nowhere. *Or maybe he'll ask some other woman in to cook it for him?* His little friend from the Korean grocery, maybe? Demi stood, stunned by the unwelcome thought, the unwelcome feeling that tumbled after it. This was absurd—low blood sugar talking, no more than that. She'd go out for supper without him, that would cure this. *And show him.* She'd go someplace special—and be sure to tell him all about it tomorrow. "Good," she said briskly as she tugged the package that contained the vintage dress she'd bought from under his elbow. "See you at nine tomorrow then, without you-know-who?"

"Oh, yeah, I've been thinking about that."

Maybe he *was* mad at her, though he wouldn't admit it. "Yes?"

"We've already discussed salary, and your terms are very generous...."

She didn't want to stand here and talk business! She tipped her fedora to a dangerous angle. Here she'd been offering to cook the brute's meal—not something she did for just any man—and he'd been brooding all along about his salary? This was why you didn't date employees!

"But I was wondering if we could work out a deal? I'd take a bit less if I could bring Burton along. Saves me the cost of a dog walker."

Was Jon so lonely that he needed a lousy, flea-bitten mutt for company? He couldn't do better than that? Preferred that to her— She stomped a mental heel on that thought. *I'm going nuts. I need food.* "Jon, if he means that much to you, then by all means bring him in. But he's on probation. One flea, one—one revolting accident and he's out of Alluroma. Forever. Is that clear?"

"Quite." He didn't look any happier than she felt. How had they gone from such effortless joy to this? She stared at him helplessly, their day like a bright, broken toy in her hands.

"Close your eyes," Jon commanded. "And hold out your hand."

"Why?" But she obeyed him anyway, then felt dizzy when she did. She wasn't used to being so...out of control of a man-woman encounter. He kept sliding in under her guard in the *weirdest* way.

Something landed on her upturned palm. She opened her eyes to find she held a bag of chocolate-covered espresso beans.

"Thank you for today," Jon said, not quite smiling. But his look warmed her to her toes. "I had a..." His words trailed away and he shrugged. "And thank you for my haircut."

"You're entirely welcome." Her own confusion was not. Nor was the unaccustomed stirring beneath her ribs as their gazes held and the moment stretched oddly. *It's called hunger, you sap!* She gave him a cool, dismissive smile, took one bean from the bag and held it over Burton's nose. He caught it in midair when she dropped it. "Burton, I trust you'll take a bath?"

"When he wags his tail side to side that means yes," Jon translated.

"I knew that!" Demi turned and stalked off into the night, chin held high. She'd eat Indian. Or maybe Thai. Or maybe she'd just wander on home after all and have a spinach salad.

She hoped Jon sat there and watched her not look back, not even once, till she'd turned the corner.

She had a horrible conviction that he did not.

CHAPTER ELEVEN

"YOU'RE JOKING," JON SAID the next morning, staring at the tie Greenley held out to him.

"The hell I am." Clearly Agent Greenley was not a morning person. "My daughter gave me this last Father's Day."

"You don't wear it, do you?" It was orange, turquoise and green, and Jon thought the animals crawling across it might be armadillos.

"Not past the front gate. Now put it on." Traffic was actually moving this morning and they were nearing the Fifties.

"This is because I told you guys I got a haircut," Jon realized, loosening his own conservative burgundy tie with reluctant fingers.

"Got it in one. You've got an image to maintain. Think of it as sleight of hand—you make the mark look where you want her to look, while you do what you need to do, or be what you happen to be, elsewhere. Hair's no longer a distraction, so now you've got to find another one. Since all the tattoo parlors are closed at this hour, this'll have to do."

"Okay, already." Jon finished tying it with a vicious jerk. "But you tell Trace I need to talk to him."

"Nothing I can pass on? He won't be stateside till tomorrow."

"Nope. Family talk." He had no real message. Just the feeling that things were slipping rapidly beyond his control.

I nearly invited her in for supper last night, and if I had, I swear I'd have asked her to stay the night. How could he pretend to be objective about Demi Cousteau? That dream last night should have set off every smoke alarm in his co-op.

The van stopped outside Demi's building and, while the driver came round to help Jon, Greenley gave Burton his farewell thump. "And I want it back—without gravy spots. Buy some of your own at lunchtime. Nothing but throw-up-then-die ties from now on, you understand?"

JON WAS FIVE MINUTES late, Demi noticed, glancing at her clock for the third time in the last half hour. She herself had been hard at work at her desk since 7:00 a.m. She'd risen at dawn after a restless night, haunted by dreams that were as vague as they were disturbing.

She'd dreamed she was standing in some vast city square, gray, cold cobblestones stretching to a bleak horizon, pigeons and people wandering in the distance, but no one came near. And she'd been whistling, whistling, whistling—something her mother had always forbidden her to do when she was a child. Caused wrinkles, she claimed. She'd been whistling for a dog—Burton? She didn't know, because no matter how she whistled, he wouldn't come to her.

And then she'd smelled honeysuckle and face powder, the scent of that truly horrid nanny who'd kept her the year when she was eight and her mother went on a tour to England over Christmas—the scent of loneliness.

Stupid dream. She brushed cheeks that were long since dry and glanced at her watch. She could tell Jon her dream and he'd make her laugh, make her see what nonsense it was.

She couldn't tell Jon—he'd know why she'd dreamed it.

Too restless to sit, she wandered into the bathroom, gave

her hair a quick smoothing with the brush she kept in the cabinet, then stared at her reflection.

She'd have liked to look radiant this morning. To show him what he'd passed up. She didn't. All her tossing and turning had taken its toll; her eyes were bruised with shadows. *And you're getting old,* she told herself spitefully. Her grandmother had found the love of her life at sixteen, half Demi's age. *And Mother hasn't found hers yet.* Some women never did.

What am I—on a roll? First Reese didn't want me, and now Jon? Which was stupid, stupid, stupid to even think about, since she didn't want Jon. End-of-her-cycle blues and blahs, that was all this was.

The hall chime rang and she brightened, which wouldn't do. *He's late,* she reminded herself, and stalked haughtily forth to tell him so.

She forgot that complaint as he rolled into view. "Oh, *please!* April Fool's was three weeks ago!" She caught one end of his tie and stared. "Why are you *doing* this—to torment me? Well, I'm not in the mood, Jon. This is hideous!" But she liked holding him this way; it gave her the sense of power she'd been missing. "What are these things—possums?"

"Armadillos, I think."

"Whatever they are, they're coming off. Now." She pulled at the knot.

"No way. Cut it out!" Starting to smile, he caught her wrist.

She liked the size of his hands, the way his fingers encircled her. She'd sooner have hopped out the window than let him see it. *My own lab tech.* What was the matter with her? "You couldn't have picked this out for yourself! Who gave it to you? An old girlfriend?" *A present one?* She attacked the knot with her free hand, starting to laugh.

Burton bumbled around her legs, yodeling anxiously—was this a fight or a romp, and how could he help?

"My mother, okay!" Jon caught her other wrist and pulled, bringing her almost nose to nose with him. "Now lemme be!"

She was suddenly laughing too hard to catch her breath.

"Y-you have a m-mother?"

"Most people do."

"Where is she?" Up to now, he'd had no reality for her outside of Alluroma. Now she wanted to know more. All. *Who are you, Jon Sutter?*

"At the Dunkin' Donuts at this hour." He let one wrist go and she returned instantly to the attack, hooked a finger behind the loosened knot and hung on tenaciously when he recaptured her wrist.

"How would you know that?" she asked as she teased the knot apart.

"She's a cop. Chief of police, in fact, in my hometown. The entire day shift except the dispatcher meet for coffee and doughnuts 'bout now."

"You're mother's a *cop?* Wears a gun?" Demi pulled the knot loose. She liked the way it came free, the way he'd gone so still under her hands. She drew the tie slowly, slowly from his neck, letting its softness caress him. She eyed the top button of his shirt. Weird how tempting it was.

"*Your* mother wears Pan-Cake makeup and sings in public for money. You live by your nose." He sounded as suddenly breathless as she felt.

"So I do." She straightened abruptly as the phone rang, and he let her go. Demi dropped the tie in his lap. "If I see this again, I'll burn it." Then she went to answer. "Alluroma, International." Her pride and joy. She'd do well to remember that. Roughhousing with one's own employee, however amusing, was hardly professional.

Still, maybe the day wouldn't be such a bad one, after all.

AND SO IT TURNED OUT—not bad, but interesting. After her victory with the tie, Jon didn't so much sulk as withdraw. Owlish and wary behind his glasses, he kept his stuffy distance, retreating unobtrusively on his wheeled stool a foot for every step she advanced.

Piqued by his fit of touch-me-not-ishness, Demi did advance. She felt as if they were dancing without music. Like partners in a tango, they were intensely, edgily aware of each other, always moving through space as one, though they were careful not to touch. The air in the lab made her skin prickle, her pulse run thready and fast. It was strange.

Blame it on springtime, she supposed. Maybe it had nothing to do with Jon, at all. She wished Richard Sarraj would return to town so she could aim all this reckless emotion at a more appropriate target.

And at the end of the day she did have word of him. "He's going with us!" Kyle Andrews crowed when Demi picked up the phone sometime after six. "Sarraj—he just left. We've been in conference since three, and he gave us the whole whopping account, Demi!"

"Congratulations!" She was happy for her art director friend, but why hadn't Richard called *her* first when he returned to the city? *Three out of three, I'm on a roll!*

"So tomorrow we're celebrating—you, me and Richard, my treat. A late lunch at La Caravelle, champagne and strategizing, to mark the beginning of a beautiful friendship. Clear your calendar, 'cause I won't take no for an answer!"

So of course she said yes. *And serves me right,* she reminded herself. She'd told Kyle that Sarraj was up for grabs. She just hadn't expected that he'd let her grab him.

"YOU SHOULD TAKE THE afternoon off," Demi said the following day. She'd come into the lab to say goodbye on her way to lunch. "It isn't fair that you're stuck in here while I'm swanning around the town."

A black swan today, she was sporting that little black suit she'd worn in the video the first time he'd seen her. Jon dragged his eyes away. "Burton and I'll take a spin in the park when I finish Sand 12." They'd zigzagged again, tracking the phantom fragrance that only Demi could smell toward its mystical source.

"Lock up and get out of here if I'm not back by six. But really, Jon, don't hang around. Go play."

"Thanks." But he had other plans. This would be the first real chunk of time he'd had to himself to search the lab. Her storerooms were crammed with cartons of supplies. He meant to inspect every box. He needed to clear Demi, and soon, then get the hell out.

Because she was getting to him. The way he'd felt when she took off his tie yesterday—she could have had his shirt, his socks and all items in between if she'd wanted them. It was time to cut and run before she stomped the prints of her high, high little heels across his heart.

"HUNG UP IN TRAFFIC," Demi predicted as Kyle consulted her Mickey Mouse watch for the fourth time in the past quarter hour.

"Must be." Kyle glanced at the magnum of Cristal champagne nestled in an ice bucket beside their table. "You know, he *was* monumentally jet-lagged yesterday." Diving into her briefcase, she drew out a portable phone. "I think I'll call the office, make sure he didn't fade on us."

Which proved to be precisely the case, Demi realized, watching Kyle's vivid face become glummer and glummer as she listened to one of her partners. So much for her celebration. "Jet lag and regrets it is," Kyle confirmed, folding her phone with a snap. "His message just missed me." She beckoned to their waiter.

"*Pah,* who needs men anyway, clients or otherwise? So tell me all about it, Kyle. What brilliant ideas do you have to launch my juice?" Demi smiled at the waiter as he popped the bottle's cork, then filled their glasses. "But first, a toast."

"To Seventh Veil," Kyle proclaimed, lifting her glass.

"He's going with that?" Demi didn't like it. The crystal pinged as Kyle nodded. *So be it.* The champagne tickled her nose—then chilled her all the way down.

"BURTON, IF YOU WERE A retriever, you'd fetch me those top boxes." Jon had checked every carton he could reach in all of Alluroma's closets and storerooms. Assuming the bottles and bags of powders were labeled correctly—and short of chemical analysis, all he could do *was* assume—he'd found nothing of interest to the FBI. Nothing of use in making bombs, nothing that could create a lethal gas. The most deadly ingredient he'd seen in Demi's lab so far was narcissus absolute, a scent so concentrated that you couldn't stay in a room with it in large amounts.

On the other hand, if Demi needed to hide anything from him, all she had to do was put it on the top shelf. He wouldn't be reaching up there till his casts came off. "Lot of help you are," he muttered, then glanced behind him.

Burton had wandered off. It was time to walk him, come to think of it. "Burt?" In the kitchen, pondering the perpetual canine problem of the refrigerator door, Jon told himself as he switched to his wheelchair. Burton had learned by now that Demi's office was off-limits, though that didn't stop him from flopping in the doorway to gaze at her soulfully. Not that Demi paid him any more heed than she did Jon.

As he rolled into the corridor, he saw him. Crouched

before the door between the kitchen and Demi's office, sniffing lustily at the crack below it. Strange, she must have shut it on her way out, something she'd never done be— *No.* That door had been open half an hour ago when Jon searched the storeroom opposite the kitchen.

"Who's there, boy?" he whispered. Burt wasn't barking. He glanced back at Jon, then returned to the gap, nose vacuuming odors from beyond the door. Demi had returned and shut it?

Or was it somebody else? A visitor who hadn't pressed the visitor's chime on entering. Jon lifted the bottle of white wine from the fridge. It looked innocent at first glance, but half-full, it would make an impression on any thief.

Not that he could exactly sneak up on his prey. The door opened inward; he'd lose a good minute maneuvering past its swing.

But as he turned the knob, he heard a metallic thump. A drawer closing, he realized. Demi's desk. So she'd returned?

She hadn't. The door swung wide enough to admit his chair. Richard Sarraj stood with his back turned, gazing out the window. With cool, contemptuous deliberation, he looked over his shoulder.

As if you didn't hear me coming? They measured each other in silence.

"Drinking on the job, Sutter?"

I am the wimp. I will not roll over there and smash this Pinot Grigio across his kneecaps, no matter how good that would feel. Jon loosened his grip on the bottle and managed a grin so stiff that it probably looked like guilt—a lush caught in the act. "Why not? It's lunchtime. Can I pour you a glass?" This guy was bad news—something in his eyes or his smile.

"No, thank you." Sarraj glanced at his watch. "I was

supposed to meet Ms. Cousteau here at three. Did she step out somewhere?"

"She stepped out an hour ago—to meet you and Ms. Andrews at La Caravelle."

"Ah? Then we seem to have had a misunderstanding."

Sarraj made for the exit, then paused. "In case I miss her, will you tell her I stopped by? To call me later?"

Establishing that he had nothing to hide from Demi? Or maybe he didn't. "Will do," Jon said cheerily, pushing his glasses up his nose. The outer door closed behind him.

"Burton, ol' boy, we've gotta have a discussion 'bout barking. You bark at squirrels in the park, you can bark at squirrels in Armani suits." Jon rolled over to Demi's desk. "What was the creep looking for?" He opened her top drawer, closed it—a metallic *whump,* but not quite as resonant as the one he'd heard. He opened her larger file drawer. "Come see if you can redeem yourself. Smell anything unusual? You got a whiff of the guy. Was he messing around in here?"

Burton poked his face in the files—they contained something edible? He nosed forward, back, then settled on one area, whuffing noisily. He sneezed, then ambled away, leaving Jon staring at a file marked Jon Sutter, which contained, when he looked in it, his original application form and his résumé. "You're sure of this?" Or maybe the dog was smelling Jon from when he'd last handled these papers?

Burton was sure of one thing only. It was past time for his walk.

"HE HAS BEAUTIFUL EYES." Sometime after the third glass of Cristal, Demi had fallen onto the subject of Jon Sutter. Now she couldn't get off it. "And I can't figure him out at all, Kyle. One minute I think I could have him if I whistled, the way he looks at me. Then the next? He's a million miles away, ice cube orbiting Pluto.''

"You're sure you really want him?" Kyle refilled Demi's glass, then her own. "I mean if he works for you, couldn't that get rather...sticky?"

"I *don't* want him," Demi said with great dignity. "I just want him to want me." They stared at each other solemnly—then burst into giggles. "I-is that too much to ask?"

"Probably. I mean it's only fair that *one* guy can resist your charms," Kyle maintained with her usual bracing heartlessness. "Sure to be character building. Besides, maybe he's gay?"

"He's not." Demi picked up a stick of celery, chased a black olive across her plate with it. "Isn't even happy some of the time, I think."

"Maybe he has a secret sorrow?" Kyle lifted the last boiled shrimp and waggled it at her inquiringly.

Demi turned it down with a shake of her head. "Then, just when I think that, he outs with this *wicked* sense of humor...."

"Sounds as if you really like him."

"I do," she admitted tragically.

"So then...maybe you *should* have him?"

"Or maybe that's precisely why I shouldn't," Demi countered with what seemed at the moment to be impeccable logic. "Now Richard Sarraj, I'm not sure I like him at all. Therefore, *he's* probably the one I should chase. Feeling like that, I should probably marry him!"

It was Kyle's turn to look distressed. "You're really interested in Richard?"

Not in the least! But she was trying hard. "What's not to like—money, looks?"

"Buns to die for?"

"Would you ladies like anything else?"

Both women froze, rounding eyes locked on each other as the waiter loomed between them. "Just the check," Kyle gurgled at last.

Demi crossed her eyes and lowered her lashes demurely—an expression she'd perfected the year they'd helped each other survive Mrs. Monroe's sixth-grade English class.

And she could still make Kyle lose it. The art director snorted, turned so pink her freckles disappeared, then exploded—just as he glided away. "You always were a rotten influence, Cousteau!"

"Who, *moi?*"

JON WAITED TILL ALMOST seven in the hope that Demi would return. At last he gave up and went home. To find his apartment filled with the aroma of pizza—finer than Demi's finest perfume—and Trace slouched in his living room, feet propped on the coffee table. "What the hell is that?" Trace allowed his socks to be thoroughly snuffled, then offered the hand not wrapped around a beer.

"Dog, I think. Burton."

"Bassett-alligator cross?" Trace headed for the kitchen. Came back with plates, more beer and a white box of take-out pizza.

"Something like that. I thought you weren't going to visit?" He studied his brother—he was tired; it always showed around his eyes.

"Decided to take the risk. Greenley said you'd been asking, and believe me, nobody spotted me."

If Trace said it, it was true. They ate with the silent efficiency of healthy men, Burton seated between them, scrutinizing the path of every bite from plate to mouth, the brown dots that served as his eyebrows screwed into a worried scowl.

After his third slice, Jon relented and fed him a crust. "When did you make it back from the Canaries?"

"Dawn, yesterday. Same flight as Sarraj, and no, he won't recognize me if he sees me again. I was back in steerage with my knees to my chin."

Tired *and* grumpy. "So Sarraj was on island for what, twelve hours? Doesn't sound like a pleasure trip."

Trace nodded. "Reporting in, receiving further orders, I'd say."

Jon handed Burton another crust. "Reporting to whom?"

His brother shrugged. "Don't know yet. Could be the captain of the *Aphrodite*—an older, ex-navy type. Or the heiress's fancy man—good-looking guy, 'bout Sarraj's own age. Or someone keeping a very low profile, pretending to be crew." Trace offered Burton a crust.

"Why not the owner herself? If she foots the bills..."

"Don't think so. We'd hoped to put an observer aboard when Customs cleared the yacht, but it didn't work out. But from what we learned afterward, the lady was... apparently drunk when Customs came aboard. Tucked up on a couch in the saloon, awake but not very forthcoming."

Jon's appetite had vanished. He handed Burton his half-eaten slice. "Apparently? You mean maybe she was drugged?"

"There was enough Valium in her cabin to trank a junior-high pep rally. Of course she could be popping pills herself. Some of these jet-setters, you'd be amazed..."

Having seen enough of Angelina's pals in modeling and TV, he would not. "Opting out. Maybe she's uncomfortable with the program," he suggested. "If she's realized she's into something nasty?"

"Could be. Or they're keeping her out for the same reason—showing her the world through rosy glasses, and please just write us another check, darling. Unfortunately she's an only child, parents dead. There's nobody we can appeal to, to yank her out of there for her own good—and for a few pertinent questions. Not while she's overseas.''

''What else?'' Involved in this as he was, Jon felt entitled to probe. Not that Trace had much more than crusts for him, either. The feds were still gathering background on the captain and the heiress's lover. Lover boy was an American from out west, political affiliations still unknown, but information should be coming soon.

On the Sarraj front, they'd traced his history back to his late teens. He'd visited Syria, then Kuwait, before returning to the States to enter college. ''If he was recruited by terrorists, that will be when and where,'' Trace predicted. ''When he went back to discover his roots. We're looking for friends he made while abroad, and we're looking for his father, because if it turns out Dad's a fanatic, and a player in a known violent group, then that's our target. Odds are he'd have sponsored his son's membership in the same club.

''Once we know who, we'll know their usual style of attack—small arms, truck bombs, missiles—know what we're looking for this time.''

Demi, Demi, Demi, what has this nonsense to do with you and me? Except that he'd have never even known she existed without Trace's suspicions. Jon listened without comment as Trace, too tired to be closemouthed, talked on, about Sarraj's hippie mother—her sad, sorry end. Sarraj's entry back into the U.S.—Customs had turned his baggage inside out and found nothing. A calculated gamble their side had lost, because now if he had a guilty conscience, he'd be even warier.

''Still, everything you've found so far could have an innocent explanation,'' Jon finally protested. ''Sarraj went looking for his father when he was old enough. The heiress likes pills and studs. Sarraj jetted to the Canaries to discuss a business deal.'' *Or to discuss me?* He'd yet to tell Trace about the notebook—and Sarraj's raid today on the office, if that's what it had been.

"I know, I know. You may be right. We run down ten dead ends for every real trail we find. But there's a smell about this one." Trace rubbed his jaw. "And we've had our first death. Once that starts happening, it's like those chains of paper dolls Emily used to cut, remember? One follows the next."

"Who?" The question came out in a croak. Burton turned to stare at him, the fur rising along his spine. The dog's eyes shifted toward the hall. Then they heard it—a brisk, won't-take-no-for-an-answer rapping.

"Who the hell's that?" Trace grabbed his plate and his beer bottles.

"Jon!" a voice called faintly from beyond the door. "It's me! Demi!"

Burton let out a yodeling bark of welcome and stormed off down the hall to scratch at the panels.

"So much for pretending I'm not home." And short of the fire escape, they were trapped.

Trace showed his teeth. "Quite the job you're doing, bro, keeping your subject at arm's length!" He slapped a last slice of pizza on his plate, remembered his shoes, jammed them under an elbow, headed for Jon's bedroom, then swung back in its doorway. "Get rid of her tactfully—but pronto!" The door closed on his scowl.

"Jon? *Burton,* tell him to open up!"

Of all the ways he'd fantasized about having her here with him, none of them had included his brother as a fly on the wall! Jon moved the dog out of his way with a look and a growl and undid the locks.

CHAPTER TWELVE

"YES?" JON OPENED the door a miserly foot or so.

But if that was a hint, Demi was flying too high to take it. "Do you like ice cream, Jon?" She nudged in through the gap. Burton danced just beyond his chair—at least *he* looked happy to see her. Maybe this hadn't been such a good idea?

"You came all the way over here to ask me that?"

Not a good idea, but now she'd have to brazen it out. "Do you?" She edged around him, her eyes sweeping the corridor. Closed doors to the right, a galley kitchen lay to the left. She entered and pulled open a drawer—odds and ends. "Though actually it's chocolate sorbet." She tried another and found two spoons. She glanced at the cabinets—bowls should be somewhere up there—then changed her mind. She felt like sharing the carton with him.

"Women eat sorbet, men eat hot dogs straight from the fridge, Demi." He was decidedly in a bad mood. "What did you want?"

Your company. She couldn't think why, now. "Well, you're a bear tonight." She moved past him down the hall. "I stopped by to tell you about my lunch with Kyle—though we only quit an hour ago. We went back to her office to look at some sketches. She's come up with a *brilliant* plan—at least she and Sarraj have."

At last she'd caught his attention. "Really?"

She chose a seat that had been pulled up to the coffee table. An open box of take-out pizza sat on the table, two-thirds demolished. If Jon had eaten all that, no wonder he was in no mood for dessert.

"What's the plan?" he asked while she opened the carton and handed him a spoon.

"Direct mail. On a scale that has never been tried before. Sarraj is going to spend *millions* to mail my scent directly to people. He— No, no, let me back up." She spooned a dollop of sorbet onto her tongue and was momentarily diverted, her senses flooding with the taste and smell of chocolate, her memories ranging from the *mousse chocolat* her grandmother made for her when she was three to the bittersweet Godiva truffles she'd bought herself last year when she returned from Boston and losing Reese.

"Ouch!" She opened her eyes as Jon tweaked her hair. "What? Oh, I was saying, first I have to tell you about Sarraj's factory. I haven't mentioned that, have I?"

He took a slow breath. "No...you haven't."

"Well, Sarraj's syndicate, the prince and all, recently bought a factory in Brooklyn that makes scent strips for magazines. It uses a new process, gels in cells, I think it is. Anyway, much more advanced, more airtight than the old methods. Guarantees that the perfume doesn't leak and doesn't degrade. When the consumer pulls off the strip— she or he smells *precisely* what I mixed. Like digital sound, only it's scent."

"Yeah—so?"

His attitude was starting to annoy her. Couldn't he see how exciting this was? "So, the usual way to promote a new perfume is to spend your millions on advertising. You give a launch party somewhere stupendous—a castle, a yacht.... And you invite everyone in the industry—all the editors and writers for the fashion and cosmetic mags, your rivals, your client and his friends, of course. All the top faces and celebs you can lure to the party. You make a buzz, in other words. The biggest buzz you can afford."

He wasn't eating, and the sorbet was too delicious to enjoy alone. She dug out a generous scoop and aimed the spoon at his mouth.

"No, thanks." He waved it aside. "Go on."

"No. Not if you don't want my sorbet. Forget it!" She offered the spoon to Burton, who'd probably been beaming her just that suggestion on all telepathic channels. The dog inhaled the treat, his tail frantic with gratitude. "*See*, Burton knows what's good, unlike *some* crabby people we know, huh?"

Watching him lick his chops, Demi decided not to dip her spoon back in the carton. She dumped it on the coffee table instead. And smelled...*what?* She turned, searching for the odor. Shampoo, somebody's shampoo, on the back of the chair in which she'd been sitting. "Did you rent this place furnished?"

"Yes, it's a sublet. Go on with Kyle's idea."

It smelled very fresh, a unisex type composed entirely of synthetics, except for some extract of nettle, a hint of balsam. And the chair had been pulled up to the table—it hit her finally. Someone besides Jon had been sitting here recently, eating pizza. *Who?*

Whoever it was, it was someone he'd made more welcome than he was making her. Demi shoved the carton into his hands. "Oh, look at the time!" She hadn't. "I really should be going." She gathered her legs beneath her.

"No, stay. You've only had a bite."

"Burton took my spoon," she said perversely. Everything was spoiled. She'd been an idiot to come here.

"So, here!" Jon dipped into the carton, then thrust his loaded spoon at her face.

She studied his offering with frigid, near cross-eyed contempt for a long moment. *It's not ice cream I want!*

The spoon didn't waver, didn't withdraw. What were they fighting for? It didn't matter; only winning mattered.

Apparently he thought so, too. When she didn't open, Jon brushed the tip of the spoon gently across her lips, leaving a sorbet smear.

Ha—think I'm that easy? She gave him a closemouthed, superior smile. *Can't make me.*

The spoon returned again. He added a thicker smear of chocolate. The metal was cold—suddenly, she was feeling...*hot.* Hot enough to melt ice cream. Sorbet. *Lick it off me!* She cocked her head and widened her eyes at him. A challenge.

Behind those glasses, he was really quite attractive in his own way, but more than his looks, she liked his stubbornness. He wasn't such a wimp, after all, was he? With insulting deliberation, Jon added the tiniest smear of chocolate to the tip of her nose. Her eyes caught fire. She lifted her chin proudly and glared. *Do your damnedest!*

With a wicked smile, he slowly—oh, so slowly—began to tilt the spoon. He meant to dribble it down her neck? Skin was one thing, her favorite black silk was quite another—he wouldn't dare!

The spoon tilted degree by slow degree. Ice cream pooled at its lower edge.

On the other hand, a member of a sex that would eat raw hot dogs by choice would quite possibly ruin the finest suit she'd ever owned to win a point. Would know nothing about the weeks she'd spent scouring designers' markdown lofts to find it. Would probably assume he could buy her another just like it tomorrow. But if she docked his salary for a year, it wouldn't replace this suit. *"You—!"* Her hand shot up as the first runnel of chocolate swelled on the lip of the spoon.

He laughed—and dumped the entire load onto her palm. *"Gotcha!"*

"Oh, yes?" She clapped her hand to the top of his head, rubbed sorbet through his lovely new haircut. They were both giggling like maniacs. "Who won? *Who?* What d'*you* think, Burton?" She bounced to her feet—it was that or kiss him, and demand to be kissed. *Kiss it off me! Kiss my neck, kiss my*—

This was utter *madness*—the champagne should have worn off hours ago! "Where's your bathroom?" Demi darted out of the room, down the corridor, grabbed the handle of the first door she came to. "Is this—"

"Not that one!" he yelled. *"No!"*

She froze, the door a foot open. God in heaven, why was he so— The air displaced by the door's opening eddied back again, and she gasped. The fragrance of a shampoo that was not Jon's—nettle, balsam, aldehydes—wafted out from the room, which if it wasn't the bathroom must surely be his bedroom?

She slammed the door and spun away.

Jon had wheeled to the end of the corridor, sat there staring at her. "Second door on your left," he said quietly.

WHEN SHE VENTURED forth some ten minutes later, her face was scrubbed free of chocolate. "I really must be going." She walked with cool reserve to his door. Stood there, the picture of bored and haughty elegance, waiting for him to let her out.

"Yeah, I s'pose it is getting late." Had she realized that someone was hiding in his bedroom? Or was this simply her retreat from their raving lunacy of the past few minutes? Maybe she'd realized how she was arousing him? Another minute of that, and given the use of his legs, he'd have scooped her up and carried her off to his— Well, no, he wouldn't, not with Trace in there. *Damn it all!* "Thanks for the ice— The sorbet."

She shrugged her indifference. "See you tomorrow, Jon. Burton?" A thread of warmth crept into her voice as she tipped her head formally at the hound. She slipped through the door and was gone.

He'd have traded three brothers and two Burtons to have her back again. Jon locked the door and headed for the bathroom sink.

Scrubbing a damp washcloth over his head, he saw Trace behind him in the mirror. They gazed at each other, unsmiling.

"Get involved with her and I'll have to pull you out, Jon."

You don't pull me anywhere I don't want to go. Haven't since I blackened your eye for you that time—what—twenty-five years ago? "She's innocent, Trace."

"You know that for a fact or do you just feel it? And lemme guess where?"

"Shuddup!"

"Women make excellent terrorists, Jon. Because men drop their guard, can't believe they could carry bombs, shoot people. But the things I've seen... Believe me, some of the worst fanatics are female."

"I believe it." *But not Demi. Never Demi.*

"You take all that lovely, fiery passion—if it's twisted, diverted? Sometimes they do it for a cause. More often they do it for a man...."

Sarraj, was he the kind of man who could inspire that kind of lethal passion in a woman? In Demi? *No.* Change the subject before they had a real blowup here. "You said there'd been a death. Who?"

"The two men who delivered the package to the *Aphrodite* in the Black Sea? The Mafia flunkies. We've been looking for them—the CIA has been, on our behalf."

"Yeah?" Jon led the way back to the living room. Burton reared up against the wheel of his chair to nudge his arm. Dogs didn't like tension. Why couldn't everybody be happy together? Jon rubbed Burton's ears, then pushed him down. "Sit."

"Well, they found the first one last night, back in Moscow. In the middle of Nijinsky Boulevard, with a tire track across his back. Nobody saw a thing, of course."

"Accident?" He tried for a tone of cool objectivity, feared it came out hopeful.

"Possibly." Trace kicked off his shoes again. "But consider the timing. Sarraj reports in to *Aphrodite*. Not two days later, this guy has his number punched. If Sarraj felt he was being watched, might he have told his pals? They decide it's time to tie up a few loose ends before we pull on them? They pick up a phone and a deliveryman's roadkill?"

The pizza sat in his stomach like a stone. *He's dead, maybe, because I left a notepad by Demi's phone? One stupid slip by me, and half a world away a man dies?* "What about—" he had to stop and cough "—the other deliveryman?"

"Disappeared that same night. He may have heard the hunt was on and gone to ground. Or maybe they got him, too, but someplace more discreet. Our people are still looking."

Jon wiped a hand across his face. "I've got to tell you something...." It wasn't just the humiliation of confessing himself a dunce, maybe a killer dunce. There was Demi. If Trace decided he'd blown his cover, that he had to leave Alluroma, what then?

IT WAS NEARLY 9:00 a.m., and Demi, already on her third cup of coffee, stared sightlessly at her computer screen, her mind on another kind of formula entirely. Mix jealousy with champagne fumes and what did you get?

Nonsense. It made no sense that Jon would have someone hiding in his bedroom last night.

Because Demi had no claim on him. If she'd interrupted a cozy tête-à-tête—Jon and Grocery Store Woman, perhaps—he would have had no reason to hide his conquest. He'd have simply introduced the two of them. *Date, meet Boss. Boss, this is my honey.* No need to stuff her in the closet.

But if she couldn't trust her own nose, then what could she trust? *If not a date's, whose shampoo did I smell?*

A recent visitor's. Yes, surely that must be it. A friend or neighbor who'd dropped in for a visit—or no—who'd picked up Jon's dry-cleaning for him. Had been nice enough to put it away in his bedroom, then had sat in her chair chatting, hair brushing its headrest. That made perfect sense.

Male or female visitor? she found herself wondering.

"You're insane!" she said aloud, and took a long gulp of coffee. Falling for her own lab tech? This was nuts!

Or maybe Kyle was right. If she was this attracted, she should have him and damn the torpedoes—or rather, bless them. Have her fling, get it out of her system so she could think again. Get back to business. The outer door chimed and she jumped guiltily, then raised one haughty eyebrow as he rolled through her door. "Aren't you two ever on time?"

And here he'd been counting the minutes till he saw her again. "Burton fell in love with a lamppost. I felt like a cad, dragging him away." Jon rolled over to her printer and picked up the output. "Four new formulas this morning already? You're a machine, boss."

"Start with the third one, please, then call me. I may have evolved beyond the first two already."

"Will do." He paused in the doorway to the kitchenette. "Forgot to tell you last night," he said casually. "Sarraj stopped by here yesterday. He said for you to phone him if he missed you at the restaurant."

"Oh, really?" Her face lit up. "Thanks!"

He should have stayed to eavesdrop but didn't have the heart for it this morning. Rolled on to the lab instead. He'd had a bad night last night.

It proves she's innocent, has nothing on her mind but perfumes, he'd tried to convince Trace last night, *her keeping me on.* If Demi were part of a conspiracy and they'd tumbled to the fact that Jon was watching them, wouldn't she have fired him straightaway?

"Nope," Trace had maintained. "That's the devil-you-know principle. As long as they know it's you who's watching, they know who to look out for. Gives them a sense of control. They can feed you false information to pass on to us.

"Or pump you—find out who you work for. If your side knows anything or if we're just curious. But if they kick you out or bump you off—"

"Hey, thanks a lot, pal!"

"If they bumped you off, then we'd know for sure we're on to something and we'd replace you," Trace continued calmly. "And next time we'd be more careful. Next time they might not spot our spy. It's much better to keep you as their special pet." But from now on he was to be on his guard. Twice as watchful.

What it boils down to is, if Demi acts as though she has nothing to hide, then she must be guilty! Jon tossed the printouts on his counter. "Burton, if I told you, you wouldn't believe. In your best-ever dream, you never dreamed this much garbage."

"WE MISSED YOU AT La Caravelle," Demi said when she reached Richard Sarraj later that day. "I understand you dropped by Alluroma?"

"Yes, I'd hoped to catch you before you left. I wasn't in the mood for a business lunch and hoped we could skip out on Kyle together, perhaps drive out to the country. I must have missed you by minutes.''

"What a pity," Demi said lightly, making a face at the far wall. Why, the rat, didn't he realize Kyle had planned that party especially for him? Or didn't he care? "Well, some other time."

Which was a dumb bit of social chitchat, because he promptly asked her for a date that evening.

"Oh, I'd have loved to, but I'm afraid I've made other plans." She had a begonia that needed repotting.

Then Sunday?

Her only other offer was her mother, who'd spend the evening interrogating her about the latest men in her life, then dissecting them one by one. Might as well please her and say she couldn't, that she had a hot date with a most eligible bachelor. *Wonder what Jon and Burton will be doing?* Demi shoved the thought aside. "That would be delightful."

"STAY," JON CALLED, loud enough for Burton to hear from his place in the supply closet. *"Sta-ay."* He opened a drawer along the far counter, tucked the rag inside and closed it silently. Catching one of his guy wires, he hauled himself halfway across the lab. "Okay, Burt."

Burt appeared in the closet doorway, ears pricked, eyes bugging with glee.

"Find the kitty, Burt! Find him!"

"What in *heaven's* name are you two doing?" Demi leaned in the lab doorway, arms crossed, dark head tilted to one side. She'd pulled her hair into a twist and secured it with what looked like chopsticks.

Jon stopped, transfixed. She was so drop-dead gorgeous with her hair up, all he could think about was letting it down again.

"Well? What's he snuffling on about?"

Burton was working his way methodically around the room's perimeter with loud sneezes and snorts and many an anxious look at Jon to see if he could catch a hint.

"We've finished your latest formula, so I'm teaching him to search. Burton, where's the kitty? *Find* him!"

"If you have a cat in here, Jon, so help me God I'll—"

"Synthetic civet on a rag, since I couldn't find any of the real. Where d'you keep it? *Kitty,* Burt! You're not even warm, sucker."

"I don't keep it. You can't make heaven out of someone else's heartache. I don't believe in caging civet cats, extracting musk from musk deer or castoreum from beavers. The fixative is the one place I always use synthetics."

"Good for you," he said quietly. Their eyes locked for a long moment, then he snatched out a shirttail to clean his glasses.

She joined him at his counter, examined the bottle sitting there. "You do realize that this particular synthetic kitty costs, pound for pound, more than a Jaguar?"

"Used less than half a milliliter. *Good* boy!"

Reared up against the side counter, Burton whined and scrabbled frantically at the drawer.

"Oh, *please*—he'll ruin the woodwork!" Demi yanked open the drawer and, holding the prize too high for Burton's frantic leaps, dumped the rag on the counter in front of Jon.

"*Good* boy!" The dog stood against his thigh, straining to see the "kitty" on the counter. Jon rubbed his ears. "Brilliant! Whattaguy!"

"If you must do this, then use this one." Demi picked another bottle off a shelf. "It costs half as much and Burton will probably adore it. It's much cruder."

"Let me have a whiff."

"You won't like it." She pulled the stopper and set the bottle before him. "At least I hope you don't."

"Never ceases to amaze me how something that smell
so horrendous in quantity can smell so wonderful in
tiny—*eeuuu!*" A foot from the bottle, Jon made a face
"*Zoo!* The entire cat house!"

"Isn't it just?" They both glanced toward her office a:
the phone rang—and in that instant Burton made his leap
for the open bottle, or perhaps for the rag. Since the bottle
was sitting on an end of the rag, it didn't much matter
which. A paw slapped down—then dragged the prize to
ward the counter's edge as the dog returned to earth. Jo
turned as the bottle tipped. As Demi shrieked and lunged—

A wave of pure cat—all the tomcats in the world and
then some—splashed across the sleeve of his shirt as he
grabbed the falling bottle.

"Oh, *ugh!*" Demi sprinted for the exhaust fans and
slapped their switch to high. "*Now* you've done it!"

Momentarily stunned, Jon dropped the stopper into
place. "Did it get you?" Burton had slunk away. This wa:
too many cats for one dog. Jon's eyes were watering, his
head starting to ache.

"I don't think— I can't tell!" She sounded stricken, al
most panicked. "Can't smell anything but you."

Smell you could cut with a knife. Smell like a bludgeor
to the head. His nose ran. The room whirled—no, that wa:
Demi, shoving his stool across the floor.

"Into the shower you go!" She was steering him to the
emergency shower in a corner of the lab.

"Can't. My casts!"

"Oh, blast—right! Then off it comes." Rounding to hi:
front, she yanked his tie above his collar, then wrenched a
his shirt, not bothering with buttons. "I can't *believe* you—
Put your hands up! Don't you *dare* touch me with tha
one!" She peeled the shirt down over his shoulders. "Yo
and your *disgusting* dog! Oh, my eyes!" She wiped he
tears against his bare shoulder, her lips brushed his skin.

"I'm sorry, Demi. Are you okay? I'll pay for it." *But right now, just keep touching me.*

"Pay for it? I'll have it out of his *hide*—and yours, too!" She stripped the shirt all the way off him, except that turned inside out, it caught at his wrists. And she wasn't about to touch his sleeve.

"Maybe you'd better go?" Or stay and tear the rest of his clothes off? His hands were trapped, and he was nearly blind with the stench. *"Damn!"*

High heels clicked across the lab, came tap-tapping back. He couldn't breathe. Scissors snicked—she was cutting his cuffs away. "There!" She clattered off with his shirt. He heard the trash can across the room bump and rustle as she dumped his rags into the garbage bag.

The ammoniac cloud lifted somewhat, but his arm was burning. Undiluted, some aromatic chemicals were corrosive. Jon sat, closed eyes streaming, taking shallow, wincing breathing, hands suspended so as not to contaminate his trousers.

Something settled on his knees—a bowl filled with water.

"Hands in there," Demi commanded.

"Thanks."

"Pah! Don't thank me. Don't even speak to me!" She caught his arm and applied something warm and wet—a sponge.

Demi had never dreamed his clothes hid such a magnificent torso, such arms, though she might have guessed, given the ease with which he hoisted himself on his chin-up bar. Jon wasn't overbuilt—he was built exactly right—and carved from marble. She finished his forearms, started on his upper arms. He hadn't taken a splash there, but she didn't care. His veins stood out above the smooth, hard muscles. His breathing had deepened. "Are you okay? It doesn't hurt?"

He murmured something wordless and shook his head blindly.

As long as he kept his eyes closed, she could keep on touching. She dropped the sponge back in its bowl, then took hold of his tie. "From now on, whenever I smell civet I shall think of you, Jon."

He laughed without sound. "I'm sorry." He didn't sound sorry.

And neither was she. Slowly, leaning close in spite of his smell, she undid his tie. Slid it off him in a lingering sexy caress. Threw it aside. *I want you. Do you feel it.* Reaching for the sponge again, she squeezed it dry, steadied herself with a palm on his bare, hot shoulder while she washed the other. She paused with the heel of her hand resting above his heart. And smiled. Oh, yes, he felt it, too. A flurry of goose bumps raced across his skin. His tiny masculine nipples stood up from their soft nests of golden hair. She dipped her sponge. "Do your eyes hurt?"

"A bit." His voice had gone husky. He cleared his throat.

She ached to put her tongue to the hollow there between his collarbones. *Soon, but not yet.* She brought the sponge to his chest, dragged it across the hard swell of his pecs—allowed one fingernail to graze an upstart bud.

He shuddered violently and caught her wrist. "Demi."

Don't say it! She heard his tone of refusal, but she wouldn't have it. He couldn't mean it. With her free hand she lifted his glasses aside. *I mean to kiss you. Tell me you don't want it!*

"Demi." He opened eyes swimming with tears—wide wet blue ocean, the pupils black and huge with desire. "Stop. I can do the rest myself."

"But—" *You feel what I feel. I can't be imagining this!* She drew the backs of her knuckles down his cheek.

"No means no, babe." He brought her captive hand to

his lips, kissed her wrist where the pulse hammered. "Boss..." Taunting, tender.

He'd use that against her? She felt her eyes tearing up with frustration. "But why?" When her every instinct cried out that his answer was yes? "You want—" *me* "—this." *Us.*

"No. I don't." He let her go abruptly, the breaking of the bond a heartless rejection.

"Liar!" She stamped her foot. *I'm not imagining! Not crazy!*

He shrugged and looked aside. "So okay. I do."

"But then *why*...?" He wouldn't look at her. She put her hand to his jaw and tried to bring his gaze back to hers. Resisting easily, he shook his head, then dropped a hurried kiss in her palm. *"Why?"* she whispered like a cheated child. His skin slowly reddened. "Jon? Look at me?"

"What makes you think it was just my—" His throat convulsed. "Just my legs that were damaged in that accident?" He went entirely pink.

He couldn't mean— Her mouth opened, then closed wordlessly. *No. Oh, no!* She glanced helplessly down at his pants, but they were baggy, as always. She whipped her eyes away even as the tears sprang to blind her.

To find in one breath that she wanted him—and in the next that it would never be? Stunned by the loss, stupid with it, she touched his head, not sure if she was giving comfort or seeking it.

He shook her hand off. She couldn't blame him. Pity was the last thing she'd have wanted. *After exposure!* That she'd forced him into having to tell her, how *could* she have been so crass? So selfish? "I'm sorry!" She dropped the sponge, then his glasses, into his lap. And almost ran from the room.

CHAPTER THIRTEEN

HE WOULD DIE and go straight to hell for such a lie! How? How could I say that? But it was all that had leaped to his addled brain. No way could he have denied his desire for her. That left mechanical failure as his only possible excuse.

But now superstition had him by the throat. For a lie like that, the punishment was only too obvious. God would make it come true! For wanting her as much as Jon did, he'd never have her.

Were Demi to crawl hot and eager and buck-naked into his bed, he still wouldn't...work. Couldn't love her. *Idiot—how could I have said that?* He should roll in there to her office this minute, take it back.

But how? Say I didn't mean it? Or that I was mistaken? Yeah, right!

And the longer Jon brooded, the more he feared that maybe he'd spoken the truth. Some sort of truth. He hadn't made love to a woman for what—six months or more? His mind shied away from the last time he and Angelina...last fall. He'd already known in his heart of hearts that they were hopeless. That he was grasping at straws. Though technically successful, emotionally the act had been a disaster.

In the months after, during his divorce, there had been no one. He probably should have climbed straight back in the saddle—anybody's saddle—but he hadn't had the heart for it. And then straight on the heels of the divorce had come his accident. So now? How was he really to know? Maybe he *had* told the truth?

No. *"No!"* he almost shouted at Burton, who looked up worriedly from nudging his leg. Still, whatever he said, he couldn't leave things like this. Jon lifted his hand to his nose—and nearly gagged. But first, whatever came after, he had to bury this cat.

An hour later, scrubbed raw but still reeking, clad in his suit jacket, which no doubt he'd throw away after today, Jon wheeled grimly toward Demi's office. He hadn't heard a peep from her this past hour. "Demi?"

Maybe she'd gone out for a breath of fresh air? All of Alluroma smelled of civet in spite of the roaring lab fans. "Boss?"

No boss—beautiful, maddening, imperious…unforgettable. Only a sheet of paper left on her desk with a note penned in her carelessly elegant scrawl.

Overwhelmed by cat—and by my own stupidity. Forgive me? I'm taking the rest of today and tomorrow off. You do, too. See you Monday at nine. D.

DEMI SPENT THE REST OF Saturday and most of Sunday lost in black and wordless brooding. She wanted him. She couldn't have him. And her own pain was nothing compared to what Jon's must be! Making love was such a wonderful part of life. How would it feel to be forever denied it? Someone as vital and generous as Jon? It was crueler than cruel.

She ironed and scorched her favorite blouse, cooked and burned a stew, bashed pots when she cleaned and furniture when she vacuumed. Paid her bills, only to seal them upside down in their envelopes with no address showing through the windows. By Sunday afternoon Demi was in a thoroughly filthy mood—which was when she recalled her imminent date with Richard Sarraj.

Given her blues, it was only fair she cancel; she'd be rotten company. But true to her present run of luck, Sarraj didn't answer his phone. So... Demi gritted her teeth and chose a flowered dress with heels to match.

With the sun sinking in a red, clear sky, they headed out of the city to a restaurant Richard liked on the Connecticut shore, his Mercedes coupe purring along like a well-fed tiger. Demi asked about his recent trip to Los Angeles, which he told her had been a rousing success. Jon was probably walking Burton about now, but she wouldn't think of that.

Just south of Stamford, Richard glanced in his rearview mirror, then hit the brakes. "Cops!" The word sounded like a curse.

As she watched the icy interaction between Richard and the traffic patrolman while he wrote out a ticket, Demi recalled that Jon's mother was a policewoman. She'd like to know more about her. Also about his father. And did he have brothers? Sisters?

Has he ever been married? She blinked. It had never occurred to her to wonder before! Yet half the men she dated had a broken marriage or two behind them. Funny, she could picture Jon married, but not divorced.

"Have a good day." The officer strode back to his unmarked car.

"Bastard!" Richard revved the engine and shot out onto the highway, then settled to an insolent fifty miles per hour. The patrol car pulled out and sped past in search of more prey.

Richard's face was crimson and his hands clenched the wheel. But they *had* been speeding. And anyone who drove a Mercedes surely could handle tickets? "You don't like the police," Demi said lightly, making a joke of it.

"They killed my mother, cops."

"What?" It was the first truly personal thing he'd ever told her. "How?"

MUCH, MUCH LATER, AFTER they'd shared an excellent and unconscionably expensive dinner at an exquisite inn in Stamford... After Demi had ignored all Richard's broad hints that he was tired and that they had wonderful accommodations at the inn—which she didn't doubt—Demi leaned back in the Mercedes' humming softness to muse about the story Richard had told about his mother.

Killed by the blow of a rifle butt to the head during a demonstration in Oregon, an attempt to save redwoods from clear-cutting. Richard had been barely twelve. Demi couldn't blame him for hating the police for that tragedy. Couldn't feel anything but sorry for him. Abandoned by his father before he ever knew him, and then to lose his mother that way? So this explained the darkness she sensed roiling beneath his polished surface.

But if she felt pity for him, she felt no closer. This would be her last date with the man. He might be everything her mother could have wished for her, but he brought her no joy. She smiled, thinking of a man and his ridiculous hound who did. Whatever tragedies he might have suffered, somehow Jon had come through them smiling. Made *her* smile.

But first, she must finish this evening gracefully. Tactfully. Richard was a client. Best to remind him of that, she told herself as he walked her to her door. "I've made great progress this week on Veil. When would you like to come in next for a sampling?"

He caught her arms and pulled her close. "I'd like a sample tonight!"

Not possible. Still, Demi firmly believed that you shouldn't date a man you couldn't kiss. "I'm afraid it's awfully late." She gave him a warmly apologetic smile, then a cool, gentle kiss on the lips.

He wanted more—took it with brutal, damp efficiency. She stiffened. He tasted of the cigar he'd smoked after supper. And more than that, he tasted—smelled—wrong. Not bad, but not for her. Not ever. She turned her head aside. "Thank you for tonight. It's been a lovely evening. Shall we meet on Tuesday? Say, three if that's convenient?"

"Oh, fine!" he said bitterly, and let her go so abruptly it was almost a shove.

Her own temper flared. But if he was churlish, still she'd been wrong to accept the date, then moon all evening about another man. "Good night, Richard." The foyer door shut behind her and she let out a great *whoosh* of relief. So much for romance!

Head high, she ascended the stairs, cataloging the familiar scents as she rose. Cat behind the door on the first-floor back. Macaroni and cheese from the bachelor who lived directly above. Baking brownies on floor two streetside— that couple had children. Floor three, her own, the scent of lemon furniture polish and the freesias she'd bought for herself on Thursday. No smells of cooking, of a man's sweaty socks or welcoming musk. The scent of a woman alone.

TWENTY PAST NINE, Monday morning, and no sign yet of Jon Sutter. Maybe she'd never see him again? Saturday, she'd forced a confession from him that would have humiliated any man. So maybe he'd simply taken his crocodile hound and rolled off over the horizon? As the outer door opened, then closed, Demi looked up with relief. "You're late!"

She'd given much thought to how she should act today. Her first impulse had been to swaddle him in tenderness and cotton wool, make it up to him somehow. But his misfortune wasn't hers to make up. And sympathy would only be a further intrusion. *Act as if nothing at all has happened. We go on as before.*

"Sorry," muttered an armload of long-stemmed roses advancing on wheels through her door. Jon's eyes peered at her above the gaudy petals.

"Oh, Jon, you shouldn't have!" If anyone owed anyone an apology!

"That's good, 'cause I didn't. We met the deliveryman on his way up. There's a card here someplace." Clutching the vase between his knees, Jon rolled awkwardly to her desk.

"Oh!" Her cheeks flamed to rival the roses. "Oh, of course, I had a date with Rich—" She shrugged, suddenly French to her fingertips. "Silly me."

Richard Sarraj, he translated bitterly. Nice recovery! Here he'd spent the weekend endlessly reliving that scene in the lab, recalling every touch of her fingers, his lips on her skin. Had cursed himself a thousand times in a thousand ways for refusing her.

While she? Demi had done what any sensible flirt would have done. She'd gone out and found somebody else to kiss, since he wouldn't cooperate. Must have done quite a bit more than kissing, considering Sarraj's blatant token of appreciation. Red roses for passion. *So she's fickle. That surprises me?* Why should a beautiful woman be otherwise?

He turned his chair and rolled toward the lab, Burton shuffling close behind. *Get on with the job, Sutton. You came here for the facts, not love everlasting.*

ALL THAT WEEK AND THE next, they tiptoed around each other, careful to rouse no feelings that couldn't be satisfied. On the surface they were coolly businesslike, forging step-by-step toward their invisible, fragrant goal.

But beneath that workaday veneer, thin and brittle as skim ice, there lurked warmth. Tension. Unanswered questions. And Demi could find no way to ask them without giving her interest away. Without risking another rejection on her part and humiliation on his. No way to ask what had happened to him in that car wreck. Was he permanently damaged? Temporarily? Partially? Entirely?

Better to just let things lie, she'd think—till the next time she caught herself wanting to grab his tie and pull him within kissing range. Blast the man. What was it about him that drew her so?

But drawn or not, she would not pursue. To care for a man who could not love her back in the most fundamental meaning of that word? She wasn't crazy. Why chase after heartache?

Or was it chasing her?

SARRAJ CAME ON THE Tuesday with burning glances and halting words of apology for his behavior Sunday night. She'd brushed them briskly aside, thanked him for his lovely flowers—which she'd installed on the kitchen table, not her desk—then kept the focus relentlessly on perfume.

"Which one did he like the most?" Jon asked her after he'd gone away.

"He doesn't seem to care." Or was that just Richard's way of getting his own back? She'd hurt his pride, so now he'd smack hers by pretending indifference to what was shaping up to be her finest fragrance ever? Whatever, he'd left the choice to her. "So we're going with Djinn 3." She shivered with sudden happiness. Aladdin's djinn. Rub the lamp and out he billows—enormous, bejeweled, dangerous, bearing three wishes to change your life. "It's going to be magnificent!"

"TO DIE FOR!" KYLE Andrews agreed a week later, sniffing the *mouillette*. She'd stopped by Alluroma with her final sketches for the ad that would carry Demi's perfume to the world. "Do *you* like it?"

"Very much," Jon agreed. Demi had called him forth from the lab to meet Kyle and see her presentation. They'd been working on the Djinn line for ten days now, and the latest trial, Djinn 57, curled his toes.

"So you're finished?" Kyle danced a little jig of comic excitement.

"Hardly!" Demi laughed. "What we have here is just the Christmas tree. Now I trim it. To create the sparkle, the nuances, the depth, I'll add another thirty-to-fifty ingredients. I could spend a year on those alone."

"You've only got a month!" Kyle said, alarmed. "Richard told me—"

"That's what he said, I know." Demi held the *mouillette* to her nose. "But I'm closing in on heaven. If I need just a *few* more weeks to—"

"Don't count on it, kid. I'd say his schedule is carved in stone." Kyle switched her attention back to Jon. "She's *always* been a raving perfectionist. We took this cooking class together in high school..."

"Enough with the soufflé!"

"She wouldn't follow the directions, kept improving it—a pinch of this, a smidgen of that," Kyle went on remorselessly. "And when the poor thing finally fell? The tantrum she pulled? We're lucky they didn't expel us—they gave us *four* Saturday detentions."

Demi sniffed. "For which she hasn't forgiven me yet!"

Having grown up with two sisters, Jon was an experienced peacemaker. He tapped Kyle's portfolio. "So show us what you've got."

Kyle had brought them a mock-up of the piece of direct mail that was the cornerstone of her ad campaign. She passed it to Jon. "Here's how it will arrive in your mail-box."

The midnight black stock was folded in thirds to make a rectangle, its edges held together with a gummed silver star. Stars spangled the dark beyond the address sticker, which read Jane Doe, Anywhere U.S.A. Along the bottom right edge was printed in white, "It costs…"

Jon followed the message around to the back. More stars glittered, along with a crescent moon. At bottom left the announcement continued, "…the earth, moon and stars!"

"So you say to yourself, 'Now what could possibly cost that much?'" Kyle prompted. "And you open it.…"

Jon nudged his finger past the star seal, tearing it, and unfolded the flyer. He sucked in his breath, then nodded approval. Demi put a hand on his shoulder and leaned cheek to cheek with him to see. "'But what price ecstasy?'" He read the inner question aloud, fighting the urge to turn his head and steal a kiss.

"Kyle, it's gorgeous!" Demi murmured beside him.

Backlit by a full moon, edged in silver, a man stood with his back to the viewer. Beyond him a woman danced— Salome, she'd shed all her veils but the last, and with the moon shining through its translucent folds.…

"You see the end of the veil that she's drawn across his face?" Kyle touched the flyer.

Demi's hand tightened on him. "Not what he was looking at," she teased.

And she was right. "The woman's…hot." With her midnight hair and her slender grace she might have been Demi, dancing for his eyes alone.

"The scent strip is the veil itself." Kyle's finger traced the veil from the man to the woman. "And here's my stroke of genius. Depending on whether this piece is mailed to a man or a woman…"

"You'd send a perfume ad to a man?" Jon was startled.

Kyle looked annoyed. "Why not? Men buy perfume for their wives, their lovers."

Demi straightened, but left her hand on his shoulder.

"You know...Jon has something. Men buy perfume at Christmas, and at Mother's Day. Beyond that, forget it. The brutes make us buy it for ourselves. And this will be mailed after Mother's Day. Maybe the launch mailing should be aimed strictly at women?"

"Richard wanted to target both sexes." Kyle crossed her arms and rocked back on her heels, on the defensive. "In fact he insisted on it."

Did he now? Jon filed that away. "Okay," he agreed, before war broke out overhead—two powerhouse, opinionated women in one room. And both of them competing for Sarraj, it looked like. *What do they see in the guy?* "So the veil is the scent strip?"

"On the women's flyer, the half of the veil covering his face is." Kyle touched the man. "So women lift the strip and sniff his cheek to sample Demi's perfume."

"And you'll choose a hunk model that any woman would be happy to put her nose to." Demi was starting to smile. "And I take it that on the men's flyer...?"

"But of course. They lift the veil from the *woman's* body, then sniff."

"You tease!"

"But it's brilliant!" Demi crowed. "Every man and woman who receives this ad will try the sample. And then we've got them."

"You think Veil will be that good?" the art director asked.

"Think?" Demi drew herself to her full height. "I know. You deliver their noses to me, Kyle—and they're mine."

After Jon had wheeled back to his lab, Kyle lingered on. "You're right," she murmured, once he was out of earshot. "He does have beautiful eyes."

Demi had been hoping her friend had forgotten that champagne-inspired confidence. No such luck.

"Have you had him yet?" Kyle persisted with her usual directness.

"Nope. I'm not mixing business with pleasure this month. *"Now..."* She changed the topic with determination. "Has Richard told you who's designing Veil's bottle and package?"

He'd been smugly mysterious about that at their last two meetings—perhaps because he could see how it irritated her? Packaging was crucial to a successful perfume launch, almost as important as the fragrance itself. And true, that wasn't her area of expertise. But still she wanted to know—*longed* to have a say in its design. Richard was cracking the money whip, was what he was doing. Reminding her that though she might feel as if Veil was entirely her baby, there were other artists involved, and that he and his mysterious prince held sway over them all.

Kyle shook her head. "He's been very hush-hush. All I can pry out of him is that the work's being done by a top designer in Paris."

"Oh, *really?*" Demi almost purred with satisfaction. "In that case, his secret's ours. I owe my grandfather a phone call...."

"Can your old pussycat find out?" Kyle had met him when she was sixteen. He was the first man ever to kiss her hand, and she was still smitten.

"Anything to do with perfume in France, my *grand-père* has a connection. Leave it to me."

"And also Jon?" Kyle asked slyly as she picked up her portfolio and stood. "Or is he available? Because if you're *really* not interested..."

Kyle with Jon? Demi's reaction was so raw, so instinctive, it stole her breath away. Her eyes narrowed to slits.

Kyle gave her a *gotcha!* grin from the safety of the doorway. "Like that, is it, huh? Then...hadn't you better do something about it?"

"Go *away*, Kyle."

She went—laughing.

CHAPTER FOURTEEN

GREENLEY WAS WAITING for Jon when he was hoisted aboard his special van that evening.

"What do you guys have, stock in this company?" Jon demanded, as the agent moved up beside him. Jon had been fighting a black mood all afternoon. Because tomorrow, at long last, was The Day, and he was terrified.

"Ex-agent owns it. He offers discretion, hires drivers you can trust. And nobody looks twice at a disabled van hanging round. Comes in handy for surveillance." Greenley leaned down to rub Burton's ears. "Got a message from your bro."

"Oh?" Demi had granted Jon the following day off. With her usual curiosity she'd demanded to know why he needed it, and he'd refused to tell her. Trace would be driving him down to Baltimore in the morning, to the orthopedic center at Johns Hopkins. Then would drive him home at the end of the day, after his casts had been removed.

"He can't make it tomorrow. We got the latest report on *Aphrodite* an hour ago. From her heading, we've been figuring she'd bypass Bermuda."

Greenley had informed him the week before that the yacht had left the Canaries, headed west. They'd been tracking her by satellite. "What's changed?"

"She altered course. Should be clearing into Bermuda any time now. Trace is scrambling to meet her. He said to tell you he's really sorry."

"Hey, the job comes first." Still, he found there was a lump in his throat when he swallowed. "No big deal."

"If...you wanted, I could take the day off. Drive you down," Greenley offered with studied indifference, his eyes fixed on the traffic beyond the van's window.

"Thanks." But letting an older brother see him with a case of the cold sweats was one thing. Letting a man who was a near stranger, however kind, see him at his most helpless...share the way he'd feel once the casts came off if the verdict went against him? *No, thanks.* "I can manage. I'll catch the shuttle down...." Coming back, he'd be— he'd damn sure better be!—on crutches, and everything would be easier.

Or would it? he wondered an hour later, sitting in his living room after he'd made his arrangements for the morning. If his right knee hadn't mended properly... *Don't even think about it.*

How could he not? The summer digs he went out on, a man without two good legs wouldn't make it up to some of the mountain sites. Unable to hike or jump or pack a load, he'd be worthless in rough country, a liability....

Sure, there was plenty of work to be done in the States, and a bad leg wouldn't affect his teaching, but for doing what he really loved... *Stop thinking!* He should drink a beer. Read, watch the tube, cook, anything to stop his mind from spinning like a hamster on its exercise wheel. *Don't think, don't worry, just pray.*

He jumped as Burton let out a bellow and galloped off down the hall, then he heard the brisk rapping. Trace, he told himself, had come to say that he could drive him after all. That all would be well, Jon could stop worrying.

A different sort of worry altogether waited on his doorstep. Not Trace, but Demi, standing with her dark head tipped to one side. She held a brown paper bag clutched to her chest. Must have come straight from Alluroma; she still wore that little red suit of hers, like a sign reading Dangerous Curves Ahead. "Yes?"

Her eyes narrowed at his lack of welcome. "You forgot this." She held out his paycheck. "Since you aren't coming in tomorrow, I thought you might like to deposit it."

"Oh...sure." He took the envelope, passed it from hand to hand. He'd give it to Greenley, and a money order would be sent to the Philippines to the man he'd supplanted. *I work for you for nothing.* Face it, he'd pay to work for Demi. To be around her.

She made no move to go. Stood there looking down at him, her dark eyes wide and puzzled. Hard to blame her. Any other man would have rolled out the red carpet by now, would be tap-dancing frantically to coax her inside. *Difficult that, with casts on.* Which reminded him all over again. Tomorrow... The night yawned before him, endless and lonely. "You...uh...wouldn't like a cup of tea or something?"

She gave him a radiant smile. "That sounds wonderful!"

In the kitchen, she put the kettle on, since he was still in his chair, too low to reach the counters. Jon watched her from the doorway, setting out mugs. Demi in his kitchen—it felt like a hand brushing over his heart. *So call me old-fashioned.*

She was talking lightly, gaily, about work...a perfume she'd smelled on a woman at Zabar's on her way over...the weather tomorrow—it smelled like rain. Nothing of consequence, just a low, pleasant babbling. She wasn't usually this talkative. The air shivered between them.

The kettle whistled. Demi turned off the burner, then paused. "You know...I'm not really in the mood for tea. I bought a bottle of wine on the way here, nothing special, but I think it'll be pleasant. Would you join me in a glass of that instead?"

He'd have joined her in a bowl of cold oatmeal if she'd asked. Anything so long as she stayed. "Sounds nice."

She brought the bottle, a corkscrew and two glasses into his living room, let him uncork it and then she poured. Her stream of bright chatter had dried up with the change of venue. They clinked glasses and neither knew what to say. *To us,* he thought suddenly.

"To life!" Her voice was husky, her eyes enormous over the rim as she drank.

It wasn't just a pleasant wine, it was paradise on the tongue, sliding down to light a fire in his stomach. "Nice." His blasted voice had dropped half an octave.

"Very." She stood and deliberately approached his chair. His skin tingled, he felt himself harden and stir. She brushed on by, moved to the lamp on the side table. "Mind if I turn this down? It's shining in my eyes."

"Yes. I mean, no." Couldn't think with her so near. He'd stopped breathing for a moment and now he had a breath to make up. He took a deep one as the lights dimmed. It didn't help. She came to sit on the arm of the couch, close beside him, looking down. She sipped again, and he watched her throat move as she drank. Found his eyes trapped by a bead of ruby at the corner of her mouth when she lowered her glass. It would be heaven to lick it away.

Her tongue flicked out neatly to capture the prize. The blood surged through his veins. *What are you doing to me, Demi?* "What?" he demanded of the gleam in her eyes, the silence stretching between them.

"I've been thinking...." She took another sip, set her glass aside. Gave him a dark, fiercely enigmatic look. Her lips parted—then her eyes slid away. Knees tight together, she lifted one foot to the side, inspected her shapely calf. Looking for snags in her stocking? Or like a cat, grooming when she was nervous? She slid a hand from knee to ankle. The nylon sizzled.

"Thinking about what?" All *he* could think of was her, what it would be to touch her, to hold her. To have her.

"What you said the other day..."

Oh, that! I take it back! The words jammed in his throat. "Uh?"

Her voice was as warm and fuzzy as the wine. "I've been thinking that... I mean, I don't know what happened...to you. But a man who..."

Who wants you like I do?

She gulped, a long slide of slender muscles. Her eyes widened to black, fringed flowers. "Who has a mouth...ten fingers, isn't really...impotent."

"Demi." He didn't know if he wanted to laugh or cry. Couldn't think what to say, only *Demi, Demi, darling...*

"And you have eyes to enjoy me," she added, speaking faster as if she feared he'd interrupt. "You have skin I can touch."

"But—" Let him touch her once and it was over. He knew all the reasons this was wrong, couldn't name a one. Could only see Trace scowling somewhere in the back of his mind, hear the echoes of Angelina's mocking laughter. *Fool again...*

"*No* buts! Don't tell me no!" She shot to her feet, knee to knee with him. "I don't want to hear it. You don't want to say it."

He didn't.

"Let's just see what...happens." Her voice held passion and the oddest note of pleading.

She really wants this. What he as a man could give her. Her hands rose to her jacket, undid the top button.... *She wants this.*

She wasn't wanting alone.

And tonight, if he loved her, he might be in casts, but

he was whole. Tomorrow held the bright hope that he'd walk again. Would soon have a working body to offer her...

But if he passed up tonight? Waited till hope became reality?

Then it might not be the reality he prayed for. Tomorrow he might learn that he'd never again be a man as strong and capable as Demi deserved.

So tonight might be his last chance.... His last night to love her in the skin of a free man... The only way he'd ever offer himself.

Time had turned to lamplit honey, sweet and slow-flowing. Her fingers undid the second button. Her fierceness had softened to a teasing, tender smile. She knew he couldn't stop her now....

Third button. He was eyes and desire—no words, no mind. The palms of his hands tingled. The blood hummed in his ears, but not so loud that it drowned out the whisper of fabric as she shrugged the jacket off her shoulders. The air snagged in his throat—she wore no blouse beneath. Only a black lace brassiere, cut low over small, high breasts. "C'mere!" he whispered.

Her eyes enormous, she came to stand beside his chair. *Demi, Demi, oh, Demi!* She looked as frightened as he was. He reached...paused. Once he touched her...

She caught his wrist and brought it quickly to her lips, laid a kiss in his palm. He shivered and closed his eyes, savoring her wetness against his skin. Sucked in a breath as her tongue explored him—the shape of his palm, the pulse at his wrist, every finger from base to tip. She bit the end of his thumb and his pent-up breath exploded in a gasp. Her smile widened, cat with cream.

Time to take the lead. He traced that smile with a fingertip, traced a line up her imperious, elegant nose, wandered through her wealth of shivering lashes. Across her sculpted cheekbone to finger her earlobe, then clasp the ivory column of her throat and follow it down. His hands burned to cup her breasts, but not yet. Let her burn, too. She'd started this blaze, but he was the fireman.

She reached behind her for the clasp of her brassiere.

"No." He caught her elbows—"Not yet"—held her prisoner, his eyes roving and exultant. "God, you're beautiful!" His hands moved to her waist—such slenderness, he could nearly span her—fingers tightened. He swayed her close, pressed an openmouthed kiss to her stomach, savoring the taste of her skin, her velvety, trembling heat. *Oh, Demi!*

Turning her, he found the button to her skirt and fumbled it loose. Slid the zipper down. Her skirt slithered down her long, long legs to puddle round her heels.

True to his fantasies, she wore a black lace garter belt, black bikinis, real stockings. Demi, his perfectionist, perfectly wonderful.

Oh, please, enough with this slow and tender! He was driving her utterly wild—looking, barely touching! And *damn* his chair. There was no way to get close to him, as close as she needed. Well, yes, there was if she only dared.

And why not? She'd come here to have her wicked way with him; it was much too late to play the timid virgin. *In for a penny...* She swung a leg gracefully over his near wheel, then the far, to half-sit astride, facing him. Then remembered she could hurt him. "Oh!"

But as she tried to retreat, he caught her waist—held her suspended. *"Oh..."* She'd yearned for a strength to match her grandfather's? Here it was. Slowly, with exquisite control, he lowered her to his lap. Her body molded to his waiting hardness. *Melted.* His fingers tightened in fierce possession—and some emotion roared through her, roughening her skin, racking her with a shuddering jolt.

Fear?

Or the wildest, strangest pleasure?

Both—delicious as the first drop of a roller coaster. *Oh, take me!* Giving herself completely to his hands, she arched her spine…let her head fall slowly back till her hair swept his knees. His lips found her breasts through the lace. *I'm yours!* Then there was no more time for thought, only feverish, trembling, unending pleasure. *Jon, my strange, funny lover!*

AFTER A LONG, LONG, cradled stillness…the darkness of her closed eyes pressed against his neck…the sound of two hearts slowing beat by muffled beat from frantic passion to sated peace, there came movement again. "Mmm—wha—?"

"Lift your legs a little—right, like that. It's bedtime, darlin'." Jon wheeled them slowly from the room. "Stay, Burt."

The dog sat down again and gazed after them mournfully. Demi giggled and waved goodbye over Jon's shoulder. "Bye-bye, Burton. D'you think we shocked him?"

"Only when you howled."

"Moi?" She bit his shoulder in punishment, smiled when he yelped—then shuddered violently. He stopped the chair to kiss her, long, hard and deep.

"You could do that again!" he noted huskily when they could breathe.

"Count on it." She'd only begun to explore him. "You know I could walk," she added as she lifted her legs to his shoulders so they'd fit through the door to his bedroom.

"Why bother when you can take the bus, leave the driving to—" His body stirred, seconding that notion.

She shivered, then sat up and sniffed warily. The room smelled of Jon, with undertones of dog. No shampoo with balsam and nettle. Perhaps she'd imagined it that other

time? *Forget it.* They'd arrived at the edge of his bed.
"Now this I call service."

"You ain't seen the half of it yet." He helped her rise
from his lap, then positioned his chair below a pair of gym-
nastic rings that hung down from the ceiling.

Waiting on the bed, she watched as he hoisted himself.
The muscles stood out in his arms and torso. The light from
the hall threw the washboard pattern along his ribs into
gorgeous relief—she caught his lean waist to help swing
him aboard. Must be quite a scramble alone. He finally lay
on his back, one leg bent with its casts holding it thus, the
other one straight. God, so he slept like that, or on his side?
My poor love!

They'd unzipped his pants earlier. Kneeling beside him,
she drew them awkwardly, tenderly off his legs, then saw
his casts for the first time. She bit her lip. "Does it hurt?"

"Nothin' hurts tonight."

Smiling, she stroked the crinkly gold that furred his hard
stomach. Still, everything from his thighs up looked in fine
working order. She'd be happy to testify how well it
worked. "But I thought you said—"

He caught her hand and brought it up to his lips. "You
cured me, Demi."

"But—"

He drew her down till they lay nose to nose, she half on
top, braced on one elbow. "And I don't mean what's down
below...." He kissed her ear, her throat, came back to her
lips.

If not that, then he meant...? Slow, liquid, their kisses
deepened. She wriggled atop him. Questions, there'd be
time for questions later, in the morning, and for answers.
All the time in the world. But right now, on this magical
night...

DIM GRAY LIGHT COMING in the spattered window... Demi
had been right, predicting rain. *Demi!* Everything returned

in a rush, every touch, every flavor, her wicked mischief and her unexpected tenderness— Jon reached for her, then realized she was up on her knees, her face hovering over his stomach. "What are you doing?"

"Memorizing you—all your smells. You smell different here—" she pressed the tip of her nose into his navel "—than you do…" Her nose quested up his body, brushed butterfly-light around one nipple. "He-ere…" There was laughter in her voice. "Or—*here!*" She stuck her nose in his armpit and snorted.

"C'mere, you beautiful bloodhound!" He caught her arms and pulled her higher. Kissed her thoroughly, then lifted her away so he could look at her. She had a trick of going limp as a sleepy tiger, trusting herself completely to his hands…. One of her tricks…. Backlit by the pearly light from the window, she was—

The light! How late was it? He'd thought dawn, but with rain clouds— "What time is it?"

She squirmed in his grip—a shrug. "Who cares? You're taking the day off. Think I will, too."

But he had a plane to catch! The van was coming at eight. "Damn!" He set her aside and rolled to look at the bedside clock—7:40 a.m.! *"Hell!"*

"What is it?" She sat up, swept her hair back.

"I've got twenty minutes before my cab comes!" Barely time for a sponge bath and to dress. He yanked the chair closer to the bed, then hoisted himself and moved over. Looked back.

Demi sat with knees drawn up, arms wrapped tight around her legs, eyes narrowed. "Where are you off to?"

"Baltimore." But suddenly he didn't want to say more. It would take too long, and he was hoping and fearing enough for both of them. And if—God forbid—things didn't work out, the last thing he'd want to do when he returned was explain. Face her pity. Pity was the last thing he wanted from Demi. "So...excuse me?"

"Of course." She turned her head away.

Damn! But he would have to make his amends later. He couldn't miss that plane. Yanking out drawers on his bureau, Jon hauled out clothes. Glanced at her in the mirror.

Still huddled into a ball, she'd allowed herself to topple backward. Was now staring blankly up at the ceiling. He grinned in spite of himself at the picture she made, then headed out the door. *Not at all happy with me.* There'd be the devil to pay when he returned. But assuming he came back whole, he'd be happy to pay in any coin she demanded. *God willing, I'll get down on my knees and grovel if she wants.*

When he rolled out of the bathroom fifteen minutes later, Demi had dressed. Her face was a serene mask except for her stormy eyes and her lips bruised from kissing. A woman who needed a good half hour of serious cuddling—but he didn't have it to give. "Demi..." *Darlin'.* "Look..."

She glanced briskly at her watch. "If your cab comes at eight, you'd better hustle. Shall I take Burton?"

He'd meant to shut him in the bathroom and let him tough it out. "Uh, oh, sure. He'd love that."

Wordless and withdrawn, she accompanied him down to the street, where his van stood waiting. If he'd been on his feet, Jon would have kissed that look off her face or taken a smack trying. But he didn't quite dare pull her down to his level. He glanced at his watch as the driver engaged his lift—8:05 a.m. The nerve jumped in his jaw. No time, but still... "Get in. We'll drive you home." Her apartment was eight blocks uptown, a detour, but it would give them a minute to talk. He'd better explain.

She started to refuse, then shrugged and stepped inside. But in the few minutes it took for the van to race to her doorstep, she focused entirely on the driver, who accepted her attentions with startled delight. Jon couldn't get a word in edgewise.

Okay, already. He'd make his apologies when she was ready to hear them. Drumming his fingers on Burton's domed skull, Jon checked his watch for the third time as the van braked. The driver rushed around to open her door and he said hurriedly, "Demi...about last night..." *Heaven would run a poor second.*

Rising already, she gave him a cool, meaningless smile. "Yes, it was very nice. We'll have to do it again sometime." *In a thousand years or so!* her tone said. "Burton? Let's go, boy." The door slid back. She tugged at his collar and the dog hopped to the street.

"I'll call you when I get back," he called after her.

Her slender shoulders lifting in another shrug, she stalked off without a backward glance, though Burton looked back, bewildered. The door slammed shut.

And Jon looked back, all the way till the van reached the corner.

As Demi paused on her stoop to pull out her keys, a man vaulted up the steps, two at a time, to join her. Sarraj, holding a bouquet of daffodils.

"Crap!" Jon swore. Damn it all to hell and back again! The van shot away downtown.

CHAPTER FIFTEEN

NOT THREE MINUTES AGO she'd sworn off all men for all time. Now here was another one in her face. Demi closed her eyes for a moment, then opened them. She hadn't dreamed it. Richard Sarraj stood before her with bouquet extended, his first smile starting to fade.

By now his gift was an embarrassment to them both. "How lovely." She accepted it automatically and automatically buried her nose in the blossoms—jonquils. She saw in her mind's eye that day, two weeks before, when she and Jon had first walked through the park. A shaft of pain shot through her temples. "Thank you. What are you doing up and out so early?" Except it wasn't. She was late, and clearly coming home in yesterday's rumpled clothes, hair tousled, eyes shadowed from a night of loving.

He hadn't missed the signs. His mouth curled downward. "Sorry to drop by like this, but I was hoping I could drive you to work."

"Umm…" She had her heart set on a long, hot bubble bath, then a nap, and then fierce, thought-obliterating work, in that order. *And no men!* "I'm afraid I'd planned to go in late today."

"Well, some other time." Richard retreated a stair step, then paused. "The reason I came—part of the reason—was that I can't make our appointment tomorrow. The venture capitalists I'm working with in L.A. have come up with a new source of money. I have to fly out this afternoon to check it out. May not be back till late Sunday."

Sunday a month from now would be soon enough. "Oh, that's a pity."

He rocked back on his heels, then steadied. "Uh, when I return, say Monday night, would you come out with me? And that's not business."

Was he blind? Couldn't he see that she was clearly involved with someone else? Or was he one of those idiots who assumed that if she'd love one man, she'd love any? He retreated a step, and she realized she was scowling. "I...don't think so." She forced her face to politeness. "It's very kind of you, Richard, and I really— I'm flattered. But I've been thinking that we're blurring the lines here. I really don't think we should be mixing business with pleasure. You understand?"

He understood he'd been snubbed. The look he gave her for a split second was—

At her feet, Burton lurched to his feet and growled. "*Burton,* hush!" She knelt and patted the hound, more to duck that unnerving stare than to quiet the dog. "Hush, you silly dog!" She looked up and gave Richard a rueful smile. *Don't make a scene. I'm not worth it. And right now, I'd probably cry on you.* Or perhaps she should threaten to do that. Nothing like tears to make a man run.

"I see," Richard said, his voice and face utterly neutral.

Perhaps she'd imagined that look? "You know, I wasn't going to mention this, but perhaps I'm in a position to save you from making a grave mistake."

"Oh?" Whatever was coming, she wasn't going to like it. There was just the faintest, nastiest hint of triumph in his eyes.

"It's about your lab tech, Jon Sutter. He made me uneasy from the start, and since we're investing so heavily in your firm, I took the liberty of checking his credentials. The man isn't quite what he seems...."

JON MISSED HIS RETURN flight, his appointment being delayed three hours when his doctor was called out for emergency surgery. With all other flights full, he settled for Amtrak, then tried to call Demi from the Baltimore station.

The phone rang again and again without answer. She had one number that she switched from home to office and back again, so presuming she'd remembered to switch it, the phone was ringing where she was. Unless she'd gone out.

Propped up in the phone booth on his new crutches, Jon found that hard to imagine. He was exhausted. *Demi, where are you, babe? And why doesn't your damn—* The answering machine kicked in. He listened to her brisk message, then, "Demi, it's Jon.... I've been thinking about you all day." He had been. Why hadn't he simply invited her along?

Except this morning he hadn't known if the day would have a happy ending or one too terrible to share. "I—" *Miss you.* Ridiculous, when they were only hours apart, but it felt like years. "I guess I'll try you again. Later. Hope Burton behaved himself." How inane could he be? "Bye." *My darling.*

Jamming the phone down, he swung back to his wheelchair and sat with a groan of relief. He dropped the crutches in the sling on its back.

He'd imagined himself striding triumphantly home, sweeping Demi up in his arms, whirling her round and round....

Instead it would be weeks before he'd built up his wasted muscles enough to support his weight unaided. And till he could actually walk, the doctor wasn't sure about his right knee, whether it would ever take the strain. But it looked good. *I'm on my way now.* The loudspeaker droned overhead. He wheeled off toward his gate, toward Demi.

"Hope Burton behaved himself," said Jon's voice. Stretched out on her couch with Burton half draped across her stomach, Demi stared toward her answering machine. He sounded just the same as before.

He wasn't.

Never had been? Her eyes swam with tears. "Bye," Jon said carelessly from wherever he was calling.

And I wonder if it really is Baltimore? All his statements were now brought into question. "What do *you* think, Burton?" She pulled a silky ear. The dog whuffled in his sleep, his warm heavy weight suddenly reminding her of his master's, Jon's arms wrapped around her in the few hours that they'd slept.

I slept with precisely—whom last night? She scrambled out from under the brute. A warm, wonderful and funny man?

Or a liar—and a thief? To say nothing of a forger! And depending on whether he'd sold those forged drug prescriptions or used them himself...

She stalked off to the kitchen and pulled the box of chocolates out of the freezer, where she'd hidden it from herself.

Lot of good that did. She'd gone out and bought the box after she'd completed her phone call to Ruggles. The real Ruggles.

Only two truffles left in the top layer. This was all she'd eaten all day. Not that it had cheered her. She popped one truffle into her mouth and handed the other to Burton, who stood at her feet, tail waving—he knew already what the sound of the freezer door opening meant. Jon was right; the dog was no dope.

I'm the dope, falling for a man from nowhere. A man with a great smile and a great line. She'd seen it happen to so many of her friends over the years, falling for smooth-talking cads. Women were unspeakably trusting—but her? If she couldn't smell a rat, who could?

"BAD NEWS?" ASKED Greenley, moving up from the back of the van the next morning. His eyes dropped from Jon's face to his legs.

"Huh? Oh, no. Good, in fact. I can use these part of the time now." Jon gestured at the crutches slung behind his chair as he gave a quick rundown on the plan—weight training, physical therapy, patience.... No, it wasn't his legs bothering him this morning.

Where was she last night? He'd called her on his arrival in the city, reached her machine. Had tried again near midnight, still no answer. She couldn't have gone out on a date, not after— So maybe she'd put the phone on mute and napped all day?

Tired as he was, he'd wakened several times in the night to wonder. It was too like all the times he'd lain awake in bed wondering where Angelina might be. *It's 2:00 a.m. Do you know where your wife is?*

Shuddup already! That was the problem with trust. It was such a fragile emotion. And hard to learn again once you'd— He tuned in to find Greenley was speaking.

"...dead or not," said the agent. "Our guess is she's—"

"*What?* I'm sorry. Back up there, tell me again."

Greenley gave him a jaundiced look, grunted and started over. Trace had arrived in Bermuda on the last flight, last night. To find that the yacht *Aphrodite* had cleared Customs in the late afternoon and that her owner, the heiress, already had departed the island by jet, bound for Atlanta.

Or rather, *some* woman had, using the heiress's passport. "Whoever it was in the scarf and sunglasses, we didn't have personnel in place to tail her. She didn't take luggage, so our guy figured she'd return to the yacht. Didn't realize she'd skipped island till Trace picked up all outgoing passenger lists on his way in through the airport. By then whoever was using her passport had landed in Atlanta."

One of the busiest airports in the country. They'd lost

her trail there. She might still be in that city, or she could easily have paid cash, assumed another name and flown on to anywhere.

"But if that wasn't her, why kill the real owner?" Jon wondered.

"Same reason as before. If she'd soured on the game plan, or finally tumbled to it? Say she'd gone all high handed. Rich women do that. Threatened to throw 'em off her yacht once they reached Bermuda? Hard to keep her drugged forever."

"But if they killed her, where's the body?" Jon asked, then supplied the answer himself. The *Aphrodite* had crossed some three thousand miles of Atlantic this past week. "Splash?"

"Easy as rubber duckies. Then, since they'd better arrive with the same number of passengers they left the Canaries with, they take on an imitation heiress a few miles off Bermuda. Somebody they've radioed to meet 'em there. Fast little powerboat zips out and puts Heiress II aboard before Customs counts noses."

"Then *she* flies away before anybody who could identify the real heiress can check her out," Jon murmured to himself. He didn't want to believe it. "Or the real owner had a spat with her lover and flounced off to Atlanta, leaving him and her crew to bring the boat home. Could be entirely innocent again."

"Butter wouldn't melt," Greenley agreed. "Too much butter for my taste, this whole operation."

And for his. As if someone, someone *very* bright, were anticipating their every question and supplying a harmless answer. "Anything else?"

"A few quickies. One. Sarraj's on a plane this minute, headed for Bermuda."

"Reporting in again?"

"I'd say so. And two. Leave the crutches here and stick

to your chair. It's your cover. You want 'em to underestimate you.''

"The hell with that! I need to practice."

"Practice at home. If the opposition thinks you can't walk, and you can, you've got an edge. Keep it."

Gritting his teeth, Jon pulled his crutches out of their sling and handed them over. It hurt. "Anything else?"

"Third and last. I'm off to Kuwait, where we finally found Sarraj's dad. Time to ask some pointed questions."

The van parked in front of Demi's building, and the driver hurried round its hood. "Involved with terrorists?" Jon asked quickly.

Greenley showed his excellent teeth. "With Mercedes-Benz."

A MERCEDES DEALERSHIP in Kuwait City! Jon wanted to smash something. He jabbed the elevator button for floor twenty-nine. *Sarraj's dad is a car dealer? And here I'm sneaking around playing cops and robbers, lying to Demi? What is this, a group delusion—we all dropped acid together?* Hadn't Trace and his Fibbie friends ever heard that sometimes a cigar was just a cigar? *That's it, I've had enough! I'm going home.*

He was going nowhere without Demi. Without... exploring what last night had meant to her.

He knew what it had meant to him. But Demi, flirt to the world? Who could have any man she pleased with just a smile? He knew what he *wanted* last night to have meant to her. But he'd given up confusing wishes with reality a long, long time ago.

When Jon entered Alluroma, Burton came galloping and yodeling to greet him. "Hiya, guy, did you behave yourself?" Jon suffered a doggy kiss, then gave him a thump on the shoulder that only brought him rollicking back for more. Where was Demi? No way could she miss this racket. "Okay, okay, I get the picture. You missed me." But Demi?

Dog prancing in the vanguard, Jon rolled into her office. Demi looked up coolly from her desk. "You're late." She turned back to her computer, frowned at the screen.

The temperature in the room was maybe forty degrees—and falling. Jon sat, the smile frozen on his face. Her scowl deepened, but she didn't look up again. Worse than he'd expected or feared. His own fault for not explaining. Wheeling closer, he cleared his throat. "Demi...about yesterday. I wanted to explain."

"No need." Her fingers rattled over the keyboard, letters and symbols marching across her screen.

What he needed was to go over there, kiss the nape of her neck, take her in his arms and hang on tight, even if she lashed out at him.

Without his crutches he didn't dare stand. But words didn't carry half the meaning of a hug. "Yes, there is. I shouldn't have left you like that yesterday. I—" He grimaced as she started typing again. "I tried to call you last night, several times, but you...weren't answering." *Where were you?*

Slender shoulders lifted in an arrogant shrug. "I was...out. Went out with Richard Sarraj. Now would you please get to work?" She hit another key. Across the room, the connected printer whirred and sucked in a sheet of paper.

He'd sat there longing for her—while she was out doing the town? Doing a creep like— *Well, I've sure been here before, haven't I?* But he had to be sure. If there was any chance that this was just hurt feelings talking... Lowering his head as if breasting a cold, breaking wave, he said quietly, "Was that just to punish me?" *Let it be that.* That he could handle.

"Oh, please!" She grabbed the edge of her desk and

spun her chair to face him, revealing eyes wide with contempt. "Don't take yourself so seriously! You were just a fling—okay?" She jerked back around to face her keyboard.

Not okay. *The last thing I wanted with you was just a fling.* He swallowed, found it hurt.

"I was curious what it'd be like," she growled without turning, "making love in a wheelchair. So now I know. Kinky...but hardly worth the effort."

Well, that about summed it up! What more was there to say? Two words, he found, as they burst out of him. "And Sarraj?" Waiting on her doorstep? Had she even bothered to wash *him* off before she went out with Sarraj? "What's he to you?"

Her dark head came up, froze as she stared at something he couldn't see beyond the far wall. "Not that it's any of your biz...but if you really must know?"

He made some wordless sound, which she took for an affirmative.

"Then understand this, Jon. You were a fling. Richard's a *catch....*"

Words like a knife thrust, angled up deftly between the ribs. He sat blinking. Pain would come later.

Demi nodded toward the printer. "Now, if you'd start with those formulas and call me when they're done..."

HE CLUNG TO HIS NUMBNESS as long as possible. You stayed firmly in the now, locking your mind on the little things, the tangible things. The cold steel of the chin-up bar beneath his fingers. The bite of the shock cord on his palms when he hauled his wheeled stool across the room. The smell of each ingredient as he mixed Demi's latest trials—bergamot, rosewood, birch-tar oil, patchouli.... The distant, bleak tread of his own heart, bumbling along in its dark and lonely cavern. *Stay numb, stay numb, so dumb, stay numb....*

He didn't. Sometime after the third or fourth formula, the pain arrived, a black crow swooping down from the sky. An expected guest, but still he sucked in his breath in surprise. This black? This sharp?

Steady... it's only pain. And if you feel pain, then count yourself lucky. Only those who live feel pain. He remembered telling himself that, his teeth clamped to keep from screaming, while they winched him up from the river gorge. If you feel pain, you're one of the lucky ones.

This was luck?

The pain this time wasn't a twisting, cracking pain like the pain he'd felt pinned to the rocks in the river while the current bent, then demolished his kayak around him. This was a tearing pain, something essential being ripped away. Something he'd tried very hard to ignore—not that ignorance had prevented its birth or its growth.

But ripped away now. *Bye-bye, hope, you were sweet while you lasted.* Demi... when had he begun to hope? How could he have dared hope? *You fool... Idiot!*

He mixed her fifth variation, then she brought him more formulas. Demi was working like a fiend today, using ingredients she'd never required before. When she dropped the printouts before him, her face was carved stone.

No stone, night before last. Her face had been soft as damp velvet against his lips. She'd lain for the longest time, braced on one elbow, her forehead touching his, their eyes speaking. Tenderness was the message he'd dared to read in those dark eyes.

Just a fling, you fool! Kinky, but hardly worth the effort. Angelina could have scripted those words. *You care for the beautiful ones, they cut your heart out. You knew that, you idiot. You've nobody to blame but yourself. Can't blame Demi. She is who she is. Lover beware....*

Well, he hadn't. He mixed the eighth variation, the ninth. She came back with more, smacked them down and stalked off. He'd have to go, too, after today. Let Trace save the world without his help. He couldn't even save his own heart from a stomping.

Will she think I'm a coward when I quit? A whiner, got my feelings hurt, couldn't take her heat? Her heat two nights ago…heat a man could have warmed his soul beside forever… *Shuddup. Just quit and go.*

CHAPTER SIXTEEN

AT FIVE ON THE DOT, Jon rolled into her office with the last trials of the day. Demi was up and staring out her window. She glanced over her shoulder as he set the *mouillettes* on her desk, then turned back again.

"I'm done and I'm going," he announced. *And I'm not coming back, babe.* The words jammed in his throat. There was a message in line before that one. "I...just wanted you to know—"

Don't say it, you fool! Keep some scrap of your pride!

Or maybe it was pride that made him say it. He owned the strength to claim his own emotions, even if that was all he owned. "Night before last— Maybe it meant nothing to you, Demi, but it meant something to me. It meant—" *Meant I know what heaven'll look like, feel like, when I get there, Dark Eyes.* "It meant a lot." He shrugged. "Anyway, I've decid—"

"So *what?*" she cried without turning. "What good is the word of a liar—and a thief?"

"Huh?"

"You know what I'm talking about—your forged prescriptions for Demerol? Valium? All kinds of filthy drugs?"

"*What?*" Burton whimpered and nudged his leg, then hustled over to Demi to jab his nose into the back of her knee, peacemaking.

"*Pah!* Don't touch me, you stupid mutt! You probably helped him!"

She whirled to glare at the dog. Her cheeks were streaked with—she was crying? She spun back again before Jon was sure. "Demi?"

She crossed her arms so hard her shoulder blades stood out like wings beneath the thin silk of her shirt. "I talked with Ruggles yesterday. The *real* Ruggles this time, not whoever you got to stand in for him."

His fictional boss back at the fictional pharmacy in Connecticut? No, he remembered, the man and pharmacy actually existed. He was a relative or friend of some agent, had agreed to provide Jon's cover.

"This time I wasn't a trusting chump! I didn't use the phone number *you* gave me. This time I called Information, got his number—a *different* number, Jon. And when I called it and reached the real Ruggles…"

So his cover was blown. The number he'd given her for a reference had connected to an FBI regional office somewhere in Connecticut. Some agent there had been designated to lie on Ruggles's behalf, to give Jon his glowing recommendation. But yesterday, if she'd surprised the real Ruggles, and he wasn't fast on his feet… *So now she knows I'm a liar.*

But a thief? "What are you talking about?"

"Oh, stop playing *dumb!*" She stamped her foot and Burton retreated, tail between his legs. "I know everything! The pharmacy wasn't sold and you weren't simply laid off. Ruggles fired you—for forging doctors' prescriptions and selling them to addicts! Maybe using yourself, for all he knew! You're just lucky he didn't want to press charges. That he let you slink off." She swiped at her cheeks, then spun to glare at him. "To me, you liar!"

She *had* been crying. The faintest, tiniest thread of emotion tugged beneath his ribs. It felt weirdly like gladness.

The rest of him was still struggling to come up to speed. She'd reached the real Ruggles, who had known and consented to Jon's using him for cover in the first place—and the man had called him a crook. *Why?* "What made you think to check up on—" He stopped as he realized how guilty that made him sound.

Demi shrugged. "Oh, what does it matter? What matters is you're nobody I could ever trust and I— I—" She drew in a shaking breath, shook her head, scooped up a book from the shelf beside her and heaved it at the wall. Burton shot around the edge of the desk and slipped into its knee-well. "*Pah!* You're fired—both of you. Now get out!"

Ruggles, who *knew* he was honest, an FBI plant, had labeled him a thief.... Jon glanced at Burton's bug eyes, peeping from cover, and his own gaze fixed on Demi's file drawer. *Ah.* Now he knew what—or rather who—had made her recheck his references! Sarraj must have checked them first himself, after he'd raided Jon's file to find Ruggles's name and location.

But that still left the essential puzzle. Why did Ruggles lie?

"Did you hear me?" Demi leaned over her desk to glare at him. Her eyes were swimming with tears.

He could have kissed them away. *I'm not what you think!*

"D'you have anything at all to say for yourself?"

Any excuse? Any justification? He had dozens if she wanted to hear them. If she possibly cared... *I'm not a thief—not even a pharmacist, crooked or straight. I'm—*

Undercover. He shut his mouth with a snap. To clear himself, he'd have to blow it. It wasn't really blown yet, just dropped in the sewer. Demi still saw him as Sutter—just a lying, sleazy Sutter. *But who—*

"Do you? Or are you just going to sit there like a lump on a log! Talk to me, damn you!"

The FBI had set him up! No way could Sarraj have painted him black if she'd called— "You did say you called information?"

"What has *that* got to do with you and—" She gulped and dropped her voice an icy, quivering octave. "Yes, that's precisely what I said. Information. Now, since you don't have anything useful to add—get out."

"No. I won't." Not while there was the remotest chance. "Not till you hear me out."

"So talk, already!"

"I...I admit everything." And soon as he got his hands on Greenley and Trace, she could add murder to the charges. "I did forge some prescriptions. A few. Mostly for Valium." She opened her mouth and he added hastily, "Mostly for nervous housewives who—"

"*Pah!* Burton could tell a better lie than that!"

Quite likely. "All right, all right, so I sold to addicts, too. But not many, Demi, and nothing really harmful—and *never* to minors."

"Why, Jon? How could you *do* something like that?"

"Uh, debts... I had some debts I had to clear up."

"Gambling debts?" Her eyes widened in horror. "Is *that* what happened to your legs? Somebody broke—"

He let out a bark of startled laughter and shook his head.

"Student loans. I'd fallen behind in my payments." Half his students at Princeton were hocked to their ears with educational loans. "Tuition to become a pharmacist, it's very..." He trailed off lamely. *Trace, I will smash your nose, rip up your black book, might even tell Mom what you've done, making me lie to Demi like this!*

"Really?" Demi swiped at a tear trickling down her face, smudging her mascara. She looked adorable.

"Cross my heart. It was wrong. I know it was, but..."

Not half as wrong as this, lying to a woman he— Jon blinked. Whom he... *Yes...I love you—mascara smudges, wicked temper and all, woman!* He reached out and wiped a tear off the tip of her nose.

Wrong move. She took a roundhouse swing at him. He

ducked and heard red nails slashing the air an inch above his head. Her brows slanted in a truly evil scowl. Like a cat, she didn't like to miss her mark, not before witnesses. "Keep your hands to yourself," she said with bitter dignity. She stalked back to the window, stood there, arms wrapped around herself as if she were chilled to the bone, staring north. "I see..." she muttered finally. "You said not many prescriptions?"

"Not many at all."

Her shoulders jerked in an irritable, imprisoned shrug.

"Not very many," he amended quickly.

"And that's why Ruggles didn't hand you over to the cops?"

"I guess. That and I promised him I'd never do it again. I think he believed me." *You believe me, too. The real me, under all these layers of lies. Look at me, Demi. Night before last, that was no lie.*

She turned and their eyes locked. His breath stopped. Demi, lying on top of him, their foreheads touching, their wondering eyes staring deep into each other's. *That was no lie. Believe it.*

She let out a shuddering breath. "If I decided to let you stay...?"

Let me hold you, touch you, and we could cut past this garbage in a heartbeat. "Yes?" he said, careful to keep all hope from his voice.

"Because I still need a lab tech, and I've no time left to train a new one... If I did let you stay, things would be entirely different, you understand?"

Oh, yes. Things were changed between them forever. *I love you, Demi Cousteau.* For what good it might ever do him, he loved her. There was no going back.

"From now on, it would be strictly business between us."

Not if I have my way, it won't. If she'd cared enough to cry...

"And you'd be strictly on probation," she added fiercely. "If I ever find you're using drugs around here—"

"Not a problem. Really, it isn't."

"Or if I *ever* catch you stealing from me, then—"

"I won't. I swear I won't." With one exception. If he found the way to steal her heart...

"And finally..." Her dark eyes widened and met his with all the impact of a tigress's glare. "If you ever mention the night before last to me...if you ever look at me as if you're even *thinking* about that night...you're fired, Jon Sutter. It never happened." She turned on her heel and moved to the window with a walk that said "See me and weep." She stood staring out into the jeweled midtown twilight. "If that's understood, then I'll see you tomorrow."

WHEN SHE HEARD THE OUTER door close behind him, Demi turned. Half blinded by stupid tears, she groped her way to her chair and sat. There, it was done. Over. Better than that, it never happened.

There'd been nothing there from the start except her overvivid imagination. Just a man; a weak, grubby man. Charming, but with some flaw in him somewhere that had made him choose the selfish way, the easy way, in spite of all his obvious abilities. *None of my business why.* Closing her aching eyes, she saw his, looking up at her. She'd leaned over him for the longest time that night, staring deep into his eyes, wondering, *Who are you, Jon Sutter? How can you touch me so?*

Well, now she had the answer to her first question anyway—a lying, petty thief! She pulled open a drawer and groped inside it for tissues, blew her nose long and heartily.

Get back to work. Instead she put her head down on her arms and closed her eyes. Willed her mind to blankness.

But if she could stop the inner wheels from turning, grinding happiness into finer and finer grains of misery, still she could not stop her nose. She whooshed out a weary sigh, breathed in…her nose twitched.

Several perfumes. Nearby. Oh, yes, Jon had brought in the last of the smelling strips for the trials he'd mixed this afternoon. All day she'd been composing like a madwoman, trying to drive him from her mind. Here were the results.

That one to the left… She reached out blindly, groped and found it. Recognized the whiff of jasmine. Its top note was just fading, the heart note stepping boldly forth. She brought it closer—and tears flowed.

It had a black heart!

She'd dived down and down today, abandoned all thought of pleasant scents to compose straight from her misery. Betrayal. Happiness slain. Anticipation murdered. Humiliation—she'd been such a *fool* for caring! Aflame with all that, the scent smoldered like a black opal.

Gorgeous, but would any woman ever wear a scent so dark? She sat up and opened her eyes. *No way.* Perfumes were created to make people happy. To bring a bit of heaven down to earth.

But Salome, dancing for John the Baptist's head? A woman dancing passion, temptation to evil, a good man's betrayal? Shimmering veils dropping one by one till the seventh revealed her gorgeously wicked heart? Here was her scent, born of sorrow.

Demi wiped her eyes, smelled it again…and smiled. It was…fabulous. Terrible and fabulous both! Her mother had the power and presence to wear such a scent. So would others—not happy women, their raging hearts on their sleeves, this scent at their bosoms. It was a "Damn your eyes!" scent.

"And damn yours, Jon Sutter!" she whispered. In the end, he'd given her something almost as precious as what he'd stolen away.

Almost.

"I'M ALL OF THE ABOVE," Trace's distant voice agreed when Jon paused in his swearing to catch a breath, "but I'd do it again."

"Why you coldhearted *son* of—"

"Your mother," Trace dropped into the gap. "I'm sorry, Jon."

"But you'd do it again!" Jon slumped back in the phone booth, head tipped back to stare at its gritty ceiling. He'd left Alluroma two hours ago. It had taken that long to call the contact number for Trace, demand they hunt him down, call them back to receive Trace's relayed instructions, which had led him at last to this phone booth in the basement of a hotel on West Fifty-fourth. A safe and private phone that Sarraj and pals could not possibly have diddled. Trace was calling from an equally safe phone somewhere in Bermuda.

And speaking while he'd been brooding. "...dropped the ball on our end and I'm *very* sorry. Ruggles reported in as instructed after Sarraj, then Cousteau, called him. Some trainee, whose next assignment will be somewhere north of Nome, I promise you, left his messages on my desk instead of contacting me. Then that paper got buried under the incoming. My fault in the end."

"Too frigging true! Why the *hell* did you set me up like that?"

"Because we'd built in a backup layer of reality in case they came sniffing. Wanted to give them a story they could buy if they didn't buy our first one. Give them a good reason you'd be sneaking and lying, even poking around in her office.''

"Because I'm a thief and a liar. Thanks a lot.''

"You're welcome. Better they think they understand you than they drop you in the river, bro.''

"Demi wouldn't—'' Jon stopped. Trace had promised to yank him out if he became involved—and now?

"Cousteau,'' Trace corrected him with a steely edge, "has just shown her true colors if you'd care to open your eyes and notice.''

"What the hell d'you mean by that?''

"She kept you, Jon. She's just learned you're a sleaze-ball, that you could steal her blind the first chance you get, and she kept you on? That's the decision of an honest busi-nesswoman?''

It was such a fragile hope he had, that Demi had kept him on because, deep down, she couldn't let go of what they'd found two nights ago. It was a dangerously foolish hope. Not one to be laid bare before a cynic like Trace. A cynic who would send Jon packing if he thought he'd lost his usefulness as objective observer. *And now I objectively love her. Is there anybody to whom I'm not lying?* Burton, maybe.

"It takes a crook to know one, Jon. And crooks are com-fortable around crooks—it's honest folks that make them nervous. The fact that she kept you on once Ruggles gave her the thief story says it all.''

"Sarraj thinks like that, but Demi—'' He saw the trap and stopped.

"If Cousteau doesn't take orders from Sarraj, then she'd fire you. And whether she thinks that way herself or not, if she *is* taking orders from Sarraj, then she isn't his lily-white dupe—she's his coconspirator.''

"If there really is a conspiracy. Find a smoking gun yet?'' *Or is this all in your head?* Maybe Sarraj was the creep son of a car dealer who hoped to make a fortune for himself and his investors with a new perfume. No more than that.

"Not yet." Trace's voice stayed cool, big brother refusing to rise to kid brother's taunts. "But when the *Aphrodite* leaves here, headed west, we nail 'em. Can't do it on British colonial soil, but once they near our coast, it's interdiction time."

"The Coast Guard?"

"Doing drug patrol. The Coasties board and search any incoming vessel they like if they suspect it might be smuggling. And either Greenley or I'll be along for the fun. They'll look for drugs, we'll look for any and everything else. The smoking gun's there someplace, Jon. I can smell it."

"I'm beginning to doubt it."

Nearly eight hundred miles to the southeast, Trace sighed. "You know it isn't uncommon, an agent undercover starting to identify with his subjects. Just something you have to expect and fight off. And when a pretty woman's involved... Honeytraps, we call 'em."

"It's not that, Trace." Well, not only that. "But I haven't found a shred of evidence to back your—"

"I know, I know. They're good. *Very* good. But trust me, there's something here. I'm not wasting your time. Now...tell me about your legs. How'd it go?"

THE DAYS PASSED AT Alluroma in grim and brittle silence.

Strictly business, as Demi had demanded. And determined to give her no excuse to fire him, Jon did his best to cooperate.

Because if Trace's instincts were right, if something wicked was this way coming, Demi stood smack-dab in the bull's-eye. And Jon intended to be there for her.

Which meant he couldn't let her fire him. Which

meant—for now—he played strictly by Demi's rules. Which meant that whenever Demi entered the lab he'd allow himself one hungry glance, then lower his gaze. Because if their eyes ever met, she'd know in a heartbeat what he was feeling, wanting. Safer to keep his eyes on the floor like a shamefaced felon.

Which opened up a whole new world of torture. Like a Victorian swain driven mad by one glimpse of a shapely limb, her ankles were driving him wild. It was anybody's guess how long he could keep playing humble lab flunkie when all he longed to do was yank her nose-to-nose and say, *"To hell with this never-happened routine! It happened like the San Francisco quake of '06 happened. Now where do we go from here?"*

Better to keep his mouth shut, speak only when spoken to. But the silence seemed to be shredding Demi's nerves, as well. Once every day or so, a weird, nonbusiness-related question would pop out, like, "Have you ever been married?" She'd asked that the day he finished Shaitan 21.

Jon nearly dropped his pipette. "Married?"

"You heard me."

"Umm…" He'd promised himself he wouldn't lie to her anymore if he could possibly avoid it. "I was…once."

"What happened?"

He tossed the dropper, then dared to meet her eyes. "We divorced."

"Oh." Her eyes slid away to the far side of the lab. "Why?"

He grimaced. In three words? Or three thousand? "She…did something I…could never forgive."

"*She* did."

The nerve ticked in his cheek. "Yeah." *It wasn't my imaginary drug crimes, if that's what you're thinking.* No crime at all, really, just a failure of generosity that appalled him. Angelina had never even understood that, in the end, it didn't matter to him whether her baby had been his or her married director pal's. Well, it mattered, but he could have forgiven.

What he couldn't get past was that she'd chosen her new career on the soaps over the baby inside her. Given the choice between staying true to her unpregnant role during a season's hectic filming or dropping out for a year to bear her child, she'd chosen her soap opera.

And he'd discovered he wasn't the tolerant, progressive husband, sworn to support his wife's career as he would have his own, that he'd always imagined himself to be. Call him old-fashioned, but something very primitive, very basic, had reared up inside him and flatly said, *Not my kid.*

Not that she'd given him the chance to say it. Only when it was a fait accompli, in the midst of one of their fights, had she thrown it in his teeth—used it not as grief to bring them together, but as a weapon, a taunt. And with that, all reason for fighting had died. She wasn't the woman he'd thought he'd married.

"Oh," Demi said again into a silence that must have stretched on for minutes. Jon jumped and focused on the vial before him. He handed it to her wordlessly, and wordlessly she went.

Only to ask him a day later, as she set out his and Burton's deli requests on the table in the kitchen, "Do you have any brothers or sisters?"

Trace had hammered into him from the start that friends and loved ones were the Achilles' heel of a man undercover. Potential hostages or revenge targets. So you drew a line and didn't cross it. No one in his family except Trace knew where he was or what he was doing.

"Or have you forgotten?" She snatched her sandwich from the bag.

"Umm, last time I counted I had one brother and two sisters."

Demi shrugged as if she didn't give a damn and moved on toward her office. She didn't eat with him nowadays. She paused in the doorway and looked back. "Where in line do you come?"

"Second. My brother's the eldest." *Please don't ask me their names.*

She didn't. She sniffed and vanished.

"Beats me," he told Burton, who sat waiting for his ham and Swiss. But somehow it felt encouraging. Later, back at his workbench, he found he was whistling.

CHAPTER SEVENTEEN

WEDNESDAY, MIDMORNING, Jon was fixing himself a cup of coffee in the kitchenette. The hallway chime sounded, the door to Demi's office banged open and a woman's voice demanded, "Have you *heard?*" It lowered and continued urgently.

Kyle Andrews? Jon set the kettle back on the burner just as Demi shrieked, "*What?* You must have got it wrong!"

"Sorry, I didn't."

"Got what wrong?" Jon stopped in the office doorway.

The art director swung to give him a grim join-the-party smile. Beyond her, Demi stood thunderstruck. "Sarraj's moved our deadline up. He wants the perfume samples mailed in three weeks."

"That isn't possible!" Demi collapsed in her chair.

"Well, it is possible—just—from my end," Kyle admitted. "But Madison, Hastings and Gurney will make him pay through the nose for it, I assure you. We don't work triple time for free. The photo shoot's scheduled for Friday. I've found my models and you're going to love 'em. Our printer's been alerted to stand by for the flyers. And Richard and I are meeting with the broker to choose our mailing lists next week. So we're on track and the tracks are greased. What about you guys?"

"No way! I've changed my whole concept since you smelled it last. It's the best scent I've ever composed, but it needs *weeks* of fine-tuning. I can't. I won't! Is the man mad?"

"Did he give you a reason?" Jon asked. *He knows we're on to him?* But rather than backing off, Sarraj was lowering his horns and going for it—whatever his goal might be?

"Something about the head of his investors' group, this mysterious prince of his, having a birthday coming up. He's decided he wants to hold the launch party on his birthday."

"That's ridiculous! You don't make business decisions on a whim."

Kyle spread her hands wide, palms up. "You and I don't, but if you've got millions to burn? It's his money."

"It's my perfume. My reputation if it flops!" Demi sailed a box of paper clips across the room. "This isn't acceptable," she said calmly as the clips tinkled down the far wall.

"But it's reality, kiddo." Kyle rolled her eyes at Jon. "Tell her."

Thanks a lot, Kyle, he felt like saying as Demi's eyes swung his way and narrowed dangerously. It hadn't hit her till now that he was here, uninvited, in her office. He mustered a foolish grin and pushed his glasses up his nose. "Hey, I don't tell her anything. She's the boss."

Kyle shot him a puzzled look and turned back to Demi. "Can you do it, boss? I know you don't want to, but can you?"

Demi jerked her gaze away from Jon and shrugged. "That's quite beside the point. I won't."

"Humor me for a moment. Could you?" Kyle asked.

Demi let out a desolate sigh. "I...suppose. Maybe. I've arranged with a friend in Brooklyn to make the juice in bulk for us at his factory once I'm done with the formula. And the gel for the flyer scent-samples. If he can rearrange his mixing schedule..."

"If he's inconvenienced, I'm sure Sarraj will pay for his trouble. And you should rewrite your bill, too."

Demi closed her eyes and shook her head. "It never was

a question of money. Not really." She turned to glare at Jon. "Don't you have work to do?" When he'd nodded and gone, lips clamped in a thin line, she burst into tears.

"Demi?" Kyle murmured helplessly.

"Don't you even ask!"

ONE WEEK LATER JON STOOD in front of a Seventh Avenue storefront, staring through the plate glass. His weight was carried more by the handles of the wheelchair he gripped than his feet. His muscles were starting to tremble. He wasn't sure if this was his normal weakness or the objects beyond the glass. Kayaks.

"Hey, you don't need some help, do you?" A salesman beamed from the store's entrance. "Want to come in and check 'em out?"

"Thanks, I'm just looking." Systematic desensitization. If he looked at them long enough, maybe his stomach would stop churning? Perhaps he should walk this way every day. He damn sure didn't mean to go through life terrified of kayaks. *Just don't mix with water.*

"Hey, that's a great hound!" The salesman sauntered over to scratch Burton's ears. "Something wrong with him?"

"Nope, he just likes to ride." Since Jon tried to limp about a quarter of the distance home in easy stages each day, supported by his chair, Burton was getting lots of joy-rides. He jumped down from the seat to inspect the man's trousers.

"Smells my dog." The guy gave him a thump, then Jon a man-to-manly-man confiding grin. "You ever tried kayaking?"

"Once or twice."

"Well, we rent out boats, too, if you ever want to do a test drive. Got a whole line of sea kayaks down on the docks near Battery Park. And we'll rebate the cost if you decide to buy one.'' He pressed a business card into Jon's hand, then swaggered back into the store.

Don't hold your breath. Jon stowed it in a pocket, clucked, and once Burton had hopped aboard, pushed on. He'd wait till he was out of Mr. Enterprise's anxious view before he made the transfer back to the chair.

A block farther on, wheeling briskly, he looked around at the repeated toot of a horn. The special van pulled in to the curb.

Greenley slid the side door open from inside. ''You guys want a lift?''

''HE SAID YOU WERE walking most evenings now,'' the agent explained, nodding at their driver. ''We quartered the blocks north of her office and what d'you know? And speaking of which, what do you?''

He'd reported in by safe phone while Greenley and Trace were gone. ''Not much since he moved up the deadline. Cousteau's working like forty devils and I'm doing my best to keep up. This is the first day we've quit on time in a week. Dem— Cousteau's mother came and hauled her off by the ear for some dinner party, or we'd still be there.''

Greenley rubbed his temples. He was looking tired. ''Anything else?''

''She went to lunch with Sarraj two days ago, and when she came back she mentioned *Aphrodite.* I'd say it's the first she'd ever heard of it.''

He shrugged. ''Or she's smart enough to cover her ass and pretend.''

Jon felt his jaw tighten. What would it take to clear Demi with these people? Saint Michael flapping down to lend her a halo? ''She thinks the boat belongs to this prince. And, no, I still haven't learned his name. But they're planning on holding the launch party aboard, four days after they mail out the sample flyers.''

"Launch party?"

"Launch the perfume. Big bash for all the industry big-wigs. Fashion and cosmetic reporters. Celebrities. Publicity. She's working up a guest list. Recommending caterers and party planners."

Greenley smiled. "Women do like that stuff, don't they?" He remembered himself and sobered. "We'll want a copy of the guest list. In fact..." He looked thoughtful. "That would make quite the event."

"What would?"

The agent lowered his voice even further. "Hijack a boatload of New York glitterati and hold them for ransom or a prisoner trade? Or blow their fancy pants sky-high? You don't think the world would sit up and notice that? That's all terrorism is, you realize. Publicity for some cause or other."

He hadn't thought. Didn't like the thought now he thought it. It went too well with the undercurrent of contempt he always sensed around Sarraj.

Or maybe that was something private between the two of them? Some instinctive antipathy, two men wanting the same woman?

"When, Jon?" From the tone of the question, Greenley was repeating himself. "When did she say *Aphrodite* would arrive here? They're still lazing around Bermuda, sippin' Dark and Stormies. Some advance notice would be nice, 'cause once that sucker moves, she can fly. We can't have her slipping by us."

"Cousteau didn't say, but I'll keep my ears open. You still mean to interdict?"

"Interdict her back to the Stone Age. If they've got anything bigger than a peashooter aboard, we'll find it." He looked up, surprised, as the van stopped before Jon's building, then called forward, "We aren't done yet. Circle around for ten minutes or so."

The driver nodded and pulled out into traffic again.

"Tell me about Kuwait," Jon said. Greenley gave him a look and he returned it squarely. From now on, if they wanted facts from him, they could pay in kind. To guard Demi's interests as well as the feds', he had to know everything.

Greenley gave a grudging sound of agreement and stretched out his legs. "Sarraj Senior... We turned his background inside-out before I moved in—military intelligence, asked the Israelis.... Nobody had a thing on him. He looks cleaner than clean except for his rep as a salesman—man's a shark. So nothing to do finally but ask. He took me out for a test drive. A Mercedes coupe, my idea of a dreamboat. After he figured he had me softened up, he came in for the kill. I hit him with my badge, then Sonny Boy."

Jon grinned, picturing it. "And?"

"Says he hasn't seen him since he was nineteen and came looking. Turns out he knew where to look, 'cause Sarraj Senior had sent his mom money for years and years to keep him."

"They hit it off? Good reunion?"

Greenley frowned. "Guy was tight on that. If I read Dad right, he thought Sarraj was spoiled—in both senses of the word. Too American. He used the words 'too late' more than once."

"Thought he wouldn't fit in?"

"Exactly. Wrong values—rotten American values. He was polite, but I get the feeling they don't think much of us out there. And even if that could have been fixed—and he's right, nineteen's too late to fix anything—there was his wife. She doesn't know Dad was married before, to Sarraj's hippie mom. And she wouldn't want to know."

Jon squirmed in his seat. He didn't want to feel pity for Sarraj. "But he was his son."

Greenley shrugged. "Guy's got two fine young sons there in Kuwait, right faith, right race, spittin' image of him. Showed me their pictures. He's very proud of them."

"So he didn't need a spoiled American son," Jon said slowly. The reason for Sarraj's rage was coming clearer. "What did he do?"

"Said 'Great to meet you, it's been swell, and could you use some cash for college?' He gave him enough for four years—back in the States."

"Paid him off. Take my money and go, you embarrassment," Jon translated. *What does a young man do when he's rejected on that level?* Rejected by a father whom maybe he's idolized throughout his childhood—ex-fighter pilot, son of the desert? Who turns out to be a car dealer, then kicks him in the teeth? No, in the pride, the heart... The resulting rage had to be enormous.

But what does he do with it?

One kind of man would take it and turn it inward, punish himself. Drugs, drink, failure to thrive. The other kind, Sarraj's kind, Jon was sure, would channel the rage outward.

But at what target? *Demi, babe, watch out, he's poison.* But surely Sarraj wouldn't target a woman? Beautiful women might be a prop he'd use to shore up his wounded ego, but— Jon looked up as the van stopped, to discover they were back at his building. "So now what?"

"So now I pick up some clean underwear, let my wife tell me why I should quit and get a real job like her brother the plumber, kiss my kid and head west." Greenley slumped even lower in his seat. "He gave me one interesting lead. Sarraj wasn't traveling alone when he came to Kuwait. He brought along a friend. Nasty customer, according to Dad. He didn't like this one at all."

"You get a name?"

Greenley nodded. "It was lover boy on the *Aphrodite*. Adam Harkness. Turns out he's Sarraj's foster brother, son of the man in Idaho who took Sarraj in when his mother died.''

Jon sat motionless, considering. "Gives him a pretty harmless reason for dropping in on *Aphrodite,* doesn't it? Visit a boyhood chum?''

"Does, doesn't it? Like I said, butter wouldn't melt.''

"Or we're spinning the conspiracy theory to end all theories.''

"Wouldn't be the first time, believe me.'' Greenley punched Jon on the shoulder, gave Burton his farewell thump. "So...I'm off to Idaho. See what turns up out there with Foster Dad. Preston Harkness. Man's a preacher, according to Sarraj Senior. Christian, but that was all he ever knew—or needed to know.''

The agent stood and slid the door open for Jon, then said, as the driver went around to operate the lift, "Call the usual number if you learn anything. *And*—'' he aimed a finger at his nose "—keep your left up till the bell rings.''

IT MEANT SOMETHING TO ME. Jon's words, for what his word was worth. They'd echoed in her mind for weeks now. Demi walked north along Seventh. It was late in the day. Her nose was addled from overuse and her eyes ached from squinting at her computer screen. She'd finally given in and granted herself a half-hour break from composing. A quick walk to the park, then back.

A bad choice. This was the same route she and Jon and Burton had taken that first day they'd walked together. The day she'd realized Jon was attractive. That she was attracted to him.

And he to her? *It meant something to me,* he'd said of their one sweet night together. She'd have sworn he was speaking the truth.

But then, she'd believed him from the start, and look where that had led her! To find herself gradually sucked in by his charm until she was trapped in the ridiculous position of yearning for a man she wouldn't touch with a barge pole? Missing the laughing companionship of their first days together? Lying in bed each night remembering the touch of his hands, his lips...mourning a future that would never be. *Damn you, Jon Sutter!*

She wasn't sure which hurt the most—missing what she'd thought they might have had, or the humiliation he'd inflicted upon her.

Tricking her into feeling sorry for him, sexually incapacitated as he'd claimed to be! She'd imagined herself his little angel of mercy—seducing him for his own good, graciously granting a poor starving man one night of exquisite pleasure.

And then afterward, feeling so proud of herself. *"You cured me, babe."* When all the while he must have been laughing inside at her—howling! *You are a fool, Demi Cousteau!*

She would not be. She hated people laughing at her, smiling or pitying.

Then don't act like a fool. Forget him. He was nothing but her lab tech, a weak man, clever with words, but with no real strength. She'd had him pegged right from the start. Should have stuck with that assessment.

"It meant something to me."

Liar!

THIRTY MINUTES LATER, breathing hard but feeling better, Demi stepped off the elevator. She was centered again, her thoughts pivoting tightly around her fragrance.

Day by day she was drawing closer to its final form.

Could smell it when she closed her eyes like a half-remembered nightmare—the burning jewel at the heart of a hellish maze. Trial by trial she'd groped toward it, blundered into dead ends, retraced her way, then pushed on.

She was *so* close. At least this she could do right, even if
she—

She stepped into her office and let out a yell. Burton
stood on his stubby hind legs, snuffling at the top drawer
of her desk.

"*You!* You get *out* of here, you stupid mutt!" She chased
him toward the lab. "Go!" Jon's dog, as sneaky as his
owner! The hound's nails scrabbled and slipped on the linoleum like a cartoon dog's in flight. "*Stupid!*" She
stopped in her doorway, hands braced on the jamb to either
side, glaring after him—stamped her foot when he turned
back to give her a goggle-eyed, reproachful "Woof!" from
the safety of the lab. Tears streamed from nowhere. Stupid,
stupid dog, almost as stupid as she was!

"Hey," Jon said mildly.

She gasped and swung to find him poised in the doorway
to the storage room on her left, a box of ingredients in his
lap. "Oh!"

"Don't pick on my dog, Demi." He rolled closer and
looked up.

It was the compassion in his eyes she hated the most.
Who was he to feel sorry for her? "Then tell the stupid
crocodile to stay out of my office! He *knows* he's forbidden
to go in there without permission!"

Jon glanced from her to the hound, who'd retreated until
only his long nose and worried eyes peeked around the far
corner. "What was he doing?"

"Sniffing around my desk." It hit her suddenly, what
he'd been after—the box of truffles in her top drawer! As
blue as she'd been these past few weeks, chocolate was
almost all she was eating. Her cheeks burned.

"I put the last samples on your desk a while ago. Guess
he smells the civet in them?"

"I suppose so," she muttered ungraciously.

"My fault for not keeping an eye on him. I apologize."

She growled something under her breath. She didn't need his apologies. Didn't need anything from him but his work. *Liar.*

"But from now on—" and suddenly she could hear the steel under his mildness "—if you need to yell at someone, Demi, here I am. Don't pick on my dog when you're mad at me."

Don't you tell me what to do! She opened her mouth to say it, saw the look in his eyes and closed her mouth with a snap. Gave a haughty sniff and retreated to her own office. Stalked straight to the far window and stood, staring out at nothing. *Who are you, Jon Sutter?*

One minute he was foolish and weak, the next he was steel. One minute she could despise him, the next she longed—

Forget it. She closed her eyes, leaned her forehead against the glass. *If you need to worry about something, then worry about work.* She stood for a few minutes more, then crossed to her desk and sat, let out a long, slow sigh, swiveled to face her keyboard—then paused.

Opening her top drawer, she flipped the box open and selected a caramel truffle. He'd liked those, she remembered.

She peered around the door into the kitchen to make sure the coast was clear. It was. Walking on tiptoe to the corner, she dropped her apology into Burton's bowl, then retreated as quietly. *Now get to work!*

MUCH LATER SHE LOOKED into the lab. "I have to go out for a few hours, Jon, to meet Kyle. She's in a snit about something."

"Oh?" He glanced up from the heater-stirrer, which was dissolving aromatic crystals into liquid. "What's bothering her?"

He was finally meeting her eyes again, Demi realized.

Though she was the one who'd forbidden it, she'd missed that silent intimacy. More than that, Jon was remembering holding her, loving her, she realized as their gazes locked across the room. She narrowed her eyes, but he didn't flinch. *You're not afraid of me, are you?* That realization ought to have angered her. Instead it cheered her, though she couldn't think why.

"She's upset?" he prodded. "About?"

"That's what I'm going to find out. Now, will you lock up when you leave?" And did he realize that this was one cautious step back on the road to trust? These past two weeks she'd made a point of leaving last. Because left to himself, a crooked employee could have walked off with a few bottles of ingredients worth thousands. *So don't rip me off. You've stolen enough from me already.*

"I could keep working till you come back. I've plenty to do."

She shook her head. "I haven't a clue when I'll be back, or even if. So don't stay past six—that's an order." Just because some sort of wary truce had been declared, was no reason to let him forget who was in charge.

He dipped his head with the faintest hint of his old mockery. "Yeah, boss."

CHAPTER EIGHTEEN

"DO YOU WANT THE GOOD news first—or the bad news?" Kyle said when Demi joined her at a table in the bar.

"Give me the good news. I could use some." Demi reached for a handful of goldfish crackers.

"Good news…" Kyle lifted a finger for a waiter across the crowded room. "Sarraj has contrived, with the help of my connected senior partner plus a *whopping* campaign contribution, to invite the mayor to your launch party—and hizonner and wife have accepted!"

"You're kidding!" Demi bit the tail off a fish.

"No, indeedy. Support city enterprises is the official excuse. The real reason is Sarraj's bucks and a chance to show the mayoral face in an election year."

"I suppose this is good." Demi bit another fish in half.

"Almost guarantees you a mention in the gossip columns."

"Then hooray for us, Kyle." Demi met the approaching waiter's eye, tapped her wineglass, held up two fingers and smiled a "Please?"

"That's what I love, enthusiastic clients! Umm, what else?" Kyle ducked under the table and came up with her briefcase. "Here's your finished flyer, minus the veil, which we printed separately. That will be applied at Sarraj's factory to cover the fragrance sample strip."

Demi sucked in her breath. "Kyle, it's gorgeous!" She'd chosen models to die for, the execution was superb. "What are you worried about? No client could ask for more than this.''

''I know.'' Kyle was never one for false modesty.

''So what's your bad news?''

The art director ran a finger around her glass. ''That's the problem. I don't really have any. But something tells me it's out there somewhere. And that it's wearing hobnail boots. Richard and I almost came to blows about the mailing lists last week. Did he tell you?'' Demi shook her head. ''Well…we're pushing Veil as the most expensive perfume in the world—bragging that it is.''

''Right. With the ingredients I'm using, it will be.''

''Well and good. That's a market niche, and other perfumes have done splendidly taking that route. So who should we be shopping your juice to? Women between thirty and sixty, with incomes of eighty thousand and upward. Doctors, lawyers, stockbrokers, heads of companies or wives of same. Inherited wealth. Roughly the same demographics as Neiman Marcus. This isn't a dimestore fragrance.''

''Hardly!''

''So Richard asked our broker for the following mail lists. Doctors, both male and female, for all fifty states.''

''What's the problem?'' The waiter arrived with their drinks. Demi thanked him and took a sip.

''Cops, both sexes, all fifty states.''

Demi nearly choked. ''*What!* They don't earn—''

''Nearly enough. I tried to tell him that. So did my mail-list consultant. Sarraj wouldn't listen. Said the police were opinion makers. Leaders in the community.''

''Maybe so, but—''

''Wait. It gets better. Richard asked for a mailing list for flight attendants, both sexes.''

''He's out of his mind!''

''I respectfully submitted the same, but he told me he

spends a lot of time flying. That flight attendants gossip nonstop, that they chat with the first-class passengers. He says they'll spread the word all over the country. All over the world.''

"But surely we can reach our target customers more directly?"

"I tried to tell him so. Then he asked for the list for teachers, private and public schools, all grades, all fifty states."

"He doesn't get it, that's what's going on, Kyle. Given the kind of money he invests on behalf of his clients, what do you figure he earns—half a million a year? He's choosing middle-class mailing lists, but he's lost sight of what a middle-class woman has for disposable income. He probably thinks everyone vacations in Bali and drives a Mercedes like he does."

"I find it hard to believe he's that stupid, but I'll tell you one thing, Dem, he's utterly pigheaded. We couldn't budge him. He added one goldplaters' list—I'd say simply to be polite, not because he believed us—and that was that. He told the broker he'd think about it, maybe call her back later and order a few more. But meantime, those are the people who will sniff your sample next week."

"Damn the idiot! Damn, *damn* all macho men who won't take advice!"

"I'll drink to that!" Kyle clinked her glass against Demi's, and grimly they drank.

"He's going to sink my perfume before it's even launched!" Demi said bitterly. "Doesn't he care?"

"Well, that's precisely what I'm wondering."

Demi picked up a fish, snapped it in two, set it aside. "What d'you mean? How could he not? Kyle, Veil will be the kind of perfume that comes along once in a hundred years. It's—"

"You care about that, and I do, but when does Richard make his money, Demi? Up front?"

"I...don't know. You mean—"

Kyle nodded. "If Richard earns his commission from the prince up front...if it doesn't depend on how well your juice sells, then...what does he really care?"

"But he should!"

"Should-shmood! If he's an honest broker, you're absolutely correct. But if he's a cynic, in this to grab the fast buck? Then maybe he's just going through the motions? Humoring us, humoring the prince till the prince's final check clears?"

"Do they have anything chocolate here?"

"Crème de cacao, I suppose. And God, no, I don't want one." Kyle waited until Demi had ordered. They drank in glowering, thoughtful silence for a while. Two men approached from separate directions, looked twice at their faces and swerved aside. "What about the bottles and packaging?" Kyle asked finally. "Did your old hunkems find out who's designing that?"

"Not yet, not by phoning around. But he's going north to Paris late this week. Said he'd be sure to catch the gossip once he got there."

"Oh..." Kyle traced another circle around her glass, stopped when it squealed. "Well. How goes the...situation with Jon Sutter?"

"Why d'you think I'm on chocolate?" Demi refused to meet her eyes.

"You seemed rather tense, last time I stopped by. And he looked miserable."

"Did he?" That was vaguely comforting. As long as she could make him miserable...

Kyle stared dreamily off over the tables. "You know, if you ever decide you don't want him..."

Demi's pulse surged the same way it did when a cab

nearly clipped her, crossing a street. "I thought you were interested in Richard Sarraj?" *Stay away from Jon!*

Kyle shrugged. "I'm rather off Richard. There's something...impenetrable about him, don't you think?"

Demi knew what she meant. "This sort of smooth, polished wall." With something hiding behind it, watching you. Something with red eyes.

"The other day, when he wouldn't listen to me about the mailing lists, I began to think I didn't like him." Kyle grimaced. "Not that I have to like a client to take his money. But Jon, I think you might have something there."

Oh, she did. She did, indeed. But precisely what? *Who are you, Jon Sutter? I know the scent of your skin. Could pick you out of a thousand men in the dark, but I can't say what you are.*

"All I'm saying," Kyle continued stubbornly, "is that a good man is hard to find in this town—any town. So if you don't want him, Cousteau, don't be a dog in the manger."

"Who says I don't?" Wanting was not the problem. Demi picked up their check and rose. "This one's mine."

"COME *ON* TRACE. You wanted me. I'm here, so call me." Jon sat in a phone booth in a bar on Amsterdam Avenue. It was long past happy hour, but tell that to the customers. If they got any happier, he'd have to find someplace quieter to take this call.

He'd waited till seven to give up on Demi, close Alluroma and go home. To find a message on his answering machine saying that the book he'd requested had come in at the public library, he could pick it up anytime. Which was code for "Contact your brother." He'd called his usual number from this safe phone and was now waiting for a callback.

He dug into his wallet and pulled out a card. Kayak Man's business card. He'd assigned himself to look at it

ten times per day. To visualize going down to his marina
and saying, "I'd like to rent a kayak."

"I'd like to rent a k-kayak," he muttered, then let out
an explosive breath. There—that was nine, good enough.
The phone rang and he grabbed it. "Took your own sweet
time!"

"Sorry," said his brother's voice. "Didn't want to call
you ship to shore—too easy for eavesdroppers. We just got
in to the dock."

"Where?"

"Coast Guard station, Norfolk. Back from interdicting
Aphrodite. She left Bermuda last night. Nailed her this
morning."

"And?" But he knew it already. The note of frustration
in Trace's voice came through loud and clear.

"Zip. She was clean as a whistle. The Coasties searched
her down to the keel, took out panels, chopped through a
bulkhead. No drugs anywhere, and the only arms aboard
were a rifle, shotgun, couple of handguns for boat defense.
Fairly standard for a big yacht. High-seas piracy is still an
issue. But they had all their permits and they hid nothing."

Butter wouldn't melt. "And I guess there was nothing
else out of order? No Rembrandts hanging in the main saloon, no bags of gold bullion, or a Stinger missile tucked
under a berth? Not even a smidgen of bomb-grade pluto-
nium?"

"Nothing but an attitude, and considering we stormed
aboard with guns at the ready and tossed hell out of their
boat, that's understandable."

"So…" Jon leaned back in the booth. "Are we wasting
our time here, bro?" *Can I go back to my own life?* Think
about making a new one? Confess to Demi and find out if
she'd ever forgive him?

"I…don't think we are."

Jon punched the side of the phone booth, then swore

silently and shook out his hand. "There's nothing *here,* Trace! You've got nada!"

"Don't I know it. But now I've met lover boy—Adam Harkness. I was wearing a Coasties uniform and standing well back, but I got a good look."

"And?"

"You know that smell you get just before lightning strikes—ozone?"

"What's he like?"

"Late thirties," Trace said slowly. "Big, smooth and smart-ass. Robert Redford with a hard edge. You can see he'd impress the women. But there's something behind the eyes.... He smiles a lot—too much. And I don't think you and I would see the joke his way, if we could see it at all."

"You've got nothing there but heebie-jeebies."

"Yep, and I've never had 'em half this bad before. They're winning every round—and I don't even know what the game is."

"You're tired."

"I am. And due to be tireder. I'm off to Helsinki. They found deliveryman number two—he hopped a boat to Finland with false papers. They're holding him for us for a few days before they lob him back."

"He say what was in the box?" Please God it was something harmless, laundry or smuggled caviar. Jon was tired, too. Tired of lies, tired of sneaking.

"So far, he's not talking. We'll see if I can prod his memory."

"Not literally, I hope."

"Nope, just a gentle reminder that we aren't the only ones looking for him. That if he doesn't want to play soft-ball with us, we can always send him back to the hardball boys who beanballed his partner."

"Okay, okay, I'm sorry I asked." It was too late to be

tenderhearted about a Russian Mafia flunkie. "Go back to the *Aphrodite.* What now?"

"Over to you, pal. She should be steaming into New York Harbor tomorrow round midnight."

Something wicked this way comes. "And then?"

"Customs takes her apart again when she clears. But I don't think they'll find anything we didn't."

"And you didn't find a Saudi prince aboard?"

"Not so you'd notice," Trace said dryly.

"He's hosting the perfume's launch party aboard that yacht in eleven days, Trace. Or so Sarraj claims."

"Could be flying in from anywhere, I suppose. Or it's all a fairy tale."

That's what he kept thinking. Of course, some fairy tales, in their original forms, would make your hair stand on end. They talked for a few minutes more, about Jon's progress in walking, news from home—their mother was demanding that Trace produce Jon or she'd know the reason why. "I keep telling her you can take care of yourself. That you're not the softy she thinks you are."

"And thanks to you both."

"She said I produce you by the Fourth—" the Suttons' annual family reunion in Vermont "—or I'm dogmeat."

Demi... For just a moment Jon could see her there, seated between him and his mother at the picnic table under the apple tree, laughing at one of his father's elaborate shaggy-dog stories, Jodi quietly appraising her, Emily bouncing in her seat to top Dad's punch line with one of her own, Burton out on the lawn making up to Emily's ancient, belligerent tomcat. If he could turn that vision into reality...lie with Demi in his narrow bed up in the attic through a long Vermont summer's night...wake with her at dawn to the sound of the mockingbirds...

"Earth to Jon. Come in, Jon."

"Uh—yeah. Where were we?"

"We were saying you report to Greenley for the next few days."

"A few more days of this is all I can take."

"Agreed, but I don't think you have to worry. Whatever this is, it's got momentum—we're moving toward something. Which means you'll have to promise to keep your eyes open and your guard up till I get back."

"Consider it promised." Jon drew a breath. "And you be careful, too."

"Always. Anything else?"

"Umm. Any more word on your heiress?"

"According to Harkness, she's off on some spiritual retreat. Said he wasn't sure where. From the way he smiled, I'd take odds he dropped her over the side himself."

Goose bumps roughened Jon's arms. Cold here, in this bar. "And the man himself—what is he when he's not playing gigolo to unfortunate rich ladies?"

"He was a doctor, a surgeon in an Idaho community hospital till he resigned last year."

"For?"

"Rumors that were never proved, charges that were suddenly dropped. But now I've seen him, I'm a believer. One rape of an anesthetized patient...and one mercy killing. The geezer who died willed his ranch to Harkness."

Demi, Demi, oh, Demi-babe! And she thought *he* was a crook? He should snatch her up and haul her off to Vermont tonight. With business partners like that... "Nice guys."

"Guys best left to the pros, Jon. You keep that in mind—you're my eyes and my ears in this, no more than that. When and if it comes to rough stuff, we'll send in the muscle."

"You hear me complaining?"

DEMI SLIT OPEN A LETTER, an invoice, and set it aside, paused, staring at a patch of morning sunlight on her office wall. *I want him.* She'd practically told Kyle as much yesterday.

I want a thief? Not even a big, bold thief, a bank robber, say, or a pirate, but someone who'd diddled papers to make pennies? This was the man she'd set against her grandfather—a man tough and capable enough to start out in the slums of Marseilles, then go on to wrest a fine living from life? A man with whom you could walk down the darkest alley in the world and feel safe? *And I want Jon?*

She wanted the man who'd held her through that long, lovely night. His strong arms, his laughter, his tenderness. That man had not been a little man, not in any way. What she'd felt for him that night had not been little. She'd had men before, but none had touched her like that. She couldn't say why that was so, but neither could she forget.

Forget him or have him, but please, please, stop this dithering! Kyle would steal him away and it would serve her right if she didn't do something soon. Demi chose another letter from the pile she'd collected from Alluroma's mailbox in the lobby, slit it open, smiled to herself as she heard the outer door open. "You're la-ate!"

"Yes." Preceded by a tail-waving Burton, Jon wheeled into the room. "We cut through the park and I stopped to pick these." He rolled closer and presented a small bouquet.

Violets, both white and lilac, tiny, exquisite. She brought the flowers to her nose. They smelled like…happiness. "Thank you." She met his eyes and felt as if she were falling upward into blue sky, with kite of joyous gold. *Whoever you are, it's you I want!*

Burton reared up to nudge the white bag on her desktop.

Demi laughed. "He smells our *palmiers.*" She'd brought them all pastry this morning for the first time in a long time. *Let us start again from today.* "Why don't you put water on for coffee while I finish this?"

"Deal." He gave her a last lingering look, took the bag and rolled into the kitchen, Burton in anxious attendance.

Demi picked up a letter. Her smile faded to puzzlement as she read its handwritten return address. David Haley...Haley...oh—*Davie*—one of Hector Domingo's ex-lovers and his best friend, a dancer on Broadway. He'd been off on a road show for months. She winced at the stab of guilt. She'd been meaning to track Davie down, ask if he'd heard from Hector and what in heaven had ever happened? But the past month had been so frantic. She had no address to reach Hector directly. All she knew was that his widowed mother and sisters lived on one of the smaller islands in the Philippines.

"So how was Kyle?" Jon called from the kitchen.

"Mmm, just fine." Demi slit open the manila envelope and a smaller letter dropped out, one addressed to her in Hector's familiar curlicues. Stuck to its front was a note, which said, "Hector asked me to send this on to you. Best, David." Quickly she slit this envelope, pulled out two pages.

"What did she have to say? You said she was upset?"

"Oh, she's a bit worried about the direct-mail campaign." She would ask Jon what he thought about the mailing lists. "But she had good news, too. The mayor's coming to our launch party." She jumped as something crashed to the floor in the kitchen. "Jon? *Jon*, are you—"

"Fine! I'm fine. Just dropped the teakettle, scared Burton within an inch of his life, that's all. The mayor? Of New York? What the hell has he got to do with perfume?"

"Not a thing, but we're going for publicity. All we can get. I'd ask the President if I thought he'd come." She unfolded the first page and read.

Demi, Demi, Demi, oh, Demi, I miss you! Kisses and *big* hugs!

I am utterly miserable and I want to come home! I
hate it here! I am no longer a Filipino, not really. I'm
a New Yorker. I miss you and I miss my friends, and
there is no decent work to be had here. They warned
me not to contact you, the men with the shiny black
shoes and the bad suits. They said you were in trouble,
too, but that only makes me worry harder. If I have
brought you trouble, I swear I will kill myself....

The blood was slamming in her ears. She skimmed faster
and faster, reached the end and started again. Hector
thanked her for sending him his paychecks while he was
in exile. As soon as he'd straightened this mess out, he'd
be back to slave night and day for her to pay her back....

She had sent him no paychecks. But then, who in the
world had?

"Publicity, yeah, that's great. Whose idea was that—
Kyle's or Sarraj's?" Jon appeared in the doorway.

"Mmm?" Men in shiny black shoes, who'd found something wrong with Hector's papers... Hauled him out of the
country overnight... Warned him not to contact her, that
she was in trouble, too. From whom? No one from Immigration had come calling, and even if they had, she'd done
nothing wrong—at least she didn't think she had.

"Demi? What's wrong?"

Something, somewhere, was dreadfully wrong. Bad news
in hobnailed boots, Kyle had called it, stomping around out
there somewhere. Stomping closer. *And it smells like a rat!*
She focused on Jon's alert face. Ask Jon, he'd know what
to—

Jon. If things were not making sense, Jon made the least
sense of all. A man who seemed forceful one minute, foolish and weak the next?

"Demi?"

A man who looked at her with honesty in his eyes—and swore he'd stolen?

"Hey!"

A man with obvious ability, the best of brains, had come seeking a dead-end job? She met his gaze as he wheeled closer—looked away. He could read her eyes as well as she read his. Her gaze settled on his hands. Hands as strong as she could have wished, hands that had made her body his own in just one sweet night.... "I... It's just this letter. From an old friend. Her lover died." Why had she said that? "Unexpectedly. I'll have to send her a card. In fact—" She folded Hector's letter, snatched up its envelope, stuffed them both in her purse. "I think I'll go do that this minute."

"Demi, stop!" he called as she fled out the door. "Hey, will you—"

She pretended not to hear; she had to think. Hector vanishing like a rabbit stuffed down a hat, Sarraj descending like a dark angel, and then Jon rolling into her life—who had sent her Jon? Coincidence, all this coming and going? Or...*what?*

SHE WANTED SOMEONE capable, hardheaded and very wise to listen to her worries, then advise her. Tell her this was all nonsense. And call her sexist, but Kyle or her mother wouldn't do. Demi wanted a man.

She could think of three who fit her needs, but the one who loved her best had taken her grandmother and vanished someplace between Paris and Grasse, Demi found when she phoned and phoned again over the next few days. Off on one of their little adventures, no doubt. Her grandfather went walkabout at the drop of a hat in his old Ferrari, and where he went her grandmother followed, happy to do so. They'd surface in a few days in Paris as promised, but till then there was no finding him. He wasn't a man for itineraries and answering machines.

Lacking her grandfather, she could have asked Reese Durand for advice, and it would have been the very best. But Demi had received an announcement of the birth of his and Nicola's daughter only last week. She no longer carried a torch for Reese—it felt funny to remember that she ever had—but still, Demi envied them their happiness. And her pride wouldn't allow her to admit that she'd yet to achieve her own. That she had man troubles—again.

Cancel Reese and that left only one person to whom she instinctively turned. And he was the last person she could ask. *Why are you here, Jon? Is your coming now just a coincidence? Or if not, who sent you?* Sarraj, to be his eyes inside Alluroma?

But why? And why would Sarraj send a man he seemed to hate?

And if not Sarraj, then who? The men in shiny black shoes who'd whisked Hector away? Immigration, perhaps?

Or maybe Hector had imagined it all? He'd always had a wonderful, if dark, imagination. Had been entranced by conspiracy theories, treating them as the most delicious sort of gossip. Perhaps his papers *had* been out of order and he'd been legitimately deported. His "paychecks" could simply be previously withheld income now being refunded to him by the IRS. And all else was smoke and mirrors and wild speculation.

Watch and wait for her grandfather, Demi decided finally. And meantime, however troubled her heart might be, her nose had work to do. She had a perfume to perfect, a staggeringly wonderful perfume, and only three days left in which to do it.

And once that was done, she would see what remained.

CHAPTER NINETEEN

"WHY ARE WE GOING this way?" Jon asked the next night as the special van turned downtown instead of up. Too tired and depressed to practice his walking, he'd called for a ride instead. He'd offered to drop Demi off, but she'd turned him down, said she had other plans.

What happened? He hadn't a clue, knew only that after that brief flicker of warmth yesterday, she'd turned back to ice. When she'd returned from sending her condolence card, they were boss and lab tech again, no more to each other than that.

"Got another passenger to pick up," the driver said, responding to the question he'd forgotten already.

The passenger was Greenley. He hopped in as the van stopped for a light in the Thirties, said something to the driver, then moved back by Jon. "When did you get back?" The agent looked as tired and surly as he felt.

"Five this morning. Caught the red-eye."

"They give you my message?" Jon had thought Demi's news about the mayor important enough to pass on in a lunchtime call.

"Yep. What'd I tell you? That's the game plan. A happy boatload of Beautiful People, with the mayor of New York taking top billing—then *kerblam!* Everything else is just window dressing, an excuse for the party."

Demi, pushing herself past exhaustion to create a masterpiece? She wouldn't see it that way. "A bomb on the boat, you think?"

Greenley shrugged. "Maybe, though I helped search *Aphrodite* this morning soon as I got in and we found squat. That was a new one, pretending to be a Customs agent. But they've got—what—eight days left to pack her full of explosives and wire 'em up?

"Or if they're planning a hostage situation instead of a boom-and-barbecue, they could be even more low-key. How many guns d'you figure it takes to keep a pack of models, cosmetics reporters and a politico in line? Two or three? Well, no, we've got caterers, too. You don't mess with caterers—all those chef's knives. Better say four guns. Bring in a few Uzis and ski masks to please the TV cameras, and hey, you've got yourself a five-star media jamboree."

"But you're not going to let it happen. Are you?" Jon added doubtfully as Greenley's smile spread, as cynical as it was weary.

"We've about run out of legal excuses to bother 'em, haven't we? From now on, we watch from a respectful distance unless and until we've got something to go on. Any bright ideas will be entirely welcome."

Dammit, you guys are supposed to be the professionals! He didn't say it. Greenley looked as if he'd welcome a fight. Jon glanced out the window as the van began to climb. They were zooming up the approach to the Brooklyn Bridge. "What the—"

"Look out there." Greenley pointed south, to the wide blue expanse of New York harbor. "The big white one, way out past the Statue of Liberty. To the left of her. See it?"

"*Aphrodite?*"

"Goddess of love, and she's a honey. Aluminum, one hundred-forty feet, displaces two hundred tons. Twin diesels, each near the size of a Cadillac. Engine room big as my whole apartment."

Jon stared a moment more at the yacht before it vanished beyond a pylon. "Anchored out instead of coming in to a dock. Like their privacy, don't they?" A mile or more from Brooklyn or Manhattan, she wouldn't be easy to watch. Not with all the shipping out there, coming and going up the East and Hudson rivers, small boats as well as large. "How many crew?"

"Five, counting Harkness."

They circled back to Manhattan, then headed uptown though the post-rush-hour traffic. "Learn anything out west?" Jon asked finally. "What's Harkness's father like?" Sarraj's foster father.

Greenley shrugged. "Couldn't get to him. Guy owns a few thousand acres of mountaintop, and his followers own more adjoining. Guards and dogs at the gate, and he wasn't coming out for a chat without a warrant."

"Followers. You said the man was a preacher?"

"Church of Hug a Tree, Carry a Gun, Spit in the Government's Eye, far as I could tell. S'pose you could call it Christian. But love your neighbor seems to come pretty far down the list, according to his, who don't much like him. But they won't say so above a whisper."

"He scares the locals?"

"Hey, come the Apocalypse, he's told them they'll either be sitting on his right hand or on his left."

The nerve in his jaw trembled and woke. "Preston Harkness is predicting the end of the world?"

Greenley chortled. "For the seventh summer in a row! The faithful all gather on his mountain for a month of praying and feasting—and wife-swapping, so the neighbors claim. Not a bad way to end things."

"Or a bad way to recruit," Jon said wryly. "I take it his congregation is growing?"

"Four hundred last summer. The sheriff makes it four hundred and seventy-four this year. They have to drive up through his town to reach the ranch, so he tries to keep a tally."

Jon drew a breath; they had only blocks to go. "Any of them Arab?"

Greenley shook his head. "Few Native Americans, few blacks—most of those Harkness's ex-buddies from Nam. Some Greenpeace types, lots of aging flower children. Sarraj is as close to an Arab as the sheriff could think of, and his dad in Kuwait would be the first to tell you that's not close enough."

"Vietnam? Harkness was there?" When Greenley nodded, Jon added, "As a chaplain?"

The agent showed his teeth as the van pulled into the curb and stopped. "Colonel. A Green Beret. Four tours in the bush, which must mean he liked it. And two things we maybe all should consider. He had a wicked rep for practical jokes. And, like most guys over there, he had a nickname." He paused while Jon descended to street level.

Jon waited for it. He wouldn't ask. Hell, he'd have to, the van was pulling away. "Okay, already—what?"

"They called him... *Prince!*" Greenley tipped back his head and, laughing, slammed the door shut. Waved goodbye.

There was nothing around to punch unless he wanted to tackle the beveled glass on the co-op's front door. Swearing, Jon rolled to the end of the block and back. How much taxpayers' money? How many men tied up, Trace flying east, Greenley west? Hector Domingo hurled off to the Philippines. His own life disrupted—and Demi! What had this farce done to Demi and him, what they might have had? Lies between lovers could be irreparable. He'd told her so many lies. And for what? Scrambling to keep up with Preston Harkness's idea of a joke?

Prince Harkness. People were given nicknames for a reason. His soldiers could have called him Presley, as in Elvis, but Prince was the name that had stuck. Why? *You're a prince of a guy, Harkness, running the FBI in circles! Running me. Running my lady.* Prince Harkness, Prince Harkness, there was something there. It made his brains itch.

Forget it. To hell with you, you crazy bastard! Jon leaned down to rub Burton's ears—and it came. *Prince of Darkness.* He shuddered violently and the dog looked up at him wide-eyed, the hair lifting along his spine. "A joke, Burton." A stupid joke.

But the joke was on whom?

"THERE SHE IS, *Aphrodite*." Swinging his coupe into a scenic overlook in Brooklyn, Sarraj nodded at the pale shape riding far out near the Statue of Liberty. "Our ship has come in at last. I thought you'd like to see her."

"Yes," Demi said politely. She'd spent a frustrating two hours over dinner arguing with Richard. Kyle was right, the man was impenetrable. Neither her charm nor her carefully reasoned arguments had pierced his smug satisfaction. Richard was perfectly happy with his choice of mailing lists; she was not to worry her pretty head. Fragrance was her area of expertise, after all, not marketing. Her nails dug into her palms. *Sexist pig!* She was coming to detest the man.

She'd asked again for the name of the designer who was creating Veil's bottles and packaging. Richard had told her to wait and see, that it was a surprise, but she'd be delighted with the results.

She'd warned him that the bottles must be delivered to her bulk mixer in Brooklyn within a week at the latest. They were about to create an enormous, nationwide demand for her perfume. Once the samples were mailed, there'd be no turning back. it would be only a matter of days before the first orders for Seventh Veil hit the 1-800 sales number he'd arranged.

If they could not meet demand with sufficient product, delivered promptly, his venture would crash. Demand for Veil would falter and die as word got around that it wasn't available. And buyers would never give them a second chance if they couldn't deliver on the first. She'd tried to tell him that, and he'd simply smiled and told her that all was in hand, it wouldn't be a problem.

No problem? She felt the problems in her *bones*. Felt as if she were riding a train, hurtling down a mountain with no brakes. Faster and faster, but bound for where?

Maybe Kyle was wrong. Maybe Richard did care that Veil was a success, but he was in over his head and too stupidly macho to admit it. Maybe he was simply a handsome, suave incompetent, assuring her, assuring Kyle and his prince that he had all in hand when he hadn't a clue? *Jon, what would Jon say?* She didn't dare ask him till she knew who and what he was. Where he fit into this puzzle.

If a puzzle even exists!

Perhaps this terror was simply her exhaustion talking, making small problems loom enormous. She meant to go back to Alluroma and work tonight. She was so close, so close.... *If I had another week, maybe two.* There was something not quite right in the soul note.

"How d'you get out to the boat?" she asked casually. If somehow she could get word to his prince? Was he really as bound and determined that the perfume be launched on his birthday as Richard swore he was? If she could make the prince see that a few more weeks would make all the difference in the world? Might make the difference between a great perfume and an unforgettable one?

"The yacht has its own tender, of course. It meets me at a marina over there." He nodded at the Manhattan shore.

"We have more than two hundred people invited to the launch party. You'll ferry them all out *there* in a little-bitty boat?" Incompetence, that had to be the answer. He wasn't picturing women in evening dress and heels, their hair mussed by a damp boat ride. The men would like it, she supposed, but the women?

Richard patted her hand. "Stop *worrying*, Demi! We'll come in to a dock for the party, allow everyone to board, then cruise from there. I promise you, everything is well in hand."

AN HOUR LATER, JON'S sense of humor had not improved. He sat in a phone booth in the lobby of a movie theater, the closest safe phone he'd been able to find at short notice. He'd come home to a coded message on his answering machine to contact Greenley. The message had been recorded not five minutes before he'd unlocked his door.

He jumped as the phone rang only inches from his ear, snatched it up. "Yeah?" He'd had enough of Greenley for one day.

"When you quit that perfume job, Sutton, can I have it?" The agent sounded in no better mood than he. "We let you off, turned the corner, and my friggin' beeper goes off. And it only beeps for bad news, which means you've got some, too. I'm out the door in twenty minutes, so listen up, 'cause I'm saying this precisely once."

The agent was flying west again, along with every other man and woman who could be spared from his station. Agents all over the country were headed west. Because yesterday, someone driving a rental van had purchased a fifty-five-gallon drum of a certain kind of fertilizer from a farmers' co-op in North Dakota. The name the buyer had given was fictitious, and his face had been Arabic, the salesman thought—though he might have been Hispanic.

"You're scrambling for that?" Jon protested. "A farmer with a suntan buys *one*—"

"Shuddup and listen! Two states away in Colorado, at *exactly* the same time, another guy, same sort of ethnic type, same sort of van, using a false name, buys fifty-five gallons of another fertilizer. You put those particular components together, you've got a bomb. A truck bomb that'll take out a skyscraper, Jon, no problem. Remember Oklahoma City?''

"Coincidence."

"That's what we're all praying. But today, not four hours ago, somebody knocked over a storage shed at a quarry in Utah. Stole two boxes of blasting caps and enough explosives to take out the Hoover Dam.

"And consider this, Mr. Show-Me. A guy came looking for work at that quarry yesterday. Casing the job out, we figure. The quarry boss says he looked Middle Eastern. Now put all that together and tell me it's coincidence!''

Jon was silent. The feds were right. One and one frequently made something besides two. But one plus one plus one? "So you think the three of them are converging somewhere out there?''

"Exactly. And where they intersect, something very, very ugly is gonna go down if we don't catch them before they put it together.'' The agent blew out a heavy breath. "So we will. Damned if we'll let 'em get away with it.''

"Good for you. But—'' Jon felt like a whiner for asking. "But what about the situation here?'' He knew even before Greenley spoke.

"You, pal, just achieved back-burner status. Our station chief has been following this investigation all along, and he's aware of the schedule. We've got—what—nine days left till party day? No sweat.''

Easy for you to say! It's not your woman.

"Meantime, your job is to keep your eyes open and call your usual number if anything changes. We'll roll up these truck nuts out west in a day or two. The kind of manpower we're throwing into this one, we'll find them sometime tomorrow, is my guess. Soon as the heat's off, I'll be back to hold your hand.''

"And if you aren't?"

"I will be, Jon, I promise. At the very latest I'll be back three days before D day. And meanwhile, the Coasties are watching the boat for us."

A divided command, divided decision-making. "I don't like it."

"Nobody asked you to. Don't like it myself. But just sit tight and be cool. We've got time."

"You might as well know one thing now, Greenley. I'm not cool enough to let Demi go out to that boat. And not her friend Kyle, either. That's nonnegotiable. So when you make your party plans, figure that in."

Greenley said nothing for almost a minute, then, "I didn't know you were calling the shots, dude. I'm not very fond of amateur hour, and believe me, our chief is less so. And Trace would tell you the same if he were here."

"But he's not."

Greenley made a sound something between a groan and a snarl. "Look. We've got nine days left to straighten this out. Till I get back, will you promise me you'll sit tight? Won't say anything to Cousteau to warn her? She's still on our suspect list even if you've got the hots for her."

"I can't promise that." Anything could happen in the next few days.

Greenley let out a long, long sigh. "Then I've got one more call to make when we're done here. I'll tell the agent in charge to pick you up for your own good—at Alluroma tomorrow if you dodge 'em tonight. They'll trump up some charge that'll hold you till Trace comes back to bail you out. You're no use to us if you're thinking with your—"

Jon hung up—it was that or smash the receiver through a pane of the phone booth. Greenley had him. He couldn't protect her from a jail cell. And his chances of convincing

Demi of her danger tonight, when he'd already lost her trust, and without a scrap of proof to show her—

The phone rang under his hand. He lifted it and banged it savagely down on Greenley's protest. *Think.* He could snatch her out of town tonight, though he'd probably have to use force to do it. The woman had a perfume to complete. But if he did that, not only would she never forgive him, but he'd have torpedoed Trace's investigation.

Which meant Trace would end up with a black mark against his name for recruiting a loose-cannon brother.

And Sarraj would be warned. Would no longer suspect, but would *know* he was being watched. Whatever his plan had been, he'd lie low for now—then try it again later. Because the hatred in Sarraj's eyes wasn't going anywhere. In the end it would find its target.

You nail him now, this time—or maybe you read about it in the papers later and know you might have stopped it. If anyone was hurt, the hurt would be on his— The phone rang again. Jon brought it slowly to his ear.

"I've got two minutes left to talk," Greenley said in a voice like dry ice. "*So*...yes or no? You promise me you'll play it my way—or we go the route described above. Don't make me do it, Jon, 'cause I will. And Trace will thank me."

"Okay." His word was barely more than a whisper.

"Say it all."

"I...won't tell her anything till you get back. That's a promise—but I'll have yours in return. That you or Trace will be here, at the *latest*, two days before the launch party."

"You've got yourself a deal." The faintest thread of warmth had crept back into Greenley's voice.

"Thanks." Jon let out the breath he hadn't realized he was holding. "And...good luck out west." They'd need it. He'd seen the west before; it stretched halfway to forever.

Three angry men in three trucks, hell-bent on destruction, would be like three scorpions hiding on a football field. It would take a miracle to find them in time.

JON MADE A POINT OF arriving on time the next morning. But Demi had been there for hours, he concluded, noting the empty mug on her desk and three more in the kitchen sink. "Demi?" He rolled through to the lab and saw the note waiting for him at his work station.

> Jon, I made a marvelous breakthrough last night! Mix these two formulas for me and see what you think. I've gone out for breakfast. See you shortly, D.

At least she hadn't signed it "Boss." Grimly he stood, pushed his chair over to the stool waiting by his chin-up bar, then walked the stool back to the counter. Sat and massaged his knee. If nothing else in life was improving, his legs were.

She returned just as he was finishing the second formula. Burton pricked his ears, lumbered toward the door, then broke into a gallop as she called, "I'm back!"

Lucky dog. There was nothing stopping *him* from rushing off to lick her hands. Jon sighed, picked up the two scent strips and followed at a pace befitting a mere lab tech.

She sat slumped over her desk, head pillowed on her folded arms, apparently unaware that Burton stood with his whiskery chin resting on her thigh. "Demi?"

Without raising her head, she opened her dark eyes and smiled at him. "G'morning."

"Are you all right?" He rolled as close as he dared, nudged Burton aside. She looked like a drowsy child. He longed to take her in his arms, pull her into his lap.

"Mmm, fine. Just haven't slept much lately." Her lashes drifted down.

"When did you come in?" His fingers curled, echoing the shape of her head. To rest his palm there, smooth her silky hair...

"Five. But I was here till...one last night. That's why I'm so..." She yawned hugely, blindly, and smiled. "Was worth it, though—least I think it was. You tell me. Have you smelled it yet?"

"Not yet." *My crazy love. Raving perfectionist.* Sarraj demanded the final formula tomorrow and she was zagging again?

"It's been too black..." she murmured, eyes closed. "Too...angry. I started it when..." Her voice trailed away and she sighed. "Anyway, I've gone beyond that now. Kept the anger, but then it unfolds to... Least I think it will."

"Here it is." He held the first *mouillette* an inch from her nose. She inhaled, held her breath, then sighed it out again. She'd sighed that way on waking, after the second time they'd come together. Lying atop him, her breath had ruffled his hair. He'd cupped his hands to her head and held her pressed against him. Had sworn to himself that he'd never let her go.

Damned stupid fool! If he'd kept to that, hadn't allowed life to intrude, to slice them apart the next morning... *We're going back to that. Somehow, some way, I swear it, babe.* They just had to survive the next few days, then he'd find some way to reach her. Find with her again what they'd shared that night.

"Close, close, *so* close," she murmured. "Now the other one?" He held the other scent strip to her nose. "*That's* it." She nuzzled past the strip of cardboard till her nose touched his hand. "That's the one!"

He sat unmoving, could have sat that way a thousand years or so, with her breath cupped in his fingers. *Oh, Demi, what you do to me!*

"Just needs a little...more frankincense. Let's up it to .07, try it again." She smiled, her breathing deepened and, just like that, she was asleep.

Are you smelling me in your dreams, along with your wonder scent? Leaving his hand at her face, Jon reached with the other, caught a strand of black silk that had spilled down her cheek, tucked it behind her ear. She'd gone wild that night when he'd nibbled her earlobe. His hand hovered over her head....

"Don't," she said without opening her eyes. One word like a door slamming shut.

He clasped his hands guiltily in his lap. "Don't what?"

She gave a haughty sniff and didn't answer. He wondered if that was good or bad? Was damned if he'd move away from her till she made him.

"I bought you something," she murmured finally, the flicker of temper gone as if he'd imagined it. "In the box there."

He noticed for the first time the large white box on her desk. "What is it?"

"Tuxedo. A proper one this time. And don't you dare slit the trousers. I bought you a pair of black sweatpants, too, in case the trousers won't fit over your casts."

So she hadn't noticed. He'd been wearing his extra-baggy pants since his casts came off, and she'd hardly been ogling his body since then. "Thanks."

"Thank Sarraj. I billed them to him. We have to look top-drawer for the launch party. It's part of the show."

"I'm invited?" He'd wondered about that.

"Of course you are. You and me, we're the miracle workers."

"And Sarraj didn't mind?"

"Not at all. He seemed really anxious to have you there."

"Nice of him." So Greenley was right, launch-party

night was *the* night. If Sarraj wanted him aboard, it wasn't to pat him on the back. *We'll see who laughs last, you suave bastard! You better believe I'll be there.*

She'd fallen asleep again while he thought. Jon touched her hair and suddenly didn't give a damn if she yelled at him. He smoothed his hand down through the warm silk, tracing the fragile curve of her skull, clasped his fingers around the nape of her neck. *Oh, Demi.* Muscles stretched tight. Her eyes were wide open, he realized. She looked up at him like a fawn about to bolt. "Go home. You're exhausted."

"Can't. I've got so much to do."

She was half killing herself, and Sarraj didn't give a damn. "Isn't it good enough as it stands?" Sarraj probably found her efforts to reach perfection hilarious, considering that her fragrance was nothing but a prop for his show. *One more thing I owe him, using her like this.*

Demi sat up and swept her hair back, throwing off his hand. "There's good enough and then there's perfect," she said coldly. "At Alluroma..." She swung to her keyboard, hit a key and a formula filled the screen. She typed in two alterations, then hit the Print key. "Mix it for me again, like this."

she'd put him on the back of it, and any longer, he'd
never get well. The heavy delivery I don't know ...

The J Falling asleep again while he in ... on another
one another and suddenly of his ... were warm at the ...
over. The sound of his ... he was ... even at the the
hearing, but if you ... it, but ... his mind that ...
hearing. It came ... to ... On these gentle, smooth ...

CHAPTER TWENTY

THEY WORKED ALL THROUGH that day and on into the night
as, trial by trial, the perfume moved toward perfection, veils
dropping one by one to reveal the smoldering heart of the
fragrance. Demi's world had narrowed to one sense, the
sense of smell. And a pair of hands—Jon's hands—to do
her bidding.

Jon worked and watched with awe, frustration, admira-
tion. His crazy lover, making something wonderful for
someone who didn't give a damn about wonders. Whatever
Sarraj was planning, it wasn't a coup in the fragrance industry. *But when this is all over, babe, you'll have made
yourself a miracle!* Even his untutored nose could tell that
Demi was right; this was a perfume that would live a hundred years or more.

Which meant there was no reason to kill herself now.
Once Sarraj was out of the picture, she'd have all the time
she needed to tweak it to perfection. *We should give him
whatever he wants and let him go.* The sooner Sarraj was
out of their lives, the sooner they could move on to what
really mattered.

Finally at midnight Jon declared a strike. They had until
three the following afternoon, when Sarraj was coming to
pick up the finished formula. "That isn't enough time!"
Demi wailed, but he towed her out of Alluroma and down
to a waiting cab.

Once she was gone, he hailed a second cab. Now that
he could stand, there was no need for the special van with

its lift. He folded his wheelchair, dropped it in the trunk, and he and Burton called it a day.

The next morning brought more of the same. Jon came in at 8:00 a.m., Demi had been there since 6:00. They had seven hours till Sarraj's deadline.

At 1:00 p.m. Jon completed a variation that made her laugh aloud with delight, hug herself and spin on her high heels. "That's it?" he asked hopefully. "You're satisfied?"

"Not quite—but it's *so* close!"

Why worry about protecting her from Sarraj? At this rate, he might strangle her himself!

"But go ahead and add the alcohol to this trial to turn it into a finished perfume. I want to wear this version and—wait!" She pulled her purse from her desk, rummaged through it, pulled out a tiny gold device. "Would you rinse this out with alcohol and fill it for me? I want to wear this one, think about it." She handed him a palm-size perfume atomizer.

At 1:30 p.m. they ran out of coffee. Since that was the fuel they were running on, this would never do. Jon and Burton rushed out to buy a pound, fresh ground at the deli. And when Jon wheeled back again, he rolled straight into an argument.

"*Please,* Richard, just one more week!" Demi's voice, passionate with conviction, shaking with strain, carried easily into the reception room. "It will be twice as good as it is now if you give me that!"

Jon grabbed Burton's scruff, halting his lunge toward the action.

"Demi, my sweet, it's perfection already. I'm more than satisfied." Sarraj's voice—suave, smug, secretly laughing. Jon clenched his teeth.

"But I am not. And since it's my name that'll be attached to this fragrance..."

"I'm sorry, but you've done everything we paid you to do and more. This is good enough."

Might as well wave a red flag at a bull! Jon wheeled hastily toward her office as Demi's voice rose half an octave—reminding him that her mother could hit E above her high C.

"Good enough? When has good enough ever been good enough? *Pah!* Richard, *smell* this. I'm halfway to heaven! You'd deny me the other half?"

Jon paused in the doorway. Holding the hand she must have thrust at him, Sarraj dipped his head obediently to smell. Jon took a grip on his wheels. *Get your nose off her or I'll—*

"You're there already. You were there from the start— the very first time I ever saw you. This will *do*, Demi." Sarraj jumped as Burton dropped his snout to the man's shoes and sneezed. His eyes lifted and swung deliberately to Jon, and still he held on to her. "Tell her," he said evenly. "It's quite wonderful, isn't it?"

He couldn't deny her achievement, even though Sarraj was using him against her. "It's magnificent."

"Good enough for the American public, wouldn't you say?"

As opposed to what? The Arab world? Or was Sarraj's world even narrower? *Whom do you not hold in contempt?* "It's good enough."

"Jon!"

"You've worked hard enough, boss. Let him have it. The customer's always right, right?" *Babe, let him go.*

She gave him a dark-eyed, murderous glare, and turned back to Sarraj. "Your appointment wasn't until three. It's only two. At least give me that hour."

Slowly Sarraj shook his head. Perhaps he would have backed down, with Demi alone. But with another man watching? "I'm sorry. But it was more convenient for me to stop by now. I want to deliver this to your mixer as soon as possible. He's promised he'll lay on another shift, mix the fragrance gel for us tonight so that my company can create the scent strips tomorrow. The day after that we mail out the flyers. We're on the tightest of schedules.''

"Then we won't keep you." Jon rolled past them to Demi's desk. He pecked out a command on her keyboard that brought up her latest formula. "This is your last version, boss?"

She was speechless with rage. But she nodded.

He hit the Print key, the printer whirred. Sarraj strolled over to collect the formula as it slid from the machine. "Very good." He stowed the paper in a breast pocket, then turned, his eyes all for Demi. "Tomorrow night my prince wishes to meet you. Entertain you royally aboard *Aphrodite* and give you his thanks. You will come?"

Over my dead body! Jon clamped his jaws on the words.

Demi shrugged and turned her back. Jon's hands curled to fists as something flickered in the man's eyes—then faded. "I'll...think about it," Demi said coolly, without turning.

Sarraj showed his teeth. "I'll call you later to arrange it. And now...my thanks to you both." He strode out of the room, a man with a mission.

Jon drew a deep breath. *Here we go.*

Slowly Demi turned. "Just whose side are you on, Jon Sutter?"

"Yours." *Now and forever.*

"*Ha!* You're fired."

"No." *Not while you need me, I'm not.*

"You *are!*" She stamped her foot and burst into tears. "Get out of my—my life."

"No." He winced as the vase holding the violets he'd brought her three days ago hit the wall and shattered. "But I'll go to lunch. Why don't we both go?" *Cool down, count* to ten, maybe sleep for a week? "Let's find a bottle of champagne. We deserve it." Seven days till D day. Seven days till this was over and he could explain.

"I have nothing to celebrate."

Let's see if I can change that. "Look, I'm going to go get my jacket and wallet. I'll be back in a minute. Okay? Meantime, could you explain to Burton it's not the end of the world?" The dog had taken refuge under her desk; just the tip of his nose showed where he lurked.

Demi rubbed her own elegant nose and nodded. Jon headed out the door. It would be all right. They'd get through this. *Trust me, Demi. Trust what you feel and we won't go wrong.*

He heard the phone ring as he reached the lab.

She was in no mood to speak to anyone. Hugging Burton, Demi glanced at the phone. Let the answering machine take it.

But she'd forgotten to switch to mute. "Hello, hello, hello," caroled an unfamiliar woman's voice. "I have an urgent—repeat—*highly* urgent message for Jon Sutt—uh, Sutter. Is anyone there? If anyone's listening, then for the love of—"

Demi lifted the receiver. "Alluroma." *And who are you?*

"Yes!" said a sexy, laughing contralto. "May I speak to Jon, please?"

Whoever this was, Demi detested the easy note of possession in her voice. "And whom may I say is calling?"

"The lady from the topless doughnut shop, not that it's any of your biz. Is he there, please? I *have* to speak to him."

Demi looked up to find Jon poised in her doorway, his head tipped in inquiry. "Oh, he's here, all right." She held out the phone and watched his eyebrows jump. At least he wasn't expecting this call. She sniffed and stalked past him into the kitchen.

Who the—? "Hello?"

"Jon?"

His jaw slowly dropped. There was no mistaking his sister's voice. "Yes?" He glanced toward the door to the inner rooms. Was Demi out of earshot?

"I have something so...*sizzling* to say to you," Emily murmured, "that you might suffer meltdown."

He'd never realized before how sultry she could sound!

Who gave you this number? Told you I was working here?

"It's *definitely* not an appropriate topic for discussion on your lady boss's phone, if you get my drift," she confided, vamping like a modern-day Mae West. "So when can we...speak?"

"Sounds like you can't wait." Trace, it had to be Trace who'd told her where to find him.

"I might...die if you make me wait."

An emergency for sure. "Never keep a hot lady waiting," he agreed lightly. So Trace feared this phone was tapped. "Can I reach you at home?"

"Yes, you can, studly."

"Then I'll call you from someplace...nice and private...in twenty minutes?"

"You do that. And just one question before you go, stud. Your boss lady sounded a mite...possessive. Should I be jealous?"

"Do you good." He hung up smartly on the smart-ass. But if Emily was right about Demi, it did him good, too. His exasperation lifted a trifle—gave way promptly to worry. If Trace had told Emily to call him, this was a crisis.

Demi glanced around the door from the kitchen. Sipping from a mug, she raised one eyebrow. The boss lady—cool, calm, infinitely haughty. So much for coaxing her into a bottle of champagne. "I've got to go out, Demi."

"So I gathered." *And I give a damn?* was the unspoken question. "Take all the time you need. You've earned it."

"I'll be back in an hour or less." He'd go to the hotel on Fifty-fourth; that should be safe enough.

"Who cares?" She vanished back into the kitchen.

"I do!" he called, heading out the door. *And when I come back, I'll start showing you how much I care.* He was done with acting where she was concerned. "Watch Burton for me?"

"*Pah,* I'm not a baby-sitter for a crocodile!"

He took that for "Yes" and left.

DEMI WENT FOR THE vacuum and focused all her raging thoughts on the vase she'd thrown—Jon's poor, battered violets. "Who does he think he is, Burton, handing over my formula like that? Who the hell *is* he?" Sarraj's man, that much was clear after today.

His man, but who else had a claim on him? *Me—or that woman?* "Who was she, Burton? Do you know her? Does she visit him? Why didn't you tell me? If I'd known he had someone, I'd never have—" She shoved the brute aside. "Oh, get *away.* Why talk to you? You're on his side!"

The phone rang. She dropped the shards of glass she'd been collecting to answer it. Jon? No reason it should be, but still her heart leaped. "Alluroma!"

"Ma chère…"

Her grandfather. She burst into silent tears and switched to French. When he'd finished speaking, she sat. Stunned. "You're quite sure?"

He snorted. He didn't speak without certainty and she knew it, but he repeated it patiently. "No designer in all of France has been given a commission to design your bottle and package, Demi. I have spent all week visiting this studio, discreetly chatting with that designer. This fact is verified. Are you sure that the man said Paris?"

It was her turn to sniff. "Quite certain. The man is an incompetent, Grandpapa, a fool. He has never launched a perfume before. He's pretending that he has matters well in hand when we're teetering on the edge of disaster."

"Perhaps he pocketed the design commission? Means to pocket any other fees he can grab from his investors, then run?"

"Run where? His reputation would be ruined forever. And his client, this prince—"

"But yes, a Saudi prince would have the means to hunt him down. You treat those people with respect or live to regret it. The prince's name, *petite?* I have many friends...."

"Sarraj never told me— Yes, I know, I know, I've been a trusting idiot—but I meet the man tomorrow night."

"I would like to meet this prince, too, very much. If there are any seats on the Concorde tomorrow, I could—"

"No, no." She drew in a deep breath. "I'm no longer your little girl, *Grand-père.* Thank you so much, but I will handle this. No. No, don't worry, all will be fine. It's a silly confusion, incompetence. No one means me any harm. And there's still time to stop it, to put this campaign back on the right path. And, Grandpapa, I have made the most *wonderful* fragrance...."

They spoke of that for a while, then of her grandmother.

She glanced at her watch. The sooner she reached the prince... But there was something else weighing on her heart. "Grandpapa," she said into a pause, "I have a question...."

He made a comforting sound. For some thirty years he'd been answering her questions.

"If you loved a...woman who was all wrong for

you...nothing like what you had ever imagined for yourself...what would you do?''

His chuckle was low and earthy. "Have her and let the rest sort itself out!"

"Really?" Suddenly she wanted to cry again. With relief this time.

"Well, the last time that happened, that was what I did. It has lasted fifty-five years so far. And your parents—no two lovers were ever worse matched. But had your father lived, I think they would still be together."

"Oh..." She smiled and wiped a tear away. He'd never told her.

"What is your man's name?" he asked comfortably.

"Jon..." It felt so *good* to say it to someone.

"Jon, a good name." He paused, then, *"Ah—*this is the lab tech you mentioned in your letter last month, the man who replaced Hector?"

"Yes...that's part of my problem. He works for me." She bit her lip, waiting for his verdict.

"He lets you walk all over him, this one?"

She laughed. "Not at all! He's so stubborn, he drives me wild."

He gave an approving grunt. "Good. The way it should be."

Her smile was wry. Her dear old chauvinist, still the wisest man she knew. "But...there is something else—and this must be a secret between you and me. He has been a thief...." She winced and waited for his roar.

There was instead a considering pause. "There are all kinds of reasons for stealing, of course. I myself, in my youth, when I was hungry.... And your grandmother, to be sure. That's how I met her. In Cairo. She lifted my wallet...."

"No!" Demi had never heard this before.

"But yes!" He was laughing softly. "When I caught her

I told her she had only to ask—so then she did, the minx...."

"I would like to hear the rest of that story sometime."

"Ah? Well, you owe us a visit. Bring this Jon with you so I can look him over, and perhaps I'll tell you."

When she hung up the phone, she was smiling. The smile lasted a minute, then faded. Her wonderful perfume, heading straight for disaster. "Not if I can help it!" She swung to her keyboard. How did you address a prince? She grimaced and typed.

Dear Sire,
There is a matter of the gravest concern to us both. It has come to my notice that....

Fifteen minutes later, she printed her second draft, read it, scowled and tossed it into the trash. Put on paper—the wrong mailing lists, the missing bottles—it sounded like lunacy. It would be simpler to tell him in person. And why not? Men listened when she spoke—well, most men. She'd go to the nearest marina, hire someone to take her out to the *Aphrodite*.... If she went now, while Sarraj was here in the city, out of her way, all the better. Just a cosy tête-à-tête between her and his prince.

"THIS HAD BETTER BE good," Jon growled when Emily picked up.

"Try bad with a capital *B*." The sex-kitten undertones had been dropped for her usual briskness. "I got a call from Trace 'bout an hour ago. He's somewhere in Russia and he wanted me to call you. Said to make sure we talked on a secure phone. I take it we're secure?"

"Yep."

"Okay, he was rushed, headed off somewhere to find somebody, and he couldn't wait to reach you at home. He sounded pretty beat. It must have been the middle of the night wherever he was, and he was in a mega-ugly mood. He made me write it down precisely and he yelled at me when I tried to ask questions. He told me not to ask anything, not to think, just take it down and read it to you. He's still a big bully." She paused for breath.

"Big brother's prerogative. Lay it on me."

"One. The box came from a secret Biosafety Level Four lab that was being dismantled for lack of funds. *Jon?*"

He continued swearing, helplessly, fluently, for almost a minute. "Go on," he managed finally. God, it all made sense! Why hadn't he seen it?

"You know what a Type BSL Four is, don't you? I looked it up after Trace hung up. What in God's name has he got you into, Jon? Level Four is where they store germs like Ebola, anthrax, bubonic plague and worse!"

"I know that, Em. Go on." Jon wiped his face. He was drenched in a cold sweat. Demi, he had to get back to her!

"Two. The man who passed the box to the deliverymen was the top researcher there. He received four million dollars in exchange for the box, and he has disappeared. Up into the Ural Mountains, Trace thinks.

"Three. Trace is going after him. Said he needs to learn about the care and feeding of the box's contents. How to safely handle it. How to store it."

"Yes." No one entered a Level Four lab without a moon suit. Not if he wanted to come out and live. If Trace learned how the box's contents must be stored, then they'd know where it was hidden. In the freezer on the *Aphrodite*, he'd bet, disguised as food, maybe a human tissue sample packaged as tripe? Or in a bottle of vinegar—or floral absolute?

"Four. In the meantime, you are not to do anything. Anything, anything, *anything*. He said repeat that three times. He said you've got time—seven days, he thought."

Seven days till the launch party, yes. God, Sarraj meant

to infect the entire party? Then what—turn two hundred contagious guests loose on New York City? A showstopper of a media event. *Top this one, suckers!*

"By 'anything' he means don't open any bottle or box if you're not sure of its contents. Jon, I want you out of there! Don't go back there, wherever there is. I'm frightened!"

"So am I, Em. But does Trace want me to scram?"

"*No,* damn him!" She swallowed a sob. "He says you're not to scare your subjects or alert them in any way. He said that's crucial. Stay put and smile, he said."

"Yes." Whatever Sarraj's original plans, he might have a Plan B, a quickie, if he thought they were closing in. Open the box on a midtown train at rush hour, say, then skip town. "Anything else?"

"Five. This is no longer a Bureau investigation. There's an interagency task force for this sort of thing. They have a strike team who'll be moving into place, he figures late tomorrow. But they won't pounce till they know who and what they're swatting and how to safely swat. So he says there will be a day or two of swearing and planning, since they have time before the event."

"Makes sense." The last thing they'd want to do was catch only half the conspirators or accidentally loose the germs during the operation.

"Six. Greenley will be your contact and your liaison with the strike force. They're rushing him back from somewhere. Look for him late tonight or tomorrow."

"Okay." He glanced at his watch. *Demi, wait for me.*

"And last. Trace says, *no matter what,* he wants you out of there before the swat goes down. He said if you make him dogmeat with Mom, he'll never forgive you. And I'm seconding that. Don't you *dare* be there in the middle of a swat! Forty or fifty supercops out to save the world, overdosed on their own testosterone? They'll blast anything that moves!''

"Probably." Without a doubt. Mincemeat, then question the mincemeat later. The nerve danced in his cheek. "That's it?"

"What more d'you *want?*"

"Well, a nap would be nice." She snarled and he added, "Now *you* listen. I want you to pack up Ralph, Augusta and Jericho and go home till you get the all-clear. And call Jodi, of course. Don't you dare tell any of 'em why. Come up with some excuse. You always were a wonderful liar, and I want you to—"

"Save your breath. Trace already gave me this sermon. My fuzzies are stuffed in their travel cages—can't you hear 'em yowling? We're out the door in ten minutes, and, *yes,* I'll fill all the cars' gas tanks, lay in food for three months, make sure Mom has a year's supply of ammunition for all her guns and Dad has enough guitar strings. And we'll chop wood all week in case there's no fuel oil next win— Jon, *please* come help me!''

"Gotta stay here and make sure you don't need all that wood, kiddo." He took a deep breath. "Just consider this another family fire drill." Their father, the school principal, was big on emergency walk-throughs.

That won a giggle from her that turned into a sniffle. He took a deep breath. "One last thing, Em. If I have my way, I'll be sending you…someone, in the next few days. Put her in my bedroom and be nice to her."

"Not that ice queen I spoke to?"

"None other. And she's not. You'll like her."

"She'd better not be a bitch like—"

"Isn't, at all. Well, maybe a little…driven." He grinned. *It takes one to know one!* They'd get along fine once they'd taken each other's measure. "Now go, be good and hug everybody.''

"And you be—" She gulped.

"Yeah, kiddo. I will. Bye." He hung up. Not as if that was the last time or anything. He shivered, moved from the booth to his waiting wheelchair—it was still faster than his feet—then spun down the corridor. *Demi!* He couldn't get back to her soon enough.

CHAPTER TWENTY-ONE

BURTON HUSTLED TO GREET him as he entered Alluroma. Jon thumped him absently. "Demi!" How was he going to tell her? "Demi?" He rolled through to the lab. "Burton, where the hell has she gone?" Out to the deli? He wheeled back to her office.

The phone rang and he raced to answer it. "Alluroma." He saw the note on her desk as he picked up. Phone jammed between ear and shoulder, he wheeled over to grab it.

"Oh, *Jon!* Hello."

"Hiya, Kyle." The disappointment was plain in his voice. He added with more warmth, "How are you?" as he unfolded the note.

Gone for the day, please lock up.

He winced—cold—but it could have been worse. Not much worse. *Where'd you go, babe?* Tonight was no night to be scouring the town for her. He refocused on the cheerful voice in his ear.

"—so you might want to tell her. Weirder and weirder, huh?"

"What is?" He folded Demi's note and tucked it next to his heart.

Kyle gave a groan. "You weren't listening at all? *Okay,* taking it from the top, my mail-list broker called me a while ago, about some other business. And she mentioned that

Sarraj had ordered a few more lists from her, and these were as weird as his first ones."

Sarraj had requested a list of all women ages twenty through sixty living in certain zip codes, with incomes between twenty and a hundred thousand.

Jon sat up straight. "What zip codes?"

"For Washington, D.C., and all its outlying suburbs. Their income level is mostly too low—my broker tried to tell him that, but Sarraj still isn't listening. And why saturate that one particular area? Women in D.C. use more perfume than other parts of the country?"

The hair prickled and rose along the nape of his neck. D.C. "What other lists has he ordered, Kyle? Demi didn't tell me."

"A U.S. military list. Officers, both sexes, all branches of the service, rank of captain and above. I suppose their income level's sufficient, but still, what's he thinking? I don't see women marines wearing Veil, do you?"

"No." He didn't see that, but... "And the rest of the lists?"

When she'd recited them all, he said numbly, "Thanks," and hung up on her midsentence. He saw it all now, at least he thought he did. *Prince of Darkness!* The man was a genius. A barking-mad *genius!*

More than that, Harkness was a magician. He knew sleight of hand. *Watch carefully, suckers,* the gold coin spinning in his left hand. Hypnotizing, lulling, holding his victims' eyes while his right hand held the hidden dagger. *Look at my launch party, suckers! Focus on that, the mayor, the pretty yacht, the photogenic event.*

Or look for those nasty Arab terrorists. *I give you Sarraj, I give you Demi, I give you an imaginary Saudi prince. Focus on them. Turn all your assumptions, all your efforts east while I make my last plans in the west.* He'd called in his faithful, would have laid up arms and food for a year in quarantine on his mountaintop.

And now Harkness swaps hands, coin to the right hand, dagger to left. *Why, look at those terrible terrorists now!* Driving their vans filled with bomb parts around and around, like three shells with a pea under none of them, drawing all the FBI's attention and manpower out west.

Which meant his real show was here—here and *now*— in New York City!

And the punch line to his joke is that he told us and still we never saw it coming! For seven years he'd been predicting the end of the world, turning himself into a joke that no one would take seriously. And now who laughs last? Seven Veils. Salome dancing...a good man's head on a platter...a nation in ruins.

His final veil was falling tonight, tomorrow and the morning after, when Kyle's flyers hit the mail. Carrying the airtight scent strips of Demi's perfume—and in those samples, a deadly plague.

The man was a tactical genius. Look at the first wave of victims he'd chosen! You want to bring this country to its knees? First, knock out the cops, the military elite, so you'll have chaos. Knock out the doctors who maybe could find a way to fight this plague—if they weren't already sick or dying. And don't forget the President and Congress, the entire Beltway bureaucracy. Their own mail might be closely examined—so send them a dose through their secretaries and their aides, their wives and lovers.

And don't forget the rest of the population. If you're sweeping a country clean, cleansing it for your chosen few, then you need to spread the plague far and wide. Send samples to the teachers, who'll cough on their students, who'll take it home to their parents and sneeze. Mail a sample to every flight attendant, let them spread it abroad through Demi's gorgeous, nearly perfect, entirely fatal perfume. Good enough for the American public—and the rest of the world, too!

He must have made a sound, because Burton reared up to rest his paws on his leg and whine. Jon reached for him gratefully. "No." He rubbed the dog's ears and pushed him down. "Ain't gonna happen," *not to my girl. Not to my world.* "Over my dead body, Burt."

So...Demi, where in God's name are you? He couldn't call down the strike force till he knew she was out of harm's way. Because they wouldn't be making fine distinctions when they ripped through Alluroma, the yacht, the bulk mixer in Brooklyn, Sarraj's scent-strip factory. Not on this mission. One maddeningly unforgettable, absolutely irreplaceable woman in their way would be one woman smashed flat, apologies to come later. Too late.

Ain't gonna happen, not to my woman. Demi, where are you!

The phone rang and he grabbed it. "About bloody time!" he snarled. "Where are you?"

"I beg your pardon?" The man's voice was deep, with a French accent, deeply amused.

"Uh, sorry, I thought you were—"

"This would be Jon, I presume?"

"It would. Who's this?"

"Alec Cousteau. Demi's grandfather. May I speak to her, please?"

"Umm, she's stepped out. Could I take a message, sir?"

"Yes. You could tell her that I've changed my mind. My wife and I will be arriving late tomorrow. If you will take down this flight number?"

"Yes, sir." There was no paper handy. Jon pulled a crumpled sheet out of the trash, smoothed it out, reached across it for a pen lying on her desk, then froze.

Dear Sire... His eyes flew down the page. God in heaven! She'd written to Sarraj's imaginary prince, complaining about Sarraj? And how had she proposed to deliver her letter?

The old man finished dictating. "You have it all?"

"Yes." Have what? Didn't matter. *Demi, she couldn't have*— He dived into the trash again, came up with another crumpled draft.

"Then there's just one other thing I need to make clear."

Cousteau had a voice like an old polished blade, honed to perfection, jabbing him back to attention. "Should you ever hurt my granddaughter in any way, you answer to me. I make myself clear?"

"She's been complaining?" And how could an eighty-something guy sound so deadly?

"Ah, well, not precisely."

"Sir, Demi's happiness is my own. Whatever she needs or desires…"

"Good." There was a thinking pause. "That is well. For you. A man who hurt my grandchild, I'd cut his heart out and feed it to the pigeons."

Ex-Foreign Legion, Jon remembered and almost smiled.

"Won't be necessary, sir. But may I ask when you spoke with her last?"

"An hour ago? A little longer?"

"She didn't say where she was going or what she was planning to do?"

"Gone to speak with her client, that Saudi prince, I would think." He swore under his breath, in French. "I had hoped to catch her in time. I'd prefer she had a man to back her."

"She has one, sir. I'm on my way." Demi aboard the *Aphrodite*—his stomach stepped off into freefall. Let him call in the SWAT team with her aboard and Sarraj and his buddies would use her as their hostage, their human shield. *No way.* He swallowed and found his voice. "But you could do one thing for me. For Demi... I need someone to make a phone call at midnight, my time.''

Because if he couldn't save her by then, he couldn't save her at all. After midnight there was the rest of the world to consider.

"THIS AIN'T REALLY FOR A treasure hunt,'' said the cabdriver. ''Rope? Doorstops? Twenty padlocks. All that chain and junk?''

''Not really,'' Jon agreed, rechecking his list. ''But thanks anyway. Couldn't have done it without you.'' They'd had eleven minutes in the hardware store before it closed. ''You got the spray paint?''

''Pink Day-Glo, since you didn't care.''

''Perfect.'' *Now, please, shuddup and drive. Lemme think.* His eyes lit on a kid bouncing down the sidewalk wearing— ''Hey, stop! That kid—I want his backpack!'' The taxi screeched to a halt, throwing Burton to the floorboards.

Minutes later they sped on their way. ''Little smartmouth would've taken twenty,'' grumbled the driver.

''Yeah, but he took forty faster.'' Luckily they'd stopped by an ATM machine. Jon glanced at his watch. Ninety minutes till dark. He was still on schedule. But, God, how long had she been aboard?

If he thought about that, he'd start howling and bite something. He set himself to arranging his bottles and gear in the pack while they crawled through heavy downtown traffic. When he was satisfied that nothing would clink or spill, he used some of his nylon line to lengthen its shoulder straps, then tried it on. A tight fit over his tuxedo jacket, but it would do.

''Here's your marina.'' The taxi pulled in to a curb. ''Well...'' They eyed each other with rueful warmth, two men who'd shared a hardware shopping spree.

Jon handed him a paper. "So remember, if I don't come back for Burton within a week, you call this number. That's Vermont. Ask for Emily. Give her my name, tell her what you've got, and if she can, she'll come get him."

The driver looked at the hound and grimaced. "What if she can't?"

"In that case, you might find he comes in handy. He could track rats."

"What would I want to track rats for?"

"Joke." Jon handed him five times the normal tip and another hundred to keep Burton in puppy biscuits. Money meant nothing at the end of the world. A plump rat would be priceless.

The driver came around to lift his wheelchair from the trunk, then help him unfold it. Jon dropped his new bolt cutters, too long to fit inside the pack, into his sling at the back of the chair, then settled into it with relief. His legs still ached from the hardware store.

"Got just one last word for you, buddy," said the driver as they shook hands. He glanced uneasily toward the locked gate and the ramp leading down to the marina's docks. "Whatever you're up to...don't do the crime if you can't do the time."

"I'll remember that." He waved goodbye, a lump rising in his throat as Burton looked back in wounded astonishment. As he cut the chain on the gate, then rolled down the ramp to the blessedly deserted docks, he silently chanted, *I'd like to rent a kayak. I'd like to rent a kayak.* Except they'd be closed by now. *So I'd like to steal a kayak. I mean to steal a kayak. Demi, Demi-darling— Shuddup, don't think about— Think about kayaks, stealing kayaks. Make mine a two-seater.*

THE VIEW FROM *Aphrodite's* saloon windows was stupendous—a spotlit Lady Liberty rearing into the night sky, and beyond her, the glittering towers of Manhattan. Demi much preferred looking out to meeting the eyes of the two men seated across this luxurious cabin.

But each time she prowled to the windows, she could feel their eyes moving over her. Could watch their reflected images in the plate glass, watching her. She held herself very stiff and tall, fighting a shiver. Something was terribly wrong here! Trouble in hobnail boots. Trouble in the eyes of that devilishly handsome man, Adam Harkness, sitting there watching her with a joke in his eyes.

She swallowed her fear and stared out the window. *Jon.* Jon was out there somewhere, beyond the black waters. Somewhere in all that distant bustle and glitter. *Jon, why didn't I tell you where I was going?* God, she wanted Jon—his sanity, his arms, his wicked sense of humor! Joyous laughter, not the ugly kind, the way Harkness had thrown back his head and laughed when she'd stepped aboard, demanding to see the prince.

She wanted Jon and she didn't care if he was somehow, some way, involved in all this. He might be Sarraj's man, but in the end, he was hers. On her side. She'd given herself to him and he had taken her.

She resisted the urge to look at her watch. "When d'you think they'll be back?" Harkness had told her—*after* he'd dismissed her hired launch and sent it on its way!—that Sarraj and the prince were still in town, attending to last-minute details for Veil's sample mailing.

But he's lying. I don't think there is a prince. She'd seen the laughing contempt in his eyes while he told her. Had wanted to slap it off his face. Knew better than to try. This man was dangerous.

"They should be back any time now," he said easily, a faint tinge of somewhere west in his voice. "Sure I can't get you a drink?"

Oh, please, would you stop asking? You think I'm fool

enough to drink with you? "Thank you, but no." She inhaled deeply, but she couldn't smell the danger. Could
smell only the roses on the dining table, away down this
long room toward the bow of the yacht. The kelp and salt
smells drifting in from the open French doors that overlooked the *Aphrodite's* afterdeck. All the smells were pleasant in this floating palace, but still her instincts cried *Danger!*

"I'd take one," said Bob, behind her. The steward,
Harkness had called him, sitting there like an obedient
guard dog. He wasn't as quick. Was too dazzled by her
legs to even consider she had a brain. *Him I could handle,
but Harkness?* She suppressed another shiver. *What in
God's name is going on here?* Why would she need to
handle anyone?

Harkness crossed to the bar that served as a visual di-
vider between the saloon and the dining area. He stooped
to open a small refrigerator, brought out wine, then three
glasses.

Demi turned. "Where could I powder my nose, please?"
She gave him a deprecating smile, medium voltage. Perhaps she'd lock herself in, wait for Sarraj. He didn't worry
her half as much as Adam Harkness did.

Harkness nodded toward the rear of the yacht. "Down
that stairway on your left, then left at the bottom of the
stairs."

If he hadn't been watching, she'd have walked straight
through the French doors to the open deck that overlooked
the stern. Perhaps there was a dinghy? She'd never rowed
a boat before, but she was a quick learner.

The stairs led her down to the master cabin in the rear
of the boat with its en suite bathroom. A sumptuous dead
end complete with king-size bed. She could look out portholes on three sides, but they were too small to slip through.

She hurried back to the corridor. It turned forward and

gave onto guest cabins, left and right, then ended in a blank wall. She could hear motors purring beyond. The engine room?

She dashed back to the master suite and into its head. Glared at herself in the beveled glass above a marble sink with gilded dolphin faucets. *You idiot!* Jon and Burton were probably strolling the West Side about now, debating between hamburgers and pizza for supper, and here she was, trapped in all this horrid luxury. She took a deep breath. *You got yourself in, so get yourself out.*

Opening her purse, she ran a brush through her wind-ruffled hair, then redefined her lips in deepest ruby. A woman used the weapons that came to hand. Weapons. New Yorkers knew them all. She scrounged through her purse. Transferred a ballpoint pen and her keys to the pockets of her red suit. Her hand bumped her favorite atomizer, filled with her latest version of Veil. She'd meant to make the prince smell it from top note to soul while she charmed him into letting her work on it more. *Pah!* She dropped it into her pocket, then considered abandoning her purse. But it was her favorite, an antique Chanel. *Not till I have to.*

Perhaps she could squeeze through one of those portholes that overlooked the stern if she took off her jacket? Worth a try. She stepped out of the bathroom and jumped a foot. Adam Harkness stood waiting, holding two glasses of wine.

Blocking the exit. Careful not to look toward the king-size bed, Demi smiled and came to meet him. "You shouldn't have!"

She took the glass he offered and looked up at him from under her lashes as she sniffed. The breath snagged in her throat, but she didn't wrinkle her nose. Something in it. *Ha—you think you can slip something past a Nose?*

"What a beautiful boat," she said huskily, and touched her glass to his. "Could I have a tour?" *Let me out of here!*

"It's not bad." He sipped and looked around the cabin as if he owned it. "But forget the tour—how 'bout a cruise? Say, three months or so. How's that sound?"

With you? In your dreams! "I get seasick." She lifted her glass, pressed her lips tight together and let the wine wet them. Definitely something! She tipped the glass higher and a dribble ran down her cheek, spilled to the shoulder of her jacket. *"Oh!"* Red wine, it would never come out. "Oh, I'm so—" She flattened a hand on his chest and leaned close. "Quick! Where's the club soda? Upstairs?" She ducked under his arm and ran, her teeth bared in a snarl as he followed, chuckling. But she was out of that room.

"Just look what I did!" *Silly me.* She showed the damage to Bob, still slouched in his chair. "Do you have a napkin, Bob? Perhaps a handkerchief?"

"One soda coming up." Harkness headed for the bar, shaking his head, laughing.

She hated people laughing at her. Bob set his glass on the coffee table, pulled a bandanna from his back pocket, and while he did so, she switched drinks. *How good is your nose, you lout?*

Not good at all, she observed while she fussed and used the soda Harkness brought her. The stain was there to stay, one more thing she owed these creeps. After that she drank Bob's glass of wine like a good girl while Harkness watched with smug amusement.

She chatted brightly for another twenty minutes, praying for the sound of Sarraj's launch, hearing nothing. *Jon, where are you when I need you?* Harkness's amusement was fading to puzzlement. She asked for another glass. Managed to switch this one with Bob, who was starting to nod, when the captain came down from the bridge deck to ask Harkness a question.

Harkness brought him over to be introduced, an older

man, vaguely military. Perhaps here was her savior? She widened her eyes in mute appeal. He held her hand a moment longer than necessary, and looked at her with something that might have been pity. Then he turned and left her to Harkness.

She took Bob's second glass of wine and went to the window, stared out at the flowing blackness and the symbol of liberty, unreachable beyond the glass.

THERE AREN'T ANY ROCKS in the harbor. No rocks, no rocks, no rocks. It wasn't really the water that scared him, Jon was beginning to realize, or kayaks. It was the rocks in the river that ate kayaks and crunched bones that he didn't like. *And there aren't any rocks out here. Not a rock in sight.*

After maybe a hundred reps of that chant and a mile of paddling he was almost starting to believe it. He'd stopped hyperventilating. His breathing had settled down to a steady huff and go. His arms were starting to stretch out and feel good. He'd forgotten how in a thin-skinned kayak the water cradled you. Lifted you up over every ripple and wave, a cold but infinitely responsive lover. *And not a rock in sight!* He laughed aloud for sheer joy, glanced behind—and yelped.

Another damn ship coming down on him! Five knots of seabound current added to their own horsepower made them move with terrifying speed. He back-paddled frantically and it slid past, a black, moving cliff. Its bow wave reared overhead—shoved him aside. The horizon swung—city lights revolving. He smacked the flat of his blade on the water to stop the flip, then sat bobbing in the ship's wake, trembling hard and swearing harder. He paddled again. And he was worrying about rocks?

Let one of those monsters plow you under and what happens to Demi? He kept a closer watch after that, dodging a tugboat towing a barge up-Hudson against the current, then a shuttle headed for Jersey. Nobody could see him out here in his red double kayak with not a foot of freeboard and no running lights.

There was less traffic as he slid past Ellis Island, then round the back of Liberty Island. The yacht lay south of the statue, farther out, but he meant to glide in from the shallows to her west. He had only one chance to do this right. It would be like climbing a mountain, something he hadn't done in years. When a slip meant death you went slow, considered every handhold once, then once again, before you trusted your weight to it. He glanced at his watch—10:55 p.m. He still had time. *Oh, Demi, love, hang on.*

CHAPTER TWENTY-TWO

SOME FIFTY YARDS OUT, he circled the motor yacht. Greenley was right, she was a honey. White as a wedding cake, a three-decker, nearly half as long as a football field. Five crew, Trace had said, counting Harkness.

Who else?

Captain, he remembered, ex-navy man. There was a light on in the top deck, in the bridge. The captain's lair—looked as if he was up there, communing with his instruments. Might have the radar on, but with any luck, the kayak would be too low-profile to read.

Aft of the bridge was where they'd store the ship's launch. He could see the boom to hoist it over the side, but the boat wasn't up there. And it wasn't hanging off the stern. *Somebody's gone ashore.* Sarraj. Maybe he hadn't come back yet?

Captain, Harkness, Sarraj. There'd be a cook on a baby this size, and a mate/engineer, who might be off, driving Sarraj's launch. Maybe a steward. Four to deal with if he was lucky, five if not. This time of night those aboard should be on the main deck, somewhere behind all those black-glass windows. Looking out? He didn't think he was visible, but he was well within rifle range and Trace had said they had guns. He swallowed hard and paddled on— dip left, dip right, glide.

There, midships on the port side of the yacht, directly below the vent stacks, could that be the door to the engine room? It had better be. The door just ahead of it might lead into the galley.

Dip, glide and dither. Jon circled around to her starboard side. The lowest deck would be the sleeping cabins—owners and guests in the rear, crew forward. With the engine room in between, since never the twain should meet on a luxury yacht. He had a friend who was a professional yacht captain, had crewed once or twice for him on boats like this. *Could have used you tonight, Wiley-boy.*

He'd have to be wily instead. Dip left, dip right. Jon passed beneath the anchor chain, stretched taut by the current. He'd thought about cutting it, but that was ridiculous, the size of those links. Still... It curved from the water up to the hawse pipe, a black hole in the white cliff of the bow. From there it would lead up on deck, to the anchor windlass, then drop down into the chain locker.

Stop stalling, you coward, get to work! He moved in close enough to touch her with an outstretched paddle, then slid down her left side, headed for the stern. There was a landing porch back there, but was there a guard?

No guard. Two miles of open water must seem guard enough. And they thought they were the predators, not the prey.

He scrambled aboard—gasping as his knees hit the teak—sat clumsily, teeth clamped on his lip while he lifted his folded wheelchair from the second paddler's hole, then his pack. He nearly dropped the bolt cutters over the side, then sat for a moment, shaking, his heart in his mouth. Without those...

He drew a breath and mounted the four steps from the landing platform to the gate in the middle of the stern. Peeking over this waist-high bulwark, he found himself staring across an afterdeck and into the main cabin. Framed by open French doors was a long saloon stretching away

from him. Fifty feet down it, Demi stood with her back to
the cabin, staring out toward the city.

Thank you, God, oh, thank you! Till this moment Jon
hadn't realized how terrified for her he really was. And
now, seeing her this close, the temptation was enormous.
*Maybe I should keep it simple? Just yell and see if she'd
run to me?* Viewed at a distance, she looked incredibly
fragile. And lonely, rejecting the yacht and everything in
it. *I'm here, love. You're not alone.*

But whether she would have run to him or no, she wasn't
free to do so. A man came to stand beside her. Blond and
big. Redford with an edge, as described. Harkness put a
hand on her shoulder—she wheeled and walked out from
under it, then out of Jon's sight. Harkness turned to watch
her with an ugly look, then followed at his leisure.

Don't waste another minute! In three, Jon had moved his
chair to the main deck and unfolded it, slung the cutter in
its sling. Had tied the kayak on a very long line so that it
hung along the port side of the boat, not visible from the
stern. If Sarraj returned, he didn't want him to see it.

Then it was show time. The chair was just narrow
enough to fit between the waist-high railing on his left and
the side of the cabin to his right. As long as he ducked
down and stayed down, they shouldn't see his head gliding
forward, just below window height. *Wheeled avenger
headed your way, guys!* Just pray to God nobody was
standing, looking out.

Midway up the left-side deck, he found that the door he'd
spotted did lead to the engine room. An oval aluminum
door with a locking wheel at chest height. You spun that
to dog it down watertight, at sea. Jon stood and opened
it—looked down some eight feet of ladder to the metal floor
of the engine room. *Crap!* He hadn't tried a ladder yet.

With bolt cutters tucked under one elbow, he made it
down, hanging most of his weight on his arms. He turned

and drew a breath. Nobody had yelled at him yet. Or shot him. It was noisy in here—the generators were running, creating electricity for all the lights on the decks above. Which meant it should be well insulated to muffle sound. *Good.*

As Greenley had said, it was a room the size of most people's apartments. With two engines as big as young Cadillacs, their fuel lines sprouting from filters to injectors to fuel tanks. Hydraulic steering lines running fore and aft. Electrical cables. Jon glanced at his watch. Five minutes was all he dared. *Make like a mad, mad beaver!*

He set the jaws of his bolt cutters to the first fuel line and snipped, then snipped again and moved on. Diesel oil dribbled down toward the spotless bilge. Whether he survived this night or not, nobody was taking Demi anywhere. Nobody was going to make a kamikaze dash to the shore to toss out a box full of death. *It ends here.*

Five minutes later, breathing hard, he stopped—to find he was smiling. Odd how wickedly seductive was destruction. Something Harkness had learned years ago? And it always amazed Jon how much faster you could tear down than you could build. They wouldn't fix all he'd done here in a night, or a week.

He noted one last time the location of the light switch and the emergency alarm, which should ring up on the bridge. You called the skipper in an emergency, not the guests. That done, he drew the can of spray paint from his pack. Day-Glo pink; he liked that.

THE HARD PART WAS where to hide while his trap was sprung. If he hid around the stern corner, he'd never be able to sprint back here in time. Jon entered the door just forward of the engine-room door—found himself standing in a short cross-ship hallway, with carpeted stairs leading up at the far end. The route to the bridge.

Aft of the stairway, around a corner to his right, he could hear the clink of cutlery, water running. The galley, complete with cook. Then to the rear of that would be the dining area. And Demi. *Not yet, babe.*

To his left a door gave onto a plush little room—a lounge, a library, with windows looking forward to the bow. Jon stowed his chair in there, then went back to the engine-room ladder and down it.

His heart was slamming double time. He glanced up at his Day-Glo handiwork on the far wall, took a deep breath—and hit the emergency alarm. Swarmed up the ladder as it buzzed here—and *please*, God, only on the bridge.

One rung from the top he banged his knee—and yelled. Bit his lip to blood, then hauled himself the rest of the way up, by his arms alone. *Damn, oh, damn, oh, crap, oh, please!* Puffing and hopping on one foot, he stumbled into the forward door. Could hear voices now. Glimpsed feet pounding down the stairs from the bridge. He staggered into the lounge and around its corner.

"What the *devil?*" somebody exclaimed, banging out the door to the deck.

"A short of some kind," said the man behind him, his voice fading as he shut the door. "Gotta be."

Two? Or was it three? And had Harkness heard them? If he had, now he'd come running, the brains of this outfit. Ex-surgeon, a man who could cut and like it. Jon held his breath, then heard a yelp of astonishment from outside. They'd be staring at his calling card from the top of the ladder.

A giant Day-Glo pink heart emblazoned on the opposite wall of the engine room, with J.S. Loves D.C. sprayed inside it. He'd meant to paint a smiley face, but his hand had followed its own path. *My lady's scarf on my lance.* And anything would do, really, to draw them down the ladder.

Right now, they probably thought lovesick Martians had landed.

He waited a moment more. Nobody was coming forward from the saloon or from the galley. *Close the trap.*

Hopping, he made it back to the engine-room door. He whipped the chain and padlock from his pack, then the bottle. He opened the door.

Three men bent over the far engine, horror-struck. Three—the mate, he supposed, the captain in his white shirt with chevrons, imitation Navy, and—*wonder of blessed wonders!*—a man dressed in spattered whites. The cook had been drawn into the drama, bless his curious soul!

Swearing wonderfully, the captain straightened—and looked up. Their eyes met, his jaw dropped, Jon dropped the bottle he held.

Eight ounces of narcissus absolute, superior grade, a thousand bucks' worth or more, smashed on the metal floor. *Nothing but Alluroma's best for you sweethearts!*

The captain yelled and lunged for the ladder.

Jon hit the light switch inside the door, then slammed it shut, spun the dogging wheel. *Oh, be fast, be fast!* He wrapped a length of chain around its rim, padlocked it. *Hurry!* Even in the dark, a captain knew his own engine room. He wrapped the other end of the chain around the metal handrail to the right of the door.

The wheel began to spin as someone turned it from inside. *Crap!* He hooked the shank of his second lock through the chain links, leaned all his weight against the door, snapped it home. Let out a shaking breath. A faint, furious hammering came through the metal.

Enjoy, boys! Narcissus absolute was supposed to be stronger than civet, he understood. Shouldn't kill them— the ventilation was excellent in there—but with luck it would muddle them.

Or make them frantic enough to find a way out.

Don't wait and see which! He hopped back to the other door, then headed for the galley. *Demi, hang in there. I'm coming.* Three down, but how many more? Harkness for sure, and now he had only one working leg.

And an attitude.

STANDING AT THE WINDOW, Demi watched Harkness's reflection prod Bob. He lifted the steward's head, then let it fall. Looked across at her as Bob snorted, then continued snoring. A shiver trembled up her limbs. She gulped and kept on staring out at the city.

"Not bad for a bimbo," he observed finally, and laughed.

She had always hated that word. "I *beg* your pardon?"

"What are you looking for—my little brother? Ritchie dances to my tune, babe. Always has, always will."

She clenched her hands and felt her nails bite deep. *You're not brothers.* Sarraj still had some human spark in him that this man had lost. But if he wasn't lying, really was the one who ruled here... She swallowed and lifted her chin. "Actually, I'm looking for my friends. They should be here any time now. You've certainly chosen an anchoring spot they can't miss." *Stop babbling.*

"What friends?" He yanked her around to face him.

"Kyle Andrews and most of Madison, Hastings and Gurney," she said lightly, looking him in the eye. "We decided to throw the...prince a little celebration, a prelaunch-party party. And my lab tech's coming along, of course. He's bringing the champagne." At the thought of Jon, she felt her eyes filling. *Oh, Jon!* She lifted her chin higher and tried not to blink.

Harkness stared at her for the count of ten, twenty, then suddenly threw back his head and laughed. He patted her cheek. "Did anyone ever tell you you're a terrible liar?"

She spun away, stalked to a chair and sat, arms folded tight.

"You need to mellow out, babe." He strolled to the bar and set out another wineglass. Reached beneath and came up with a pill bottle. He shook a pill into his palm, then looked up at her and grinned. Dropped it into the glass.

No way in the wide world! She glanced aft—no help in that direction—then forward. Run to the captain? Her eyes rounded.

An orange ball—no, it was an orange!—was bowling softly along the carpet toward her. Must have come from the dark hallway some forty feet forward, which led to parts of the yacht she'd yet to see. *What? Who?* Innocent as a child's toy, eerily purposeful, it rolled on, bumped the side of her couch and stopped.

She glanced casually back at Harkness, who was pouring wine into the glass. He picked up a spoon and stirred. She leaned over to set her purse in front of the orange and when she did so, she caught its scent.

Civet.

Demi straightened and stared blankly at Harkness. *Her* civet, that crude grade that Burton had pulled over on—she smiled. *You!* She stood and walked over to the bar, drawing Harkness's gaze away from her prize.

She looked down at the drink to hide the triumph blazing in her eyes. *Oh, my crazy, crazy, wonderful lover!*

But now what? Harkness must have thirty pounds on Jon, and two legs to his none. And he was vicious where Jon was gentle. It would be no match at all. *Unless you brought someone with you? Or someone's coming to save us?* That was Jon's message? *I'm here, hang on tight till help comes?* Looking down at the drink, she barely nodded and hoped he saw.

But meanwhile, till their rescue arrived—what?

Harkness pushed the glass across the bar till it nudged her hand. "Drink up, gorgeous."

Stall. She lifted the glass, turned it round and round without looking up at him. Don't meet his eyes if he knew when she lied.... "How about a deal? You tell me what's going on here, then I drink?"

"How 'bout you drink and then I tell?"

"No deal." She set the glass down and strolled back to the windows. Refused to look toward the hallway. *Jon!*

Harkness loomed behind her, glass in hand. "Drink it."

She turned, took it, smiled politely. "No, thank you."

She poured it on his shoes.

As he looked up from the damage, his eyes told her she'd made the worst possible move. He grinned, reached for her—

And a faint, extended rumbling sounded from somewhere forward. His head snapped around.

From the corner of her eye, Demi saw movement. She turned—to see the Statue of Liberty gliding serenely away. *"Oh!"* A second more and she realized—the yacht was moving, not the Lady! They'd swung off to one side. As she stared, the boat slowly swung back to its original bearing.

Another rumble from forward. *"Son* of a—" Harkness lunged toward the noise, then spun on his heel to glare at her.

"What is it?" It had to be Jon. It *was* Jon!

"It's the anchor chain running out. Something's—" He grabbed her by the arms, swung and dropped her onto a chair. Shoved a finger in her face. "Stay *right* here."

She gave him a dazzling smile. Anything that worried him was ducks by her! "Where would I go?"

"It's a mile or more to the closest shore, so don't even think about going over the side."

She crossed her legs deliberately and leaned back.

"Believe me, sunshine, if I knew how to swim, I'd have swam by now."

"It's 'swum'." He patted her cheek. "So stick around, beautiful, it's gonna be an interesting night." He turned and went forward, not quite running.

She wiped her cheek, waited a moment, then hurried after him. *Jon, oh, God, Jon, tell me you didn't come alone!*

In the hallway, she skated to a halt and spun left, sniffing. Civet! The smell came from here, a kitchen. "Jon?"

No Jon, but the smell drew her to a counter, then a reeking bowl of oranges, perfume to her nose. *I shall always think of you when I smell civet,* she'd told him. Her eyes were filling and not from the stink. She brushed them and saw the note tucked under the bowl.

Another rumble came from the bow. Demi unfolded the note and read.

> If you love me, then run to the rear of the boat. Get in the kayak you'll find on the left-hand side and wait. If anyone comes for you but me, then cast off and row for home.
>
> P.S. Do same if you don't love me.

HE'D FOUND A WINEGLASS and a bottle of champagne in the galley fridge, already opened. As Greenley said, make 'em underestimate you. Seated in his wheelchair on the bow, Jon set his filled glass on the deck, then took a sip from the bottle. Not half-bad. He poured half a cup into his palm, splashed his face with it, rubbed his hair, then breathed deep. *Let's do it.*

The anchor windlass was a lovely old-fashioned sort, with a wheel. Turn it slightly counterclockwise and it eased the brake. The anchor chain ran out slowly. Turn it more and it let the brake off entirely. He let it off.

There was a hesitation as the current nudged the bow. Then two hundred tons of boat swung ponderously sideways on its slackened leash, drawing more chain up from the chain locker as it drifted backward, away from its fixed anchor. The chain made an excellent racket—steel links clattering down the deck, then rattling down through the hawse pipe and into the water. Down in the engine room, the captain would be throwing twelve kinds of fits.

But can you hear this aft? Jon let out some thirty feet of chain, then turned the wheel clockwise to stop it.

The yacht straightened out again on its longer tether. He checked his watch, 12:01 a.m., then stared north past the Lady. *Nothing.* If Cousteau called at midnight, how long after that? Not long if he could convince them. In a true emergency they'd swat first and plan later. *God, Greenley, I hope you're back!* He'd told the old man to ask for him.

And where is everybody? Maybe they'd also swat first and question later. Shoot him from the bridge. He hadn't thought of that. Bit late now. He turned the wheel, let out fifty racketing feet. *Come to me, Harkness. Come pick on somebody your own size.* He laughed aloud and set the brake.

"Oops." His glasses. He drew them out of the breast pocket of his tuxedo and placed them on the end of his nose. *Harmless geek, that's me. Geek in a penguin suit.* He remembered his wineglass and picked it up. Heard hurrying footsteps. He tipped the bottle and drank—tipsy geek—then looked aft to see him coming, Harkness at last.

Putting a hand to the windlass wheel, he smiled at the man. "I'm terribly sorry, but I think I may have broken it. Doesn't work like the one on my brother-in-law's putt-putt." He eased the wheel slightly and the chain creaked, then crept out inch by clanking inch.

Harkness loomed overhead. Couldn't be as tall as he

looked from down here, surely no more than six-foot-three to his own six?

"Who the *hell* are you?"

"Demi's lab tech. Jon Sutter. Sorry I'm late for the party." He glanced down at the creaking chain. "Should this be *doing* that? I never should have messed with it. Here."

He thrust the champagne bottle at Harkness and swung the wheel all the way left. "There, that's bet—*oops*. No…" The yacht fell off to port, its chain roaring up from the locker and rumbling down the deck. "Definitely broke it. Sorry. Well, have a drink. Cheers." He lifted his wineglass as if to drink, and Harkness threw off his stupefaction.

"You friggin' *moron!* Get away from there!"

His chair was blocking the brake wheel. The boat was gathering way. "Sorry. Here, let me hold that." Jon took his bottle back. Harkness shoved his chair backward. The man leaned down, cursing and frantically spinning the wheel to the right.

The brake caught. The chain groaned, slowed, then tautened. Harkness looked up with bared teeth—and Jon splashed his glass full in the man's face.

Civet. He knew what that felt like.

Harkness gasped, must have inhaled—let out a strangled yell. Clawed at his eyes. Jon grabbed the lab bottle from his side pocket, pulled its stopper and emptied the rest of the civet over Harkness's hair and shoulders as he fell to his knees.

He whipped his chain out of hiding, wrapped it twice around the man's throat and hauled him down to the deck. Padlocked him to the anchor chain. Took a punch or three doing it, but well worth it. Panting, Jon rolled aside. Pulled himself up the windlass to his feet—one anyway—hobbled back to his chair and sat. "That's not too tight, is it?"

Harkness didn't answer, but from the way he was swearing, Jon supposed it wasn't. "I've got one question to ask, then I'll leave you alone," he said when Harkness paused for breath. "Where're the germs?" If they'd already been loosed, he had to know. Maybe they still could be contained.

Harkness yelled and kicked at him, caught his shin with one foot. Jon gasped and wheeled back a foot. Found his breath. His hands were shaking. "It's over, Harkness. Nobody's coming to help, so save your breath. Tell me."

He learned a few choice phrases he'd never heard before. But he mustn't forget Sarraj, due any time now. Jon gritted his teeth and rolled over to the wheel. Let the brake off maybe three inches. The chain groaned and slid that far and Harkness let out a shriek.

"You do understand what happens if I let it all the way off?" He would never do it, not for two whole kneecaps and all the tea in China. Not to have Demi's love for all his life could he do it. It made him sick to his stomach to even say it.

But a man who could consider killing the whole world was warped enough to expect evil from others. Had been warped, poor bastard; he and Sarraj both. "The chain goes out that hole in the deck. You're attached to that chain. You won't fit through that hole." But two hundred tons of yacht backing down on the chain would make him fit.

Harkness made a horrible high-pitched sound—and talked. The virus was in a sealed bottle in Sarraj's factory in Brooklyn. Waiting to be handed to the workers tomorrow. After Sarraj left them, they'd mix it into the scented gel, having been told it was a fragrance component. They'd make the sample strips, send the finished flyers off to the bulk mailer—and die four days later, about the time the samples hit America's mailboxes. By then the *Aphrodite* would have skipped her own launch party and put to sea with provisions for three months.

Not my world. "Thanks." Jon checked the wheel, tightened it as hard as he could, then headed aft as fast as he could roll. *Demi, are you waiting?*

MAYBE IT WAS THE WINE, or the lack of sleep, or maybe she was simply in shock from the past few hours. Demi waited in the kayak, praying that whoever Jon had brought with him was big enough and tough enough to handle Harkness. Finally she noticed there was only one paddle. And only two seats in the kayak. Would Jon leave a friend aboard with these louts? He would not. *The second seat was for her.*

"Oh, my *God!*" She scrambled out of the kayak, up onto the stern platform—she'd had to tow it back there to get in, in the first place. Her heels! She dived headfirst back into the boat and nearly tipped it, finding them. She was cursing in three languages when she came up for air. *Jon, oh, no, Jon!* Maniac lover. To the kitchen first, she decided, stepping into her shoes. Find a good knife and then—

"Hey," he said from the deck just above her.

"You!" She flew up the steps. "I may kill you myself, you—" She kissed his lips, his eyes, his ear, the top of his head. She was crying. "*Damn* you, how could you—" She turned forward. No one was coming. "Did you have a gun?" There was a gash on his cheek, she tasted blood. He smelled of champagne and civet and his own wonderful self. The scent of her crazy lover.

"Don't like 'em much. Come on, we've got to go. Don't have much time." He pulled her down for one kiss, a long, deep one.

They broke apart at last and she stared at him. "Who the hell *are* you?" And did she care when he kissed like that?

"Later, love, every bit of it." He glanced at his watch. "It's after midnight."

"You turn into a pumpkin?" He already had, or something much better.

"Something like that. Can you help me down the steps?"

His breath hissed out as she helped him rise from his chair. She wedged her shoulder under his arm. "When did you learn to walk?"

He laughed, but there was pain behind it. "If you can call it that!" They staggered down the steps, wavered across the deck—and he dropped by the kayak. Let his breath out in a ragged whoosh.

"You're hurt!" She kissed him again.

"A few dings. Let's get out of here."

Without her help, she doubted if he could have slithered into the kayak. He touched her cheek as she leaned over him, crying. "I'm fine, babe. Get in."

She'd lost a shoe, her best Italian pumps. She scrambled back for it, straightened and glanced toward the Lady—and saw the lights of a little motorboat gliding in. "Oh..." Sarraj standing behind its wheel, staring at her. Alone, no prince at his side.

Jon was swearing softly as he tried to crawl from the kayak.

She looked from him to the approaching boat. "It's Sarraj. Do you work for him, Jon?" His look of incredulity was answer enough. *Thank God.* Still, he was utterly spent. "Stay there."

"Demi, he's dangerous!"

She didn't answer. She smoothed back her hair, wiped her eyes and turned. *Sarraj, my dark angel.* Her mother would have adored him. She dug her hands into her pockets and stood there, waiting.

The craft kissed the right side of the yacht. Sarraj bounded to the platform, whipped a line around a cleat,

then straightened, staring from her to Jon in his kayak.
"Demi!"

"She hasn't a clue," Jon said, looking up at him.

Sarraj ignored him. "I'm sorry you brought him along."
He grasped her arm and turned to peer forward. "Where
are the others?"

"Up there, someplace. We were just leaving."

"I'm very sorry, but you can't." His fingers tightened.
"Go to the saloon and fix yourself a drink. I'll be there in
a minute to explain everything."

"Is Jon invited, too?" She wanted to be sure. And was,
as Sarraj's face went as blank as a stone.

"Sutter stays here. Go forward, my sweet. Now."

"Do as he says, Demi." Jon's voice was tight and flat.
Pah. She didn't look at him.

"Demi, do it."

In your dreams! Reaching out, she caught Sarraj by his
tie, pulled herself up on tiptoe to look deep into his eyes.
Widened her own. "Richard, do you love me?" A question
to set any man back on his heels.

He blinked. "I...could."

And maybe in some other lifetime? "A pity." She pulled
the hand holding her atomizer from her pocket. Sprayed
him square between the eyes with Veil, at a perfume concentration, eighty-seven-percent alcohol.

He yelped—grabbed for his eyes, and she spiked his in-
step. He yipped and she shoved him backward toward the
water.

He dug in his heels and swept out one arm, knocking
her flat. *"Oof!"* No way would she let him hurt Jon! Panting, she sat up, yanked off one heel and reversed it.
Crawled across the deck to where he stood, cursing and
rubbing his eyes.

Reaching his feet, she swung her shoe high—then saw
the white blade of Jon's kayak paddle slicing in from the

water. Her unstoppable lover, swinging for the bleachers. The blade caught Sarraj behind his knees. He yelled, tilted—Demi grabbed his ankle and pulled. The splash as he hit the water drenched her. She spat like a cat, wiped her face and crawled over to the kayak. "Should we help him out?"

"Are you nuts? Untie his boat from that cleat, push it, then come *on,* babe!"

She cast off his boat. "But, Jon—" Richard was making a terrible fuss at the rear of the platform, thrashing and cursing and trying to climb out. "If he can't swim?"

"He was going to put a plague in your perfume, Demi. Now will you—"

"*That's* what they were...?" She got into the boat. Looked back as they shot away from the yacht. "Then drowning's too good for him!"

"Besides, they'll fish him out." Jon nodded toward the north.

It took her a moment to pick out the moving lights from the city's beyond. A plane, no, a chopper, she realized as she heard the beat of its rotors. Two helicopters. She turned her head and found a third, then a fourth, converging on the yacht. "Who's that?"

The kayak shot past the bow of the *Aphrodite,* headed for the Jersey shore. Jon was paddling like a madman. A spotlight leaped forth from the lead chopper, bathing the yacht's stern in a blaze of light. The second chopper hovered over its bow, a deadly fire-eyed insect, and lit it to daytime radiance. As they slid in close to Liberty Island, then turned north, skulking along its rocks, Demi spotted a boat coming from Brooklyn, something half as big as the yacht herself, white with a red slash on its bow, throwing sheets of spray.

"Who *are* all these people?" Black against the light, men were sliding down lines from the chopper to the deck, pouncing on something up at the bow. The kayak slipped around the shoulder of Liberty Island and the chaos vanished. "Jon?"

He lifted his paddle and let them glide. "SWAT team. Coast Guard, FBI, probably city police. A pickup party, I imagine."

He was panting softly. She leaned back to touch his face. He kissed her fingers. "Careful or you'll tip us."

"And who are *you*, Jon Sutter? Immigration?"

He laughed aloud, joyously and wholeheartedly. Shook his head and paddled.

"FBI?"

He dipped, smiled, dipped again and shook his head. "Would you believe an archeological chemist? Professor thereof? On sabbatical, of course."

She shook her head and, twisting farther around, leaned as close as she dared. "If you're lying—or even teasing me—I swear I'll tip us both and hope you sink! Now...the truth?"

He put his paddle down and leaned to meet her. "That is the truth. That's all you'll ever have from me, Demi, from now on."

She had more than that from him already! Demi smiled, cat with cream. She'd had time, while she stared out the *Aphrodite's* windows, to count the days. Realize what day of the month this was and what that signified. But that was a secret she'd tell him later.

They kissed, their lips barely brushing. The kayak wobbled and they broke apart, laughing. Hungering for more. "So is Sutter your real name? And Jon?" How could he ever be anything to her but Jon—gentle, crazy, awesomely capable, infinitely dear to her heart?

"Jon Sutton."

Sutton... Demi Sutton, she could live with that. She'd keep Cousteau for her professional life. "Jon Sutton..."

she said softly, and leaned again to touch the cut on his cheek.

"At your service, my love."

As I am at yours, forever more. She sniffed—"Well, I should hope so!"—then gave him a slow, wicked smile as he paddled on.

HARLEQUIN SUPERROMANCE®

Loving DANGEROUSLY

They're tall, dark and dangerous. Exciting. The kind of men who give women thrills—and chills. The women are daring, strong, compassionate—and willing to take a risk. Danger may threaten, but together the hero and heroine can face any challenges. Even the challenge of love.

Look for these upcoming *Loving Dangerously* books:

Where were you when the storm blew in?

Snowbound

Three stormy stories about what happens to three snowbound couples, from three of your favorite authors:

SHOTGUN WEDDING by Charlotte Lamb
MURDER BY THE BOOK by Margaret St. George
ON A WING AND A PRAYER by Jackie Weger

Find out if cabin fever can melt the snow this December!

Available wherever Harlequin and Silhouette books are sold.

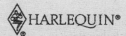 

BESTSELLING AUTHORS
IN THE SPOTLIGHT

.WE'RE SHINING THE SPOTLIGHT ON SIX OF OUR STARS!

Harlequin and Silhouette have selected stories from several of their bestselling authors to give you six sensational reads. These star-powered romances are bound to please!

THERE'S A PRICE TO PAY FOR STARDOM... AND IT'S LOW

$1.99 U.S.
$2.50 CAN.
Special Offer

As a special offer, these six outstanding books are available from Harlequin and Silhouette for only $1.99 in the U.S. and $2.50 in Canada. Watch for these titles:

At the Midnight Hour—Alicia Scott
Joshua and the Cowgirl—Sherryl Woods
Another Whirlwind Courtship—Barbara Boswell
Madeleine's Cowboy—Kristine Rolofson
Her Sister's Baby—Janice Kay Johnson
One and One Makes Three—Muriel Jensen

Available in March 1998
at your favorite retail outlet.

PBAIS

KEY TO MY HEART

Unlock the secrets of romance just in time for the most romantic day of the year— Valentine's Day!

Key to My Heart
features three of your favorite authors,

**Kasey Michaels,
Rebecca York
and Muriel Jensen,**

to bring you wonderful tales of romance and Valentine's Day dreams come true.

As an added bonus you can receive Harlequin's special Valentine's Day necklace. FREE with the purchase of every *Key to My Heart* collection.

Available in January,
wherever Harlequin books are sold.

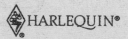

**Look for these titles—
available at your favorite retail outlet!**

January 1998
Renegade Son by Lisa Jackson
Danielle Summers had problems: a rebellious child and unscrupulous enemies. In addition, her Montana ranch was slowly being sabotaged. And then there was Chase McEnroe—who admired her land and desired her body. But Danielle feared he would invade more than just her property—he'd trespass on her heart.

February 1998
The Heart's Yearning by Ginna Gray
Fourteen years ago Laura gave her baby up for adoption, and not one day had passed that she didn't think about him and agonize over her choice—so she finally followed her heart to Texas to see her child. But the plan to watch her son from afar doesn't quite happen that way, once the boy's sexy—*single*—father takes a decided interest in *her*.

March 1998
First Things Last by Dixie Browning
One look into Chandler Harrington's dark eyes and Belinda Massey could refuse the Virginia millionaire nothing. So how could the no-nonsense nanny believe the rumors that he had kidnapped his nephew—an adorable, healthy little boy who crawled as easily into her heart as he did into her lap?

**BORN IN THE USA: Love, marriage—
and the pursuit of family!**

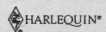